Emma Blair was born in Glasgow and now lives in Devon. She is the author of twenty-nine bestselling novels including *Scarlet Ribbons* and *Flower of Scotland*, both of which were shortlisted for the Romantic Novel of the Year Award.

For more information about the author, visit www.emma-blair.co.uk

GOODNIGHT, SWEET PRINCE

Emma Blair

SPHERE

First published in Great Britain in 1999 by Little, Brown and Company
This paperback edition published in 2011 by Sphere

A CIP catalogue record for this book
is available from the British Library.

ISBN 978-0-7515-4747-4

Printed and bound in Great Britain by
Clays Ltd, St Ives plc

Sphere
An imprint of
Little, Brown Book Group
100 Victoria Embankment
London EC4Y 0DY

An Hachette UK Company
www.hachette.co.uk

www.littlebrown.co.uk

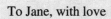

To Jane, with love

Now cracks a noble heart. Good night, sweet prince;
And flights of angels sing thee to thy rest!

Hamlet Act V, Scene 2

Chapter 1

'What!'
    Tommy Riach dropped his gaze to stare at the floor, writhing inside. 'I'm sorry, Dad,' he mumbled.

'That's not bloody good enough. Expelled from school! What on earth possessed you, boy?'

How could he explain? He couldn't, simply not having the words. The streak of rebelliousness that ran through him was deep as any canyon and, to him anyway, defied description.

Jack Riach sighed, removed the dark glasses he wore and ran a hand over the sockets where once his eyes had been. He loved his son with all his heart and yet there were times when he could have knocked the bugger senseless. 'Smoking and drinking, you say.'

'That's right,' came the whispered reply.

'Wait till your mother finds out. She'll be beside herself. Cry herself silly no doubt. What do you make of that?'

Tommy was lost for an answer, hating the thought of

hurting his mother in any way. Or his father come to that.

'Do you have cigarettes on you now?'

'Yes, Dad.'

'Then you'd better light up. Why the hell not. If that's what you want to do.'

'Thanks, Dad.'

Tommy quickly fumbled for the packet of ten he had in his jacket pocket and moments later smoke was curling towards the ceiling.

'And, according to you, it's happened before. This was the second occasion you were caught.'

'Yes.' That again was said in a whisper.

Jack came to his feet and crossed to the window where the cold November light played across his face. For some reason he found himself remembering the war and what it had been like before he'd lost his sight. There had been so many young men only a few years older than Tommy, most of them now dead. Buried over there in France and Belgium. Somehow that put things into perspective. Smoking and drinking weren't so bad after all. Insignificant really. Nor was being expelled from school.

Jack recalled . . . and shuddered inwardly. 'So what are we to do with you now?' he queried softly.

'I've no idea, Dad.'

'Another school?'

'That's up to you.'

Jack smiled wryly. 'Is it indeed. I would have thought it was up to you. What's the point of sending you off to another school if you're only going to be expelled again. Don't forget this isn't the first time we've had trouble. You seem to have a real talent when it comes to that.'

Tommy looked round for an ashtray already knowing

there wasn't one. He flicked ash into the fireplace instead. 'Are you asking or telling?'

'Don't be impertinent, boy,' Jack growled threateningly.

'I didn't mean to be.'

'Then I'm asking.'

Tommy considered school which he loathed. It seemed so . . . senseless. All right, it was necessary to learn the fundamentals, reading, writing etc. But beyond those a total waste of time as far as he was concerned.

Jack suddenly laughed.

'Dad?'

'Wee Linda Millar.'

Tommy flushed, knowing exactly what Jack was referring to. 'She's moved away.'

'So what in the hell has that got to do with it? Can you imagine what it was like for me to have to face her father.'

'She agreed, Dad. It wasn't as if I forced myself on her. She was as keen for me to look at her drawers as I was to see them.'

'At that age!'

Tommy shrugged. 'Curiosity, part of growing up I suppose. I don't know.'

'You were only ten at the time, Linda eight. And you weren't peering at her drawers but what was underneath. What I could never understand was why you didn't lock the toilet door.'

It hadn't only been the toilet with Linda, Tommy reflected with amusement. No indeed.

It struck him then that was another thing he hated about school, all chaps together. Not a female in sight, discounting matron that was. It simply didn't seem right to him. Unnatural.

'How's the book coming along?' he inquired casually.

'Fine, as far as I know. Your mum says it's going well.'

'She's always a good judge.'

'So far anyway.' Jack paused, then said, 'Are you trying to change the subject?'

Which was precisely what Tommy had been hoping to do. 'I just wondered, that's all.'

Liar, Jack thought. Though full marks for trying. He turned and returned to his chair which he eased himself into. He might be blind but there wasn't an inch of the house he didn't know like the back of his hand or could find his way round. He'd be meeting his great friend Andrew that evening, this was something to discuss with him.

Tommy flicked the remains of his cigarette into the fireplace. 'Can I go now?'

'If you wish.'

Tommy hesitated in the doorway. 'Dad, I'm really sorry. Truly I am.'

'I know that, son,' Jack replied softly. 'Now go and make your peace with your mum. If you can that is.'

Tommy left Jack to his thoughts.

'Well,' Andrew Drummond mused. 'That must have been a bit of a shock for you and Hettie.'

Jack groped for his pint and lifted it to his lips. It was a Friday night when he and Andrew always met up, when possible that is, in the local pub. They'd been doing so for years.

'You can say that again.'

'How's Hettie taking it?'

'As you'd expect. Feeling ashamed, which is hardly surprising considering her background.'

4

Andrew recalled the Hettie of old, a farm worker and Jack's paid mistress before the war. Now his wife, and the best wife Jack could have had. He'd always thought highly of Hettie. More than that.

Jack slowly shook his head. 'What's to become of that boy? I wish I knew. There's a wild streak in the lad which most certainly doesn't come from me.'

Andrew couldn't help but laugh. 'That's rich, Jack Riach! Who are you trying to kid? Talk about self-delusion. You were as wild as they come when young, as many a lassie could have testified to.'

Jack had the grace to look shamefaced. 'You're exaggerating.'

'In a pig's ear. As you well know, if you're honest that is.'

'I'm always honest,' Jack protested halfheartedly.

Both men laughed.

'Besides which, you were hardly an innocent yourself. Particularly where the lassies were concerned.'

'True,' Andrew mused. And wonderful days they'd been too. He had many fond memories of his youth.

'Do you remember . . .'

The pair of them fell to reminiscing.

'I suppose I could always buy another farm,' Jack declared later at the kitchen table where he, Hettie and Tommy were having a late-night supper. He'd originally been a large landowner but had sold up on returning from the war because of his disability.

Hettie frowned. 'Whatever for?'

'Not for me of course, but Tommy. We could hire a manager to teach him the ropes. And I'd naturally be on hand to advise.'

A thoroughly appalled Tommy stared aghast at his father. 'Are you serious, Dad?'

'Quite. We've got to do something with you and since you've decided you've finished with school then that would seem the obvious thing.'

Tommy's knife clattered on to his plate, all thought of food forgotten. 'It's a terrible idea. Completely ridiculous.'

Hettie gazed coldly at him, still furious over what had happened. The shame of having a boy expelled! She was quite mortified and hated to think what the good people of Dalneil would say when the news got round. 'And why is it ridiculous?' she snapped.

'It just is, that's all.'

'I should have thought it would have appealed,' Jack said mildly.

'Appealed! Grubbing around in the dirt for a living. No thank you.'

'Don't speak to your father in that tone of voice,' Hettie admonished, fighting back the urge to slap Tommy. Damn it, but she was close to tears again.

'You'll have to get a job of some sort, you certainly can't sit around here for the rest of your life,' Jack went on.

'We had hoped you'd go to university one day. Which is hardly likely now,' Hettie glared.

'I'd never have got into university, Mum. My marks must have told you that. I'm just not clever enough.'

'You're clever enough all right,' Jack stated. 'What you mean is that your marks, and I admit they have always been poor, merely reflected the fact you wouldn't apply yourself. That's a different matter entirely.'

Tommy's lips thinned. He could hardly deny the accusation because it was true. Lack of application and a certain amount of laziness on his part. 'I'm still not going to be a farmer,' he muttered stubbornly.

'What then?'

'I don't know yet. I'll think of something.'

'Hmmh,' Jack mused. 'The old McPherson place is up for sale, and at a reasonable price too, I understand. It doesn't have a lot of acreage but would do to get you started.'

Tommy came abruptly to his feet. 'Farming's out, Dad. It may have suited you once upon a time but it would never suit me. I mean that.'

'Sit down and finish your supper,' Hettie gestured. She was beginning to realise for the first time just how spoilt Tommy had become, and wilful with it.

'No thank you, I've had enough. Now if you'll excuse me.'

Jack sighed, thinking along the same lines as his wife. His expression had become strained when the kitchen door clicked shut.

'There were a few moments there when I could easily have clouted him. Little sod,' Hettie hissed.

Jack silently agreed with her.

Tommy, not yet bothering with the candle, threw himself on to his bed and stared up into the darkness. There was an awfully big adventure out there somewhere waiting for him, he'd known that for years. But what? That was the question to which he didn't have an answer.

An African explorer maybe. That would be jolly interesting. But how did you become one of those? He could just imagine himself cutting a swathe through the jungle, fighting man-eating lions and the like.

A grin crept over his face. A big-game hunter, that

was another possibility. Or big-game hunter *and* explorer. There was no reason why you couldn't combine the two.

These fantasies were something he'd never confided to a single soul, certainly not the chaps at school who'd have ragged him rotten.

School, he wasn't going to miss it one little bit. Thank God his father had agreed those days were over. For the most part they'd been boring in the extreme. Tedious beyond belief.

Just as being a farmer would be. That was the very last thing he wanted, the very notion made him squirm.

When younger he'd dreamt about being a pirate, hoisting the jolly roger and all that. But in the end he'd had to concede that was too fanciful, not to mention impractical. As far as he knew there just weren't any pirates nowadays. All sadly gone.

'Ho ho ho and a bottle of rum,' he murmured, and laughed quietly.

Tom Riach, the feared and dreaded pirate. Chests of gold, silver and jewels captured on the Spanish Main. And women, oh yes there would be lots of those. Lots and lots. All sorts and types. All swooning at his feet. Fabulous women and oodles of booty, what a life, he reflected. How glorious that would have been.

The awfully big adventure was definitely out there waiting for him. No doubt about it.

And one day it would happen.

The next morning Andrew was in the process of getting dressed when a sudden pain lanced through his stomach causing him to gasp and bend over.

'What's wrong, Andrew?' a concerned Rose, his wife, demanded.

The pain lanced again, though this time not so severely as before.

Rose hurried to his side, her brow furrowed. 'Darling?'

He managed a weak smile. 'Indigestion I think. It just caught me unawares, that's all.'

She laid a hand on his arm. 'Come over here and sit down for a bit.' It was unusual for Andrew to suffer from indigestion, almost unheard of actually. Normally he could eat the richest of foods without suffering any ill effects. The legacy of years of army cooking, he sometimes joked. A regular officer until resigning his commission to take over the family distillery, he'd been stationed in Ireland for the duration of the war.

Andrew straightened. 'There's no need for that. I'm fine now.'

'Are you sure?'

He took a deep breath. 'Whatever, it's gone.'

'Can I get you anything. A tablet perhaps?'

'No, Rose. But thank you anyway.'

He stared into her eyes, thinking how beautiful she was, and how much he loved her. It had always worried him that the twenty-year age gap would one day affect their marriage, but it never had. Although . . . well childbearing had proved a different matter. Rose had never been the same after Drew had been born. Where previously she'd revelled in their lovemaking that had all changed with the arrival of their son.

'I suppose I'd better get on,' Andrew smiled. 'Mustn't be late for work. What would the staff say.'

'Indeed,' Rose agreed, also smiling. Andrew was a stickler for timekeeping and made it a point of honour to always be at his desk on the dot. Mr Kelly, his book-keeper, was forever declaring you could set your watch by Andrew.

'I'd only have a light breakfast if I was you,' Rose suggested. 'You don't want to bring on that indigestion again.'

He nodded. 'A slice of toast and cup of tea will do me.'

Rose started to turn away to continue with her dressing which she was only halfway through.

'Rose.'

He drew her to him and once in his embrace tenderly smoothed her long, as yet uncombed, hair. 'Do you ever have any regrets? About us I mean.'

She frowned. 'What a silly question. No, of course I haven't. Now why suddenly ask that, for goodness sake?'

He continued smoothing her hair. Then, on impulse, he brushed his lips over hers. 'I'd hate to take you for granted.'

'You hardly do that. At least, I don't think you do.'

'Nor do I, Rose. You're probably the best thing that's ever happened to me and I'll never forget that.'

How sweet he could be at times, she thought. Sweet and romantic. She'd been extremely lucky to meet Andrew Drummond. 'I've never regretted a single day of our marriage, so there. And that's the God's honest truth.'

'Me neither,' he confessed.

'Good, that's that out of the way. Now you'd better hurry up or you will be late.'

'Heaven forbid,' he laughed.

He was troubled, she thought, not knowing why. There had only ever been one bone of contention between them and that hadn't been mentioned in years. Was that it? Was that what had prompted his question?

She was acutely aware of his eyes riveted on her back as she walked away from him.

*　　*　　*

Nancy Thompson ran a hand over her weatherbeaten face, wishing there could be just one day in her life when she didn't feel totally and utterly exhausted. No wonder so many of her kind died relatively young, worn out by the unremitting toil and harshness of their situation.

Nancy was a bondager and had been for two years since the age of twelve when her mother had taken her along to the Hiring Fair to find her a labourer, or hind as they were called, who'd take her on.

That day she'd caught Bill McCabe's eye and the deal had been struck. Shortly afterwards she'd gone to live with him in the cottage he'd been allocated by the master.

There were many outside the Border valleys who knew nothing of the bondagers' life and would have been scandalised to think such a thing still existed. But exist it did, although it was not quite as prevalent as it had once been. Slavery some called it, serfdom by others.

Bill, a short squat man of twenty-three who could never have been called good-looking by any stretch of the imagination, pushed his plate away. 'Any more tea in the pot?'

'There should be some left.'

Bill grunted, Nancy's cue to fetch the pot and refill his cup. When that was done she went to the sink where she emptied the remains into a draining dish.

Bill scraped back his chair, picked up his cup and crossed to the fire which he sat in front of. There he lapsed into a brooding silence which was common for him at that time of night.

'Annie McGillvary's baby's due any day now,' Nancy declared. Annie was another bondager who lived in the next cottage along with her hind.

Bill didn't reply.

'She's scared about it as it's her first one. Some of the older women tell terrible stories, you understand. Enough to put the fear of God into anyone. You'd think they'd know better.'

Nancy got on with the clearing up, then started on the dishes. As she washed she thought of her ma whom she'd never seen from the day she'd joined up with Bill, nor was ever likely to again. She'd been the oldest of three children whom her mother, another bondager, had been only too pleased to be rid of.

Bill glanced at the battered clock on top of the mantelpiece. Almost time to go to bed. The best part of the day as far as he was concerned. He enjoyed his bed, with Nancy in it.

Prior to Nancy his bondager had been a lassie called Pat. Pleasant enough, to begin with anyway. But then she'd started to show a tendency to nag which hadn't pleased him one little bit. He couldn't bide a nagger. And so she'd had to go to be replaced by Nancy. If he missed Pat at all it was because she'd been an excellent cook, far better than Nancy whose meals were nothing out of the ordinary. Still, he reflected philosophically, you couldn't have everything.

'Right,' he announced a little later, noting that Nancy had finished at the sink. 'We'll go through.'

Nancy didn't dislike what was coming next, nor did she particularly like it either. It was simply one of the many things expected of her.

How long before she fell pregnant? she wondered. And what then? Would Bill renew her yearly contract or find someone else to take her place?

Bill wasn't a great one for children. He'd said so on a number of occasions.

Nor would he ever do what she'd asked many a time which would have greatly lessened the chances of her getting in the family way. He was far too selfish about his own needs and gratification for that.

Thankfully that night, which wasn't always the case, he was quick and soon snoring his head off.

The next thing Nancy knew he was shaking her and telling her it was time to get up.

Another hard slog stretched wearingly ahead.

'That's enough for today,' Jack Riach declared, and yawned.

Hettie glanced up at him in surprise, having been taking his dictation which she'd later type out and place with the rest of his manuscript. A manuscript which was growing steadily towards completion.

'What's up? You've given me a lot less than usual. Isn't it coming for you?'

Jack shook his head. 'It's Tommy, I'm worried about him and it keeps intruding on my mind.'

Hettie closed the large notebook in which she'd been writing and laid it aside. 'Would you like some coffee?'

He considered that. 'No, what I'd really like is a dram.'

'At this time of day! It's far too early.'

He grinned sheepishly at her. 'Rules are made to be broken, Hettie. I've always said that.'

'Even though.'

'And we could really break them by you joining me for a couple.'

'A couple now, it was only one a moment ago.'

He shrugged. 'Will you fetch the bottle or will I have to do it myself?'

'I'll get it.'

'Still happy with how the book's coming along?' he asked as she poured the drinks.

'If I wasn't I'd say. You know that.'

'Then it's fine?'

'Believe me, Jack, it's fine. I'm just dying to know how it's going to end, that's all.'

He laughed softly and tapped his nose. 'That's for me to know and you to wonder about. Besides, I'd spoil it for you if I told you the ending in advance.'

'I don't believe you know what it is,' she teased.

'Oh, but I do.'

'Maybe you're fibbing.'

'Now why should I do that?'

'You just would, being you.'

'I never tell you the ending, so why change now?'

'Rules are made to be broken, Jack, you just said so.'

He laughed. 'Point taken. But I'm still not giving you the ending. That remains my little secret.'

Truth was he didn't have an ending yet which was unusual for him. Normally he knew it early on, if not before he actually started to dictate.

'Where's Tommy?' he queried.

'Gone out for a walk, I believe. He mentioned something to that effect after breakfast.'

'Well that certainly won't do him any harm.'

'No,' Hettie agreed.

Jack sighed.

'You are worried about him, aren't you?'

'Very.'

'So am I. It's only natural.' Hettie paused, then said tentatively, 'Jack?'

'What?'

'There's always the army. It would be a good career for him. Or one of the other services.'

Jack's expression clouded over and then darkened even further. 'No,' he replied harshly. He finished what was left in his glass and immediately held it out for a refill.

'It was only a suggestion.'

'You weren't there, Hettie,' he said so softly she almost couldn't hear. 'Oh I know you've heard people, including myself, occasionally speak of it. And you've read about it. But the reality . . .' He trailed off, mind filled with awful, terrible memories.

'That was in the war, Jack. It's peacetime now.'

A grim smile slashed his face. 'Peacetime yes, but for how long with that fellow Herr Hitler in power. He's already gone into Czechoslovakia and once he's conquered that, what next?'

Jack shook his head. 'There could well be another war, Heaven forbid, and before too long either. It doesn't bear thinking about. Certainly not for us who were in the last one.'

'Do you think . . . it really could happen, Jack?' Fear was clutching her insides as she asked that.

'You wouldn't believe people could be so stupid, and yet they can. It's possible, Hettie, very very possible.'

He took a deep breath, then said bitterly, 'I loathe and hate the Germans, you've no idea how much. Because of them millions died, not to mention the untold misery they caused. If they drag us into another carnage then I hope their entire race roasts in perdition for all eternity.'

Hettie didn't know what to answer to that so said nothing. She could well understand Jack's feelings though she didn't entirely agree with them. It seemed to her there had to be many decent Germans, that stood to reason after all. You could hardly condemn an entire nation, no matter what that nation had done.

'So the army and other services are definitely out,' Jack stated. 'Understand?'

'Yes,' she whispered.

'Not another word on the subject.'

Hettie was sorry she'd brought it up in the first place. She should have known better.

'Push,' Nancy urged.

Annie McGillvary's lips were drawn back in a wolfish snarl. 'I'm trying,' she gasped. 'I'm bloody trying.'

The onset of pains had been sudden and violent. Nancy had tried to get her friend home to have the baby there but that hadn't been possible. Which was why Annie was now lying on her back in a field, legs drawn up and splayed, while Nancy was doing the best she could. It wouldn't be the first time a bondager had birthed in a field, it was quite a common event.

Annie screamed, eyes bulging. Her whole body convulsed.

If only it hadn't been such a raw day, Nancy thought, but what did you expect at this time of year. The wind was whistling all around them causing a nearby hedge to rustle and sway.

It was going to be quick, even the inexperienced Nancy knew that, which was something of a relief. 'The head's coming,' she exclaimed excitedly. 'I can see it now.'

Annie couldn't believe such agony was possible. It was as if she was being ripped in two. Literally torn apart.

'Push,' Nancy urged again.

'I fucking well am!'

Nancy wished one of the older women had been with

them but Annie had insisted she go with her. One in accompaniment was all that was allowed.

Now the head was born and the shoulders were straining to be free. Blood and goo were dribbling down the inside of Annie's icy-cold thighs.

This time the scream was the most horrendous yet, a scream whipped off by the wind to be lost in the distance.

A mercifully short while later it was all over, Annie having collapsed in on herself after the final titanic push. 'A boy or girl?' she croaked.

Nancy held the child to her breast, partially covering its blue-tinged body with her smock. 'A boy.'

Nancy glanced at her friend through eyes filled with tears.

'And the wee mite's dead.'

Chapter 2

'It's Andrew and Rose,' Hettie exclaimed, ushering them into the room where Jack and Tommy were.

'This is a pleasant surprise,' Jack smiled.

'We were on our way to my sister Charlotte's and thought we'd drop by,' Andrew explained. Charlotte was married to the Dalneil minister, John McLean, and lived in the village manse.

'Take a seat,' Jack declared, coming to his feet. 'I don't suppose you'll refuse a dram.'

'Only if it isn't Drummond,' Andrew joked, knowing full well Jack kept nothing else.

'And you, Rose?'

'A small one with water would be nice.'

Tommy felt the foursome should be alone and decided to take himself upstairs. 'I'll leave you lot to it,' he stated affably.

'No, you stay, Tommy. Our visit here concerns you,' Andrew replied.

'You've grown since I saw you last,' Rose observed. 'Quite the young man now.' Then, teasingly, 'Is that the hint of a moustache I can make out?'

Tommy blushed. He'd always fancied Rose Drummond rotten, though of course she was far too old for him, not to mention married.

Hettie laughed. 'Shame on you, Rose, you'll embarrass the lad. That's cruel.'

Andrew's statement had intrigued Tommy. Concerned him? In what way? he wondered.

'Would you like a hand there?' Andrew queried, moving to Jack's side.

'If you'd pass them out.'

'Aye, no trouble at all.'

'Any excuse for a dram,' Hettie said, though not entirely unapprovingly. Whisky and Scots went together. Some men just needed a wee bit of restraint, that's all.

Jack shook the bottle he was holding. 'The damn thing's empty, Hettie. Is there another in the larder?'

'Isn't there always. I'll go and fetch it.'

Rose eyed Tommy kindly, having known for years that he had a soft spot for her. 'You've left school I understand.'

'Expelled,' Jack qualified. 'Let's not be mealy-mouthed about it. The bugger was expelled, kicked out for smoking and drinking.' He paused, then added, 'Who knows what else he was up to either.'

'You mean lassies?' Rose further teased.

This time Tommy went scarlet.

'The thought had crossed my mind.'

'Well, Tommy?' Rose queried, still with a teasing tone.

He was tongue-tied, being asked such a thing by Rose. 'Well?'

'Fat chance of that at an all boys school,' he finally managed to stammer in reply.

'I contrived to meet a few when I was at school,' Andrew commented drily. 'No doubt it was the same with you.'

Hettie breezed back in with the new bottle. 'It's lovely having some company. We were listening to the wireless earlier but there wasn't much on.'

Jack listened a lot to the wireless for obvious reasons. It was a great solace to his blindness.

'We're not intruding then?' Rose queried.

'Och no, you and Andrew could never do that. The pair of you are always welcome in this house as you well know.'

'What's the occasion at Charlotte's?' Jack inquired of Andrew.

'Nothing special. A natter and some supper, that's all.'

Andrew noted that Tommy was looking uncomfortable, and apprehensive. He smiled inwardly.

'Smoking and drinking,' he said to Tommy. 'A touch of the cratur I hope. Do you like whisky?'

Tommy nodded.

'And yet I see your dad hasn't given you a glass.'

Jack hesitated for the briefest of moments. 'I suppose it's all right. You are sixteen after all. Straight or with water?'

'Straight please, Dad.'

Andrew grunted his approval. 'I'm delighted to hear you like whisky, lad, for that's what I've come to talk to you about.'

Tommy couldn't imagine why. He was quite bewildered.

'*Slainthe!*' Jack toasted, raising his own glass.

'How's the book coming along, Jack?' Rose asked after

she'd had a sip. 'Andrew never mentions anything about what's said at those get togethers of yours on a Friday night.' Which wasn't true, though Andrew was selective. He had told her about Tommy and discussed the matter with her.

'He won't let on the ending and I'm dying to know,' Hettie chipped in, eyes twinkling.

'Nor will I.'

'You horrible thing,' Rose said, now teasing Jack.

'What I have taken down so far is extremely good,' Hettie declared, immensely proud of Jack and his writing. 'Nor would I say that if it wasn't so, as you all know.'

'I look forward to reading it then.'

'And as always you'll have one of my free copies,' Jack retorted.

'Thank you.'

'Getting back to whisky,' Andrew said, sitting beside Rose on the settee. 'Would you be interested in making a career in it, Tommy?'

That startled the youngster. 'I beg your pardon?'

'You heard me. Would you be interested in making a career in it? With Drummond Whisky to be more precise. As a traveller for the firm.'

Jack was dumbfounded. 'Are you serious, Andrew?'

'Never more so.'

'Well,' murmured Jack. Tommy working for Andrew, that would be perfect.

'Tommy?' Hettie prompted, also delighted by this suggestion which would solve all their problems.

'I, eh . . .' Tommy swallowed. 'I honestly don't know.'

'You wouldn't start off as a traveller of course,' Andrew went on. 'You'd have to learn the ropes first. From the bottom up so to speak. But given time and progress you would eventually go on the road for me.'

Tommy's mind was whirling. His first reaction was to reject the offer, but that would be ill mannered and his parents would be furious. A traveller for whisky hardly matched being an African explorer and big-game hunter.

'Speak up, son,' Jack enthused. 'You can't just say you don't know. This is an ideal opportunity and one you're lucky to have, considering the circumstances.'

Andrew laughed and waved a hand dismissively. 'His being expelled makes no difference to me. It shows spirit, that's all. A quality I much admire. The trick is to harness that spirit . . .' He treated them all to a beaming smile. 'In this instance with spirit of another kind. If you'll pardon my little joke.'

He rounded again on Tommy. 'The remuneration wouldn't be much to begin with, but fair, I promise you that. And there would be a yearly review.'

'This is very kind of you, Andrew,' Hettie declared.

'Not really, it depends how you look at these things. Anyway, in life it's often who you know, eh?'

Tommy finished his whisky which he didn't even notice going down.

'Well?' That was Jack again.

Tommy was horribly aware of four pairs of eyes staring intently at him. 'It's . . . an awfully big decision to make just like that,' he prevaricated.

'Quite right too,' Rose declared, taking his side. 'It is an awfully big decision. One that should be thought through. He's showing sense.'

Tommy shot her a smile of appreciation.

'I understand.' Andrew nodded.

Jack's lips thinned. As far as he was concerned Tommy

should have jumped at the chance. What was there to think about? Damn all, in his opinion.

'Can I speak to you, give you my decision in a couple of days' time?' Tommy asked Andrew.

Hettie was aware of how displeased Jack was and was none too happy herself. But Rose was right, there was absolutely no point in forcing the boy.

'Of course,' Andrew replied.

'That way a mistake won't be made,' Rose said, again coming to Tommy's aid.

'Then we'll leave it at that for now,' Andrew agreed.

Tommy knew there was going to be all hell to pay when the Drummonds had gone.

Nancy paused in her darning and shook her head. These socks had almost had it, she thought. They'd been darned so many times there was nearly more darning than original wool. She idly wondered if other men were as hard on socks as Bill.

She glanced up and frowned when there was a knock on the door. Now who could that be at this time of night? Had to be Annie over for a blether she presumed.

She was wrong. She gasped in surprise when she opened the door and the master was revealed. 'It's you, sir.'

'Aye, me.'

Nancy wasn't sure what to do, being all alone. 'If it's Bill you want I'm afraid he isn't here,' she said.

The master already knew that which was why he was there, it being the one night a week the labourers went to the pub. 'Damn,' he muttered, pretending disappointment.

'Can I help you, sir?'

The master banged his hands together. 'Fiendishly cold night. Is there any tea going?'

'I can put the kettle on if you wish.'

He immediately stepped past her. 'Then do that. Nancy, isn't it?'

'Yes, sir.'

Once inside the master glanced around. At least she kept a reasonably neat and tidy house he reflected, though it wouldn't have mattered if she hadn't.

He brought his attention to bear on Nancy now busy at the sink pump. An attractive figure, as far as he could make out that was. And the face wasn't bad either. He was going to enjoy this.

Nancy was nervous, so much so her hands were trembling. She wished Bill had been there.

The master removed his coat and tossed it aside where it fell across a chair. His jacket followed the coat. The pub was open for a good hour yet, plenty of time for what he had in mind.

Damn the wife and her monthlies, it was so inconvenient. There again, it gave him the opportunity to branch out when he wished. Not that he always needed an excuse when the mood took him.

'It won't be long, sir.' Nancy smiled, busying herself, wondering why he'd taken off his jacket as well.

Nice smile, he thought. He walked towards her, stopping a few feet away. His eyes fixed on the bulge of her breasts.

Nancy knew then with a certainty why he'd come. A hand flew to her mouth. She'd heard it went on, of course, the other women whispered about it from time to time but never really discussed it openly.

She swallowed hard, hoping against hope she was wrong

and it really was Bill he'd come to see. Please God that was the case.

'Lovely little creature, aren't you,' the master said in a husky voice, suddenly filled with desire.

Nancy edged sideways. 'Please, sir.'

He smiled, a smile that quickly transformed itself into a leer. The blood was pounding in his veins. 'There's nothing to be afraid of, Nancy. I'm not going to do anything you ain't done before. How old are you, lass?'

She told him.

Young and no doubt juicy. Just the way he liked them. Slowly he began undoing the front of his trousers.

Nancy whimpered. She could try and dodge round him and flee the cottage. But if she did escape, what then? She and Bill would be out on their ears, no doubt. She felt like an animal caught in a trap.

'You'll enjoy it, girl, I promise.' Not that he gave a damn whether she did or not. All that mattered was *he* did.

Nancy's vision blurred. This was a nightmare. She'd been sitting at home, totally at peace with herself and surroundings. Then that knock on the door and . . .

She gave a muffled scream as he grabbed her.

The master got up from the floor where Nancy lay spread-eagled. Like shagging a bloody corpse, he thought in disgust. Worse than useless. At the very least she might have struggled but hadn't even done that. He wouldn't be coming back again, he decided. Wasn't worth it. He liked his women to have some oomph in them, a bit of appreciation. But her . . .

Nancy didn't open her eyes till she heard the door click shut.

*   *   *

'Christ Almighty, what's happened to you?' Annie McGillvary exclaimed. She too was alone, Hector having also gone to the pub.

A dishevelled Nancy fell into Annie's arms. 'Oh Annie, Annie,' she sobbed.

Annie guided her friend over to a chair and sat her down. 'Now what's this all about?'

'The master . . . the master . . .' Nancy broke off and shook.

Annie sighed. Bastard. It was obvious now what had happened. 'He called on you, I take it?'

Nancy nodded.

'Did he hurt you?'

'Not really,' Nancy choked.

'Then count yourself lucky. He's been known to do that before. Belle Gibbons was black and blue after one such visit. The swine punched her all over.'

Nancy was thankful she'd been spared that. 'It was so unexpected, Annie. So very unexpected. Suddenly he was there and then minutes later . . .'

Annie wished she had some drink in the house, but unfortunately didn't.

'I've only ever had Bill until now you see,' Nancy babbled. 'And I had time to think about that, get used to the idea before he bedded me. But with the master . . .' She shuddered. 'I thought I was going to puke.'

'There there,' Annie crooned, stroking her friend's cheek. 'It's all over now. Finished and done with.'

'I feel so . . . dirty inside. Dirty as sin.'

'But you shouldn't. It wasn't your doing after all. What happened is common enough hereabouts. If a master takes a notion to a bondager then that's that, she has no say in the matter. None at all. The only thing to do is grit your teeth and let him get on with it. That's the way it is, Nancy love.'

'It's so unfair though,' Nancy sobbed.

Annie smiled bitterly. 'You've never said a truer word. Unfair it is, but that's the way of the world I'm afraid.'

A traveller for Drummond Whisky, Tommy reflected, staring up at his bedroom ceiling where light from his candle cast flickering shadows. That meant a car, which would be terrific, something he'd always wanted. He had an aptitude for mechanical things and was sure he'd make an excellent driver.

He closed his eyes and imagined himself as a racing driver whooshing round bends, then opening up on the straight, going at a fantastic speed.

The car would be in British racing green livery of course, and he would be the premier driver in the whole country. He saw himself receiving the winner's cup and all the admiring glances, mainly from women, coming in his direction.

The champagne would pop and froth, then he'd be pouring it into the cup and drinking deeply. A god, that's what you must be at a moment like that, a veritable god.

Tommy sighed and brought himself out of his reverie. He had a decision to make and it wasn't easy. Even with the inducement of a car.

The thing was, what was his alternative? Run away from home, take his chances like that? It was a possibility of course, one he'd been mulling over. Trouble was he didn't have any money to back himself up. If he did run away it would be with only a few measly pounds in his pocket. He was practical enough to know that wouldn't get him very far.

Working for Andrew Drummond wouldn't be too bad, he thought. Andrew was a decent man and, by all accounts, a good employer. He could do a lot worse. Oh aye, he could do that.

It would be a start, he rationalised. And you had to start somewhere, even if the jungles of Africa were your ultimate aim.

Tommy sighed again, already knowing what his answer was going to be when he next saw Andrew.

'What have you been up to?' Bill McCabe slurred as Nancy came into the cottage. He was clearly drunk, though not belligerently so. His eyes were rheumy and squinting slightly.

Nancy had already tidied herself before leaving Annie's, which she did when Hector had arrived in. She explained where she'd been.

Bill grunted.

'How was your night out?'

'Och fine. The usual.'

She'd discussed with Annie whether or not she should tell Bill what had happened, and decided she wouldn't. There was nothing Bill could do about it anyway except be upset. Which he may or may not be, she wasn't sure.

'Would you like some tea?' she asked.

He shook his head, then belched. 'Not on top of that I wouldn't. It would be spoiling good beer.' Bill yawned and stretched. 'It's bed for me. I'm fair done in and that's a fact.'

Nancy found herself staring at that part of the floor where the master had taken her, remembering anew the ghastliness of it all.

'You all right?'

She nodded.

'You look a bit funny like.'

'Do I?'

He lurched towards her. 'What were you and Annie talking about?'

'Nothing much. The things we normally talk about.'

Bill didn't believe that. Even in his befuddled state he could sense something was amiss. 'Come on, what was it?'

She hadn't been going to but should she now change her mind? 'Mainly the baby Annie lost,' she lied.

'Oh!' That explained it. 'She'll soon have another if Hector has anything to do with it. You take my word. He enjoys his oats does Hector.'

Just like you, she thought. Just like you.

'See to the fire and come on through. I'll be waiting.'

Not tonight, she wailed inside. Not after the master. That would be too much to bear.

But go through with it she'd have to. She knew that, even though she would feel total revulsion and hatred against men and their rutting ways throughout it all, and afterwards.

The master sat astride his horse watching three of the bondagers, one of whom was Nancy, hard at work. His expression was dyspeptic.

What a disappointment that had been, he reflected. And, now he thought about it, an insult to himself. Why, halfway through he'd almost felt like giving up there and then.

An insult right enough. And he wasn't a man to take insults. By God, he wasn't. A corpse, he thought yet again. That's precisely what it had been like. Shagging a bloody corpse.

Small flakes of snow started to fall, causing him to glance up at a heavy, grey leaden sky. There had been the smell of snow in the air for days and now it had arrived.

His horse whinnied and then snorted, making him smile. He remembered that she didn't like snow. It made her nervous, especially falling snow.

Nancy paused in what she was doing to catch her breath, well aware that the master had been staring at her. Now what was going through his mind? she wondered. Was he thinking about the other night or something else? Beside her Annie, who'd gone back to work the day after she'd given birth, toiled relentlessly on.

The master, noting that Nancy had stopped, glared at her which sent her instantly back to the task in hand. He smiled inwardly. You'll have to go, bitch, he decided. Nobody insults me and gets away with it.

He wheeled his horse about, intending to return home for a hot meal and drink.

McCabe would go at the end of his contracted year, and with McCabe would go that Nancy.

His mind was made up and once that happened he never changed it.

Tommy halted to gaze at the Drummond Distillery, a building he'd known all his life though he'd only ever been inside on very few occasions. Now he was seeing it in a quite different light.

He had an appointment with Andrew in ten minutes and mustn't be late. That would never do, Hettie had impressed on him when he'd been sluggish in getting ready. So here he was, in best bib and tucker, about to take the plunge that would alter his life for ever.

It wouldn't be too bad, he told himself yet again. A start anyway, if nothing else. And the awfully big adventure was always out there waiting for him. He knew it was. That was something he must cling on to, never forget.

He suddenly smiled to himself, remembering the car that would one day be at his disposal. A car to take him all over the country and even down into England.

Sucking in a deep breath he continued towards Drummond's and his immediate destiny.

'Is it true?' Bill demanded, voice loaded with anger.

Nancy, who herself had only arrived home a few minutes previously, glanced round at him. His expression was frightening.

'Is what true?' she gulped.

'That the master came here and you displeased him.'

Oh Christ, she thought. 'Who told you that?'

He balled his hands into fists and advanced on her as she swiftly retreated. She'd never seen Bill like this before.

'Never you mind, is it true?'

'How do you mean, displease?'

'Exactly that, you stupid bitch.'

Her breath was coming in short pants while her skin had gone cold all over. A different sort of cold to that caused by the weather. 'Who told you?' she repeated.

'I said it doesn't fucking well matter. All that does is you displeased him.'

Nancy hung her head in shame. 'He turned up one night when you were at the pub and forced himself on me. I had no choice, Bill, believe me. If I hadn't given in you and I might have been turfed out.'

'And we still might,' he hissed. 'If you were going to open your legs for him the least you could have done is make a good job of it.'

'I'm sorry,' she whispered.

'Sorry! That's no bloody use. None whatsoever.'

She felt the tears begin to well, her thoughts muddled at that moment. 'He's such a horrible man, Bill. You've no idea what it was like.'

Bill made an exclamation of disgust and moved away. He wanted to smack Nancy, knock her from one end of the room to the other. What had been a secure little billet was now in jeopardy.

'You must have known he'd tup you at some point, young and pretty as you are. It's to be expected. It's his right after all. He's master, ruler of all on his land.'

She couldn't help herself. 'Have you no thoughts for me? No consideration for my feelings?'

'Sod your feelings, I care nothing for those. Not in these circumstances. A complete let-down I heard. Worse than useless.'

Nancy doubted that had come from Annie, or even Hector via her. The origin must be the master himself.

'What's a little shag, eh? Nothing, nothing at all. Happens every night of the week. The trouble with you, lady, is you're high and mighty. 'Tis a fault in you I've noticed many times. And now you've displeased the master. God damn you!'

'I didn't mean to displease him,' she replied, now almost hysterical. 'I didn't mean to do anything.'

The anger suddenly evaporated in Bill and he sagged where he stood. He was fond of Nancy, in a funny sort of way. In fact, if he was truthful, he felt . . . quite affectionate towards her. As much as he'd felt towards any woman that is, which wasn't saying a great deal. Now this . . .

He ran a hand over his face. Crossing to a chair, he slumped into it.

'Bill?'

'Aye?'

'I am sorry. Please believe that.'

'Aye, sure,' he muttered.

Nancy was trying to bring herself back under control, the momentary hysteria having almost got the better of her. She'd wondered how Bill would react, now she knew. No concern about her wellbeing, only that she'd displeased the master.

'Well, what's done is done I suppose,' Bill mumbled. 'Can't help that now. No use crying over spilt milk as they say. Except . . .' He swung on Nancy. 'If he calls again you put things right, you hear?'

'Right?'

He grimaced. 'I don't know what was wrong but whatever it was don't do it again. Make sure he goes out that door with a smile on his face and a spring in his step. Now promise me?'

She nodded.

'Let me hear you say it.'

'I promise, Bill.'

'You want to stay here, don't you?'

She nodded again.

'Then that's what you've got to do. And just pray to God he does come back. Or at least forgets the whole matter. The master isn't one to cross or upset, Nancy. Believe me. He's got a black heart that man. Black as coal.'

Bill lapsed into one of his brooding silences and after a

while Nancy turned away and got on with their evening meal.

'I've got a surprise for you,' Rose announced to Andrew.

He glanced up from his Sunday paper. 'A surprise?'

'A nice one too.'

'So what is it?'

Rose was enjoying this, and had been looking forward to the moment. 'Any ideas?'

He considered that, then shook his head. 'None at all.' A surprise? He couldn't imagine what.

'I'm going to have a baby.'

Chapter 3

'A baby!' Andrew exclaimed, stunned.

Rose smiled at his reaction. It had been eleven years after all since Drew had been born. She'd quite convinced herself she'd never have another child. That Drew was all there was.

Andrew leapt from his chair, the paper falling to the floor. He swept Rose into his arms and whirled her round. 'Darling, that's absolutely wonderful! I can't tell you how pleased I am.'

'I think you are,' she laughed in reply.

He stopped and stared at her, eyes blazing with pleasure. 'How far gone are you. I mean, is it certain?'

'It's certain, all right. And I'm three months gone. I wanted to be absolutely sure before telling you.'

Like Rose, Andrew had come to believe they'd never have another child. And now this. Right out of the blue.

'It'll be a little girl of course,' Rose declared. 'I've always wanted a girl and that's what we're going to have. I'm convinced of it.'

'Now hold on, Rose,' Andrew cautioned. 'Let's not get carried away. It might not be a girl . . .'

'It will,' she interjected firmly.

'But it might not be, I don't want you being disappointed. As far as I'm concerned as long as the bairn is born healthy with all its bits and pieces in the right places then that's all that matters.' He'd been about to add, with no after-effects to its mother, then changed his mind.

Now he came to think of it, there had been an added glow to Rose of late, and some sort of difference about her. 'How do you feel, my love? Any morning sickness?'

'If there had been you'd have known about it, silly. And I feel wonderful. Absolutely on top of the world.'

'Have you been to see the doctor yet?'

'Several times. He says there's nothing to worry about. Everything is exactly as it should be.'

Andrew breathed a sigh of relief. A baby! He was still grappling to take it on board.

'If you don't mind I thought we'd call her Mary after my mother.' Mary Seaton had died from influenza when Rose was young, leaving her father Willie to bring both her and her brother Ian up on his own. Until Willie had married Georgina, who'd then become their stepmother.

Andrew frowned. 'I've nothing against that, but isn't it unlucky to name a baby before it's born?'

'Nonsense!' Rose retorted. 'There's nothing unlucky about it. Old wives' tales. So you agree?'

'If it's what you wish.'

'I do. Very much so.'

'And a boy?'

She waved a hand. 'It's a girl, a boy's name won't come

into it. Trust me, I know. We women have intuitions about such things.'

That might be, Andrew thought, but he didn't like her building up her hopes about the baby's gender. He didn't want her being disappointed. He had heard of cases where it had been difficult afterwards when the wrong, or unexpected, sex had turned up.

'Now I want you taking good care of yourself,' he stated brusquely. 'No more horse riding for a start. Far too dangerous. Especially at your age.'

'My age!' she exploded mildly. 'I'm only thirty-two.'

'Even so, it's old enough to be pregnant. We mustn't take any chances. I insist on that.'

'Do you indeed,' she teased.

'I do. Most emphatically.'

She'd already decided to stop riding, but wasn't going to let Andrew know that. Let him think she was obeying his wishes. 'All right, no more riding,' she pretended to concede. 'Anything else?'

'A sleep every afternoon.'

'Whether or not I'm tired?' That again was said in a teasing manner.

'Precisely. And alcohol is completely out.'

She had to smile, not being a great drinker at the best of times. She was far too mindful of her figure for that. As a teenager she'd been inclined to plumpness and had got into the habit of watching her food and alcohol intake as a result.

'Agreed, Rose?'

'Agreed.'

He relaxed a little. 'Now, how about Drew?'

'What's he got to do with it?'

'Are we going to tell him?'

A smile twisted Rose's lips. 'I think we'd better. I'll probably begin to show before long anyway.'

'Then you can tell him.'

Rose laughed. 'Me! Why me? Why not you?'

'Because ... because ...' He couldn't think of an answer.

'Might it be because you'd be embarrassed?'

'Not at all,' Andrew blustered.

'I think so.'

'Then you think wrongly.'

Rose knew she didn't. 'I know what, we'll compromise,' she suggested. 'We'll tell Drew together.'

Andrew could see he wasn't going to wriggle out of this one. Well, if it had to be done so be it. Though he'd have much preferred Rose to have had a word on her own. 'When?'

'How about after lunch?'

He nodded. 'We'll do it then.'

Mary Drummond, Rose mused to herself, not for the first time. That had a fine ring to it. And Mary it would be.

Drew, home from school two days previously for the Christmas holidays, stared aghast at his parents. 'You're expecting!'

A smiling Rose nodded while Andrew glanced away.

Which meant ... At their age that was disgusting! No, it was more than that. It was obscene. Why, his pa was positively ancient while ma was ... He just couldn't credit his mother and father were still doing *that*.

'Are you pleased?' Rose prompted.

'We certainly are,' Andrew added in a mumble, supporting his wife.

'I suppose so,' Drew replied hesitantly. He was nothing of the sort. He was far from pleased. Apart from anything else it meant he was going to have to share the limelight. Or worse still, be completely shoved aside while all attention would be focused on this new addition to the family.

'It's going to be a little sister for you,' Rose declared, still smiling.

Andrew sighed. 'You don't know that for definite, Rose.'

She rounded on him, continuing to smile. 'I told you earlier, Andrew, it *will* be a girl. I'm positive.'

Drew couldn't get over the fact his parents still did it. He wasn't supposed to know the facts of life, they certainly hadn't been explained to him by Andrew and Rose, but he had picked up the rudimentaries at school. And incredulous he'd been too when he'd heard them. He found it amazing that people actually did that to one another. The very idea made him sick.

He stared at his mother, seeing her through new eyes. And disapproving eyes they were too. 'When?' he stuttered.

'In the spring, darling.'

He hoped he was at school when it happened. 'That's nice,' he managed.

Rose positively beamed. 'I'm glad you approve.'

Huh! Drew thought bitterly. It was as if his childhood had somehow, suddenly, begun to slip away. Right now he wanted to be on his own, think this through. It had never entered his mind; why the whole idea was preposterous, that his parents still went in for that sort of thing. He'd considered them well past it.

'Is there anything else you want to ask?' Andrew queried gruffly.

Drew shook his head.

'Fine.'

Drew wanted out of there, away from that room, the very house itself. And his parents. He'd run to the distillery and back. Further probably. Run as fast as he could, like the wind.

A few minutes later that's exactly what he was doing.

'So how did you get on?' Hettie asked Tommy who had just returned from his first day's work.

He pulled a face. 'Uncle Andrew wasn't joking when he said I'd be starting at the bottom. I've been humping sacks of grain all day.'

Jack chuckled.

'It's not funny, Dad! My back feels as though it's broken.'

'My wee lamb,' Hettie sympathised.

'You'll soon get used to it,' Jack stated. 'It won't take long.'

Hettie was recalling her time on the farm when a few sacks of grain had been nothing to her. But she'd been brought up differently from Tommy whose life to date had been one of ease.

Tommy flopped on to a chair and sighed, 'I won't have any trouble sleeping tonight.'

'Why don't you go and have a nice bath and then we'll eat directly afterwards.'

'I doubt I've enough energy left to go up those stairs, Mum. I'm whacked.'

Tommy gazed down at his hands, grimacing to see the beginnings of blisters. He couldn't help but glance at the clock and figure out how many hours there were till he had to return to purgatory.

'Of course you've enough energy,' Hettie declared in a no-nonsense tone. 'Now on you go. You'll feel the better for a bath, I promise you.'

Tommy groaned, 'I suppose so.'

'I know so,' Hettie stated.

Tommy pulled himself out of the chair, finding he was already starting to stiffen up. He'd be like a board before long, he reflected ruefully.

Tommy was so tired he fell asleep in the bath and Jack had to wake him up for supper.

'Why are you wriggling like that?' Nancy demanded. 'You've been fidgeting all evening.'

Bill glared at her, and mumbled a reply.

'Eh? I didn't hear what you said.'

'A boil!' he exclaimed. 'On my arse. It hurts something chronic.'

Nancy grinned. 'I was wondering why you were squirming in bed last night. It's not like you to be so restless.'

Bill shifted his position yet again. 'Damn thing.'

'How do you know it's a boil if it's on your backside? You can't see there.'

'I had a good feel earlier. It's a boil all right. And a big juicy bugger at that.'

Nancy had a think. 'My ma used to say that bread poultices were the very dab for those. Shall I make you one up?'

Bill gritted his teeth. He didn't like the idea of Nancy fiddling around with his backside, but he'd do anything for some relief. He grunted in reply.

'Is that a yes or no?'

'Yes damnit!' he swore.

'Right then, I'll get on with it. You'd better strip off.'

Bill was shy about that. He and Nancy might sleep together but nudity was something else.

She guessed what was bothering him. 'It's the only way, Bill. Unless you want to go on suffering.'

Which was the last thing he wanted. 'Aye, all right,' he answered ungraciously.

Nancy put the kettle on to boil while Bill got out of his trousers, deciding to stay in his long johns, until the poultice was ready.

Nancy crumbled bread into a bowl, ready for the water, then rooted around for some bandages she knew she had somewhere. She was going to enjoy this, she thought gleefully.

'I've never had a bread poultice before,' Bill said. 'Will it hurt?'

'Och, not to a big man like you. Nothing you can't cope with.'

Bill grunted again.

Nancy laid out her scissors in preparation for what was coming next, humming to herself in the process.

'Will you stop caterwauling,' Bill complained, nerves on edge. 'You sound as if you're being strangled.'

'Thank you very much,' she replied sarcastically, thinking that was it, the poultice was going to be as hot as she could make it.

'Well, you do.'

Bill ran a hand through his hair. He hated being unwell, positively loathed it. Not that having a boil was being unwell, far from it. But it was the same sort of thing in a way. It meant he wasn't a hundred per cent and that made the grafting more difficult.

Nancy waited till the kettle was fully boiling before removing it and pouring some of its contents into the bowl, clouds of steam issuing from both bowl and kettle.

In the interim she'd made up a pad of muslin on to which she now scooped the bread, mashing it down with the back of a tablespoon.

'Drop those long johns and lean across a chair,' she instructed. 'And hurry up if you want the benefit of this.'

Bill did as he was bid, feeling a proper fool with his naked backside sticking in the air.

Nancy approached him with the steaming pad in one hand, bandages and scissors in the other. She was doing her best to keep a smile off her face.

What a ridiculous sight, she thought. If Bill could only see himself. Better still, if others could. Especially those he worked alongside.

'Now then,' she declared, and slapped the poultice across the large boil that had erupted on his left cheek.

Bill howled and jerked.

'Keep still!' she snapped.

'It fucking burns.'

'Och, don't be a big jessie. Hold still.'

Bill's teeth were clamped shut, his eyes firmly closed. It was as if he was being branded.

'Next we'll get this bandage on to keep it in place,' Nancy said quietly.

Bill wished he'd never mentioned the bloody boil. This was terrible. 'Hurry up,' he gasped.

Nancy sadistically pushed down on the pad which made him writhe in agony. Oh, but this was grand. It wasn't often she had the upper hand where a man was concerned.

Her bandaging was far from expert, and she wasn't at

all sure the pad would remain in place, but she'd done her best. When the poultice cooled it would begin to draw, hopefully sucking all the poison out.

Nancy had to stop herself from slapping Bill resoundingly on the rear. That wouldn't have amused him one iota, though it certainly would her. 'Now how about a cup of tea? That'll cheer you up?' she suggested.

Bill began tugging at his long johns, keeping his face turned away from Nancy so she didn't see the tears in his eyes. He gave her another grunt.

Nancy resumed humming, much to Bill's annoyance. Only this time he didn't complain or pass comment.

One of the lassies in the bottling department glanced up as Tommy appeared. Here was a bit of sport, she thought, nudging her pal Irene in the ribs and nodding in Tommy's direction.

'Well, if it isn't Little Lord Fauntleroy himself,' the lassie, whose name was Bell Mathieson, called out.

Irene giggled, as did several of the others present.

Tommy reddened slightly and hurried on his way. He knew all these women, who lived in Dalneil and the surrounding area, but by sight only. Their being 'common', he hadn't had any truck with them in the past.

'Hello, Lord Fauntleroy, come on over here and give us a big smacker,' Irene declared brazenly.

Tommy's face reddened even further. This was awful, not to mention humiliating.

'Och, you're no interested in a wee runt like that, are you, Irene?' Isa Weir said, tongue firmly in cheek.

'He might not be wee all over,' Irene instantly retorted, which raised a filthy laugh.

'Is that right, Mr Riach?' Bell queried, heavily accenting the Mister. 'Are you no wee all over?'

'But big,' Hannah McIlroy added.

All the girls kept working during this teasing, their hands deftly moving as they corked, labelled and finally boxed the ever moving line of bottles that clattered between them.

Tommy desperately wanted to make a withering reply, but couldn't think of one. Then he stepped on something on the floor that sent him skidding, nearly losing his balance and falling over.

Bell and her companions screeched with laughter.

'It's a bit early for him to have been at the whisky already,' Sandy McAlpine commented loudly.

'He's too young for whisky. Aren't you, Mr Riach?' Isa Weir jibed.

Mr Balfour, the gaffer, came back into the department having been to the toilet. 'What's going on here?' he demanded.

The women immediately fell silent.

Mr Balfour harumphed and swept them all with a disapproving glance. 'Ah, Tommy,' he smiled. 'What can I do for you, lad?'

'Nothing, sir. I'm just passing through.'

Mr Balfour nodded. 'On you go then.'

Hannah McIlroy sniggered as Tommy passed her. '*Are* you big?' she whispered.

Rose had already run her bath and was waiting for it to cool before getting in. Meanwhile she was sitting in front of her vanity table brushing her hair. It was mid-afternoon.

She stopped brushing to stare at her abdomen reflected in the mirror, smiling to herself at the thought of what was inside. Their baby, little Mary.

45

She couldn't remember when she'd last been so ecstatically happy. It was as though all the colours in the world had somehow been made brighter. Shining as never before.

Rose sighed with pleasure. This pregnancy was proving quite different to the one she'd had with Drew. Then she'd been depressed and irritable, while this time round she was just bursting with energy and enthusiasm. That difference was yet another reason she was convinced she was carrying a female child.

Oh what fun it would be having a daughter. The fun of dressing her and all the other little joys that made having a daughter so different to a son.

A doll's house, she thought, they must get one of those. Then she remembered the doll's house she'd had when young and how much she'd enjoyed that. She'd spent hours at a time playing with it, all on her own, no need for other company.

She wondered if her father Willie had held on to the doll's house or if it had been thrown out or given away. It was quite possible it had been kept, in which case she would have it brought here for Mary. And the dolls that went with it.

The idea excited her. Her old doll's house and dollies, Mary would adore those.

She made up her mind to telephone Willie that very evening and inquire about them.

'How does it look?' Bill queried anxiously.

Nancy stared at the cavity where the boil had been, thinking it a right mess.

'Well?' Bill demanded.

'The poultice has done the trick.'

Bill uttered a sigh of relief, thinking that was that then.

Nancy wished she knew more about boils. The cavity and flesh directly round it were purple and red, shot through with whitish feathery lines, and the whole thing was still very angry in appearance. She wondered if Annie had any ointment she could put on that might help.

'I'm going to wash the area down and put on another bandage,' Nancy declared. 'That'll have to do for now.'

'It's still sore.'

'Aye, bound to be. But you're on the mend.'

'Thank God for that,' Bill mumbled. It was going to be lovely to sit down properly again, and lie on his back of a night.

'Just stay where you are till I get things ready,' Nancy instructed, and moved away leaving Bill bent over a chair with his long johns wrinkled round his ankles.

What she hadn't told him was that another boil had started to appear close by the original.

Andrew pulled Rose closer to him. 'That was wonderful. Thank you,' he crooned.

'It was wonderful for me too,' she replied coyly.

Andrew could only wonder at their recent lovemaking, a complete turnaround to what it had previously been. It reminded him of the times before Drew had been born.

She was actually eager now when he approached her, compliant to his wishes. What a change from the mental distance he'd endured for years when he'd felt, or at least that was the impression he'd got, she was only allowing him out of wifely duty.

If this was what a second pregnancy did to her then he praised the day it had happened.

'Oh, I forgot to say, I rang Pa when you were out at the pub with Jack,' Rose informed him, her voice warm and cosy, just like the body pressed against his.

'Oh?'

'He and Georgina would like us there for Hogmanay.'

'Indeed.'

Rose stroked a naked thigh. 'We haven't been to see them for ages, Andrew. I think we should go.'

'You want to then?'

'Very much so.' She smiled up at him. 'Besides, I have an ulterior motive for visiting The Haven.' That was the name of the estate Willie owned.

'Ulterior motive? Sounds intriguing.'

She told him about the doll's house and wanting to bring it back with them.

Andrew frowned. This business of Rose insisting the baby was going to be a girl really worried him. The idea had quite taken her over.

'So what do you say?' she prompted.

Andrew was always slightly uneasy about going to The Haven and visiting Georgina, though since his marriage to Rose nothing had ever been mentioned between them about the affair they'd once had. Or the fact that the son Willie thought was his, was actually Andrew's own. Not for the first time he thanked the Lord that young James, a year older than Drew, took after his mother in looks.

'I don't see why not,' he conceded. It had been a while since they'd been to The Haven; if anything a visit was overdue.

Willie was a long-standing friend of his from army days when they'd served in Ireland together. It was after the war, while passing through the area, that he'd met up again with Willie and through him Georgina and Rose.

Rose knew about the affair with her stepmother and had long since forgiven him, or at least come to terms with it. She had no inkling about the true parentage of James – and pray God she never found out.

'Drew will enjoy it,' Rose persisted. 'He and James get on so well together.'

'True enough.'

'Shall I accept their invitation then?'

'Of course. I'll look forward to it.'

Rose snuggled up even closer and moments later her hand was on his groin, instantly arousing Andrew again.

He marvelled at the change in her.

'Kiss me,' she whispered.

He did a lot more than that.

Andrew was day-dreaming, which was quite unlike him at work, when there was a tap on his office door. He roused himself. 'Come in!'

It was Mr Kelly, the book-keeper. 'Am I disturbing you, sir?'

'No, not at all, Mr Kelly. What can I do for you?' He noted that Kelly wasn't carrying any files, papers or the like.

Mr Kelly was only a few years older than Andrew but, with his white hair and thick bushy eyebrows, might have belonged to the next generation up. He was a small wiry man who always moved quickly and with apparent determination.

Andrew, feeling he couldn't do it all by himself any more, had advertised a few years previously for a book-keeper and Kelly had been one of the applicants.

Kelly was a local who'd moved to Edinburgh in his late teens where he'd taken up employment with an insurance company. A confirmed bachelor, he'd sent in the application because he wanted to return home to live with his ailing widowed mother. Within a short time of taking up his new post Kelly had proved himself indispensable and had certainly lightened Andrew's workload. Andrew thought the world of him.

Kelly cleared his throat. 'I've just heard the news, sir, about Mrs Drummond, and I wanted to offer my congratulations.'

'Why, thank you, Mr Kelly.'

'No doubt you're delighted, sir.'

'Indeed I am. As is my wife.'

For a brief moment Kelly thought of the children he'd never had and never would. If there was a regret in his life, that was it. It would be a fine thing to have children of your own, especially a son and heir like Andrew. But that was not to be. Truth was, he'd never felt comfortable in female company. Not in that respect anyway. He'd never have admitted it to a soul but they scared him somewhat. The idea of having to be physical with one would have sent him running a mile.

Andrew glanced at his watch. 'I'll tell you what, Mr Kelly. Shall we have a dram on it?'

Kelly was shocked, though he did his best to try and hide it. 'Aye, if you wish, sir,' he replied reluctantly, heartily disapproving of drinking while working. And certainly before noon as it now was. But Andrew was the boss.

A few minutes later both men were holding fully charged glasses, Kelly wondering if he should take it upon himself to propose the toast or leave that to Andrew.

Andrew did the honours. 'To the new baby, eh?'

'The new baby, sir.'

Kelly grimaced as he swallowed his dram, not being

much of a drinker at the best of times. The spirit made his eyes water.

'And will you convey my best wishes to Mrs Drummond, sir. I'd be obliged if you did.'

'I shall indeed, Mr Kelly. You can rest assured.'

Kelly placed his empty glass on Andrew's desk. There had been some matters he'd wished to discuss with Andrew but now decided to leave them till later.

'Is that all, Mr Kelly?'

'Yes, sir. Thank you, sir.'

'Then how about another . . .'

'No, no, sir. I must be getting on.' And with that Kelly hastily left the office.

Andrew chuckled quietly when Kelly was gone. A funny old stick, but his heart was in the right place and he certainly knew his job.

Chapter 4

Nancy shook her head. 'It's getting worse, Bill. You've three whoppers now and signs of another on its way.' The cavity belonging to the original boil also remained unhealed. This despite the ointment, borrowed from Annie, that she'd rigorously applied.

Bill swore.

'I honestly don't know what to do. I think you're going to have to go to the doctor.'

Bill straightened up with a jerk. 'That'll be the day. I'm not going to any doctor. I don't trust them. Quacks one and all.'

'There's nothing else for it that I can see.'

He turned and glared at her. 'No doctor, understand!'

'All right, it's your funeral.'

He gingerly felt the boils and groaned. They were like red hot pokers stuck into his bum. He was tired, even more than usual, not having slept properly for nights.

'Shall I put on some more ointment?' she queried.

'Aye, go ahead.'

'Though it doesn't seem to be doing any good.'

'Put it on anyway.'

'Then bend over again.'

This was getting past a joke, she thought as he presented his backside to her for a second time. At which point one of the boils burst sending a dribble of thick, yellow pus running downwards.

Nancy winced at the sight, thinking how horrible it looked. Very nasty indeed. 'Perhaps you should take some time off work?' she suggested.

'Don't be soft, woman. I can't do that. No work no pay, and that means you as well, for if I don't get paid then neither do you.'

She'd been well aware of that. 'It was only an idea.'

'And a stupid one at that.'

'There's no need to be abusive, Bill. I'm only trying to help.'

He stared into the roaring fire, biting his lip as she began mopping up the pus. He was damned if he'd go to any doctor. Not only did he not trust them, they were expensive to boot.

The barman at The Sheugh glanced at Bill in surprise. 'What are you doing here, Bill? It's not your night.'

'There aren't any rules that I always have to come in on the same night I take it?' he snapped in reply.

'Of course there aren't.'

'Then give us a dram and a half pint.'

Bill stared moodily about him as the barman got on with his order. It wasn't his night but he'd desperately wanted a drink to take his mind off these effing boils that were driving him mad.

He wasn't pulling his weight at work, he knew that only too well. Not that he'd said anything to any of the others, none of their bloody business that he had boils on his arse.

And where was it going to end? One had led to two and that to three with another on its way. Was he going to have a whole backside full before he was finished? The thought of that brought a cold sweat to his brow.

'There you are, Bill,' the barman declared, placing his drinks before him.

Bill grunted, fished out the correct money and paid for them. There was enough in his pocket for a few drams, thank God. Anything to ease the pain and discomfort.

As the pub was nearly empty the barman considered lingering to chat, then decided against it and moved away, guessing Bill wanted to be left alone.

Bill picked up his dram and threw it down his throat, giving a small cough afterwards. He'd just had to get out of the cottage. He didn't know what it was about Nancy lately but she sure as hell was getting on his wick. Everything she did seemed to irritate him.

Why hadn't she been able to cure these boils! She was a woman, after all. Women could do these things. Patsy certainly would have been able to. Patsy would have had them cleared up quick as a wink.

Go to the doctor indeed, he sneered to himself. No bloody fear. He'd much rather swallow his money than give it to those charlatans.

He thought of John Bald whom he'd grafted alongside a few years back. A grand bloke had been John till he'd fallen ill and gone to the doctor with pains in his chest. Well, that had been the end of John. Six months later he was dead and planted. So much for going to the doctor.

The bastard had been quick enough to take John's cash all right. Oh aye, he had that. And a fat lot of good it had done John. No good at all.

Bill crooked a finger at the barman and indicated he wanted another dram.

He again thought of Nancy, certain she was laughing at him behind his back. Bitch. How dare she laugh at him, he couldn't help having boils. They were the last thing he wanted. And she found them funny.

He placed more money on the bar when the dram arrived, not speaking to the barman or the barman to him.

Irritating, that's what she'd become. Annoying in the extreme. The second dram swiftly disappeared followed by a gulp of beer.

A slight numbness was taking hold of him which eased his pain. A few more drams and he wouldn't be feeling much at all. Perhaps he might get a decent night's sleep later on.

And then the bandage that Nancy had secured round him somehow slipped, to fall off his buttocks altogether.

Fuck, he swore inwardly. She couldn't even put a bandage on properly. Now he'd have to go to the bog and do something about it.

He was raging inside as he headed for the toilet.

Nancy sat in the dark, wrapped in a warm shawl. She'd let the fire almost die out. She was waiting for Bill to come home; he was a lot later than she'd anticipated.

She enjoyed sitting in the dark letting her mind roam free. Sometimes she thought about things, other times nothing at all. She found great solace in this, particularly the latter.

She'd seen the master watching her again that day, his expression inscrutable, those hard eyes of his fastened on to her. She'd found it scary.

She wondered if he'd call again, dreading that he might, shuddering at the memory of him pawing at her, driving himself into her flesh. It had been sheer humiliation and a frightening violation.

She started when there was a rattle at the door which then swung open.

'Bill?'

He swore, and lurched towards her, knocking over a chair in the process. 'Where are you?' he slurred.

'Here.' She rose and went to meet him.

Bill reached out and grabbed the front of her smock. 'Why are we in darkness?'

'I like it that way sometimes. You know that.' Christ, he was pissed, she thought, the reek of alcohol wafting over her as he swayed on the spot.

'The bandage fell off in the pub. A proper tangle I was in,' he snarled.

'I'm sorry.'

'And so you should be. Can't you do anything right? Can't you even put on a fucking bandage so that it stays up properly?'

'I did my best.'

'Well, that's not good enough. You hear. Not good enough.'

He threw her from him. 'You stay here the night. I don't want you in my bed. It'll be more comfortable without you.'

He staggered from the room, stumbling several times as he went.

Nancy stared after him for a few seconds, then returned

to her chair and sank into it. Couldn't do anything right? Was that really true or just the drink talking?

She'd often felt alone in her short life but never more so than at that moment. Alone, and worthless.

Nancy dropped her head into her hands and sobbed in despair, hot salty tears coursing down her cheeks.

'Despite his moans and groans I think he's settling into the job,' Hettie said to Jack. 'Do you agree?'

'It would seem so.'

Hettie was happy to have that confirmation, glancing up at the ceiling beyond which Tommy's bedroom lay. As was usual with him since starting at the distillery he'd gone to bed relatively early.

Was it her imagination or was there a change in him? He seemed more grown up somehow, more mature. She was certain there was an air of gravitas about him that hadn't been there before.

Hettie sighed with contentment. Children, they were just one long worry from the day they were born. Nor did it end when they left home and got married, she'd been told. Even then you kept on worrying yourself sick about them.

Not that she'd have changed anything. It must be appalling to be childless, she reflected. Particularly for a woman whose whole being craved to reproduce.

Men had that urge as well, she thought, but not in the same way as women. Their urge was for sex, to plant their seed, whilst a woman's was to give birth. The completion of the cycle which she'd seen so many times on the farm, from the earth and ever-changing seasons, to the animals in the field.

Jack suddenly smiled, a beam that lit up his face. He began to chuckle.

'Jack?'

'Huh?'

'What's wrong with you?'

He was still smiling broadly. 'Nothing. Nothing at all.' He'd just come up with the perfect ending for his new book but wasn't about to tell Hettie that.

'Are you sure?'

'Absolutely positive.'

He chuckled again. It was a cracker all right. An absolute cracker.

Tommy, shoulders hunched against the cold and hands deep in his coat pockets, trudged on his way home for lunch. He hoped Hettie had something warm and filling to serve up, he was starving.

He halted when he heard a drone in the distance and, shading his eyes, glanced up at the sky.

What a beautiful sight, he thought, the plane's sleek lines gripping his imagination.

And then the plane went zooming overhead affording him a full view of its underside. One of those new fighter planes he'd read about, he decided. Had to be.

His heart was in his throat as he watched it recede into the distance, thinking what it would be like to fly one of those. Even more exciting than a racing car for you were operating in three dimensions as opposed to only two.

For the space of a few moments the Spitfire was silhouetted against the weak, watery winter sun. A shining bullet of pure power. Then it was lost in cloud.

Tommy sighed. What he wouldn't have given to be the chap in its cockpit, a lord of the air as all fighter pilots were.

For the rest of the way home he envisaged himself at

the plane's controls, putting it through its paces. Banking left, right, diving, pulling out of the dive at the last possible moment. A dashing daredevil to be regarded with awe wherever he went.

For the rest of that day the fantasy kept popping back into his mind.

'Glasgow!' Rose repeated in delight.

'I have to go down on business and thought you might like to come with me. You could do some Christmas shopping while I'm tied up, then we could have the evening together and stay overnight.'

Rose's mind was already racing, the shops she'd go to, what she might buy. 'It sounds wonderful.'

'I thought you'd be pleased.' He suddenly frowned. 'I need the Rolls looked at anyway. I can't quite put my finger on the problem but there's been something wrong with it of late. Probably only a bit of fine tuning but while in Glasgow I'll take the opportunity of putting it into the dealer's for a check over.'

The Rolls had originally belonged to Andrew's father Murdo, in fact had been his pride and joy, and had come to him on Murdo's death. The old lady was getting on in years now and several times he'd thought about replacing her with a newer, more updated model. Thoughts he'd always eventually dismissed, coming to the conclusion on each occasion that there was no reason why the car shouldn't last him out. A Rolls was special after all, built not only for the luxury and perfection it provided, but to last.

'The day after tomorrow, you say?' Rose queried.

'That's right.'

'You might have given me more notice.'

He laughed. 'I might have done if the idea had not only come to me this morning.' He paused, then added, 'Besides, the break will do you good. You've been cooped up here for ages.'

'I shall shop for baby clothes,' Rose announced enthusiastically. 'Apart from Drew's christening gown we haven't anything left of his. Anyway, this time round I'll want pinks not blues.'

Andrew sighed. There she went again, determined it was going to be a little girl. 'Perhaps neutral colours to start with?' he suggested. 'Until we know what's what.'

Rose fixed him with a withering stare. 'Oh ye of little faith, Andrew. I've told you to trust my instincts on this.'

'Even so . . .'

'Not another word,' she interrupted. 'You'll only spoil my fun if you go on and on.'

'I'm just thinking of you, Rose,' he said lamely.

'I appreciate that. You don't want me to be disappointed, and I won't be. You could put money on it.'

Andrew recalled a period in his life when he'd been addicted to gambling. An embarrassing affair that had ended up with Murdo having to pay off his debts. He cringed inside at the memory.

'It'll be an early start,' he declared. 'You'll have to be up and ready. I shan't be hanging around as I have appointments to keep.'

'I'll be ready,' she assured him.

Crossing to Andrew, eyes sparkling, she pecked him on the cheek. 'You're a darling man, Andrew Drummond, and I love you very much.'

'As I love you.'

The smile she gave him contained the promise that she'd be showing her gratitude, and love, later on that night.

Drew stood in the window watching the Rolls drive off to Glasgow, angry and jealous that his parents had not taken him with them. Despite his pleadings the answer had been an emphatic no.

He thought of the forthcoming child his mother kept burbling on about non-stop. It was 'Mary this', and 'Mary that', and 'when Mary comes I'm going to' . . .

He loathed this Mary before she was even born. Loathed and detested her.

'Are you all right, Master Drew?'

He turned from the window to find Christine, one of the maids, staring at him in concern.

'Why shouldn't I be?'

His tone was rude, she thought. There were times when Master Drew needed his arse skelped, which he certainly would have had if he'd been hers.

'You just looked a bit upset, that's all.'

'Haven't you got something to do?' he answered coldly.

Skelped and skelped again, Christine told herself. The little bugger was spoilt rotten. 'Plenty,' she replied equally coldly and swept away, leaving him to it.

Drew was instantly contrite, knowing he shouldn't have spoken to Christine that way. But he hadn't been able to help it. Besides, she was only staff after all, no one of real importance.

At least he'd be going to The Haven for Hogmanay, there was that to look forward to. He and James would have lots of fun together. As he would with Grandpa Willie.

That helped dissipate his anger somewhat. Hogmanay at The Haven would be great.

'How about this, sir?'

The necklace was eighteen strands of eighteen-carat gold roped together by a length of fine gold wire. Andrew liked it immediately, but would Rose?

'It's very nice,' he murmured.

'And tasteful, sir. Definitely that.'

Andrew glanced at the assistant, then back again at the necklace, trying to imagine it round Rose's neck. During their stay in Glasgow he too was searching for a Christmas present, making himself find the time to do so.

'How much?' All items in the shop, Glasgow's most exclusive and prestigious jeweller's, were unpriced.

The assistant told him.

Expensive, Andrew thought. But he'd wanted the best and you had to pay for that. Besides, it was to be more than just a Christmas present. It was also a celebration of Rose's pregnancy. In other words, a very special gift to mark both occasions.

The assistant moved away to return with another necklace. 'There's this one, sir.'

Andrew shook his head. That one didn't appeal at all.

'We have others.'

'No, no,' Andrew interrupted, making up his mind. He tapped the double-stranded piece. 'This will do admirably.'

'A wise choice if I may say so, sir. Very wise indeed.'

Andrew reached for his cheque book. There was something else he intended buying Rose before returning to the hotel.

The thought of it made him smile.

* * *

'For me?'

'For you, my angel.'

Rose stared quizzically at the fancifully wrapped box, wondering what it contained. The box was about a foot long and several inches wide.

'Well, aren't you going to open it?'

She laughed. 'Don't hurry me, Andrew. Let me enjoy speculating about what's inside.'

He watched her closely as she attacked bows and ribbons.

'Oh, Andrew,' she breathed when the lid was off and the tissue paper unfolded. 'It's beautiful.'

Rose laid the box on the bed and pulled out a pale pink négligé edged with matching hand-made lace. A nightdress of the same colour, also edged in lace, was revealed underneath.

She held the négligé up against herself, then ran a hand over the smoothness of the fabric.

'It becomes you.' Andrew smiled.

Pure silk, Rose thought. Trust Andrew.

'Pleased?'

'Of course.'

He indicated the nightdress. 'And there's that to go with it. I was rather hoping you'd wear them both tonight.'

She smiled wickedly. 'I can imagine what you have in mind, you old seducer.'

'Anything wrong with that?'

'Not in the least.'

Rose placed the négligé beside the box and whisked out the nightdress, which shimmered in the overhead light. 'Why don't you try them on?' he teased.

'Not yet, thank you very much. We'll never get any dinner if I do.'

'I can always have it sent up. That and champagne.' The wicked smile returned. 'You are impatient.'

He went to her and caught her into his arms, drinking in the sweet smell of her. 'You're right. We should wait. Tonight will come round soon enough. And in the meantime I want to wine and dine you. My favourite girl.'

She cocked an eyebrow. 'Does that imply there are others?'

'Don't be silly. I've never looked at another woman since marrying you, and you know it.'

'Do I?' Now it was her turn to tease.

'It's the truth. You're all I want and ever will. Where women are concerned that is.'

'Is that a fact?'

'It's a fact.'

It could be so good between them at times, she thought. So very good. 'There's only one drawback about the nightdress,' she said softly.

He frowned. 'Which is?'

'I don't have to put it on to know it'll be tight fitting. Give me another month or two and I won't be able to get into it.'

He hadn't considered that, nor had thought to mention to the saleswoman that his wife was pregnant. 'I can always change it. Though not tonight, the shop will be closed by now.'

'I don't want you to change it. I was only telling you, that's all.'

'There are still those couple of months,' he murmured, and blew gently in her ear.

'Indeed there are. And *after* Mary arrives.'

He wanted her there and then, to strip her naked and
. . . He broke their embrace and cleared his throat.

'What's wrong?'

'I'm having evil thoughts.'

She laughed, gathered up her négligé and nightdress and
draped them over her pillows.

'Rogano's,' he breathed huskily, his imagination running riot.

'Can we still have champagne with our fish?'

'You can have whatever you want, Rose. A bucket of
the stuff if you wish. Tubsful of the stuff if it'll make
you happy.'

He'd temporarily forgotten she wasn't supposed to be
drinking, she thought gleefully, testament to his 'evil
thoughts', as he'd put it. 'I don't need champagne for
that. Simply being with you is enough.'

A lump came into his throat as he gazed deep into
her eyes.

'The table's booked for eight thirty. We'd better get a
move on,' he said eventually.

Ever since seeing the Spitfire Tommy had been reading
up on the air aces of the Great War. What splendid chaps
they'd been, heroic in the extreme. Flying their Spads,
Sopwith Camels and SE15s.

He closed his eyes, picturing himself high aloft in one
of those fabled machines, a white streamer attached to the
back of his helmet crackling behind him as he shot down
yet another Hun.

'Stop idling, boy! You're being paid to work not day-
dream,' Mr Kelly snapped, having stopped in front of
Tommy's desk.

Tommy's eyes flicked open. 'Sorry, sir,' he stammered.

'And so you should be.'

Kelly stared sternly at Tommy who'd come to help him in accounts. The lad was a liability in his opinion, couldn't add for toffee, forever making mistakes, having to go over columns of figures again and again and still getting them wrong more likely than not.

'Then get on with it. And remember I'll be keeping an eye on you at all times.'

'Yes, sir.'

Tommy busied himself once more with the ledger book open before him. How boring this was, how excruciatingly boring. One long yawn.

Tommy stared at the ledger's pages, but it was the skies over France and Germany he was seeing.

'Is there something in the dictation you can't make out?'

Hettie glanced across at Jack, having stopped typing for the past few minutes while transcribing her notes. 'No, I was just thinking.'

'Now there's a dangerous occupation,' he joked. 'About my book?'

Hettie sighed. 'No, Rose. Envying her really.'

Jack could hear a wistfulness in her voice. 'In what way?'

Hettie decided to take a break and got up from her chair. 'Would you like a cup of coffee?'

'Not for me.'

'I would. I won't be long.'

Jack waited patiently till she returned and sat opposite. 'It's unlike you to be envious, Hettie,' he said softly.

'I suppose it is. But in this case I am.'

'Is it the baby?'

That startled her. 'How did you guess?'

'A couple of things you've said recently.'

Silence fell between them while Hettie sipped her coffee, then nibbled the biscuit she'd brought in to go with it. 'The book is coming along well,' she declared.

'And I'm still not telling you the ending.'

'I've given up all hope of that.'

'Good, let it surprise you.' He paused, then said, 'Shall we go for a stroll after you've finished?'

'If you wish.'

'I could use some fresh air blowing round my cheeks.'

Me too, she thought. She and Jack often went for a walk which she always enjoyed. She'd describe anything that might be different and there were always people to stop and pass the time of day with.

'The baby,' Jack said, bringing the subject back to that.

Hettie gazed into her cup. 'It would be nice to have another child. I think Tommy missed out on not having a brother or sister.'

'I agree,' Jack stated. 'But as they say, man proposes, God disposes. It apparently wasn't his will for us to have another.'

'Or Rose, until she suddenly fell pregnant again. So, in our case who's to say. It might happen yet.'

'It might.'

'And wouldn't that be wonderful, Jack! I'd be so thrilled.'

'Who knows,' he teased. 'Maybe these things are catching.'

'Maybe,' she grinned.

That cheered Hettie up and her gloominess and self-introspection vanished.

'Why don't we go out for that walk now and you can finish your typing when we get back?' he suggested.

'Would you mind?'

'Not in the least.'

Jack decided he was going to buy Hettie a puppy for Christmas. It would need lots of attention and could give her something to fuss over. It would hopefully stop her being so broody.

Chapter 5

'Where's Mum?'

Andrew laid his whisky aside to gaze at his son. He'd been lost in thought, remembering the days when he'd been young. Those and times in Ireland as a Second Lieutenant. Other memories too, some of which he wasn't proud of.

'Gone to Aunt Charlotte's,' Andrew replied. 'She shouldn't be too long I wouldn't think. What do you want her for?'

Drew shrugged. 'Nothing much.'

'Can I be of any help?'

Drew shook his head.

How well did he know his son? Andrew wondered. Probably as little as Murdo had known him at that age. And older come to that. Murdo had seemed forever tied up at the distillery just as he supposed he was.

He gestured to the chair Rose usually sat on. 'Come and join me.'

Drew viewed Andrew with suspicion, this being rather out of the ordinary. 'Why?'

'Just for a natter, that's all. No other reason.'

He had nothing better to do anyway, Drew decided, heading for the chair. Truth was he was bored rigid and impatient for their departure to The Haven. With James about there was always plenty to do there.

'A penny for them?' Andrew probed.

Drew didn't really enjoy being alone with his father whom he found stern and forbidding at times.

Drew shrugged.

Andrew reached for his drink and had a sip. 'We don't get enough time together, you and I.'

And even less when the rotten baby arrived, Drew thought bitterly. He was getting heartily sick of his mother forever going on about it.

'Then what shall we talk about?'

Drew was beginning to wish he hadn't accepted the invitation to sit down. 'Anything you like,' he mumbled.

'What about when you grow up and one day take over the distillery?'

Drew blinked. 'You mean when you're dead?'

That made Andrew smile. 'Before then I hope.'

'Maybe I don't want to run the distillery. Maybe I'll want to do something else.'

Andrew stared at his son in astonishment. That possibility had never crossed his mind. 'But it's yours, your inheritance,' he stated slowly.

'So?'

'So it's your duty to take over where I leave off. If nothing else, think of the people who rely on you for employment. What about them?'

'Whoever bought the distillery would keep them on, I suppose.'

Andrew's expression became grim. 'Don't you understand? It's Drummond single malt whisky, it should be owned and run by a Drummond, not someone else. An outsider.'

'Maybe I'll have a baby brother and he can run it,' Drew said slyly. 'Just as you took over when my uncle Peter was killed.'

'Don't ever mention a baby boy in front of your mother,' Andrew swiftly rebuked him. 'You know she has her heart set on having a girl.'

'But she might not.'

Heaven forbid, Andrew thought. Heaven forbid. He saw off what remained in his glass and, rising, crossed to the decanter. That possibility was something he'd been trying desperately hard not to think about.

Drew was enjoying his father's discomfiture, watching Andrew keenly through slightly slitted eyes. 'Mum doesn't know it's going to be a girl after all. She's only guessing.'

Andrew had a quick gulp from his glass, then topped it up again. 'We'll simply have to wait and see what happens,' he said gruffly.

Drew secretly hoped it would be a boy. It would be a sort of revenge. Then he had an alarming thought. 'There won't be any others after this one?'

Andrew returned to his chair. 'It's feasible I suppose. Why not.'

'But . . . but . . .' Drew stopped spluttering and gazed at his father in horror. 'You're so old. So ancient. Why, you're almost as old as Grandpa Willie.'

That hurt, Andrew reflected. It truly did. He was sensitive enough about the twenty-year age difference between himself and Rose without that kind of statement being made.

'Ancient, am I?' he repeated, forcing himself to chuckle.

'You've even got white hair.'

Andrew self-consciously touched a patch above his left ear which had lost its natural auburn colour and was now a distinct white. 'Only in parts,' he attempted to joke.

'It's still white.'

There was a long silence between them, then Andrew said slowly, 'You resent this child, don't you, Drew?'

Drew didn't reply.

'Don't you?' That was said softly, but with an edge to it.

'Yes,' Drew eventually whispered.

'But why? Won't it be nice having a brother or sister?'

And then the dam burst, the pent-up resentment Andrew had so correctly recognised. Drew blinked back tears. 'I just can't believe you and Mum . . . at your age. It's . . . unbelievable . . . horrid . . .' He broke off, trembling all over.

An embarrassed Andrew did his best not to show his emotions. 'It's perfectly natural, Drew, when people love one another as we do. That's what happens between them.'

Drew didn't want to hear any more of this or discuss the matter further. 'I think you're both disgusting!' he shouted and, leaping from his chair, ran out of the room.

'Drew! Come back here!'

When his son didn't Andrew contemplated going after him, then decided it was probably best not to.

'Oh dear,' he sighed. They were going to have problems with Drew. He might come to terms with the inevitable, but Andrew had his doubts.

Should he tell Rose about this conversation? She'd be

dreadfully upset and that was the last thing he wanted in her present condition.

He'd leave it a while and talk to the lad again. Yes, that was what he'd do. A month maybe, perhaps more. After all, it was early days yet. It was only a short time since Drew had been told of Rose's pregnancy.

'Children,' he breathed. What a handful they could be.

He knew it must be his imagination, but he was certain he could hear Murdo laughing in his grave.

'Enjoying yourself, Mr Kelly?' It was the distillery's Christmas 'do' and every single member of staff was there. A great deal of food had been laid on plus crates of Drummond whisky. And should the latter run out there was always plenty more where that came from.

'Oh aye, very much so,' Kelly lied in reply. He didn't enjoy this sort of occasion one little bit.

Andrew gazed about him, thinking it was going well. But then it always did. He spotted Rose chatting to Bob Mowbray, one of the maltsters. Bob was shortly due for retiral and would be sorely missed.

Over in a corner Tommy was starting on his fourth dram. He didn't realise it but there was a rather silly grin on his face, the effect of the other three.

This was a bit of all right, he was thinking. Free booze and all you could eat. It certainly beat that ledger book he'd been struggling with earlier.

'This is rare, isn't it,' Bell Mathieson, from bottling, said to her pal Irene.

Irene patted her stomach. 'I'm full as a pig, so I am. I can't remember the last time I guzzled so much.'

'And it's good stuff too. Not plain like we get at home.'

'Aye, it is that,' Irene agreed.

Bell nudged Irene with her elbow. 'There's Tommy Riach. Fancy going over?'

'What for?'

'To talk to him, you eejit.'

Irene considered that. 'I don't think so. He's posh, Bell, management and all that. No' one of the workers like us.'

'That doesn't make any difference on a night like this. Even Mr Drummond and his wife speak to everyone. Real friendly like.'

Irene studied her friend curiously. 'Have you got a notion, Bell Mathieson?'

'What do you mean a notion?' She knew exactly what Irene was getting at.

'For Tommy Riach.'

'Och, away and bile yer heid. He's far too young. I don't go in for cradle snatching.' Bell was the grand old age of eighteen.

'You seem keen though.'

'I'm nothing of the sort,' Bell retorted. 'I only suggested chaffing with him. Look, he's all alone, standing by his ownsome.'

Irene studied Tommy. 'He is quite handsome, I give you that. But no' for us, Bell. When he gets a girl it'll be some high falutin lassie. Don't forget who his da is. A famous writer and all. Not to mention stinking rich from all accounts.'

'He is attractive though,' Bell mused.

'And they say he's got a big one.'

Bell laughed. 'Don't be daft. That was only a joke yon day in the department to embarrass him.'

'Maybe so. But there are those who swear it's true.'

'Never!'

'I'm telling you.'

'And how would they know?'

Irene shrugged. 'Search me. Perhaps one of them found out for herself and passed on the word.'

Both females were virgins and would have hotly denied being anything else. Yet, as was common amongst their kind, they would pretend otherwise when it suited them. A wink here, a glance there, a knowing look when certain types of remarks were passed. They saw it as good fun and all part of being grown up.

'Here, my glass is empty,' Bell observed.

'Have you finished that already!'

Bell giggled. 'It doesn't half go down quickly when they're giving it away.'

Irene nodded her agreement. 'May as well make the most of the situation then, eh?'

'You're dead right there.'

They looked over at a long trestle table festooned with bottles. It was strictly help yourself.

'Shall we?' Bell proposed.

'I'm with you.'

In unison, they moved towards the table.

'Are you getting tired?' Andrew queried anxiously as Rose joined him having left Bob Mowbray.

'Not in the least.'

'I don't want you overdoing things. Perhaps you should have a sit down for a while.'

Rose laughed. 'Stop fussing like an old mother hen, Andrew. I'll sit down if I need to.'

'Just make sure you do,' he cautioned.

She touched him lightly on the hand. 'You really are sweet.'

'I do my best,' he smiled.

'I think I should mingle again. What do you say?'

'We'll do so together.'

It was getting terribly hot in there, Rose reflected, and she was beginning to perspire a little. Another ten or fifteen minutes and she'd retire to cool off and check her make-up.

'Why so cheery?'

A startled Tommy turned to find he was being addressed by Bell Mathieson with Irene beside her.

'You were scowling as if you had a bad smell under your nose,' Irene explained.

Tommy laughed softly. 'Was it as obvious as that?'

Bell nodded.

'I was thinking . . .' He hesitated. 'Perhaps I shouldn't say.'

'Go on,' Irene urged.

Still he swithered, then the alcohol got the better of him. 'I was thinking about Mr Kelly. He's been getting at me all afternoon. The man makes my life a misery.'

'Oh?' That was Bell.

'He hates me for some reason. I'm sure of it.'

'I find that hard to believe,' Irene commented.

'It's non-stop niggle as far as he's concerned. I just can't seem to do anything right.'

'Surely you're exaggerating.' Bell frowned.

'Not in the least. I got one lousy column of figures wrong this afternoon and that was that. He wouldn't get off my back until it was time to go.'

Tommy glared across the room at Kelly who was deep in conversation with Davey Grant, an elderly engineer. 'Bloody swine,' he muttered.

'It's that bad, eh?' Irene smiled, trying to lift Tommy's spirits.

'Worse. You've no idea. I can't wait to get out of his

clutches and into another department. Thank God I'm not here as a trainee book-keeper. Life under him would be ongoing hell.'

Bell nodded her sympathy. They were lucky with Balfour their gaffer. He might be a hard taskmaster but he was very fair. 'I've heard you're eventually going to be a traveller for us. Is that right?'

'That's right.'

Bell's eyes lit up. 'That's a smashing job so it is. And well paid too I should think.'

'Very.' Tommy preened. 'And I'll have a car. Well, I'll have to being on the road.'

'Jammy you.' Irene beamed.

Kelly was now forgotten as Tommy set out to impress the girls. 'It's a very responsible position you know. And terribly important.'

'Oh aye,' Bell agreed, thinking there was something rather angelic about Tommy's appearance which she hadn't noticed before. It appealed.

'You must be awfully clever,' Irene declared, her eyes shining also.

'Not where columns of figures are concerned,' Tommy joked, and they all laughed.

'You're really nice,' Bell grinned.

Tommy went slightly red. 'Why thank you very much.' Then, not to be outdone where compliments were concerned, and thinking it only polite anyway, 'And so are the pair of you.'

'Och, we're just wee working girls,' muttered Irene. 'That's all.'

'You're still nice. And easy to talk to.'

'Do you normally have trouble talking to lassies then?' Tommy stared at Bell. 'Depends on the lassie.'

Bell nodded her understanding.

'Well I'm going to get myself another dram,' he declared. 'How about you two?'

Bell and Irene instantly swallowed the remainder of their drinks. 'That's very kind.'

He took their glasses from them. 'I'll only be a couple of minutes.'

'We'll be here,' Bell retorted.

'We're not going anywhere,' Irene added.

Bell thoughtfully watched Tommy's retreating back. Like an angel, she thought again.

'Pity there isn't any dancing,' Irene commented.

'Aye, true enough.' Bell wouldn't have minded getting up with Tommy Riach.

'I could really go a bit of the jigging.'

'Me too.'

Pity about his age, Bell reflected. And the difference in class between them.

'I think we'd better be getting you home,' Bell declared to Tommy some while later.

'But why? I'm enjoying myself. Aren't you?' he slurred in reply.

'You've had enough, Tommy. Any more and you might make a fool of yourself.'

Despite the fuzziness in his head Tommy could see the sense of that. He had had quite a lot. He tried to tot up how many, but couldn't. He quietly burped and the taste of whisky flooded his mouth.

'Have you got a coat?' Bell queried.

Tommy nodded.

'Then you get that while we get ours. We'll walk you back.'

'Will you?' He was delighted.

'You might fall down or get lost otherwise. We can't take the chance. It would be awful for someone going to be a traveller to disgrace himself.'

'Oh, the humiliation,' Tommy replied in a mock tone.

'It would be too. Especially if Mr Drummond got to hear of it, which he probably would.'

'It might even get you the sack,' Irene chipped in.

Tommy shook his head, and held up crossed fingers. 'My dad and he are like that. He'd never sack me. Not in a million years.'

'I wouldn't count on that,' Bell replied sternly. 'Now come on, let's be out of here. It's almost finished anyway.' She gazed about her. Many of the staff had already taken their leave, though Mr and Mrs Drummond were still present.

'Aye, all right,' Tommy consented. 'But just a last dram before we go.'

'No,' Bell stated firmly.

'Another won't hurt.'

Bell stared into glassy eyes. 'In your case it would. Now do as you're told and that's an end of it.'

'Bossy women,' Tommy sighed.

With Bell and Irene flanking him on either side they headed from the room.

'Christ!' Tommy exclaimed, and went tumbling on to the road.

'He is well and truly pissed. Even more than I thought,' Bell said to Irene.

Irene smiled. 'It won't do him any harm. At least he didn't make an exhibition of himself inside and that's the main thing.'

'Aye, you're right there.'

Neither girl was particularly perturbed by drunkenness, it being a common enough state of affairs. Neither was exactly sober herself.

'Upsadaisy,' Bell declared, grabbing Tommy by the arm and hauling him to his feet.

'I slipped on the frost,' he mumbled sheepishly.

Bell and Irene didn't bother arguing. 'Not far to go now,' Bell informed him, as they started off again. To stop Tommy weaving she hooked an arm through his.

Just before Tommy's house Irene hesitated. 'I'll let you take him up to the door,' she said to Bell, giving Bell a fly wink. She then hung back as Bell and Tommy completed the last few yards.

'Must be quiet. Don't want to wake the parents,' Tommy whispered.

'Now you go straight to bed, you hear?'

'I hear,' Tommy answered, the same silly grin that had been on his face earlier now back again.

There was a few seconds hiatus between them, then Bell kissed him full on the mouth.

Tommy was momentarily taken by surprise, more so when a probing tongue found his. Taking hold of Bell he pressed her hard against him.

Bell squirmed away when a hand started moving towards her breast. 'Goodnight, Tommy.'

'Goodnight, Bell.'

'Don't fall up the stairs now.'

'I won't promise.'

She pecked him swiftly on the cheek, after which she rejoined the waiting Irene.

Tommy crept inside.

*   *   *

Hettie, lying awake with Jack fast asleep alongside her, heard Tommy come in. She could tell from his erratic footsteps that he'd had a few.

Tommy's bedroom door clicked shut and silence again descended on the house.

He was growing up, Hettie thought, pleased yet worried at the same time. He was still her baby after all. Her wee son.

She rolled over and cuddled up against Jack. Now Tommy was back safe she too could go to sleep.

'Well?' Irene demanded as they continued on their way.

'Well what?'

'Is it a big one?'

Bell knew she was being teased. 'A real whopper. Absolutely enormous. I nearly fainted when I held it.'

Irene's jaw dropped open, such was the sincerity in Bell's voice. 'Did you really?'

'Oh aye, I took it out and gave it a waggle. Huge as a donkey's it was.'

'You're having me on.'

'Who me!' Bell replied, pretending innocence and not succeeding.

Irene laughed, knowing she'd been had. 'I actually believed you there for a moment.'

'We did kiss though.'

'I saw that. What was it like?'

'Just a kiss, that's all.'

'Nothing special?'

'Maybe. Maybe not,' Bell prevaricated.

'Anyway, you just remember he's no' for the likes of us so don't go setting your cap at him.'

Which was a great pity, Bell reflected. Despite the fact

he was younger than her that's exactly what she'd like to have done. She'd taken quite a shine to Tommy Riach.

It was Christmas Eve and Bill was sitting staring grimly into the fire. Every so often he grimaced slightly and shifted his position.

'Would you like a cup of tea?' Nancy queried.

Bill glared at her, then shook his head.

She decided not to bother either. 'Is it bad the night?'

'Of course it's fucking bad, you stupid bitch.'

Nancy winced. 'I only asked.'

'Then don't.'

The silence between them stretched on and on. Eventually Nancy rose and put some more coal on the fire. That would be it for the evening, from there on the fire could just die down.

It was the last thing Nancy wanted to say, but she felt she had to, mentally preparing herself for the abuse that was bound to follow. 'You're going to have to give in, Bill, and go to the doctor. You can't go on the way you are.'

The look he shot her was one of sheer malevolence. 'Don't mention doctor to me. You know how I feel about those bloodsuckers.'

'There's no alternative, Bill. I've done everything I can. What's worrying me is you could get a worse infection. What then?'

He didn't reply.

'Then it would become even more serious.'

Bill's lips set into a thin, determined line. 'I will not spend my hard-earned money on a doctor.'

Temper suddenly flared in her. 'Then go on suffering. And hell mend you!'

'Quiet, woman!' he snapped viciously.

Nancy came to her feet. 'I'm off to see Annie and Hector. I won't be too long.'

'What are you going there for?'

'Because I can't stand this atmosphere any longer, that's why. Now is there anything you want before I go?'

'No.'

'Right then.'

He listened to her take her shawl from the peg behind the door and whirl it round her shoulders. There was the snick of her hand on the latch.

'Nancy.'

She paused, and turned. 'Aye?'

'I'm sorry.' He almost choked on the apology but got it out nonetheless.

Nancy immediately softened. 'I'm on your side, Bill. I think you sometimes forget that.'

He swallowed hard. 'I know.'

'Then will you do something for me. Please?'

'What's that?'

'Reconsider the doctor. For your own sake.'

There was no answer.

'Bill?'

'The money . . .'

'To hell with the money,' she interrupted fiercely. 'You're in agony with those boils. If money's what it takes to get rid of them then spend the damn stuff. And just be thankful you've got it to spend.'

Bill took a deep breath. Nancy was right, he knew that. But what she was proposing went against the grain. Completely so.

'I'll think about it,' he mumbled.

Nancy knew then she'd won. 'You do that.'

There was a gust of icy cold air and she was gone.

*   *   *

'All aboard!' Andrew called out.

Drew opened the rear door of the Rolls and dived inside. At long last they were on their way to The Haven.

'Here, where are your manners? What about your mother?' Andrew admonished. 'Ladies first, don't forget.'

'He's anxious to be off, that's all,' Rose smiled.

'Even so.'

'Sorry, Mum,' Drew said from the interior of the car.

'And so you should be,' Andrew replied, though smiling now. Turning to Rose he said, 'I'll drive slowly and carefully, I don't want you to be bumped in any way.'

His concern really was touching, Rose thought. If she'd told him once she'd told him a dozen times she wasn't made of porcelain. 'Not too slowly or it'll take us all day to get there.'

She kissed him tenderly on the cheek, glanced round at Drummond House which they'd only be gone from for a few days, then was helped to her seat by Andrew.

A few minutes later the Rolls was purring on its way.

Chapter 6

'Andrew!'

Willie Seaton came bustling down the steps of The Haven to shake his son-in-law and old friend warmly by the hand. 'How wonderful to see you again.'

'And you, Willie.'

James Seaton, face alight with excitement, came running after his father. Drew, who'd shot out the opposite side of the Rolls, joined him.

'Rose, my darling,' Willie beamed, and hugged his daughter tight.

'Be careful, Dad. Don't forget my condition.'

Willie immediately released her. 'I do apologise, for the moment there I'd quite forgotten.' He eyed her from head to foot. 'And don't you look radiant with it.'

'I can't tell you how happy I am.'

'You don't have to, it's obvious.'

Andrew glanced sideways at James, eternally thankful that the boy didn't take after him. The secret of

James's true parentage remained safe between himself and Georgina.

'Let's get out of this cold,' Willie enthused, grasping Rose by the arm. 'I'll send someone out to get your luggage.'

'Be back later!' James shouted, as he and Drew dashed off.

'Children nowadays,' Willie said, shaking his head. 'Always so impatient.'

'I doubt they've changed all that much since we were that age,' Andrew commented drily as they mounted the steps towards the front door.

Georgina, who was waiting in the drawing room to greet them, wore a navy blue fancy print frock enhanced by a softly draped streamer tie collar of lustrous plain tone satin. Soft shirrings accented the moulded hip-line while the circular flare-cut skirt showed off the smart uneven hemline.

She hadn't changed much since the last time they'd met, Andrew noted. Still the attractive woman she'd always been. For some reason he found himself self-conscious of the greying at his temples.

Georgina took Rose by the hands and gazed at her in delight. 'We were so pleased to hear your news,' she declared. 'We'll discuss it all later when we're alone and can talk freely away from these men.'

Rose laughed. There had been a time when she'd disliked Georgina, resented her for taking her mother's place. But those feelings and emotions were now long gone. It was hardly Georgina's fault her mother had died.

'So, who's for a snifter? You two will be needing one after your journey,' Willie proposed.

'Not for me thank you,' Rose smiled. 'I'm keeping a

strict limit on my alcohol intake on account of Mary.' The sojourn in Glasgow had proved a minor exception to that rule.

'Mary?' Willie frowned.

'That's what I'm going to call the baby when she arrives. After you know who of course.'

Georgina was also frowning. 'You seem awfully certain it's going to be a girl.'

'I am,' Rose replied confidently. 'There's no doubt about it being a lass. Isn't that so, Andrew?'

He shrugged. 'So you say.'

'I've never been more convinced of anything in my life,' Rose added.

'I naturally approve of the name,' Willie mused. 'But I think you shouldn't have your heart so set on the gender.'

'That's what I've been telling her,' Andrew commented. 'It's going to be a terribly big disappointment if it's a boy.'

'It won't be. Wait and see. And by the by, Father, do you still have my old doll's house?'

'Doll's house?' Willie repeated. 'I really have no idea. Georgina?'

'I've none either. If it is still around it's probably up in one of the attics.'

'Then I shall look for it there,' Rose stated. 'I want it for Mary.'

'You're not going wandering round any attics,' Willie rebuked her. 'I'll send up one of the staff. If it's there it'll be found.'

'And my dolls. I want those as well.'

'Dolls as well,' he agreed, and turned his attention to Georgina. 'Now what can I get you, my love?'

'Something soft would be lovely. Tonic water if we have it.'

Willie nodded his understanding. Georgina was most abstemious where alcohol and rich food were concerned which was why she'd retained the youthful figure he so adored.

'And you, Andrew?'

'Drummond please.'

'What do you have planned for this evening?' Rose inquired of Georgina, for they'd arrived on Hogmanay itself.

'A quiet night with just the family. We'll undoubtedly have a number of first-footers after the bells are rung, but until then it'll be only us. Willie thought lots of people and noise wouldn't be appropriate in the circumstances.'

That was a relief to Rose. The last thing she wanted was to be involved in a big get-together which would have been too tiring by far. As it was she'd retire fairly soon after the new year had been seen in.

'Sounds splendid to me,' Andrew declared.

'Good,' Willie nodded.

Rose couldn't help but glance at the spot where her brother Ian had been murdered by an intruder. What a ghastly memory that was. She still carried a sense of guilt about the way she'd mercilessly teased Ian when he'd been alive. Ian whose life, so full of promise, had been ended at such an early age.

She'd visit the grave before returning home, and that of her mother. She always did when at The Haven. And while with her mother she'd tell her of little Mary.

Willie gave Andrew his glass, the last to be handed round. 'A toast?' he queried.

Andrew's expression became troubled. 'Can I propose one?'

'Of course, old boy.'

Rose was expecting a toast to the new baby, wrongly so as it transpired. Andrew was thinking about current events in Europe.

'To the continuance of peace,' he said softly.

'Aye,' Willie murmured, his good humour abruptly vanishing. 'I'll certainly drink to that.'

'Peace,' Willie echoed.

'I'm glad that's over,' Willie sighed, ushering Andrew into his study. It was nearly six a.m., the last of the first-footers having just departed.

He went straight to the decanter, poured two hefty measures, gave one to Andrew and slumped into a comfortable leather chair, indicating that Andrew do likewise.

'I always find Hogmanay a funny old time,' Willie mused, lighting a cigarette. 'Somehow neither one thing nor the other.'

'I know what you mean.'

'One moment you're happy as Larry, the next sad as all get out. At least that's how it affects me.'

'Same here. More or less.'

Willie regarded Andrew keenly. 'And what do you think 1939 holds?'

Andrew shrugged. 'All sorts I should imagine. Some good, some bad.'

'Will it be war?'

Andrew briefly closed his eyes, then slowly opened them again. Were those dreadful horrors to return? It made him go cold all over just thinking about it. 'It certainly seems to be heading that way. I wish I could say otherwise but I can't.'

'Please God you're wrong.'

'Oh aye, I couldn't agree more. Please God I am.'

Both men fell silent, remembering the previous conflict. They had been lucky to have spent it in Ireland which, though still dangerous, had been nothing compared to the Western Front and other theatres.

'At least . . .' He trailed off.

'What, Willie?'

He gave Andrew a weak, sickly smile. 'Our boys are too young to get caught up in any new hostilities. There's that to be thankful for.'

'Indeed.' The relief in Andrew's voice was evident.

'They're too young and we're too old. Past it, Andrew, you and I, well and truly.'

'Bloody Germans,' Andrew hissed through clenched teeth. 'Don't they ever learn? Weren't the millions who died on all sides enough for those butchers?'

'It was Versailles and the French. The conditions of the peace treaty were too harsh thanks to the Frogs. The Jerries have never forgiven either them or us for that. Particularly Herr Hitler, and he's the one who counts.'

'This country isn't ready for war, we all know that.'

'If it did happen all over again do you think . . .' Willie broke off and swallowed hard. 'We could lose this time round?'

The prospect of German domination was an appalling one. Those arrogant, heel-clicking, cold-hearted bastards strutting up and down every street in the land. Andrew's hand tightened on his glass till the knuckles shone white.

'We have to face the possibility.'

'Surely the Americans would come in again?'

'We could only hope and pray so. Without them, and even with the might of the Empire behind us, I would fear the worst.'

'Christ,' Willie swore.

Andrew saw off what remained of his drink. 'Can I?'

'Help yourself.'

'You?'

'Aye, I will.'

Andrew was dog tired, bed would be more than welcome when he got into it. He thought of Rose already well tucked up and fast asleep. Waiting for him to join her.

'It's been a long day,' Willie yawned.

They talked about the threat of war for a short while longer, then both men headed off to their respective rooms.

'Please, Dad?'

Andrew glanced at his wife. 'Well, Rose?'

'It won't hurt for him to stay on a few days longer. He's enjoying being with James so much and there's no company for him at home.'

'I'll personally put him on the train,' Willie assured Andrew. 'He won't come to any harm.'

'Please, Uncle Andrew?'

Andrew thought back to the conversation he and Willie had had late on Hogmanay, thankful again these boys were not older. 'All right,' he consented.

Drew whooped with glee and did a little jig on the spot while James laughed and clapped his hands.

'Well, that was a popular decision it seems,' Andrew commented to a smiling Georgina.

For a moment, no more than that, she was looking at him the way she once had when they were lovers. And then it was gone. 'Yes,' she agreed.

That had jolted Andrew, made him feel uncomfortable. He wasn't proud of the fact he'd cuckolded Willie, though to be fair he wasn't the one who'd made the running.

On the other hand if he'd been more strong-willed he wouldn't have got involved no matter how hard Georgina had tried to seduce him. But in those days women had been a weakness of his, a weakness he'd overcome since marriage.

'I mustn't forget the doll's house when we leave in the morning,' Rose said. That had indeed been discovered in an attic. One of the maids had spent several hours cleaning it up so that it was again fit to be played with.

'We won't forget it,' Andrew assured her. 'You have my word on that.'

On impulse, Rose crossed to him and kissed his cheek. 'Thank you.'

'Or the dolls,' he added.

'I have to go out on the estate for an hour or two. Do you want to come with me, Andrew?' Willie asked.

Andrew considered that. 'Yes, I would. I'll enjoy the exercise.'

'While they're away we can have tea and another natter,' Georgina smiled to Rose.

Rose ran a hand over her forehead. She was feeling tired and would really have preferred an afternoon nap. She also felt strangely drained which was quite unlike her. Perhaps she could do both, natter and nap, before the men returned.

Rose came groggily awake. 'Andrew?'

He sat on the edge of the bed beside her. 'You should start getting ready for dinner.'

'Is it that late?'

He stroked her hand. 'This is the third time I've been up to see how you were.'

'I must have been more tired than I realised,' she apologised.

'It's entirely natural, considering. You are expecting after all.'

'Little Mary,' she grinned.

'Little Mary,' he agreed, knowing that would please her.

'Georgina and I had a lovely chat,' she said. 'We've had quite a few since you and I arrived.'

'Anything in particular?'

'Oh, my pregnancy, after the baby arrives, local gossip. That sort of thing. Women's talk.'

Rose sat upright and sucked in a deep breath. 'I feel a lot better for that sleep.'

'Shall I run your bath?'

'Please.'

He stared her straight in the eyes. 'I do love you, Rose.'

She smiled. 'I know. And I love you. Very much.'

She grasped the hand that had been stroking hers and laid it on her bosom.

Andrew knew this wasn't an invitation to lovemaking but rather a gesture of affection, that she simply wanted to be touched by him.

They sat in blissful silence for a short spell, then he roused himself. 'I'd better attend to that bath, otherwise I'll be wanting to get in there with you.'

Rose gave a low laugh and swung her legs out of bed. A laugh that became a gasp when a slight wave of nausea swept over her.

'Rose?'

'It's nothing. I think I'm just hungry, that's all.'

'You're eating for two we mustn't forget.'

'That's something I'm trying not to do,' she chided in reply. 'Now on you go and see to the bath so that I can get on.'

Rose watched him fondly till he'd left the room, then reached for her dressing gown, the nausea having disappeared.

She started to hum, a jaunty traditional tune that she remembered from her youth.

'I think it's going to snow,' Andrew said, peering up at a leaden sky. 'It has that look about it.'

Rose snuggled even deeper into the fox fur coat she was wearing. 'Wouldn't it be wonderful to be marooned somewhere. Just the pair of us.'

He chuckled. 'Hardly.'

'I think it would.'

'Do you now?'

'Oh yes,' she replied brightly. 'Just you and I, snowbound in a little croft somewhere. With nothing to do but . . . entertain ourselves.' The latter was said meaningfully.

'You brazen hussy, Rose Drummond.'

'With a roaring fire to keep us warm.'

'I see,' he murmured, delighted by her mood.

'It would be so romantic, don't you think?'

'Oh, undoubtedly.'

'And I like it when you're romantic.'

'Aren't I always?' he teased.

'Most of the time. Especially when you buy me things.'

He laughed. 'Is that what this is all about. You want something?'

'Could be,' she demurred.

'Such as?'

'Oh, I don't know.'

He was thoroughly enjoying this. 'Yes you do. Now come on, out with it.'

Her eyes sparkled but she didn't reply.

'Rose?'

'Why don't you try and guess.'

'I've no idea what you're after, honestly.'

'But try and guess.'

He pretended to be serious. 'A gold watch. Diamond bracelet?'

Rose giggled. 'Wrong.'

'A new wardrobe then.'

'Nope.'

He tried to think. Now what could it possibly be. 'Can you give me a hint?'

'Hint schmint. No schmints.'

She was getting outrageous now, he thought. 'If I didn't know better I'd say you'd been at the bottle.'

'Who me!' That was expressed with a combination of mock outrage and innocence.

'Yes, you, my sweetest darling.'

'As if I would. And it not even noon yet.'

He glanced at his watch. 'It's not far off.'

Rose sighed with contentment. She was enjoying this journey which, for some reason she couldn't quite fathom, had a rather surreal air about it. The Rolls might have been a gilded coach, she a fairytale princess and Andrew a . . .

'Kiss me,' she commanded.

He gazed at her in astonishment. 'I beg your pardon?'

'Kiss me.'

He leant across and pecked her on the mouth. 'How's that?'

'Not good enough. I want a proper kiss.'

'But I'm driving.'

95

'So pull over and stop. We're hardly in the middle of dense traffic.'

Which was true enough. They were the only car on the road and hadn't passed another vehicle for the past twenty minutes or so. 'If you insist.'

'I most certainly do.'

'Right then.'

He turned into a natural layby and killed the engine. 'You asked for it,' he declared, reaching for her.

The kiss was long and passionate, yet tender at the same time. A kiss between man and wife still very much in love with one another.

'There,' he murmured when the kiss was over.

'You still haven't guessed what I want you to buy me.'

'I'm stumped, Rose. Haven't the foggiest. Is it going to cost me much?'

'An absolute fortune.'

'Then so be it. Now what is it?'

'Lunch.'

He blinked. 'Lunch?'

'That's all.'

'Are you hungry?'

'Not yet, but I'm getting that way. I will be soon.'

What had got into her, he wondered. Not that he was complaining, far from it. 'Then lunch you shall have. The most expensive and lavish to be had in these parts.'

The smile on her face suddenly froze into a hideous grimace.

'Rose?'

She grunted and clasped her middle.

'Rose, is this another game? Because if it is it isn't funny.'

'Sore,' she complained. 'Pain.'

Alarm flared in him. 'What sort of pain?'

Rose swallowed. 'I think . . . I think . . .' She swallowed again. 'Oh Andrew, I'm bleeding.'

He swore viciously. 'Are you sure?'

The look in her eyes told him she was. 'Must get you to a doctor,' he said, fumbling with the ignition key.

Rose whimpered.

He turned the key and nothing happened, not a flicker of anything from the engine. He desperately tried a second and then a third time with the same result.

Rose leant forward, still clutching her middle. This wasn't happening, she kept telling herself. It wasn't happening!

Andrew banged the steering wheel in frustration. Mustn't panic, he thought. That was the last thing to do. He forced himself to take a deep breath and then try the key again. The engine remained lifeless.

'I had the damn thing seen to while we were in Glasgow,' he said through gritted teeth. 'They assured me everything was fine, that the old lady was running smooth as a nut.'

Rose jerked. 'It's coming, Andrew!'

He stared at her, appalled. 'The baby?'

She managed to nod.

'Jesus Christ.'

There were now tears flowing from her eyes that had nothing to do with the pain she was experiencing. 'Mary,' she choked. 'My wee Mary.'

Andrew knew it to be useless but nonetheless tried the key again, praying the engine would miraculously start. It didn't.

He was frantic. What in the hell to do?

Then he saw her, a girl in the field opposite. She was

walking parallel to the road, heading in their direction. He immediately threw open his door and slid out.

'I won't be a moment,' he yelled to Rose, already sprinting towards the girl.

'Don't leave me, Andrew!'

'I'm not!' he yelled back over his shoulder.

Nancy Thompson stared in amazement at the stranger bearing down on her. She frowned, wondering what was going on. The man was clearly in distress.

'We need your help. We need your help!' Andrew cried.

He vaulted a low stone dyke to stand beside her. 'It's my wife, she's miscarrying,' he blurted out.

Nancy glanced at the Rolls, then back again at the distraught stranger. 'In the car?'

He nodded vigorously. 'Please do what you can.'

'Let's go,' she declared. They clambered over the dyke and hared across the road.

Nancy's mind was in turmoil at this rapid turn of events. She wrenched Rose's door open and peered inside.

Rose had slumped over both seats, her face contorted in agony, tears still flowing.

'Oh my angel,' Andrew groaned.

Nancy thought of her friend Annie McGillvary and the baby born dead in a field. At least she was now experienced in these matters.

'The master's house is about half a mile away,' she informed Andrew. 'It would be best if you drove there while I try and comfort the lady.'

'Engine won't start,' Andrew explained. 'I've tried it again and again.'

A spasm racked Rose's body.

Nancy knelt just inside the door and hurriedly undid

Rose's coat to reveal a blood-stained gaberdine suit. There was no doubt about what was happening.

'We'll get this skirt off,' Nancy said.

Andrew reached in and took Rose's hand while Nancy busied herself. 'I'm so sorry, Andrew. I'm so sorry,' Rose choked.

'It's not your fault.'

'Wee Mary. My wee bonny Mary.'

Andrew was horribly aware of the doll's house sitting on the rear seat with Rose's memorabilia alongside it. The sight of that ensemble sickened him.

Nancy pulled the skirt free, having slid it out from underneath Rose's bottom, and tossed it on to the road. It was ruined anyway.

'Where is this house? Which direction?' Andrew demanded of Nancy. 'Has the owner a telephone?'

'Straight ahead,' Nancy replied. 'You can't miss it. And no, there isn't a telephone.'

Andrew swore.

'I'll run there anyway. There must be a car . . .'

'Don't leave me, Andrew,' Rose pleaded, her hand tightening in Andrew's. 'I want you here if I should die.'

'You're not going to die,' Andrew swiftly replied, not knowing if that was true or not.

'I feel I am.'

'Well, you're not,' he delivered sternly.

Nancy had rucked up the half-slip Rose had on and was now removing the fashionable frilly knickers underneath.

'It hurts so much, Andrew,' Rose whispered.

'I know.'

Nancy used the already sodden knickers to wipe away some of the blood awash on Rose's thighs. The birth hadn't yet happened but was obviously imminent.

Andrew felt so helpless standing there. He should really go to try to fetch a doctor but his leaving would only cause Rose more anguish. He fully understood her wanting him there with her.

'Is it a constant pain or are they coming and going?' Nancy asked Rose.

'All the time.'

'I have whisky in the glove compartment. Is that any use?'

Nancy shook her head. 'Not unless you want some.'

'No.' He did really.

Nancy had noted the well-packed luggage rack. 'Do you have any towels in your cases?' she queried.

'I'm afraid not.'

'I'm so sorry, Andrew,' Rose repeated in a whisper.

'I said it's not your fault. These things happen and there's nothing we can do about them.'

Nancy mopped up fresh blood that had oozed out, this darker in colour than the rest.

'It's going to make a mess of your nice leather seats,' Nancy commented.

'Bugger the sodding seats, they're unimportant,' Andrew snapped back.

'I was only saying.'

Andrew bit his lip, then apologised. He was beside himself.

'I understand, sir. Don't worry. No offence taken.'

'It isn't fair,' Rose mumbled. 'It just isn't fair. What have I done to deserve this?'

'You've done nothing, darling. I promise you.'

Andrew realised that Rose had stopped crying while her eyes had taken on a slightly glazed look.

'Andrew . . . Andrew . . .' Rose threw back her head

and shrieked, causing the veins in her neck to stand right out.

'Dear God,' Andrew muttered, fighting back tears of his own.

Rose shrieked repeatedly, each cry a knife in Andrew's heart, until finally, and thankfully, it was all over.

To his dying day Andrew never told her that the foetus had been male. When asked he'd lied and said they couldn't make out what sex the baby was.

Chapter 7

'She's asleep now,' Sister Eason whispered.

Andrew stared dully at Rose who'd been given a strong sedative. What a nightmare this had all been. What an awful, terrible nightmare. He gently unclutched the hand holding his and laid it on the bed.

'How do you feel?'

He glanced at Sister Eason. 'Pardon?'

'I said, how do you feel?'

Andrew shook his head. 'As you'd expect I suppose.'

'Well you come away with me now and I'll give you a cup of tea.'

'I don't want to leave her.'

'She won't wake for hours, Mr Drummond. I assure you your wife won't know you've left her bedside.'

'But . . .' He trailed off. The sense of inadequacy he was feeling was now even more profound than it had been earlier.

'Come along, tea and a biscuit. That's an order now.'

He'd have the tea, but not the biscuit. He wouldn't have been able to hold that down.

'You're in a state of shock, Mr Drummond,' Sister said once they were outside the screens surrounding the bed.

'I suppose I am.'

There were three other beds in the small ward which was part of Leithan Cottage Hospital. Leithan itself was a middling-sized market town approximately twelve miles from where Rose had lost the baby.

There had been a car which had stopped, the couple in it bringing him and Rose to the hospital. He couldn't remember if he'd thanked the girl who'd helped them. Nor did he know her name, she'd never said what it was.

'Would you prefer coffee?' Sister asked once they were in her office.

'Tea's fine.'

'I could give you something stronger if you wish.'

'No, tea please.' He wouldn't have been able to keep that down either.

Dr Laidlaw, a middle-aged man with a jolly, cherubic face, came into the office. 'Ah, Mr Drummond. I was just on my way to see you.'

Andrew, who'd sat down, stood up again.

'Sister?'

'The patient is asleep.'

Laidlaw nodded. 'Good. Sleep's what she needs. The more the better.'

It was the question Andrew hadn't been able to ask up until then. 'Is she going to be all right, doctor?'

'Oh aye, she's a healthy young woman. Physically there shouldn't be any after-effects and there's no reason why you can't have another child in time. So put your mind to rest, Mr Drummond.'

Andrew sagged with relief. 'Thank you.' He sucked in a deep breath. 'Have you any idea what caused the miscarriage?'

'None at all I'm afraid. Nature does that sometimes for no apparent rhyme or reason. It just happens.'

'And she'll be all right?' he repeated.

'As rain, given time to recover. Now that could take a while, she's been through quite an ordeal as you know. Rest, rest and more rest is my recommendation. Her body has taken a battering but it'll mend itself. I don't envisage any problems there. As I said, she's a healthy young woman.'

'Would you like to wash up before your tea?' Sister Eason queried of Andrew.

'Yes . . . I would, thank you.' There was a smear of blood on the back of his hand that needed to be got rid of.

'Can I make a suggestion?' Laidlaw said.

Andrew nodded.

'Wash up, have your tea and then book into an hotel. Your wife will be here with us for the rest of the week at least. And you might want to change your clothes.'

Andrew glanced down at his rumpled suit which also had blood on it. 'Yes, of course. But I don't want to leave Rose.'

'She'll be asleep for ages yet. That draught I gave her was a strong one. There's plenty of time for you to get yourself sorted out.'

Andrew saw the sense in that. He would need some place to stay after all. He closed his eyes and frowned. 'My luggage is with the car which broke down. The police said they'd send someone from a local garage to fetch it.'

'Sister, why don't you get on the phone and find out what's what. You might also ring the Strathspey.'

To Andrew he explained, 'That's a comfortable hotel only several streets away. Nice and handy for the hospital.'

'I'll arrange everything,' Sister Eason declared.

'Is there anything I can give *you*, Mr Drummond?'

'You mean a prescription?'

'That's right.'

'No, I'm fine.' Andrew laughed bitterly. 'Well hardly that, but you know what I mean. I can cope.'

'You're certain of that? It's no bother to give you something.'

'I'll cope, I assure you. Now I'd better go and get washed.'

'Turn left as you leave the ward,' Sister Eason smiled. 'And your tea will be waiting for you when you get back.'

Andrew stopped outside the office to stare at Rose's screened bed.

There was a lump in his throat big enough to choke on as he tore his gaze away and made for the toilet.

A thoroughly shaken Georgina hung up the phone. The call had been from Andrew to tell them what had happened. He'd asked if Drew could stay on even longer than they'd arranged. He'd also requested that Willie explain the situation to Drew.

Poor Rose, Georgina thought. And how ghastly to miscarry in a car in the middle of nowhere. What a dreadful plight for the pair of them to have been in.

At least Rose was in safe hands and being well looked after. Andrew had said the attention she was getting at the hospital was first-class.

She crossed to the bell tug and pulled it, then went to

the window to watch Drew and James playing on the lawn. She could see they were having a whale of a time.

'You rang, madam?'

Georgina turned to face Sadie, the maid who'd answered her summons. 'Find one of the men and ask him to get Mr Seaton. He's needed here at the house as soon as possible.'

'Yes, madam.'

'Drew!'

An ashen-faced Drew had jumped up from where he'd been sitting and fled the room when Willie had finally concluded what he'd had to say.

'Drew!' Willie called again, to no avail.

'Let him go,' Georgina counselled. 'He'll return when he's ready.'

'I need a drink,' Willie declared. 'That wasn't the easiest of tasks.'

'No it wasn't.'

A few moments later James appeared. 'Have you finished?' He glanced around. 'Where's Drew?'

'I think he wants to be alone for a while. Your father had some bad news to give him,' Georgina replied.

Drew forced his way into the middle of some bushes and, not bothering that the ground was freezing cold, sat down. In the distance he could see The Haven, from which he'd run non-stop.

His breathing was laboured, his chest heaving. His thoughts were in turmoil.

It was as though . . . as if . . . he'd actually *willed* the child to die. He shuddered and tightly clasped his hands together to stop them shaking.

He'd loathed that child, detested it. Resented its coming. Why, hadn't he actually admitted the latter to his father?

And why? Jealousy, that's why. Because the baby would take away, had already taken away, the spotlight being solely on him.

And now the child, wee Mary as his mother had insisted on calling it, was dead, gone for ever.

Guilt racked him. If he hadn't had such evil thoughts Mary might still be alive. Alive in Mummy's tummy waiting to come into the world, instead of . . .

If he'd loathed Mary he now loathed himself even more. What sort of boy was he to hate an unborn child? Despicable, that's what. Totally despicable.

If only he could do something, if only there was some way to make amends. Take back those thoughts, have things as they were. But there wasn't, and never would be.

Drew sobbed, filled with self-pity and disgust.

Then there was his mother. She too could have died, what then? He simply couldn't imagine life without Rose. The comfort of her touch, the warmth of her embrace. Basking in her love.

'Oh, Mum,' he croaked. 'Please forgive me. Please. I didn't mean any of it, honestly I didn't.'

But that was a lie. He had. He'd wanted the baby gone, disappeared. Which was precisely what had occurred.

A great fear took hold of him. Fear of God. For wasn't he a murderer, killer of his own sister?

He might not have stuck a knife in the child, but what he had done was as good as killing her.

He unclasped his hands and rammed a finger across his mouth, biting hard on its flesh and bone.

This was a day he'd remember and regret for always. Of that he had no doubt.

No doubt at all.

'Is there anything we can do, Andrew?' a heavy-hearted Hettie asked, glancing yet again at Jack sitting listening to her. 'Well let us know if there is. You only have to say.'

'What's happened?' Jack demanded when she'd come off the phone.

'Rose lost her baby.' She went on to give the details.

Tommy, also in the room, stared from Hettie to Jack and then back again. He remained silent.

'And there's nothing we can do?'

'Not according to Andrew.'

'Damn,' Jack muttered. Then, 'Damn,' again. Andrew must be in a frightful state, Rose a great deal worse. 'Did he mention when they're coming home?'

'That hasn't been decided yet. The weekend perhaps, or the beginning of next week.'

Tommy laid aside the newspaper which he'd been pretending to read, in reality day-dreaming. 'Shall I put the kettle on?'

Hettie smiled her gratitude. 'That's a good idea, son.'

'He's finally nodded off,' Georgina announced to Willie on rejoining him after a lengthy absence. The clock informed her it was just past midnight.

'He took it very badly I'm afraid,' Willie commented morosely.

'He did that. Even worse than I would have expected. He was sodden when he got back and will come down with a cold I shouldn't wonder.'

'Did he say anything further?'

Georgina shook her head. 'Nothing more than those

few words when he arrived in. Even James couldn't get him to speak.'

Willie recalled the conversation he'd had with Andrew about what 1939 might hold. Neither of them had even considered this possibility. Their speculations had been entirely national and international, not domestic.

'It's a blooming shame,' he said rather weakly.

'Aye, it is.'

Georgina produced a wisp of hanky and blew her nose into it, her eyes suddenly wet with tears.

'Come here, lass,' Willie said huskily.

She crossed to him and sat on his lap, curling her body against his.

'It's times like this we should be thankful for what we've got,' he murmured.

'Yes.'

He gently stroked her hair, then the arch of her neck, thinking what a lucky man he was.

Andrew was hollow-eyed and haggard-looking as he sank on to the wooden chair beside Rose's bed. He'd had a word with Sister who'd informed him that Rose had been given another draught of sedative in the middle of the night.

Some while later Rose's eyes blinked open and she gazed uncomprehendingly at the ceiling above her.

'Rose?'

She slowly turned her head to look at him. For a few seconds there was no expression at all, then the hint of a smile twisted her lips. 'Hello.'

'How are you?'

Her hand fluttered, and he reached over and took hold of it. He noted how cold it was.

'Tired.'

He nodded.

'And . . . empty.'

They stared at one another, understanding and love flowing between them. In a way, they'd never been closer.

'I thought I might have imagined it, but I didn't, did I?' she said in a faint, tortured voice.

'No.'

'In the Rolls . . . and there was a girl.'

'A farmlass who helped. I never caught her name.'

Rose nodded imperceptibly.

'Are you hungry?'

Rose considered that. 'I'm not sure. I don't think so.'

'You're going to be fine, Rose. Tiptop. The doctor has assured me there's no reason why we can't have another child.'

He immediately wished he hadn't said the latter when her face contorted.

'Wee Mary,' she breathed.

Andrew bit his lip.

'I didn't see . . . I never saw . . .'

'Ssshh, Rose,' he crooned, squeezing her hand.

'So empty,' Rose repeated. 'So very, very empty.'

All the goodbyes had been said, the thank yous made, and now Andrew, at long last he felt, was taking Rose home. She halted outside the main door and drew in a deep breath. 'Freedom,' she joked.

Andrew laughed. 'I can well understand you saying that. Even with the best of care and attention hospitals can't be fun.'

'They certainly aren't.'

He took her by the elbow, carrying her case in his other

hand. 'Now watch these steps. I don't want you taking a tumble and ending up inside again.'

'Heaven forbid.'

She was putting a brave face on it, he thought, his heart going out to her. He couldn't wait to get her ensconced again at Drummond House.

At the bottom of the steps Rose paused and glanced around. 'I thought you said the Rolls was here waiting for us.'

His expression became grim. 'No, I said the *car* was. That's ours, the red Austin Twenty over there.'

'And the Rolls?'

'I sold it and bought the Austin as a replacement.'

She didn't have to ask why he'd got rid of the Rolls, she knew why. And was extremely grateful for it. Many men might not have been so thoughtful, or sensitive. 'Is it a good runner?'

The moment of tension had passed. 'So I was assured by the garage. It's jolly comfortable too.'

She was hobbling slightly he noticed as they walked over to the Austin, but that was only to be expected. It shouldn't take her long to be properly back on her feet again.

'Jack, Hettie, it's good to see you!' Andrew exclaimed, coming to his feet as they were ushered into the drawing room.

Hettie immediately flew at Andrew and threw her arms around him, squeezing him hard.

'Here, hold on there, Hettie. You'll crack my ribs,' he protested. Years of hard graft on the farm had left Hettie unusually strong for a woman. At least, the sort of woman Andrew was used to.

Hettie pushed him away, but kept hold of him, staring deep into his eyes. She nodded at what she saw there. 'Where's Rose?'

'Upstairs resting. She's tired from the journey.'

'I'm not surprised after what she's been through. Are we your first visitors?'

'No, Charlotte's already been and gone.' Charlotte was Andrew's sister, the minister's wife.

'Can I see Rose, or is that not a good idea?'

'Go on up and have a natter. Jack and I will remain here and do the same.'

'If that's all right then. I'll only stay a few minutes.'

During this exchange Jack had made his way to a chair. 'So how is Rose really?' he asked when his wife had left them.

'Drink?'

'No thanks.'

Andrew went to the mantelpiece and leant against it. 'To be honest, Jack, I'm not quite sure. Up one minute, down the next. An enigma at other times.'

Jack could hear the strain in Andrew's voice although Andrew was doing his best to disguise it. 'We felt for the pair of you when we heard the news,' he said with meaning. 'It must have been awful.'

'It was, Jack, believe me.'

'Right there in the car?'

'I stopped the bloody thing and then it wouldn't start again. Lucky for us a local girl was on hand to help out. Otherwise I don't know what I'd have done.'

Jack grunted his sympathy.

'Are you sure you won't have a drink? I could certainly use one.'

'Aye, well on you go then.'

Jack listened to the chink of glass on glass. 'When are you going back to work?'

'I haven't really thought about it. That's been the last thing on my mind,' Andrew replied over his shoulder.

'Can I give you a piece of advice?'

'Of course. Fire away.'

'Get back as soon as you can. What's done is done, there's no point dwelling on it more than you have to.'

'But Rose . . .'

'It was your loss too, old boy. Don't forget that. You too are grieving. Just don't wallow in it, that's all. Remember the saying, life goes on.'

'You're a hard man, Jack Riach,' Andrew mocked.

Jack recalled being told he'd lost his eyes, and then learning how badly scarred his face was. 'I've had to be,' he replied drily. 'There are certain things you simply have to come to terms with. If you don't you go under.'

Andrew realised to what Jack was referring, and was instantly contrite. 'I'm sorry,' he stated quietly.

'Don't be. Just take my point on board. That's all I ask.'

'I'll return in a couple of days. I need some time to be with Rose.'

'That's understandable. In the meanwhile why don't you drop by the distillery. I would imagine many of them are worried about you.'

'I hadn't thought of that,' Andrew mused, giving Jack his whisky.

'There's a lot of goodwill towards you and the Drummond family in that place. You've always been good and fair employers, after all. And they like and respect you as a man, same as they did your father. They care about you and yours.'

'Stop it, Jack, you're embarrassing me,' Andrew mumbled, pleased Jack couldn't see he'd gone rather pink.

'Well, it's true.'

Andrew resumed his spot by the mantelpiece. 'Sometimes you wonder what it's all about, don't you, Jack?'

Jack laughed. 'Oh aye, you do that.'

Rose had stayed in their bedroom all day, taking her meals there. Andrew was therefore surprised when later that evening Rose suddenly appeared, to smile wanly at him.

'Darling!' he cried in delight.

'I want to talk to you,' she explained, pulling her dressing gown more tightly about her.

He immediately set about stoking up the fire, throwing fresh coals on it. 'Rather chilly in here,' he commented.

'That doesn't matter. I'm only down for a moment.' She hesitated, then went on, 'I hope you don't mind but I've asked the staff to make up a bed for you in one of the guest rooms. I need to . . . well, be on my own.' She stared beseechingly at him. 'I hope that doesn't offend you?'

'Not in the least.'

'It's just . . . That's how I want it for now.'

'If that's what you want then so be it. I'm not offended at all. I certainly don't want to disturb you during the night by tossing and turning or something silly like that.'

She smiled her relief. 'I knew you'd understand.'

'Of course I do. Perfectly.'

'Then I'll go back on up again.'

He watched her head for the door, a wraith of a figure that made his insides ache. 'Rose?'

She turned to him, a strange look on her face. 'Yes, Andrew?'

'Am I allowed to kiss you goodnight when I come up too?'

Rose nodded.

'Then I shall.'

She smiled wanly again.

It might have been a trick of the light, or purely his imagination, but she seemed to float from the room.

'Mr Drummond sir!'

Andrew stopped, *en route* out of the distillery. As Jack had suggested he'd come in and spoken to a few of the staff, chiefly Mr Kelly. He'd let it be known he'd be at his desk the following Monday morning. Punctual as usual, he'd informed Kelly, whose response had been a wry smile.

'Miss Mathieson, isn't it?' he said when the girl came hurrying up.

Bell blushed with pleasure that he knew her name. 'From bottling, sir.'

'So how can I help you?'

'I've been elected, sir, by the rest of bottling, including Mr Balfour the gaffer, to give you this.' She thrust an envelope at Andrew.

He stared at it in astonishment. 'I see.'

'It's nothing much, sir. We wanted to get flowers but there's none to be had for love or money this time of year. So we've made do with that.'

The envelope was addressed to himself and Rose.

'It's a card, sir, signed by all of us. I hope you don't think we're being forward, sir.'

'Not at all Miss Mathieson.' He remembered Jack's words of the night before. This was no token, but something heartfelt. 'Tell everyone that Mrs Drummond and I thank them. Tell them . . .' He had to break off and clear his throat which was suddenly clogged with emotion. 'We're deeply touched.'

'I'll get back then, sir.'

'Yes, you'd better.'

Bell saw enormous sadness etched into Andrew's face, and he somehow appeared older than she recalled. Not that she was used to being in his actual presence, but had often observed him in passing. He regularly went through the department, often having a chaff with Mr Balfour when there.

Andrew cleared his throat a second time as Bell hurried off, her long black skirt swishing over the floor.

Touched, he'd told Miss Mathieson. Truth was, it went even deeper than that.

Much.

The Scots have a word dwam which means a daze, or state of mental abstraction. Rose, lying in bed, was in exactly that when her door burst open and Drew came charging in.

Next moment, tears streaming down his face, he was wrapped in her arms, his own hugging her as tightly as she was him.

'I'm sorry, Mum, I'm sorry, I'm sorry. . .' he sobbed over and over again.

'There there, Drew,' she crooned, starting to rock slightly. She thought he was upset because she'd lost the baby and had no idea of what this was really all about – his guilt in believing he'd caused her to lose it, and put her life in jeopardy as a result.

Drew gazed up at her, his adored mother. The sweet, comforting, familiar smell of her filled his nostrils.

'Rose?'

She glanced at the open doorway where Andrew stood framed.

'Just leave us alone for a few minutes, please.'

'Fine. Willie and Georgina are here.'

She knew that, otherwise Drew wouldn't have been. 'I'll get up shortly.'

'Right then. I'll tell them.'

'Dreams,' Drew whispered. 'Bad dreams, Mummy.'

'About me?'

'Yes.'

She stroked his hair. 'There's no need for that. I'm fine, as you can see.'

'It was all my fault.'

'Don't be silly, poppet,' she laughed. 'Of course it wasn't. You had absolutely nothing to do with it.'

He wanted to tell her about his thoughts, had intended doing so, but now faced with her found he couldn't. The words simply wouldn't come. He laid a wet cheek on the swell of her breasts.

'I've missed you so much,' he mumbled instead.

'And I've missed you. Dad and I both have.' That wasn't quite true, she not having given much thought to Drew, being used to him being off at school anyway. But it was clear the boy needed reassurance.

'I'm going to be good from now on,' he declared. 'Extra specially good.'

'That's nice.'

'I promise you, Mummy. I promise you.'

Chapter 8

Nancy was scrubbing the floor, and hard graft it was too after a long day in the fields. But it had to be done along with all the other seemingly endless household chores. Sometimes she felt she'd already died and was living in hell.

She sat back on her haunches for a breather, laid down the brush and massaged her red, chapped hands. How long before arthritis set in? The bugbear of most people, male and female, who did the same sort of job as she and Bill.

He was sitting by the fire staring into it, his features hidden from her by the angle between them. She wondered what he was thinking, if anything at all. He was as still as a stone statue.

At least his boils were now a thing of the past, thank the Lord. The doctor had soon sorted them out. You'd have thought he'd have shown a little gratitude, however grudging, at her having talked him into going. But not one bit of it. The only reference he ever made of his several visits to the doctor was to complain how much money it had cost him.

Jesus, he was a mean bastard. Tight as a midge's arse. You'd have imagined at Christmas he might have given her a wee something, a minding, albeit that wasn't really the custom amongst adults, at least working-class adults like themselves. Not him, not Bill McCabe. Not even a sweetie or plain handkerchief.

Still, she reminded herself, there were worse than Bill about. Oh aye, far worse from what she'd heard. She should count herself lucky.

'Bill, can we speak?'

There was no reply.

'Bill?'

He stirred himself. 'Wheesht, woman.'

She got up, wincing at the pins and needles which suddenly stabbed her legs, and went to him. 'We should speak, Bill, and now's as good a time as any I suppose.'

He glared balefully at her. He was in a filthy temper, though there was no reason why he should be. He just was, that was all. 'Have you finished the floor?'

'Not yet.'

'Then I'd get to it if I were you.'

'It'll be done soon enough. Even I have to take a break. I'm not a bloody horse, you know. Or come to that, you'd give a horse more breaks than you would me.'

'You can be right yappy at times,' he snarled.

'Can I indeed.'

Nancy dried her wet hands on the pinny she was wearing, noting that the pinny would have to go in the wash. 'It's not long now till our contract comes up,' she stated. 'Have you any idea what's going to happen?' She was referring to the yearly contract between Bill and the master.

Bill hawked into the fire which caused her lips to thin in disapproval. She'd repeatedly asked him not to do that, considering it a foul habit, but he always ignored her. She sometimes thought he did it just to spite her.

'None at all,' he replied sourly.

Nancy sighed. If the contract wasn't renewed then it meant the Hiring Fair and a new master to find. It also meant leaving this cottage which she'd grown fond of. Like hinds, there were a lot worse about.

'You and he get on well enough, don't you?'

They had, he thought bitterly. Though not recently. Not since the master's calling on Nancy and going away displeased. Stupid bitch, why couldn't she have put herself out a bit. Done some play acting if that was what was required. He didn't know a great deal about women but had realised the majority of them weren't past that when it suited them.

'Well?' she prompted.

'Leave me alone. I want some peace.'

'You're not answering my question.'

He glared at her again, fighting back the temptation to slap her one. He would have enjoyed that. Christ but she could be irritating. Like an itch that never stopped no matter how much you scratched it.

'He wasn't too happy with me a while back, those bastarding boils. But that's over and done with. In the past so to speak.'

'So he will be renewing the contract?'

'How the fuck am I supposed to know!' Bill suddenly shouted. 'The master hardly takes me into his confidence.'

'There's no need to get shirty about it, Bill McCabe. I've every right to ask after all.'

'Have you now,' he sneered.

'Yes I do. If you're out then so am I, and all the upheaval and uncertainty that goes with it.'

He'd already made up his mind that if he was out he was getting rid of Nancy. It just hadn't worked between them. Oh, she was fair enough in bed, though not a tremendous cook. Certainly nothing like Patsy when it came to the pots and pans. He'd been thinking more and more of Patsy recently, regretting his split with her.

'I'm off through,' he declared, standing up and yawning. He rubbed the bristles on his chin, making a rasping sound.

'It's early yet.'

'So what? There aren't any rules about when I have to go through, are there? I mean, I am a free man where that's concerned.'

This time it was she who glared.

'I'll be waiting,' he smiled ominously, and left her fuming.

'You're hurting, Bill,' Nancy complained later on. She was bone dry as was sometimes the case just before her monthlies. Usually Bill was understanding, but not on this occasion.

'Tough shite,' he hissed, and thrust even harder.

Nancy gritted her teeth.

Bill grinned to himself. He was getting a little of his own back for her being so bloody irritating.

'Hello, Tommy, how are you getting on?'

He came up short as Bell Mathieson joined him. They and others from the distillery were on the way home for the evening.

'Oh it's you, Bell.'

'In the flesh.' She shivered. 'I can't wait for spring to get here. I hate this cold and snow.'

He resumed walking as she fell in beside him. 'Where's your pal Irene? You're usually with her.'

'She's off the day. Down with the flu.'

'Aye, there's a lot of it going round.'

'Have you had it yourself?'

He shook his head. 'Not so far, touch wood. How about you?'

'Me neither I'm happy to say.'

'That's good then.'

'It was a shame about Mrs Drummond's baby,' Bell commented a little further along the road. 'How is she doing?'

'Fine, as far as I know. Well as could be expected.'

'It must be awful to lose a baby,' Bell reflected wistfully. 'And imagine, in a car as well. That's what I heard.'

'It's true,' he nodded.

'Poor woman. It must have been real humiliating for her. I mean, can you imagine. Your skirt pulled up and . . .'

'That's enough, Bell,' Tommy interrupted quickly. 'I don't think we need to go into the sordid details.'

She smiled. 'Have I embarrassed you?'

'Not in the least,' he lied. 'I just don't think it's something we, or anyone else come to that, should be talking about.'

'Aye, maybe you're right.'

'Certainly not like that anyway.'

She glanced sideways. What a catch he would be. Good-looking, not to mention charming. He'd make a fine husband, she thought not for the first time.

Bell giggled.

'What's up with you?'

She tried to keep a straight face, and couldn't. Did he have a big one or not? She'd never find out. 'I was just thinking of something that was said when we were working,' she replied, which was true enough. Her face creased even more.

'So are you going to tell me what it was?'

That made her giggle again. 'It wasn't important. Forget it.'

Tommy dug his hands deeper into his coat pockets. It was a raw night and going to get worse. He hoped his mum had some soup waiting, just the dab in weather like this.

'Did you enjoy kissing me?'

That startled him and caused him to flame scarlet. 'What sort of question is that?' he protested.

'An honest one I should have thought. So, did you?'

He looked away and muttered something inaudible.

'I didn't hear that.'

'Of course I did.'

'And I enjoyed kissing you. Even if you were drunk.'

'I wasn't that bad!'

She laughed mockingly. 'Pull the other one, Tommy Riach. You were stotting. I doubt you'd have made it back if we hadn't been there to help you.'

'Nonsense.'

'Kid yourself if you like, but it's true. Stotting drunk enough to piss your pants.'

'I did nothing of the sort!' he retorted, scandalised.

She had him on the hop, she thought gleefully, considering it great sport. 'I never said you did, only that you were so bad you might easily have done.'

'You're exaggerating.'

'I don't think so.'

'Yes you are.'

'Am not.'

'Are so.'

'Not.'

'So.'

They both burst out laughing at the absurdity of this exchange.

'You're fun, Bell.'

'And so are you, Tommy. We get on well together you and I.'

He couldn't deny it. They did.

'There's a dance a week on Saturday. Are you going?'

'A dance? I haven't heard of it.'

'Aye, in the hall. There's to be a proper band and everything.'

'You mean Scottish dancing?'

'No, dance-hall dancing. The real stuff. Irene and I will be there. We wouldn't miss it. Should be a good night.'

Tommy had not been to one of the local dances, never having had the inclination to do so. He now wondered about this one.

'So are you going?' she queried.

'I shouldn't think so, Bell.'

'Why not?' She was trying to mask her disappointment.

He shrugged.

'That's no answer.'

'I just don't think so, that's all.'

'You could always come with Irene and me if you're shy,' she teased.

He was tempted, he had to admit. And it would be nice

to dance with Bell and maybe kiss her afterwards. Yes, he would certainly like that. 'Who else will be there?'

'Village folk and others from round and about. They won't all be young either. Quite a few of the older people will turn up. These dances are always popular.'

'Tell you what, I'll think about it. How's that?'

Again she was disappointed, certain that meant no. He was turning her down. Served her right for inviting him in the first place; she should have known better.

'We always go to the pub first and have a bevy or two,' Bell persisted. 'That puts a rosy glow on things.'

'They wouldn't serve me. They know I'm underage.'

'Ach, I wouldn't worry about that. They turn a blind eye on occasion. As long as you behave yourself that is. Which I'm sure you would, being a gentleman and all.'

A gentleman! He almost preened.

She laid a hand on his arm. 'It would be lovely if you came, Tommy.'

He looked into her eyes, then glanced away. 'Would it?'

'Oh aye.'

'I'm back!' Tommy called out. He was starving.

Hettie appeared and stared steadily at him. 'Was that Isobil Mathieson I saw you with, son?' She knew fine well it was, having watched the pair of them saying goodbye through the window.

'Yes, we walked down together. She's usually with her friend Irene but Irene's off ill with this flu that's going round.'

That placated Hettie a little. She followed Tommy on through to where Jack was. 'Good day?' Jack inquired cheerily.

'All right.'

'The dreaded Mr Kelly still got it in for you?'

Tommy grimaced. 'In spades, Dad. The man's a menace.'

'Well, it's just something you'll have to put up with for now.'

Tommy crossed to the roaring fire and vigorously rubbed his hands. 'When's tea, Mum?'

'Shortly.' She was still eyeing him suspiciously.

'Is there soup?'

'Vegetable broth.'

Tommy smiled in anticipation.

'That'll put hairs on your chest,' Jack chuckled.

'And yours,' Tommy retorted.

'Oh, I gave up hoping years ago. It never worked for me I'm afraid.'

'Tommy and Isobil Mathieson walked home together,' Hettie said casually.

'Oh?' That was Jack.

'Terrible family, you know. No better than tinks. That father of hers has a dreadful reputation in the district.'

Tommy stared at his mother in dismay. 'I was only talking to her, Mum, being friendly like. There's no harm in that, surely?'

'Not as long as it's only talking and nothing else.'

'They are a pretty rum family,' Jack agreed. 'And as your mother says, no better than tinks. Though I have to admit old man Mathieson has always been pleasant enough to me.'

Tommy now knew what his mother was driving at, which both amused and annoyed him. What she was really saying was that it was an unsuitable relationship which mustn't develop any further.

Hettie saw that Tommy had got her meaning and nodded slightly. There might be nothing between him and Isobil Mathieson, but if there was she would nip it right in the bud. The likes of Isobil, or Bell as they so commonly called her, weren't for her Tommy.

Andrew hesitated outside their bedroom door, or Rose's bedroom as it had become since her return from hospital. It was another night when she'd gone to bed directly after the meal, leaving him to spend the rest of the evening alone.

A glance at his wristwatch told him it was just past eleven. Silently he partially opened the door and poked his head round, the light from the corridor spilling into the dark interior.

Rose's eyes were shut, her breathing steady. She was fast asleep.

He stared at her for a few seconds, wishing he was there beside her. Wishing . . .

Taking a deep breath he closed the door again, the only sound being a small click as the lock engaged.

Rose smiled to herself as she listened to his retreating footsteps.

McFarlane, the groom, touched his forelock. 'Morning, Mrs Drummond,' he said.

'Good morning, McFarlane. How are you today?'

'Never better, Mrs Drummond. Thank you for asking.'

She went to a stall where a brown horse with white facial markings stared mournfully at her. The mare snickered in recognition.

'And what about you, Strumpet? How are you?'

She scratched the mare's ears. Strumpet rubbed and tried to lick her arm in appreciation.

'I'm just about to take her out for her morning exercise, Mrs Drummond,' McFarlane informed Rose.

Rose had been in two minds up until then, but now being with Strumpet decided her. 'Don't bother, McFarlane. I'm going to change. I'll take Strumpet out myself.'

McFarlane raised an eyebrow in surprise, but said nothing. It wasn't his place to comment.

'It's been a while, hasn't it, my pretty,' Rose crooned, Strumpet whinnying in reply. Somehow the delighted animal knew that it was to be ridden by its mistress for the first time in many months. The mournful look had vanished.

'So have her saddled up and ready for me, McFarlane. I shan't be long.'

'Yes, Mrs Drummond.'

Rose kissed the horse on its nose, suddenly feeling light as air inside. She was going to enjoy this.

Nancy picked up yet another stone and threw it into the canvas bag she was dragging alongside her. When the bag was full she'd take it to the edge of the field and empty it.

Stones were forever being unearthed by ploughing in this particular piece of land which was why, once a year, they had to be collected and removed. On this occasion the back-breaking work had fallen to her.

She paused to wipe away sweat and catch her breath. There were hours to go before the dinner break, and then the long afternoon stretched beyond that. It was going to take her two days at least to do what was required.

For some reason she found herself thinking of the lady in the fancy car. A sorry episode if ever there was.

Nancy sighed, remembering the fine clothes the woman had been wearing. What a pity they'd been ruined, though that probably wasn't much of a loss to someone so obviously wealthy.

Why, no doubt the woman had wardrobes full of clothes, all as fine and expensive. The loss of a single suit would be nothing to her. Despite herself, jealousy stabbed through Nancy.

They must live in a big house, she reflected, with servants, lots of them to attend every need and whim. She smiled, trying to imagine herself in such a position.

The husband had been a good-looking chap too, beautifully tailored and manicured. She laughed aloud comparing him to Bill McCabe. What a joke!

Oh, to be well off, she thought wistfully. Wouldn't it be wonderful. Rich instead of grubbing around in a field picking up stones for a living. That and all the other hardships she had to endure.

How old would the lady have been? Difficult to say really. Though certainly much younger than the husband.

Nancy gingerly touched her face. How rough and weatherbeaten it was, brown from continual exposure to the elements. Totally unlike the lady's skin which had been smooth as velvet.

Oh well, she mentally shrugged. There was no use worrying about it. Her lot was as a bondager and all that entailed. A daily grind from early morning to late at night, out grafting rain or shine.

She glanced down at her hands, calloused and dirty, her fingernails chipped and broken. Now the lady's hands had been . . .

'Stop it, Nancy Thompson!' she declared aloud. This

was daft, utterly pointless. She'd been born to what she had and nothing on this God's earth was going to alter that.

Still . . . and she smiled softly. A lassie could dream, couldn't she? Even if she had nothing else but dreams.

She bent again to pick up what seemed to be the millionth stone of the morning.

Hettie glanced at Tommy in exasperation. 'Will you stop prowling and sit down!' she exclaimed. 'You're giving me a headache with all that constant movement.'

Tommy halted in his tracks. 'Sorry, Mum.'

'What's wrong with you, lad?' Jack queried.

'Nothing. I'm just . . . restless, that's all.'

It was Saturday night and he knew precisely why he was restless. He couldn't stop thinking about the dance being held later on and wishing he was going.

And he still could, if he really wanted to. Except he wouldn't. For to go would mean meeting Bell and his mother was right about her; Bell was most unsuitable for someone of his background and prospects.

'If you're that restless why don't you go for a walk?' Jack suggested.

'Good idea,' Hettie nodded. 'It might get rid of some of that energy bottled up inside you.'

'Aye, on you go,' Jack prompted. 'Give us a little peace.'

Tommy grinned. 'Am I upsetting you that much?'

'Yes,' Hettie stated emphatically. 'You are.'

'All right then, I will.'

'Round the village twice at least,' Hettie said. 'And don't come back till you've calmed down a bit.'

'I won't.'

And with that Tommy was gone.

*   *   *

'He isn't going to show,' Bell whispered to Irene, adding lamely, 'not that I really expected him to.'

'There's plenty of time yet,' Irene replied, glancing at the clock behind the bar. The pub was full, all the tables already taken when they'd arrived, which was why they were having to stand.

'There's Isa Weir and Hannah McIlroy,' Bell said, spying their two pals from bottling who'd just come in. Isa's boyfriend Ronnie was already there waiting for her to join him. He immediately waved to the pair who went over. Ronnie also worked in the distillery.

Irene stared down into her now empty glass. 'Are you for another?' She laughed. 'As if I have to ask.'

'Of course I am.'

'Right then,' Irene declared as Bell finished her drink.

'They say gin makes you sin,' Irene giggled, and headed off for refills.

Chance would be a fine thing, Bell thought glumly.

Tommy was standing across the road listening to the hum emanating from inside the pub. He could see several people he recognised through the window opposite, but not Bell.

He could go in for a drink, nothing more, he told himself. Bell had assured him he'd be served as long as he behaved himself.

Only if he did that he'd get into conversation with Bell and then it really would be difficult not to be persuaded to go on to the dance.

Did he fancy Bell? Actually fancy her that is? It was a question he'd been trying to avoid answering.

He'd certainly enjoyed kissing her. That warm mouth

and tongue, her eager body pressed up against his. An experience he'd love to repeat. And could. All he had to do was cross the road and go through that door. Nothing could be easier.

God, but he was tempted.

'I'm gasping for a fag,' Irene said quietly to Bell. Being in a public place she could hardly light up.

'Nip to the toilet then.'

'Do you mind?'

'Not in the least.'

'Will you wait?'

Bell eyed her friend dyspeptically. 'Well, I'm hardly about to piss off and leave you. Talk about a silly question.'

'You might get chatted up in the meantime. Find a click.'

Bell gazed about her. 'I shouldn't think so. But I promise you, if Don Juan appears and I get swept off my feet, I'll still be here when you get back.'

'Well, there's no need to be sarcastic,' Irene retorted.

Bell laughed. 'Away and have your cigarette.'

As Irene left her Bell's gaze fastened on to the doorway. There was still no sign of Tommy. He'd never said he'd come, she reminded herself. No promise had been made so none had been broken.

But it would have been lovely if he'd turned up.

'The trouble with Tommy is that, apart from Eric Taylor, and Eric's away at school, he doesn't have any friends in the village,' Jack commented to Hettie. The Taylors were a local naval family, the father, a high-ranking officer, usually absent at sea.

'That's true,' Hettie nodded.

'Eric has always been around in the past when Tommy was on holiday. Different now of course.'

'Eric will be home again at Easter. They'll get together then no doubt.'

'No doubt,' Jack echoed. 'The pair of them have always been thick as thieves. Ever since they were wee they've run together.'

Jack drew in a deep breath. 'Too much time on his hands after work, that's his trouble. All he does is kick around the house. Never really goes anywhere.'

Tommy *was* rather at a loose end in the evenings, Hettie reflected. What he needed was a hobby. Certainly an interest of some kind.

As long as it wasn't Isobil Mathieson, she thought grimly. She might have come from humble stock herself, but Tommy was not only her son but Jack's as well. That made all the difference.

Tommy had a certain status in life. And would be a wealthy man when the time came to inherit, which should never be forgotten. Least of all by him.

'We should make a move soon,' Irene said to Bell.

'I'm not in a hurry. Are you?'

Irene shook her head.

'Well then. I don't want to arrive at the beginning of the dance. I much prefer getting there when it's in full swing.'

'Aye, you're right.'

'My turn this time,' Bell declared, taking Irene's glass, which had rapidly emptied again.

Tommy had slowly walked the length of Dalneil's main

street, and was now retracing his steps equally slowly. His eyes flicked sideways when he came abreast of the pub.

He hesitated for the briefest of moments, then continued walking, listening to the hum from the pub fading behind him.

Chapter 9

Andrew was annoyed as he strode home from the distillery, the fountain pen he'd used for years having leaked all over his shirt. He intended changing it and then returning to work, which was a damned nuisance as he had a great deal to get through that day.

He wondered what Rose was up to as he climbed the stairs. She hadn't mentioned earlier that she had anything special on so she should be around somewhere. Unless she'd gone out riding which she'd been doing a lot of lately.

He came up short outside her bedroom where the door was ajar, frowning at what he saw within.

'Rose?'

'Hello, Andrew. What are you doing back at this hour?'

He explained to her as he went inside. 'Are you actually playing with those things?' he asked incredulously.

Rose was sitting beside the doll's house she'd rescued from The Haven, her childhood dolls propped against it.

'Yes, it's fun.'

'I see,' he murmured.

'Now don't look so disapproving. I said, it's fun. There's no harm in that surely?'

'None at all.'

Rose began laying out a porcelain tea set, placing a cup, saucer and plate in front of each doll. 'This is what I used to do when I was young,' she smiled disarmingly. 'And I always served scones to go with the tea. They all adore scones.'

There was a peculiar quality to her voice, he thought. It was as though . . . she actually was somehow young again.

'We're having a guest today,' Rose declared. 'A very special guest. Aren't we, dollies?

'Yes, Rose,' she said, pretending to be one of the dolls answering her.

'And who's that?'

'Mary. Mary's coming to visit.'

Andrew went cold all over. 'Mary?' he queried softly.

'Our Mary. Our little Mary. Isn't that right, dollies?

'Yes, Rose.' That was supposed to come from another of the dolls.

He swallowed hard. Had she gone mad or something? A feathery sensation of alarm raced up and down his spine.

'Do you wish to join us, Andrew?' Rose asked.

He shook his head.

'You'd be most welcome. Wouldn't he, dollies?

'Most welcome, Rose.

'Andrew likes scones too. He often eats them. Don't you, Andrew?'

He nodded.

'In fact they're a great favourite of his. Just as they are of yours.'

'Rose, eh . . .' He cleared his throat. 'Are you feeling all right?'

'Of course, darling,' she replied, eyes wide and beguilingly innocent.

'You seem to be taking all this . . . very seriously.'

'But naturally.'

'And this talk of . . . Mary. It, eh . . .' He trailed off, lost for words.

'What about her, Andrew?'

'Mary doesn't exist, Rose. She's dead.'

Rose's smile seemed to stretch on and on for ever. 'I know that, Andrew. I miscarried her in the Rolls. Remember?'

'Then why are you speaking about her as if she was alive?'

Rose came to her feet and the bizarre magical spell that had surrounded her abruptly splintered. 'It was only a game, Andrew. Nothing more. There's no need to look so concerned.'

'But I *am* concerned, Rose. What you were doing is hardly healthy.'

Rose turned her back on him. 'We all handle grief in our own way, Andrew. This happens to be mine. My way of dealing with things.'

He went to her and grasped her shoulders. 'Oh, Rose,' he whispered.

She shook him off. 'I'll get you another shirt. That one's quite ruined.'

Rose swept from the room leaving him staring after her. This was worrying. He'd have to speak to the doctor about it.

'McCabe!' The master crooked a finger indicating that Bill come to him.

'Yes, sir?'

'You're not a bad worker, McCabe. When you haven't got boils on your arse that is.'

'Thank you, sir.'

This was amusing the master who'd never forgotten, or forgiven, his displeasure with Nancy. He'd intended letting Bill go, but had changed his mind about that. What he now planned was better.

'The contracts are nearly up,' he stated.

This was the moment Bill had been dreading. 'Yes, sir. Next month.'

The master nodded, and didn't instantly reply, intentionally keeping Bill on tenterhooks.

He was for the chop, Bill thought in despair. Oh well, he'd been expecting it anyway.

'Do you wish to remain on?'

Bill's heart leapt. 'Oh yes, sir. I do.'

'Hmmh.'

'Very much so, sir. Nancy and I are happy here.'

'Indeed,' the master mused. 'Are you indeed.'

Bill's mouth had gone dry as he waited to hear his fate. Why didn't the damn man just come out with it?

'Then remain you shall,' the master said after a suitable, tantalising, pause.

Bill touched his forehead. 'Thank you, sir. Thank you kindly. You won't regret it, sir.'

'You, but *not* your woman. I don't want her around any more.' The master smiled inwardly.

'Me but not Nancy, sir?'

'That's correct. The choice is up to you. If you wish to stay you'll have to find yourself another female. Is that clear?'

'Quite, sir.'

'So what's your answer?'

'You want it right away, sir?'

'I do. Here and now.'

Bill took a deep breath. He was fed up with Nancy anyway, her and her irritating ways. This merely sorted the matter, making it easier for him.

'I'll tell her tonight, sir. Spell it out like.'

'Good, McCabe. Good. You shouldn't have trouble finding a replacement, a chap such as you.'

'No, sir. I shouldn't think so, sir.'

'That's settled then. Go back about your business.'

'Yes, sir. Straight away, sir.'

So much for Nancy Thompson, the master thought with grim satisfaction. His displeasure had been revenged.

'And that's the long and short of it,' Bill declared, having waited till he'd finished the evening meal before announcing the news.

Nancy's face mirrored her shock. 'He wants you but not *me*?'

'That was the deal.'

'And you agreed, just like that?'

Bill was having trouble holding her gaze. 'He demanded a decision there and then.'

'Did he?'

'Yes,' Bill stated emphatically. He'd go out, he decided.

He had a few bob in his pocket which would buy him a couple of pints. A celebration in a way now he knew what was what. At least he wouldn't now have to suffer the humiliation of the Hiring Fair, standing there like so much meat in a butcher's shop window. And who knew what a new master would be like? This one was bad enough without his having the misfortune to land worse.

He would still have to go to the Hiring Fair of course in order to find another female, but that was something to look forward to, the boot being on the other foot so to speak. He felt quite cheered at the prospect.

'You're a bastard, Bill McCabe,' Nancy said levelly. 'A black-hearted bastard. And after all I've done for you too.'

He pushed his plate away and belched. 'You ain't done no more than you should. Would be expected.'

Her eyes flashed anger. She was still trying to come to terms with the bombshell he'd dropped. Not that she had any tender feelings for Bill, that didn't come into it. It was simply they were a team and rubbed along together well enough. Now uncertainty loomed before her.

And what if she didn't find another hind? What then? That would be a catastrophe. Farm work and bondaging were all she knew.

Bill rose. 'I'm off out for a wee while. I'll see you when I get back.'

'Bastard,' she repeated.

Bill waited till he was outside and away from the cottage before bursting out laughing.

Nancy tensed as Bill's hand crept under her nightie. The smell of beer and stale breath hung heavily over them.

'Don't even think about it,' she hissed.

'There's no need to be like that, Nancy. It's only a shag after all. You like it as much as me.'

She pulled away from the groping hand. 'If you don't stop right this minute I swear I'll go through to the kitchen, get the carving knife and stick you with it.'

The hand was immediately withdrawn. She would too, he thought. Nancy didn't make idle threats.

'Aye, all right then,' he muttered, well put out. And a little scared too if he was honest.

Nancy knew that sleep would be a long time in coming. How dare he! To expect that after what he'd done to her. Talk about bare-faced cheek!

A month was all she had left in this cottage, no time at all. And then what?

Of one thing she was certain. There would be no more shagging with Bill McCabe. He'd had his lot where that was concerned. And if he tried to force her it would be the carving knife.

Her mind was still spinning when Bill began to snore.

'So what do you think, doctor?' Andrew asked, having just recounted the story of the doll's house and the imaginary Mary coming to tea.

Dr Lesley was in his mid-thirties and popular with the folk of Dalneil. He wasn't only a good doctor but had an easy bedside manner which went down well.

'It could be a breakdown of some sort,' Lesley mused. 'Have there been any other symptoms?'

Andrew glanced away, finding this next bit embarrassing. 'She won't have anything to do with me sexually since the miscarriage. We're sleeping in separate beds.'

'I see. Though I can't say I'm surprised. What Mrs

Drummond has been through is bound to have taken its toll. Mentally that is. She'll need a period of adjustment. It's quite normal.'

'I can understand that.'

'Was eh ... everything all right in that department beforehand?'

'Not really,' Andrew replied quietly.

Lesley waited for him to elaborate.

'She hasn't been very keen since our son was born. It was as though it had become a chore to her. That she was only doing her duty.'

'And previously?'

'A very loving and passionate woman, doctor. I certainly didn't have any complaints.'

'Which has all changed since the birth of Drew.'

Andrew nodded. 'She did perk up after falling pregnant the second time. For a while it was as it had once been between us. I took her to Glasgow and that was like a second honeymoon. Then the miscarriage and now separate bedrooms.'

'Hmmh.'

Lesley leant back in his chair and studied Andrew thoughtfully. 'My initial reaction is to say leave things as they are. I'm a great believer in doing nothing rather than something for something's sake.'

Which made sense to Andrew. 'Only what if she is, has gone ...' he could hardly bring himself to say the word ... 'mad.'

Lesley sighed. 'That is a possibility of course. I have to admit. It wouldn't be the first time the trauma of miscarriage has had that effect on a woman. Put her over the edge.'

'If you'd seen and heard her with the doll's house,'

Andrew said, and shook his head. 'It frightened me I can tell you.'

'I'm due to drop by and see her sometime soon anyway, so while there why don't I do a wee bit of subtle probing. Sound her out in certain matters, more so than I would normally. That way I can make an evaluation.'

'Fine, doctor.'

'I'll telephone and make an arrangement with her.'

'You don't think . . . I'm being an alarmist, do you?'

'Not at all. You love your wife and are naturally concerned for her well-being. You were quite right to come and speak to me about that concern.'

Lesley rocked forward in his chair. 'Is she home tomorrow?'

'All day as far as I know.'

'Good. I'll ring then.'

'Thank you, doctor.'

Lesley took Andrew by the arm as he was escorting him from the surgery. 'I'm sure there's nothing really to worry about, Mr Drummond. Not in the long term anyway. But in the meantime we may as well just see what's what.'

Andrew felt a lot better as he drove away. Simply articulating his worry had been a great relief.

Andrew woke with a start and sat bolt upright in bed. Sweat was streaming down his face and shoulders.

He'd been back in Ireland, watching Alice, the woman he'd been going to marry, burning to death. Hearing the shrieks and screams from within the human torch she'd become.

'Christ,' he muttered, and ran a hand over his forehead, a hand he noted was trembling. He was thoroughly shaken.

Alice whom he'd adored and whom the Fenians had burnt alive when they'd set fire to the family home. She'd died with her mother and father.

The nightmare had been so vividly real he would have sworn he was actually there witnessing what had occurred. The tormented shrieks and screams were still reverberating round inside his head.

Alice whom he'd loved with all his heart before meeting Rose, and whose death he'd revenged by killing the bastard McGinty responsible for the atrocity.

He'd set ablaze the McGinty home in retaliation then shot and killed the family before throwing McGinty himself back into the conflagration to perish in flames as Alice had done.

Andrew fumbled with the bedside lamp and switched it on, flooding the room with soft yellow light. It had all happened so long ago, so many years before, and still it haunted him.

He'd often wondered what his life would have been if Alice had lived to become mistress of Drummond House. There would have been no Rose then, no Drew. And of course no miscarriage in the Rolls.

McGinty . . . seeing the man's face and still hating him for what he'd done. He hoped again, as he'd hoped many times in the past, that the Fenian bastard was roasting in everlasting hell.

He and Rose must try for another child as soon as possible, he decided. Surely that was the answer to the problem that had arisen from the miscarriage. And if she did fall pregnant, not forgetting how long it had taken for her to become so the second time, pray God it was with a lassie, the daughter Rose so desperately wanted.

The first thing was for them to resume normal relations.

A period of adjustment Dr Lesley had said. Well, that was fine, but a period was exactly that, a space of time which, by its own definition, must eventually come to an end. His immediate aim must be to bring that end about sooner than later.

A holiday perhaps? That might help. The pair of them thrown together without any work to intervene. Definitely a possibility to which to give some serious thought.

The trouble was the distillery, which he always loathed leaving for anything more than a few days. How bound he was to that building and what it produced! But he must put things in perspective, he told himself. Rose was his wife and her well-being, not to mention their marriage, must take priority.

Not just a week's break but a month at least. And somewhere far away, distance being essential in his opinion. A balm to help heal the deep wound afflicting Rose.

Andrew held his hands in front of him to see that they'd stopped trembling. His breathing was also back to normal.

He lay back and closed his eyes, recalling scenes from his childhood. His father Murdo and brother Peter. Peter whom he'd never really got on with and who, being the elder, should have inherited if it hadn't been for France and the war.

How he wished he was in bed with Rose. To feel her close, touch and cuddle her. Not for sex, that was the last thing he wanted at the moment, but for her presence and the reassurance that went with it. The sheer solace that man and wife should find in one another.

He could go to her now, explain how disturbed he was, that he'd had a nightmare. But he wouldn't, knowing that to be wrong. It would be putting pressure on her which she didn't need.

A picture of Rose with the doll's house flashed into his mind causing him to shudder. That had been scary, truly frightening. What if she had gone over the edge never to return? How dreadful that would be.

The shrieks and screams inside his head were gone now. The image of Alice faded to a pale shadow of that which had woken him.

Loneliness could be a terrible thing, he reflected, as could memories. Especially in the middle of the night when all sorts of ghosts and horrors, some real, others imagined, walked.

Jack Riach listened in sympathetic silence as Andrew recounted the story of the doll's house. The two of them were in the pub where they did their best to meet up every Friday night.

'Dear me,' Jack whispered when Andrew was finished.

'I thought a holiday might be a good idea. A long one to try to take her mind off matters.'

'It certainly wouldn't do any harm.'

Andrew gazed morosely into his dram. 'Lesley called in to see her then came over and spoke to me at the distillery afterwards.'

'Oh?'

'He was very hopeful and did his damnedest to put my mind at rest. He said he couldn't detect anything abnormal in Rose, that she was simply a woman trying hard to cope with an extremely difficult situation.'

'There you are then,' Jack smiled.

'Except he wasn't there that day in the bedroom. He never heard her voice or saw the look in her eyes.'

'That bad, eh?'

'Worse than you can imagine. It made me feel sick. I honestly thought I might vomit afterwards.'

Jack didn't reply to that. If only there was something he personally could do, but what? Be a friend, there when necessary. A shoulder to lean on, an ear to bend.

Andrew threw the whisky down his throat and then had a long pull from his pint. 'Anyway, I don't want to bore you with my problems any further.'

'You're not boring me, Andrew, honestly.'

Andrew could hear the ring of truth in his friend's statement. 'Thanks, Jack.'

'A problem shared after all.'

'Indeed.' Andrew smiled. He glanced around, his gaze fastening on a young couple sitting in a corner. They were both locals, recently married.

He couldn't help but thinking how attractive she was. A full-bosomed lassie with chestnut-coloured hair and, somehow, provocative features. He felt an old familiar stirring. It had been a while after all.

'Another drink?' he said gruffly to Jack, rising from his chair.

'Aye, sure.'

When he returned he repositioned himself so that the girl was completely out of his line of vision.

'There's a page here addressed to you,' Rose declared across the breakfast table.

'Me!' Andrew exclaimed in astonishment. This was something new, Drew never wrote specifically to him.

'It says "Dear Dad".' Rose smiled, handing the page across to Andrew.

'Wonders will never cease.' He took the page.

He began to frown as he read first one side then the other.

'Well?' Rose prompted.

'Drew wants me to know that when he grows up he definitely intends taking over the distillery. That he's looking forward to it and is sorry if he ever gave me the idea he might do otherwise.'

'I see,' Rose murmured. 'And did he give you such an idea?'

'There was some talk one day about the possibility of his not following in my footsteps as I followed in my father's and he in Grandpa's.'

'You never mentioned.'

Andrew shrugged. 'I was surprised but didn't really think him serious. I also got the impression it was a bit of a tease, that sort of a thing.'

'His recent letters have been strange,' Rose mused. 'Though don't ask me how. I'm not entirely sure.'

'It's probably just his age. All children go through peculiar phases. I know I certainly did.'

As had she, Rose reflected. Particularly during puberty. That had been a most difficult time for her. But it couldn't be puberty with Drew, he was still far too young for that.

There again, Andrew was thinking. The strangeness of his recent letters could well be the result of late events. Yes, that was it no doubt, he decided. The miscarriage.

Andrew was right about that, though he didn't appreciate how badly affected Drew was, not being aware of Drew's assumed guilt.

'Have you ever considered becoming a Sunday school teacher?'

Tommy gaped at his mother. 'I beg your pardon?'

'You heard me. Have you ever considered becoming a Sunday school teacher?'

'Why should I do that?' an aghast Tommy queried.

'You might enjoy it and it would give you an interest outside work. I'm sure you'd be welcomed with open arms.'

Tommy couldn't think of anything he'd like less. The very notion was preposterous. 'Lassies do that. There isn't a single male amongst them.'

Hettie smiled inwardly. The whole point, though she wasn't about to tell Tommy that. Not only were the teachers all lassies but, without exception, ones from good families. Who knew, it might be the start of something.

'I think you'd be rather good at it myself,' Hettie went on. 'It could be very interesting.'

Interesting, his foot. Boring beyond belief more likely.

'You were aye keen on Sunday school when younger,' Hettie declared. 'You used to love it.'

He had too, Tommy thought. 'That was then and now's now,' he stated firmly.

'I always thought you had a wee fancy for Miss McKeown, Mrs Ure as she is now, who taught you. You spoke about her often enough.'

'Did I?' Tommy replied, pretending innocence. He'd worshipped Miss McKeown who'd been the dishiest of all the teachers. The *only* dishy one, he now recalled.

'There are probably Miss McKeown types there now,' Hettie declared slyly.

Then, deciding she'd said enough for the moment, 'Anyway, it was only a thought.'

Miss McKeown types? Now that might not be as daft a suggestion as it had first seemed.

*   *   *

'Come on, girl, come on!' Rose urged Strumpet, flicking the mare repeatedly on the flanks with her crop.

Rose started to laugh from the sheer pleasure and exhilaration of the gallop. Her heart was thudding nineteen to the dozen.

A stone wall, or dyke, loomed into view which she decided to jump. Then she and Strumpet were soaring through the air to land with only the slightest of bumps.

'Faster, girl, faster.'

Strumpet did her best to respond. Her mane was streaming, her nostrils flared in the extreme. Somehow the mare found it within herself to quicken the pace.

Rose knew she could be badly hurt if she came off at this speed, and didn't care a jot. Being hurt or even killed didn't matter, all that did were the sensations she was experiencing. Glorious sensations that were causing her blood to race and her spirits to soar. She felt as though she'd transcended this world and was inhabiting another.

'Give her a good rub down and feed, McFarlane. She's deserved it,' Rose instructed, patting the exhausted mare's nose. Strumpet was too exhausted to even whinny a response.

McFarlane took in the mare's sweat-stained and heavily lathered coat beneath which she was both heaving and trembling. He glanced at Rose, then back again at Strumpet.

'You have had a ride today, Mrs Drummond,' he said in a neutral tone. She'd completely knackered the bloody beast, was what he was actually thinking.

'I have indeed.'

McFarlane couldn't remember the last time he'd seen a

horse in such a state. As for Mrs Drummond, she looked done in as well.

'I'll be going out again tomorrow,' Rose informed him.

'Yes, Mrs Drummond.'

'Shortly after breakfast, same as today.'

'Strumpet will be ready and waiting.'

'Good.'

Rose kissed the mare, after which she wheeled about and strode from the stables, leaving a somewhat perplexed McFarlane behind. He'd found the look in her eyes quite unnerving.

Chapter 10

'God, this is tedious and never gets any better,' Bell commented to Irene, the pair of them halfway through the morning shift.

'Aye, well just be thankful we've got work. There's plenty in this country don't.'

'True enough. That wage packet at the end of the week is always welcome and no mistake.'

Irene sighed. 'I'm gasping for a fag.'

'When are you not?' Bell teased. 'I swear that when you die you'll come back as a chimney.'

'There are plenty worse than me,' Irene protested. 'Besides, who can afford to smoke all that much at the price of ciggies. It's scandalous so it is.'

'If you stopped think of the money you'd save.' Bell was teasing again knowing there was little likelihood of that.

'And the enjoyment I'd be giving up,' Irene countered, hands moving deftly over the line of bottles passing before her. 'You have to have some pleasures in life.'

'Well I know what mine is,' Hannah McIlroy called over. 'And it sure as hell isn't fags.'

That raised a laugh from the other girls with a few lewd comments and digs being made.

'That last dance was a bit of a disappointment,' Sandy McAlpine declared.

'In what way?' queried Isa Weir.

'The usual talent. No new faces. I didn't think the band were all that good either.'

'The dance seemed all right to me.'

'Of course it did,' Bell said. 'You had Ronnie in tow, love's young dream and all that. No wonder you had a good time.'

'Have you done it with him yet?' Sandy inquired with a twinkle in her eyes.

'I'm not saying. It's a secret between the pair of us.'

'Which means you haven't,' Irene snorted.

'It does nothing of the sort. It means exactly that. I'm not saying.'

'One thing about your Ronnie,' Sandy went on. 'He does have a lovely bum. I've always thought that.'

'Me too,' Hannah chipped in. 'Though of course I've never seen it in the raw. What's it like, Isa?'

'Is it all hairy?' Bell further teased.

Isa shot Bell a contemptuous glance. 'He's a man, no a bloody monkey for Christ's sake.'

'That doesn't answer the question.'

'It's the only answer you'll get out of me, Bell Mathieson.'

'It really must be love the way he was slobbering all over you,' Irene grinned.

'He doesn't slobber! Not over me or anything else.'

'Aye, all right, keep your shirt on. It's only an expression.

Though I could have sworn I saw him foam at the mouth at one point.'

'Really!' exclaimed Sandy McAlpine.

'Really. The sort mad dogs get.'

Sandy burst out laughing while Isa glared. Though, if she'd been honest, she was enjoying being the centre of attention.

'You lot are just jealous. That's your trouble,' Isa sniffed.

'As if.' Bell smiled.

'I didn't see you there with anyone.'

'I was with Irene,' she protested in a mock fashion.

'You know what I mean.'

'Maybe that's because I'm choosy.'

Isa was instantly outraged. 'That's an awful thing to say. You can't get more choosy than my Ronnie. He's a dreamboat.'

That produced a guffaw all round.

'What world do you inhabit?' Sandy jibed.

'Maybe she needs specs,' Bell leered.

'Ronnie a dreamboat,' Irene repeated, and cackled.

'I seem to remember you fancied him at one time,' Isa retorted. 'But he wasn't interested. That's because he's got taste.'

'Taste, my arse. He can't have that if he's going out with you.'

'Well, if you're talking of arses yours is certainly big enough.'

Now it was Irene's turn to be outraged, being very sensitive about her somewhat largish bottom. 'Bitch!'

'No more than you.'

Bell was grinning to herself, that barb had really hit home with Irene.

'Balfour!' Mrs Reid, one of the older married woman, suddenly warned. The chatter immediately ceased.

Bell glanced over to see that Mr Balfour had indeed reappeared in the department having been absent for the past half hour. He was accompanied by Tommy to whom he seemed to be explaining something.

Bell wasn't sure what her reaction was to seeing Tommy; her emotions were mixed. All she could think was how well he looked. She paused momentarily to wipe a stray wisp of hair from her forehead.

Balfour and Tommy, the gaffer talking non-stop, made their way slowly along the length of the department to pause only a few feet away from Bell.

She smiled at Tommy who couldn't have failed to notice. There was no response, none whatsoever. Not even a flicker of recognition in his eyes. Then he and Balfour were continuing on their way.

Bell dropped her gaze, stung to the quick. That had hurt, really really hurt.

It had been as though she didn't even exist.

'Well, I'm off to bed,' Rose announced, rising from the easy chair she was sitting in. They'd only retired from dinner fifteen minutes previously.

Early yet again, ridiculously so, Andrew thought in dismay. It was as though she didn't want to spend any time in his presence. Or at least, as little as possible.

'I was hoping you might stay up for a bit so we could chat,' he said.

Rose hesitated. 'About what?'

'Nothing in particular. Just chat, that's all. Spend a cosy evening together.'

'I'm tired, Andrew. Bed's the best place for me.'

'If you say so, Rose.' The disappointment was clear in his voice.

She went to him and pecked him lightly on the cheek. 'That'll save you looking in later.'

More disappointment. 'Goodnight then.'

'Goodnight.'

'Oh, Rose!' he said as she was moving away.

She stopped and turned, a quizzical expression on her face.

'I was wondering, how about the pair of us going for a ride this Saturday afternoon? I haven't ridden in ages and the exercise would do me good.'

The quizzical expression became one of slight irritation. The last thing she wanted was to go riding with Andrew, much preferring her own company.

'Still, if you don't wish to.' He smiled thinly when she didn't answer.

'No, it's not that,' she lied, desperately trying to come up with a reason for his not accompanying her.

'But?'

There was no way round this, she realised. She could hardly go out by herself and leave him behind. That would be too much like a slap in the face.

'No buts, it'll be fine,' she replied, trying to force enthusiasm into her voice.

'I shall look forward to it, Rose.'

'As shall I.'

Like two strangers, he reflected after she'd gone. That's what they'd become, like two strangers.

Rose stopped brushing her hair and stared at herself in the vanity mirror. Why was she being so horrid to Andrew? She did love him after all. And yet day after day, night after night, she found herself rejecting him. Pushing him away. Ignoring him.

Tears welled in her eyes to run down her cheeks. Large fat tears like escaping diamonds, each sparkling and dancing in the light.

She sobbed. Sorry for herself. Sorry for Andrew. Sorry for everything. Sorry for being born in the first place.

She really did try with Andrew, but somehow, something always came between them when she made the effort. She wanted him there, and didn't. Loved him, yet at other times hated him.

He was going away on business for a few days the following week which suited her down to the ground. Or did it? Why, oh why was she so confused, so muddled, so utterly wretched?

The baby of course. She knew that. It was the obvious answer. The doctor at the hospital had warned her there might be a period of emotional flux, but she'd never expected anything like this.

Would she ever be right again? Could she ever return to the Rose who'd married Andrew? The sweet uncomplicated young woman who'd been so full of hope for the future?

Things had changed with the advent of Drew, she was aware of that. Her feelings had altered, a coldness creeping in where there had only been warmth before.

She'd never denied Andrew, she reminded herself, even while knowing that wasn't entirely true. There had been nights where excuses had been made, a slight upset, or illness, exaggerated. But basically she hadn't denied him, though her heart wasn't in it.

And then the second pregnancy and what a difference that had made. She'd discovered joy again, and a taste for the pleasures of the flesh that had long lain dormant.

She thought fondly of Glasgow and the hotel room where they'd made such wonderful love. Then revulsion swept over her at the memory, causing her to shiver slightly.

A female Jekyll and Hyde was what she'd become. One moment this, the next that. A quite different animal entirely.

Perhaps she should call Andrew upstairs, invite him to stay the night with her. The poor man had his needs after all, and where Andrew was concerned they were considerable.

What if he tired of her excluding him and sought his pleasure elsewhere? How would she feel about that?

It would bother her, naturally so. And yet would it? She wasn't sure.

Part of her would be jealous, another part relieved. But which part would be the greater? For wouldn't he only be seeking what she was refusing him?

She could hardly blame Andrew if he did elect to cheat on her. He was no saint, not by a long chalk. What she knew of his past history, and she was sure there was a great deal she didn't, proved that.

What a useless creature she was, Rose thought, wiping away the still flowing tears. No good to anyone any more, least of all her husband who loved her as much as she loved him.

It was as though a great glass barrier had been built, a barrier she could see through but could neither get through nor over. A shimmering teasing tantalising barrier.

Reaching out she picked up one of the dolls she'd placed

earlier by the side of her mirror and clasped it tightly to her bosom.

Tears continued to flow as did her sobbing.

'Oh Mary,' she whispered.

'I'm going to miss you dreadfully,' Annie McGillvary said to Nancy. The pair of them were mucking out a cowshed, or byre as they called it.

'And I'll miss you and Hector. You've been smashing friends to me.'

'You'll find another man at the Fair. Handsome lass that you are. The buggers will be queuing up.'

Nancy laughed. 'I doubt that.'

'And you're young. Lots of work left in you which is one of the ways they'll see it.'

There were only days to go and . . . Nancy paused and drew in a deep breath. She was scared, frightened of what lay ahead. The uncertainty of it all.

'He's a swine your Bill,' Annie declared vehemently, her pitchfork thudding into the mound before them.

'Not *my* Bill any more,' Nancy corrected her, thinking with satisfaction that she'd kept her word to herself. Bill had gone without since the night he'd broken the news to her, and most unhappy he'd been about that too. It was the threat of the carving knife that had dissuaded him from forcing the issue. As time had gone by, much to her grim amusement, he'd become more and more bad tempered, the reason for that obvious. Nor had he hit her which she'd again put down to the threat of the carving knife.

'Aye, true enough,' Annie agreed.

Nancy suddenly became aware that she was being watched. It was as if she had a burning sensation between her shoulders and back of the neck. She swung round and there, standing in the shed's open doorway, was the master.

He was staring at her, an amused, triumphant, smile playing across his lips.

He was gloating, she thought. No other word for it, gloating. Well, as long as that was all he did she didn't care.

She returned to work and, when she looked again at the door several minutes later, he was gone.

At the conclusion of the hymn the congregation sat and the Reverend McLean, Andrew's brother-in-law, announced that they would now be joined by members of the Sunday school.

There was a slight rustling amongst those present when the children, herded by their teachers, filed in.

This was what Tommy had been waiting for, the arrival of the Sunday school teachers. Now what were they like?

He was pleasantly surprised, having been expecting the worst. Several of them weren't bad-looking at all. One of them he recognised, a lassie he hadn't seen in years. The others were unknown to him.

It was the last girl who really caught his eye. Hardly a ravishing beauty but she certainly had something that, as far as he was concerned, made her stand out.

Should she or shouldn't she? She hadn't been going to but now Nancy decided she would. She halted and turned round for a last glimpse of the cottage she'd just vacated.

There it was, the grey stone building that had been her home, and which she'd probably never see again. A place of memories, none of them happy ones.

Mist was swirling and eddying, rapidly becoming thicker

by the minute. She caught a glimpse of one of the bondagers but couldn't make out who.

Her goodbyes had been said the previous night, and sad they'd been. Annie had wept and wished her all the best. As had Hector, though he hadn't wept. Well, being a man he'd hardly do that!

Others had come to the cottage to mutter their farewells, the women mainly, with a number of dark looks being cast at Bill sitting silently by the fire.

He would also be going to the Hiring Fair that morning but hadn't suggested they travel together. He hadn't left yet and she had no idea if he was taking the same route as herself or another.

No words had been said between them earlier. She'd served him breakfast which he'd eaten, then, with a grunt, he'd gone out about some task or other. He still hadn't returned when she'd closed the door behind her and set off.

Well, it was finished. She and this place. She and Bill McCabe. It was a new day and a new beginning. A chapter in her life had finished, another was about to open.

There was one final look at the cottage, after which she hurried on her way. Plunging deeper and deeper into the ever-thickening mist, praying to God she didn't get lost.

The Fair would be over by early evening. To get lost and miss it could prove a catastrophe.

Andrew smoothly changed gears as he rounded a bend. He wouldn't have taken this road by choice but a new customer in the area had necessitated the different route.

'Leithan 2 Miles', the sign informed him. The small town where Rose had been in hospital after the miscarriage.

No, he wouldn't have come this way at all if he could have prevented it.

Andrew frowned as he entered the town; there seemed an awful number of people around. Far more than he would have expected. As he got closer to the centre the crowds became more dense.

Something was going on, had to be. And then he recalled that Leithan held a Hiring Fair once a year round about this time. That must be it, he thought. He'd arrived on Fair day.

He'd heard of Hiring Fairs but never actually been to one. He found the concept of what went on there rather intriguing and wondered if he should stop off and take a look around. He was rather hungry after all, and Leithan would be as good as any place to have a bite to eat.

Nancy shivered and tugged her navy blue shawl more tightly round her shoulders. This was awful, even worse than she remembered. The humiliation of it all made her cringe inside.

So far three hinds had stopped and talked to her, all moving on again. Several others had stood off and given her the once-over but not approached, one of these a horrible older man with black teeth and an inturned eye. The thought of going to bed with him had made her flesh creep.

She'd arrived later than planned, which hadn't helped matters, but the weather had held her up.

She stamped her feet to try and bring some feeling back into them.

Andrew had walked past the girl before it dawned on him that he'd seen her before. Though how he should know one of these wretched creatures he couldn't imagine.

Perhaps she bore a resemblance to someone, could that be it? No one sprang to mind.

'Toffee apples, sir. Would you like a toffee apple?'

The speaker was standing behind a barrow displaying them. His expression, as he studied Andrew, was hopeful.

Andrew shook his head. Toffee apples indeed!

'Have you got the kiddies with you, sir? I'm sure they'd like one. They don't come no better or tastier than my toffee apples.'

Disgusting-looking things, Andrew thought, perusing the items in question. 'No thank you,' he stated gruffly, and began retracing his steps.

In some ways the Fair was proving a bit of a disappointment. He'd expected there to be more novelty about it. Hoop-la stalls, coconut shies, those sort of things. Well, there were a few in evidence, but only a few.

There she was again, the girl he'd thought he'd recognised. The white scarf covering her head and tied underneath her chin, topped by a black straw hat, didn't do her any favours, he reflected. But then that was the same headgear worn by the other women standing about waiting to be hired for farm work.

The girl moved and now he could see her face quite clearly. He did know her, he was certain of it.

But from where?

'Excuse me?'

Nancy had noticed the well-dressed man heading in her direction but hadn't really paid any attention to him, not dreaming for one moment that he'd stop and talk to her. 'Yes, sir?'

'You don't recall me, I take it?'

Nancy shook her head.

'You helped my wife a while back when she was in difficulty. We were in a parked Rolls-Royce when she started to miscarry.'

Nancy's face lit up with amazement. 'Of course, sir!'

'So it is you. I wasn't absolutely sure.'

'A terrible thing to happen, sir. Right horrible so it was.'

'I don't know what we'd have done without you. And I never even thanked you afterwards or got your name.'

'Nancy, sir. Nancy Thompson. And you don't have to thank me, I only did what anyone would have done. How is the lady, sir?'

'Fine, well on the way to recovery.'

He owed this girl a debt of gratitude, Andrew thought. Five pounds perhaps, that should cover it. 'So you're here looking for a job, eh?' he said affably.

'A hind to be more precise, sir.'

'A hind?'

'Man, sir. Farm labourer. They take me on then contract themselves to a farmer. The farmer won't employ a hind without a woman, sir. He gets two for the price of one that way.'

Andrew shook his head. 'I must confess I know little about the system.'

'It's called bondaging, sir, and that's what I am, a bondager.'

Andrew was trying to digest this, understand it properly. 'You say you're waiting for a man to pitch up and offer you employment. Correct?'

'Yes, sir.'

'Any man?'

'Whoever'll have me, sir.'

There was clearly more to this than Andrew had thought. 'And what exactly would your duties be for whoever takes you on?'

'Keep his house, sir. That and work for the farmer.'

'Keep his house,' Andrew repeated slowly. 'You mean live with him?'

Nancy nodded.

Andrew was shocked. Why, this was no more than a form of prostitution. If he was understanding things correctly that was. 'Live with him as . . .' He cleared his throat. 'Man and wife?'

'Aye, sir. That's the way of it.'

'Dear God,' he whispered. He really had had no idea. This was barbarous. And it disturbed him hugely.

How old was Nancy? Difficult to say really. Her weatherbeaten face no doubt added years to her.

'Fourteen, sir,' she answered when he asked.

Andrew was appalled. Fourteen! And condemned to a life like this. At the mercy of whichever male should take a notion to her. Prostitution was precisely the word for it and of a most revolting type. His thoughts were whirling.

'What happened to the man you were with?' he queried.

Nancy briefly explained about Bill and the part the master had played in her ending up at the Hiring Fair that day.

By the time she'd finished Andrew had come to a decision. As he'd reminded himself, he owed this girl a debt of gratitude, and pay it he would. To hell with five pounds, he could do a lot better than that. And would.

'Are you hungry?'

She blinked at him in astonishment, thinking that a strange question. 'Yes, sir. I didn't bring anything with me and can't leave here in case I miss an opportunity.'

'A hind,' Andrew said grimly.

'That's right, sir.'

He glanced down at the small cloth-covered bundle by her feet. 'Are those your things?'

She nodded.

'Then pick them up and come with me, Nancy Thompson.'

'Sir?'

'I'm hungry as well so I'll explain what I have in mind over a hot meal.'

'In mind, sir?'

'You heard me.'

'I don't understand, sir. Are you a farmer?'

Andrew laughed. 'No, distiller. I make whisky.'

'Then what would you want with the likes of me, sir? I know nothing about whisky except that I enjoy a taste when I can get it.'

'You drink whisky?'

'I have, sir. Though not often. Don't get the chance you see.'

Andrew nodded his approval. 'My sisters were brought up to drink whisky, a family tradition. So you'll fit right in.'

'I still don't understand, sir.'

'You will. Now grab hold of that bundle and let's go.'

Confused and bewildered Nancy did as she was bid. She liked and instinctively trusted this man.

Andrew had ordered their food at the bar and now rejoined a nervous Nancy. 'It won't be too long,' he declared, placing a half pint of beer in front of her. His was a pint.

'I've never been in a pub before,' she stated quietly. 'It's . . .' She trailed off and glanced about her.

'Just relax, Nancy. There's nothing to be worried about. I assure you.'

'What do you intend, sir? You still haven't said.'

He regarded her thoughtfully. 'How would you like to work as a maid in a big house? You'll have your own bedroom and lashings of good food. The work is hard I grant you, but nothing like you've been used to I shouldn't think. And you get one whole day off a week.'

'I don't know nothing about being a maid, sir,' Nancy protested.

'That's all right, you'll soon pick it up. It's fairly simple really.'

A maid? Nancy was thinking. No more being outside in all weathers, no more Bill McCabe, or someone like him, to have to deal with. No more having to open her legs night after night whether she felt like it or not.

'Would I get paid, sir?'

'Of course.' Andrew mentioned a sum which, albeit modest, was enough to impress her. 'So what do you say?'

'Oh yes, sir. Thank you, sir. I'd be only too pleased to accept and you'll find me a grafter.'

Andrew smiled with satisfaction, pleased he'd been there to come to her aid. His debt had been paid.

'Can I ask your name, sir. Last name that is. I remember your wife calling you Andrew.'

'Drummond. Andrew Drummond. My wife and I live in Perthshire. A village called Dalneil. I don't suppose you've ever been to Perthshire?'

167

Nancy shook her head.

'A beautiful part of the country. More rugged than round here, more spectacular you might say.'

'Am I going there today, sir?'

'Indeed you are. With me in my car.' He laughed at the expression on her face. 'You've never been in a car either, I take it?'

'No, sir.'

'Then it'll be a new experience for you.'

'Yes, sir, Mr Drummond, sir.'

'Mr Drummond will do fine. Now . . .' He had a swallow of beer. 'I want to hear all about being a bondager and get to know something of your background.'

He listened in stony silence as she recounted her tale.

Chapter 11

A ndrew halted the car when Drummond House came into view. It had been a long drive, but a cheery one. Nancy was an excellent companion with a dry, sometimes bawdy, wit. Andrew had warmed to her and felt quite relaxed in her presence, as he hoped she was in his.

'That's it,' he declared, pointing.

Nancy gaped with stupefaction. It wasn't just a big house, it looked the size of a castle to her. It was huge! The master's house was teensy by comparison.

'Well?'

'I'm going to actually live *there*?' she replied in a strangulated voice.

Andrew chuckled. 'That's right.'

Nancy swallowed hard and then shook her head. This was unbelievable. Who would have thought when she started out that morning this was where she'd end up.

'It's beautiful, Mr Drummond.'

Beautiful? Yes, he supposed it was. He gazed at the

house with fresh eyes trying to see it as someone would for the first time. 'Thank you, Nancy.'

Andrew strode into Rose's bedroom, formerly theirs, to find her lying on the bed staring vacantly at the ceiling. He frowned in irritation. She seemed to be forever lying down of late. When she wasn't out riding, that is.

She turned her head to gaze at him. 'Hello, Andrew. Good trip?'

'It went very well, as expected.'

He crossed and sat beside her. 'I had a bit of a surprise earlier. One I've brought back with me.'

'Oh?'

'Do you remember the girl who helped you in the car the day . . .' Choose your words carefully here, he warned himself. 'The day you were taken to hospital?'

'Of course I remember.'

'Well, on the way home I stopped off in Leithan and . . .'

Rose swept into the kitchen where Nancy was enjoying a bowl of cock-a-leekie soup. Up to that point she hadn't been able to recall the girl's face, but she did the moment she saw it.

Nancy immediately came to her feet and attempted a smile.

'I thought I'd better give the lass something after the journey she's had,' Mrs Moffat, the cook, explained, wiping her hands on the large white apron she always wore while on duty. 'Just to tide her over like. She'll eat properly with the rest of us later on.'

Rose nodded her approval. 'Quite right, Mrs Moffat.'

She brought her attention back to Nancy. 'How are you, Nancy?'

'Never better, Mrs Drummond, thank you very much.'

'You're to work for us, I understand.'

'That's right. Your husband came across me at the Fair and kindly offered me a position. So here I am, ready to begin right away if necessary.'

Rose laughed. 'I think tomorrow morning will be time enough for that. Meanwhile we'll have to get you settled in.'

'Thank you, ma'am.'

She studied the girl, her emotions mixed. The sight of Nancy brought back such painful memories. And yet, she was enormously grateful for the help the girl had given her. Things had been bad, but might have been a great deal worse if Nancy hadn't been there.

No, Andrew had done the right thing she decided. One good turn deserved another after all.

'We don't employ a housekeeper here,' Rose explained to Nancy. 'I take care of those duties myself.'

Nancy nodded.

'It keeps me busy you'll appreciate. Gives me something to do. Now then . . .' Rose took a deep breath. 'I'll return in fifteen minutes, which should give you time to finish that soup, and we'll take it from there.'

'Thank you, ma'am.'

'I hope you'll be happy here, Nancy.'

'I'm sure I will, Mrs Drummond.'

Rose left the girl to her cock-a-leekie, one of cook's specialities.

'It really is the most disgusting business,' Andrew declared angrily, pouring himself a dram. He and Rose had just retired from dinner giving him the first real opportunity to tell her about Nancy.

171

'I have heard of bondaging. Though I can't say I know all that much about it.'

'Slave labour, that's what it is. A combination of that and prostitution in my book. The whole rotten system should have been abolished years ago.'

Rose nodded her agreement. It sounded awful.

'She was at the Fair, out of a job, because she didn't please the farmer who raped her.'

'Raped her?' Rose repeated in a whisper. That was dreadful.

'Forced himself on her as his right of employer. Have you ever heard the like?'

Andrew slumped into a chair facing Rose and had a sip of whisky. 'She's had a hell of a life. I felt immensely sorry for her when she told me about it.'

He paused, then said, 'I presume it *was* all right me bringing her here. I mean, you don't object? It just seemed the least I could do.'

'Of course it's all right, Andrew. She'll be a welcome and useful addition to the staff.'

'She's only fourteen. Imagine having to live with a man as his wife at that age. Not only that but work like a trojan into the bargain. The sort of hard physical labour an Irish navvy might balk at.'

Rose settled deeper into her chair, intrigued by what Andrew was saying.

The pair of them talked and talked, mainly about Nancy, and for the first time in ages Rose didn't go early to bed.

Christine, who had the room next to Nancy's, stuck her head round the door. 'It's rise and shine,' she announced.

Nancy immediately slid from underneath the bedclothes.

It was early, but a later rise than she was used to. She couldn't wait to start her duties.

'Get washed and dressed and I'll be back for you,' Christine said and disappeared, closing the door behind her.

Nancy stretched and yawned. She'd slept well, the bed being warm, cosy and comfortable. Best of all there hadn't been Bill McCabe to contend with. That in itself was a sheer delight.

She wondered if Bill had found someone at the Fair. Bound to have done, she thought. Bill wouldn't have any problem there. She wished the newcomer to the cottage well. Especially if the master took a fancy to her.

After she'd washed at the bowl and jug of water provided she hastily donned the uniform Mrs Drummond had allocated her the previous night. The uniform was used but that didn't matter. It was only a little loose at the waist, otherwise it fitted perfectly.

She was ready and waiting when Christine returned.

There were five other girls who worked at Drummond House as maids, all of whom she'd met the night before. They were a friendly bunch and clearly all got on well together. Nancy had been made to feel completely at ease from the moment she'd arrived.

'Morning, Kelly!'

Kelly stared after Andrew who'd just strode past him. He had not seen Andrew in such a good humour for a long while.

Well, long may it continue.

'What was the war really like, Dad? You rarely mention it.'

Tommy and Jack were alone, Hettie having gone out visiting. She wouldn't be home again for a good hour yet.

Jack had been thinking about his book, mulling over the next section. 'The war?' he repeated softly, mind flashing back over the years.

'As I said, you rarely talk about it.'

'That's probably because I don't want to.'

Tommy could hear the wistfulness in his father's voice, that and more.

'The war is a period best forgotten about,' Jack said.

'Was it that awful?'

Jack could recall it so vividly it might have happened only yesterday. The sights, the sounds. Faces of comrades killed in the terrible carnage, Peter Drummond, Andrew's elder brother, among them. The mud that had claimed so many victims, men sucked screaming to their deaths. Others blown to smithereens. Arms, legs, body bits flying through the air . . .

'Dad?'

'Pray to God, son, that there is never another one. That's all I can say.'

'And yet the papers think there will be.'

'I know. I shudder when your mother reads them to me. The news fills me with dread.'

Another war, it seemed inconceivable that anyone, any sane person that is, would allow it to happen again. 'It's your birthday next week,' Jack said.

'Seventeen, quite grown up, eh?'

Seventeen, Jack thought, just the right age for war. Old enough to be brave, too young to know any better. It was the smell he remembered most vividly, he reflected. The rank stink of all-pervading fear.

'A land fit for heroes,' Jack smiled gruesomely. 'That's what they promised. A land fit for heroes. Only they never delivered. That wasn't what the poor bastards came home to at all. They were lying, the politicians that is, lying in their teeth. I've never believed or trusted a politician from that day to this.'

'Did you . . . kill anyone, Dad?'

Jack sucked in a breath. There was one in particular that had stayed with him. He'd been cowering at the bottom of a shell hole in no-man's-land when Fritz had jumped in beside him. There had been several seconds of stunned silence while they stared at one another, each surprised to find the other there, then he'd fired his revolver twice and that had been the end of Fritz. He'd spent sixteen hours in that shell hole with the corpse before being able to get away.

Fritz had been a middle-aged chap, quite portly too, wearing a thick gold wedding ring so there had been a family back in Germany. A woman suddenly widowed, children suddenly fatherless.

He'd escaped in heavy smoke. Diving, ducking, weaving, jinking to the safety of their own lines, tumbling into the trench like a frightened rabbit into its burrow.

'Dad?'

'Yes, son?'

'I asked: Did you ever kill anyone?'

'Not that I was aware,' he lied.

'Oh. I thought you might have done.'

'Perhaps I did. Often you simply never saw the result of what you were firing at.' Well, that was true enough.

'But never hand to hand?'

Jack was shaking inside though he didn't show it. Fritz in the shell hole, the bayonet slash that had disembowelled a young lad who'd shrieked and shrieked as his guts spilled out from between his fingers. And then there had been . . .

Jack shook his head, feeling he might drown in the memories as so many had drowned in the mud.

'Don't ever think war is glorious,' he said, voice tight as a drum. 'That's the last thing it is, believe me. And I should know.'

Pack up your troubles in your old kit bag and . . .

Jack was unable to cry having lost his tear ducts along with his eyes. If he had been able he'd have wept.

Rose was *en route* to having a lie down when she spotted Nancy, busy dusting, through an open doorway.

Fourteen, Andrew had said she was. A mere child, a baby really. And to have been through what she had. How she sympathised with the lass, especially the rape.

Rose couldn't imagine what that must have been like. To be taken against your will, forced. It was ghastly beyond belief.

Fourteen. She wondered what Mary would have been like at that age. Certainly not as mature as Nancy, Heaven forbid. She tried to conjure up a picture of Mary at fourteen and, strangely, it was Nancy's face she saw. Nancy, but different. A more youthful Nancy, an innocent Nancy. Nancy as a child should be at fourteen and as Mary would most certainly have been.

A laughing Mary, a giggling Mary, a wide-eyed Mary with her whole life before her.

As she would have been. *Should* have been.

Rose stifled a sob and hurried on her way.

'I'd be delighted for you to become a Sunday school

teacher,' John McLean, the minister, said to Tommy, who'd called on him at the manse.

Tommy had given this a great deal of thought and decided Hettie was right, it was a good idea. The lassie who'd particularly caught his eye that morning in church was called Barbara McTaggart. Her father was a local landowner in a smallish way. He'd found that out through discreet inquiry.

'Now when would you care to start?' John asked with a smile.

'This Sunday seems as good a time as any.'

'Even better. Then Sunday it is.'

'Fine then,' Tommy declared, rising from where he'd been sitting. 'I'll be there.'

The minister also came to his feet. 'Would you like a cup of tea before you go? My wife has just made a lovely chocolate cake which I'm sure you'd enjoy.'

'No thank you. I'd best be going.'

John shook Tommy warmly by the hand. 'I know you'll be a splendid success as one of my teachers. And, I daresay, the others will appreciate the male company.'

Yes please, Tommy thought, with Barbara McTaggart firmly in mind. 'I'll see myself out. I know the way.'

'Sunday then, Tommy.'

'Sunday.'

That was it, he'd done the deed, Tommy mused when he was outside. He just hoped he wasn't going to regret it.

Somehow he didn't think he would.

'The mistress has just never been the same since losing the baby,' Pattie Williams declared to Christine, as the two maids shared their mid-morning break.

'Things are all higgledy-piggledy right enough,' Christine agreed. 'You simply don't know where you are nowadays.'

Unknown to either, Mrs Moffat was in the larder listening to this conversation. The cook's mouth was a thin slash, for she too was worried about Rose. It was getting close to the point where she was going to have to speak to Mr Drummond. Only that very morning she'd asked Rose yet again for the coming week's menus and Rose had put her off saying she'd have them soon enough. Not at all like the Rose of old, and not good enough.

'In my opinion she should get a proper housekeeper. That would solve everything,' Pattie went on.

Christine nodded.

'Then things wouldn't be at sixes and sevens no more.'

'Maybe it's just a passing phase and she'll get over it,' Christine mused. 'I have an auntie who went a bit funny after she lost a baby. It didn't last long though, a couple of months at most I seem to remember.'

'I do feel for Mrs Drummond. I mean, you have to. For that to happen right there on the road.'

'Aye, poor woman.'

'No wonder she's been strange ever since. It's quite understandable.'

'Understandable all right, but that doesn't make it any easier for the rest of us. We're carrying the brunt.'

'Lucky for her Nancy was there.'

'Aye, real lucky so it was.'

The entire staff knew by this time how Nancy had come to be employed by the Drummonds, though weren't aware of the full situation. Nancy had merely said she'd worked on a farm and left it at that, glossing over the business of the Hiring Fair and bondaging. According to her she'd bumped into Andrew while looking for a new position and that had been that.

Christine finished her tea and sighed. 'I suppose we'd better get back to it.'

'No rest for the wicked, eh?'

'None at all.'

Mrs Moffat only emerged from the larder when both girls had departed from the kitchen.

Rose looked across the room when there was a tap on the door. She resisted the temptation to switch off the bedside lamp as Andrew would probably see the light go out. 'Come in, darling!'

Andrew had been downstairs swithering about whether or not it was too early to have this discussion. In the event he'd decided it wasn't.

'Reading I see.'

Rose laid the book aside. 'A novel I bought a while ago.'

He went to her and sat on the edge of the bed. 'Interesting?'

'So so. A romantic story that has its moments.'

A romantic story, was that a good sign or not? He had no idea. 'I've been meaning to talk to you, Rose.'

Somehow she knew what was coming and sighed inwardly. She'd been expecting this.

He reached out and took her hand. 'I think we should try and get back to normal. Have things as they were.'

She stared at him but didn't reply.

'It has been a while now and . . .' He cleared his throat. 'I miss you.'

Rose could well guess what it was he really missed. 'You have been patient, Andrew,' she conceded.

'I've done my best.'

'But it is early days yet.'

His heart sank to hear that.

'I don't know I'm up to . . . well . . . you know.' She glanced away and gently removed her hand from his.

'We could leave that for now. But I do believe we should be sleeping together again. Sharing the same bed. Don't you agree?'

Rose closed her eyes. This was difficult, and it wasn't as though she didn't sympathise with Andrew, she did. But the last thing she wanted was him back in the marital bed knowing full well that, despite what he might say or promise, it could only lead to the inevitable. That was Andrew.

'I need more time, darling,' she murmured.

Now it was his turn not to reply.

'Please?'

His determination melted. 'Of course. If that's what you wish.'

'I do.'

'Only . . .' Why did he feel he was about to propose something that was obscene. 'The sooner we get together again the sooner, God willing, we can have another child.'

'Another child,' she repeated slowly. 'A replacement for Mary you mean?'

'Not a replacement. You can't do that. But another child.' Hopefully a girl, he prayed.

For some inexplicable reason Rose found herself wanting to scratch Andrew's eyes out. Which didn't make any sense at all. Another child was the obvious answer. Then why was she so reluctant to try for one? That was a question to which she didn't have an answer.

'Rose?'

'I'm suddenly awfully tired, Andrew. I should sleep.'

Disappointment bit heavily into him. That and a certain amount of anger. She was being so unreasonable, but then that had been more or less the case since her miscarriage.

He thought of Glasgow and how good it had been between them, desire instantly taking hold of him. He would have given anything for it to have still been like that.

'I'll let you rest then,' he said, reluctantly getting up.

She gave him a smile of gratitude. 'Thank you.'

'But we must talk again about this.'

'We will, Andrew. I promise.'

He didn't believe her. At least, she wouldn't do so willingly.

Her bedside light snapped out as he closed the door behind him.

'Fascinating,' Jack murmured, Andrew having just recounted Nancy's story to him. And fascinating was precisely what he did find the story.

'Only fourteen too. A mere chit.'

'I've never heard of this bondaging. It's new to me.'

'Well, it still goes on, though it should be against the law in my opinion.'

Jack groped for his pint and had a swallow. This had certainly caught his interest and he was wondering if he could do anything with it. 'Can I meet the girl?'

Andrew stared at his friend in surprise. 'I suppose so. But why?'

'There's a book in this. I can smell it.'

'A book,' Andrew mused. He hadn't thought of that.

'But I'll need to chat to her first. Find out all the detail that I can. The ins and outs so to speak.'

Andrew considered the matter. 'I've no objection to you speaking to her, Jack, though it's up to her whether or not she'll agree.'

'Naturally. I didn't assume otherwise.'

'You sound quite keen?'

'I am, old bean. I am.'

'Then I'll tell you what, why don't we leave it for a couple of months. Let her find her feet up at the house. Then I'll broach it with her. How's that?'

'Capital. I'll be finished what I'm doing now and open to fresh ideas.'

Andrew was amused by this turn of events.

'Hello again.'

Barbara McTaggart smiled at Tommy who'd joined the ranks of Sunday school teachers that morning. 'Hello. How did you get on?'

He shrugged. 'Not too bad. I'm being allowed to take my own group next week.'

'That's good.'

She'd been smaller than he'd expected, and a little prettier. He liked the dark green of the eyes now studying him closely. 'Which way do you go?' he asked.

She told him.

'Why don't I walk with you for a bit. Unless you've another arrangement that is?'

'No,' she replied slowly. 'I haven't.'

'Right then, Barbara, walk together we shall. You don't mind me calling you Barbara I hope?'

She laughed. 'Well, you can hardly call me Miss McTaggart as the children do.'

He laughed as well.

'And my friends call me Babs.'

'Babs,' he repeated. It suited her.

'You're working at the distillery I hear.'

'That's right, training to be a traveller. In a few years' time when I've learnt the business I'll be on the road.' He didn't even bother to try and keep the pride out of his voice. 'Impressed?'

'Oh very,' she teased.

'It'll be well paid and I'll have a car. Though it isn't what I want to ultimately do.'

'Oh?'

He regarded her thoughtfully, wondering why he was even considering confiding in her. 'It'll have to be a secret though, just between the pair of us.'

She was intrigued. 'Cross my heart and hope to die if I breathe a word. That suit you?'

He nodded.

'Then come on, spill the beans.'

'An African explorer,' he announced triumphantly.

She stared at him in amazement. He was pulling her leg, surely. 'An African explorer,' she repeated, dazed. That was an ambition to say the least.

'And big-game hunter.'

Now he was having her on. 'I see,' she murmured.

He caught her by the arm having heard the disbelief in her voice. 'Honestly.'

'Well you . . .' She wasn't quite certain what to say. 'Certainly aim high.'

'Why not?'

'Why not indeed.'

'And one day I will be these things. I've sworn it to myself.'

He was serious, she realised. This wasn't a leg pull at all.

'Now you won't let on to anyone, you promised.'

'Our secret. Just between the pair of us.'

He beamed his approval at her.

There was more to Tommy Riach than met the eye she thought. Daft or not, she liked him for these absurd ideas. For absurd they were.

As for Tommy, he was thinking how much he liked Babs McTaggart. In fact he liked her a lot which was a most satisfactory state of affairs. Just what he'd been hoping would be the case.

Andrew came groggily awake as the naked figure slid in beside him. 'What . . . ?'

'Ssshh, darling,' Rose purred, placing a finger over his lips.

Rose! And naked. He was stunned.

Rose ran a hand over his chest, then slipped it inside his pyjama top. She wasn't quite sure why she was doing this, only that she had an overwhelming urge to make love. Her whole being craved it. To feel him inside her, for the release that would bring. Nor would the latter take long, in the first instance anyway.

Andrew was trying to collect his wits, this being completely and utterly unexpected. He groaned as her other hand found him and began teasing.

'My darling,' she crooned, shifting herself into the position she wanted. Her need was more urgent than she'd ever previously known.

Rose freed Andrew from the confines of his pyjama bottom, then sat astride him. A swift wriggle and he was in place.

'Rose?'

'Ssshh.' The finger again over his lips.

Andrew smiled wolfishly as she began to move. This was his dream of months come true.

As time passed he marvelled at how passionate, demanding and insatiable she was. It was as though she was trying to draw the very life force out of him.

When he awoke next morning it was to find her gone. All that remained was the sweet smell of her scent.

Chapter 12

Andrew frowned and glanced at his watch. 'Is Mrs Drummond coming down this morning?' he asked Pattie Williams who was serving breakfast.

'She's already had something and left, sir. Went riding I believe.'

His frown deepened. That surprised him. To go off without a word after what had happened the previous night. Odd to say the least.

His frown turned to a smile as he recalled their lovemaking. Rose had been simply . . . tempestuous. At one point her cries were so loud he'd feared she must wake the entire household. Luckily Drew, whose bedroom adjoined the one he was now using, was away at school otherwise he'd have been bound to hear.

Oh, but it had been wonderful, particularly after such a long spell of celibacy. He couldn't have asked for better. The sheer intensity on Rose's part had brought a whole new dimension to their lovemaking.

He hoped he was in for a repeat bout later that night.

'Come on, come on, you bitch!' Rose yelled into Strumpet's ear. The horse was running faster than it had ever run before, the countryside a blur flying by.

Rose's eyes were starting in her head, her expression one of ecstatic pleasure as the small whip she was carrying rose and fell.

McFarlane was appalled when Rose returned Strumpet to the stables. To bring the horse to such a state was downright cruelty.

'I'll take her out again tomorrow morning, McFarlane,' Rose announced.

'If you don't mind me saying so, the beast should have a few days' rest to recover. She's been going some.'

Rose eyed the groom coldly. 'I beg your pardon?' There was steel in her voice.

'The beast should have a few days' rest, Mrs Drummond. She might break down otherwise. That or do herself some real damage.'

'What are you implying, man?'

'Nothing, Mrs Drummond. Nothing at all,' he replied hastily. 'I'm only giving you my advice as a groom should. Whether you follows it or not is up to you.'

'Are you being impertinent, McFarlane?'

Christ, he thought. He was going to get the sack. And at his age where would he find another position? This one suited him down to the ground. 'No, Mrs Drummond. I'm sorry if it sounded that way. I certainly didn't mean it to.'

Rose relented. Perhaps Strumpet did need rest. But that wasn't a reason why she couldn't still have a ride. 'I'll take Moonbeam out then,' she said.

Moonbeam was Andrew's horse, a powerful gelding that McFarlane considered far too strong for Rose. But he had no intention of saying so, not after their last exchange. He touched his forelock. 'I'll have Moonbeam saddled and waiting, Mrs Drummond.'

'Good.'

She glanced over at Moonbeam's box, the animal staring back. A thrill of anticipation ran through her. 'You're not to mention this to Mr Drummond, understand?'

McFarlane nodded.

Now that should really be a ride, Rose thought gleefully.

Andrew was perplexed. Rose had been cold and distant all the way through dinner. You wouldn't have believed it was the same woman who'd come into his bed the night before. It was like comparing an iceberg to a fiery furnace.

'From what I'm told Nancy is doing rather well,' he said, swirling the contents of his after-dinner dram round in its glass.

Rose didn't reply. It was as though she hadn't heard.

'Rose?'

She blinked and seemed to come out of a reverie. 'Did you say something?'

'That Nancy is getting on rather well.'

'Yes. Yes she is. I'm pleased with her.'

'Is something wrong, darling?'

Rose cocked an eyebrow. 'Why do you ask that?'

'You don't seem to be . . . quite yourself this evening.'

'No?'

'No,' he stated emphatically.

'I wasn't aware of the fact.'

There it was again, that distant tone to her voice. As if

she was there and at the same time not. He had a distinct feeling of irrelevancy.

Should he or shouldn't he? He'd fully intended mentioning the previous night and how stupendous it had been, but now . . . in her present mood?

Well, of course he should. It had happened after all. It hadn't been a dream on his part. The smell of scent lingering round his bed earlier bore testimony to that. The smell of scent and his general feeling of well-being.

'Shall I now be moving back in?' he asked with a smile.

Rose stared blankly at him.

His smile began to slip. 'Shall I be moving back in, to our bedroom that is?'

She turned her face away from him, a face that had grown completely expressionless. 'Not yet, Andrew.'

'But I thought . . . hoped . . . after last night?'

'I need more time. I told you.'

'But that was before you came to me.'

'Well, it hasn't changed.'

He sighed with disappointment. 'Will you be coming again to see me?'

Rose didn't reply.

'Please say you will. For God's sake, Rose, don't make me beg. I am your husband after all.'

'Yes, you are,' she whispered.

Andrew was totally confused. What he'd thought was a break-through apparently wasn't.

'It was so good, Rose. So very good.'

She should never have gone, she thought. But she had been unable to stop herself. It was as if she'd been driven by demons.

Fear took hold of her. A fear she couldn't put a

name to. She abruptly stood. 'I'm going up now. Don't disturb me.'

'If you wish.'

She turned to look at him and for a brief moment there was a terrible torment in her eyes. Then it was gone.

'We'll work this out, Andrew, I promise.'

'I hope so.'

When he later passed her door light was showing underneath. As asked, he neither knocked nor attempted an entrance.

Heart heavy as lead he went to his own room.

'Tommy Riach walked Barbara McTaggart home from Sunday school yesterday. The second time he's done so,' Irene informed Bell who was working alongside.

That jolted Bell. 'Who's Barbara McTaggart when she's at home?' she replied nonchalantly.

'Some stuck-up cow with airs and graces. Part of the gentry. You wouldn't know her.'

'Do you?'

Irene laughed derisively, considering that a joke. 'Only what I've heard. She doesn't mix with the likes of us, the peasants.'

'And Tommy walked her home from Sunday school?'

'Twice apparently. She's a teacher there as is Tommy now.'

Bell paused momentarily to stare at her friend. 'He's what!'

'A Sunday school teacher. Joined the Holy Rollers.'

'Shit,' Bell muttered. That *was* a turn-up for the book.

'What are you two gabbing about?' Isa Weir called over.

'Don't be so bloody nosy!' Bell retorted hotly.

'Oh, pardon me for breathing,' Isa replied, voice dripping sarcasm.

They might be pals but that didn't stop Irene sticking the knife in. 'She's very pretty I hear.'

'Who?'

'Barbara McTaggart of course.' Then, teasingly, 'Do you think it's a romance?'

'How the hell should I know. I neither know nor care.'

Liar, Irene thought smugly.

There were lots of questions Bell wanted to ask, but wouldn't, not wishing to show any interest. But underneath she was upset, just as Irene had intended.

It might have been an Arctic wind blowing in as Rose entered the kitchen. A red spot on either cheek betrayed her inner fury. 'I want a word, Mrs Moffat,' she stated.

The cook, whose hands had been deep in a bowl of flour, wiped them on her pinny. 'Yes, Mrs Drummond?'

'I believe you've spoken to my husband to say you're unhappy with the way I'm managing things.'

Mrs Moffat glanced at Christine and Jamesina Laing, the latter another maid who was also present, as was Lena Johnstone the young scullery maid. Whatever was to be said should have been said to her alone and not in front of others. This was a breach of etiquette and undermined her authority.

Rose didn't give a damn about any of that, being hell-bent on having it out with the cook. 'Well?'

'Perhaps we could speak later.'

'We'll speak now!' Rose declared forcefully.

'Come on, Jamesina,' Christine whispered. It was best

they got out of there and fast. Lena, a slow but kindly girl, stood transfixed, not knowing what to do.

'Remain where you are,' Rose snapped to Christine and Jamesina who froze in their tracks.

'I have talked to Mr Drummond,' Cook acknowledged slowly. 'I considered it my duty to do so.'

'Why not me?'

'That didn't seem appropriate as it was regarding you.'

Rose took several steps forward, her gaze riveted on Mrs Moffat's eyes. 'Not up to the job any more is what I understand you said.'

Mrs Moffat blanched slightly. True enough, that was what she'd said, though not so bluntly. 'You have been ill, Mrs Drummond, and are taking some time to recover. I merely suggested it might be an idea to employ a housekeeper to take the strain off you.'

Rose's lips twisted into a sneer. 'Then *my* suggestion is that if you're unhappy here you hand in your notice.'

Mrs Moffat wasn't a woman to be bullied, not by anyone. 'I see,' she replied, anger in her voice.

'But if you do you won't be getting a letter of recommendation to take with you. Any letter I, or Mr Drummond, might write would be quite to the contrary.'

That was it as far as Mrs Moffat was concerned, her blood now up. She wasn't going to be spoken to like this, and certainly not in front of other members of staff. 'I'll pack right away,' she declared.

Christine sucked in a breath. They couldn't lose Mrs Moffat! It was unthinkable. Mrs Moffat was a brilliant cook who ran her kitchen like clockwork.

'You'll serve a month's notice. That was agreed when you were taken on,' Rose said, eyes flashing.

'Why should I bother with that when I won't be getting a letter of recommendation. Not that I need one, I have plenty others from previous employers. No, Mrs Drummond, in the circumstances I think it best I pack my bags and leave today.'

Rose hadn't been expecting this. To dismiss Mrs Moffat certainly, but not for the cook to leave virtually there and then. 'Do as you must,' she answered.

Mrs Moffat removed her apron, neatly folded it and placed it on the table. Then she swept past Rose and out of the kitchen without a backward glance.

Rose wondered why she felt defeated, as if she'd been got the better of.

Roast beef was scheduled for that evening, she remembered. That shouldn't be too difficult to cope with. She'd oversee, she decided.

'Put that apron on,' she instructed Christine. 'You're acting cook until we hire a replacement.'

'Bloody Norah,' Christine muttered when Rose too had gone.

'You did *what*!' Andrew exploded.

'You heard me. I had it out with Mrs Moffat and she resigned. She left this afternoon and good riddance I say.'

Andrew was furious. 'But she was . . .'

'I will not be criticised by any member of staff,' Rose interrupted. 'Especially behind my back. That was unforgivable.'

'It wasn't exactly a criticism, as I explained to you. She was simply showing concern and thought a housekeeper would take a weight off your shoulders.'

'Huh!' Rose sneered. 'You can be a fool at times,

Andrew. Quite naïve where women are concerned. It was criticism all right, and most unwarranted. I've been running the house perfectly.'

'Then why would she come to me?'

Rose shrugged. 'Jealousy maybe.'

That astounded Andrew. 'What on earth would she be jealous of?'

'I don't know. But I've always suspected her of being a bitch underneath, and this only proves it.'

'And you let her go without a reference?'

'She had plenty others she told me and wouldn't be needing one from us.'

'What about pay?'

'She didn't work a month's notice so forfeited anything already owed. She broke the contract, not me.'

Naïve with women – he resented that. He might have many faults but naïvety, with either gender, wasn't one of them. He thought Rose had behaved disgracefully and would never have told her of his chat with Mrs Moffat if he'd known this would be the outcome. His one consolation was that Mrs Moffat wouldn't be long out of employment, she was too good a cook for that. She had a sister in Stirling, he recalled. He would send a cheque there and ask for it to be forwarded. That and a note stating his regret at her departure.

'I've already drafted out an advertisement for a new cook,' Rose declared. 'We won't be without one for long.'

How Rose had changed since the miscarriage, Andrew thought. She'd become almost a different person, and not one he was sure he liked. He still loved Rose, there was no doubt in his mind about that. But did he like her?

That was something else again.

*   *   *

'I appreciate it's a silly complaint and I probably shouldn't be bothering you with it, but there we are.'

Dr Lesley regarded Andrew across his desk. 'There's nothing silly about indigestion, particularly persistent indigestion, it can be extremely painful.'

'I've tried everything I can think of but it just keeps coming back.'

Lesley nodded his sympathy. 'You've been under a great deal of pressure recently, Mr Drummond, perhaps that's the root cause. Pressure manifests itself in all manner of ways. Now what exactly have you taken?'

Andrew reeled off a list of pills and potions.

'I have a mixture that's usually very helpful. We'll try that. In the meantime I suggest you eat only light meals for a while. Do you smoke?'

'No.'

'That's good. Smoking can often lead to various stomach upsets. As can alcohol. I presume you drink?'

Andrew treated the doctor to a wry smile. 'I'm a distiller, of course I drink. Whoever heard of one who doesn't.'

Lesley matched Andrew's smile. 'A rhetorical question I suppose. I'm certainly not adverse to a dram myself.'

'Drummond's I hope,' Andrew said quickly.

'Oh, always.'

'Then I'll see you get sent over a case.'

Lesley beamed. 'That's most generous of you.'

'Not at all.'

'But for now can you try and keep your consumption down to a minimum. That should also help.'

Andrew pulled a face. 'That's torture, doctor, not a cure.'

Emma Blair

'Well, temporary torture, Mr Drummond. Just do your best.'

Lesley rose and crossed to a large, ancient, cabinet which he opened. He rummaged for several moments before finding what he was after, a bottle containing a white mixture.

'There we are,' he declared, placing it in front of Andrew. 'The instructions are on the label.'

'Thank you.'

Lesley sat again and made a pyramid with his hands. 'Now, how's Mrs Drummond?'

A look of anxiety creased Andrew's face. 'Physically she's fine. Goes out riding every day. But mentally . . .' He took a deep breath. 'She's becoming even more irrational.'

'I see,' Lesley murmured. 'And eh, relations between the pair of you. Have they resumed?'

Andrew found this line of questioning extremely difficult not to mention embarrassing. 'She did come to me one night. But one night only.'

'And was that a success?'

Andrew coloured slightly. 'Very much so. But with hindsight even that was irrational.'

'In what way?' Lesley saw Andrew's hesitation. 'I am your doctor don't forget, used to keeping confidences. The more information I have the better it is for me to diagnose correctly. Besides, I hear all sorts in this surgery. Things that would not only surprise but astound you.'

'She acted rather out of character,' Andrew stated in a low voice. 'Far more enthusiastic than I've ever known her. Quite bizarrely so when I came to think about it.'

Lesley leant back in his chair to consider that. 'The mind is a weird and wonderful device, Mr Drummond.

If only we understood it more. I think the best thing is
if I pay her another call at the house.'

'You won't mention this conversation?' Andrew asked,
alarmed.

'No, I'll pretend it's a routine call just like the previous
one I made.'

'That's fine then,' a relieved Andrew sighed.

Mrs Drummond was beginning to worry him, Lesley
reflected. Perhaps he should refer her to a specialist.

He'd decide that after he'd made his call.

'What's up with your face the night?' Agnes Mathieson,
Bell's mother, demanded.

'Nothing.'

'Then why is it like fizz?'

Bell wasn't about to say why that was so. Agnes would
have been mortified, not to say furious. As for her da,
sitting snoring in a chair, if she'd told him what was
running through her mind he'd probably have clouted
her one.

She stared at Agnes's prematurely aged face, fag dangling
from the corner of her mouth. Her hair was unkempt,
greasy and straggly at the ends. Her dress was old and
stained, fit only for the midden.

As for her da, he defied description. And he smelt abom-
inably, but then he always had. It was a rare occurrence for
him to have a bath.

Bell gazed about her. What a dump, hardly fit for pigs
far less humans. Dirty too, clart everywhere. In the next
room she could hear her two younger brothers going at
it again. Why oh why were they forever fighting? Scruffs
the pair of them.

She was the only one in the family who kept herself

decent, natural pride made her do that. The boys took the piss from time to time but she always answered loftily that it was because of her job. She had to be presentable for that. It was necessary.

That usually shut them up as they knew how reliant the family was on her regular money coming in. Without her pay packet they'd be in a right old state and no mistake.

She thought of Tommy Riach and the lovely home he no doubt came from. Everything there would be spick and span, just like the home she intended keeping when she got married.

'So why like fizz?' Agnes demanded again.

'Bad day at the distillery,' Bell lied, and shrugged. Which satisfied Agnes who left Bell to it.

Bell closed her eyes and conjured up a picture of Tommy. He'd be a wonderful husband. Kind, probably generous, caring. And a good provider, unlike some she thought, meaning her da. Oh aye, a traveller for the distillery was bound to earn stacks.

It would be idyllic being married to Tommy. But there was fat chance of that. The man in the moon would come visiting first.

No, he'd probably marry this Barbara McTaggart or someone like her. She had no chance, as Irene had told her months back. She and Tommy Riach came from two different worlds and nothing would ever change that.

Resentment filled her. Why couldn't she have been born into a decent family. Why had she been landed with the parents she had, and the background that went with them. Life was cruel right enough.

Bell wrinkled her nose in disgust when her da broke wind, following that up with a loud belch.

She'd go to see Irene, she decided. She had a couple

of bob in her purse and hopefully Irene might have the same. She'd suggest a visit to the pub.

Anywhere, to get away from this dump.

Rose hung up the telephone. That had been Georgina, her stepmother, wondering if she'd be interested in a shopping trip to Edinburgh. Of course she would, nothing would be nicer. And so they'd agreed to meet up the following week, booking into the same hotel where they'd spend the night.

It would be fun, she thought. And she did need some new clothes. Well, she always needed those.

Andrew was enthusiastic when she mentioned it later on that day, thinking a break from the house and Dalneil would do her the world of good.

Dr Lesley's report had been positive which had cheered him. Rose was depressed but, despite her bouts of irrationality, coping very well.

Time, Lesley had assured him. It would just take time.

'I don't know about you but I'm ready for lunch,' Georgina declared, having just bought a black gabardine suit that she considered did wonders for her figure. It had a slim little curved-in waist, big billowing push-up sleeves and a simply gorgeous jacket that flared at the sides with ripples in the back. On seeing her in it Rose had said she looked like a film star.

'There's just one other department I'd like to visit before then. You don't mind, do you?' Rose pleaded.

'My feet could do with a rest.'

'Mine too, but this won't take long. I promise you.'

Georgina heaved a sigh of resignation. 'Oh, all right. But not too long, mind.'

'You're a darling, Georgina.'

'Children's clothes?' Willie Seaton frowned.

'That's where we went. And believe me, Rose would have spent hours there if I'd let her.'

'But why on earth would she be wanting to look at children's clothes. She's not expecting again?'

'If she is she didn't mention and I didn't ask. It didn't seem right to after what she's so recently been through.'

Willie lit a cigarette. This was damned odd.

'But it didn't finish there. Later that afternoon she insisted we go into a toy shop. And again would have stayed for hours if I'd been willing.'

'You must have said something then, surely?'

'I did try to probe a little but without success. Rose wouldn't be drawn.'

'Did she buy anything?'

Georgina shook her head. 'Neither in the children's department nor the toy shop. She just seemed to want to browse.'

He regarded her steadily. 'So what did you make of it all?'

'I found it rather . . . I know she's your daughter, Willie, and this isn't exactly the nicest of words, but I found it rather creepy.'

'Creepy,' Willie mused.

'Definitely so. It quite spoilt the day for me.'

He laughed. 'It can't have spoilt it that much going by the amount of money you spent. Even by your standards you excelled yourself.'

'It's the prices, darling,' she lied smoothly. 'They've gone up dreadfully. I didn't buy more than I would normally.'

'Well, it's certainly your last shopping trip for a while. Another like that would bankrupt me.' The latter was nonsense of course but he felt he had to put some curb on her.

'About Rose,' she said, getting away from the subject of money. 'Do you think you should say something to Andrew?'

'I could do,' Willie replied reflectively. 'Telephone him at work and speak to him there. On the other hand, the fact she went to those places might not have any significance whatsoever.'

'It was still creepy,' Georgina insisted.

Willie wondered if his wife wasn't exaggerating matters. Perhaps Rose had been searching for a present and hadn't found anything suitable.

Yes, he decided. That was far more likely to be the case.

'You sent for me, Mrs Drummond?'

'Yes I did, Nancy. I'm going to have a tea party with my dollies and thought you might like to be our guest.'

Nancy stared at Rose in amazement. 'That would be ever so nice,' she replied slowly, wondering what on earth was going on. Mrs Drummond playing with dolls!

Rose smiled beatifically. 'I brought the dolls and their house back from our visit to The Haven you know. They were mine when I was young. Did you have dolls, Nancy?'

'I'm afraid not.'

'What a pity. Such a shame. Anyway, let me introduce you to mine.'

Nancy struggled to keep a straight face. This was ridiculous. But play she would if that was what was required.

Chapter 13

'I really loathe that man,' Tommy declared vehemently, referring of course to Mr Kelly. 'He makes my life a misery.'

Babs McTaggart glanced sideways at him in amusement. He was walking her home from Sunday school as had become their weekly custom. 'Surely he can't be that bad.'

'He is, believe me. I don't know why but he has a go at me every opportunity he gets.'

'Are you sure you're not upsetting him in some way?'

'Well, if I am I'm not aware of it. I think he just doesn't like my face.'

Babs laughed. 'That's ridiculous.'

'No it's not. You must have met people you've taken an instant dislike to for no rhyme or reason. I know I have.'

Babs looked up at the sky. It was a beautiful June day, neither too hot nor cold. Just right in her opinion.

Somewhere in the distance crows were cawing, a peaceful sound she always thought.

Tommy was wondering if he dare take her hand. Up to now they had simply walked together. There hadn't been any physical contact. But what if he took her hand and she pulled it away again? How embarrassing that would be.

He thought briefly of Bell Mathieson, a different sort of girl entirely. He wouldn't have had any qualms about taking her hand. In fact, Bell would probably have taken his long before now.

'I'm enjoying this, but then I always do when I'm with you,' he heard himself saying, and blushed.

'And I enjoy being with you, Tommy,' she replied quietly.

'That's good then.'

An uneasy silence fell between them.

'I'm sorry about Mr Kelly. It must make life difficult for you,' she commented eventually.

'It does. Everything else at the distillery is fine with the exception of him. I wish he'd suddenly retire or drop down dead.'

She immediately halted and stared at him, her expression one of horror. 'You don't mean that.'

'I do.'

'No, you don't. You can't seriously wish anyone dead. That's an awful thing to say.'

He could see how deeply he'd offended her, and should have known better, Babs being a devout Christian.

'I suppose I was just letting my tongue run away with itself,' he conceded sheepishly.

'Don't forget, Tommy. "As ye give so shall ye receive", and that includes thoughts and ill wishes. They'll always come back on you.'

Her words were wounding, pointing up a charitable lack in himself. He felt ashamed.

'Still, it's only human,' she said, resuming walking. 'What we have to do is overcome those human frailties.'

'You're right, Babs. Of course you are.'

He frowned when her house came into view. It was such a short journey between the church and there and it always seemed to fly by. 'How about us walking a bit further?' he proposed.

'Oh, Tommy, I'd love to. But I have to get in. Lunch is always served promptly.'

He couldn't mask his disappointment. 'I understand.'

'It must be the same with you?'

'Well, not exactly promptly. Not on the dot so to speak. My mum is a little bit more easy going than that. But yes, there is a general time when it's dished up.'

'And your mum would hardly be pleased if you were late.'

'Hardly,' he agreed.

'There then.'

He kicked a stone which went skittering away. The rest of the day would seem interminable after this. Stretching on and on until it was time to go to bed. Sundays could be exceptionally dreary.

'Tell you what,' she said. 'We could meet up again after lunch. How about that?'

He instantly brightened. 'That would be wonderful, Babs.'

'Knock at three and I'll be ready.'

'On the dot, like your mum and her lunch.'

They both laughed.

'Where are you off to in such a hurry?' Hettie demanded.

'I'm going for a walk.'

It was quite unlike Tommy to be so eager to do that. She put two and two together and came up with four. 'Who with?'

He coloured slightly. 'Why does it have to be with someone?'

That confirmed it to her. It was a lassie all right. 'Oh, I just thought it would be, that's all.'

He briefly considered fibbing by naming Eric Taylor, on holiday from school, but decided against that. 'Anyway, I must go,' he declared, and rushed from the room.

'You thinking what I'm thinking?' Jack queried from his chair.

'A girl. No doubt about it.'

'Well, good luck to him.'

'Hopefully a lass from Sunday school. That would make sense.'

'Possibly. But don't you go interfering. Let things take their own course.'

'Interfering, me! The very idea.'

Jack chuckled. 'As if you would,' he said sarcastically.

At least she could find out who the girl was, Hettie thought. A wee word here and there would soon give her the answer.

They stopped under a large chestnut tree, one of the very few in the area. 'I used to come here for conkers when I was a lad,' Tommy said. 'Me and my pal Eric. We both climbed up it once and I fell out. I was lucky I didn't hurt myself.'

He gazed up into the branches in fond memory, remembering the sheer terror he'd felt when he'd slipped and gone plunging earthwards. He'd laughed about it afterwards but it hadn't been funny at the time.

'Did you steep your conkers in vinegar? I believe that's what you do to make them really hard.'

'Sometimes. Other times I baked them in the oven. It's considered cheating but I used to do it nonetheless.'

'I doubt there'll be any chestnut trees in Africa,' she said, tongue firmly in cheek.

'Africa?' For the moment he couldn't see the connection.

'When you go there as an explorer and big-game hunter.'

He realised he was being teased. 'But all sorts of other trees. The exotic kind. All shapes, sizes and colours of the rainbow. They'll be a wonderful sight.'

'What about snakes?' She shuddered. 'I've never seen a live one but the very thought . . .' She broke off and shuddered again.

'They've got snakes there that eat you alive,' he informed her. 'I read that in a book. Some poor chap went to sleep and when he woke up a huge snake had swallowed most of his leg.'

'You're having me on!'

'It's true,' he protested. 'They had to kill the snake and cut it in two lengthways to release his leg which was already part digested.'

Babs grimaced in disgust. 'And you seriously want to go to a place like that?'

'Oh yes, and I will. It'll be the most terrific adventure. The sort most people only dream about.'

Dream, she thought, not for the first time. That described Tommy perfectly, a dreamer. Well, it was no bad thing. Dreams of that nature were harmless, if kept in perspective. The reality of life invariably proved quite different.

Tommy found himself staring at her bosom, a gentle swell beneath her dress. He couldn't help but wonder what it would be like to . . .

'Tommy?'

He roused himself. 'Sorry.'

'What a strange expression you had on your face.'

'Did I?' he queried, pretending innocence.

'You looked transfixed.'

Transfixed in imagination, he thought. Most definitely so.

She moved closer. 'Are you all right?'

'Yes I . . .' He couldn't stop himself, didn't want to. His arm curled round her waist bringing her into an embrace. Her eyes opened wide but she didn't protest.

Then his lips were seeking hers, and finding them.

'Drew, I wish you'd stop following me around everywhere. It's very disconcerting.'

The boy shuffled his feet.

'Can't you find something to do?' Andrew asked mildly.

Drew glanced up at his mother, guilt heavy within him. If it hadn't been for him she'd never have lost the baby. The fault for that was all his.

'Well?' Andrew prompted.

'I've been thinking, Dad.'

'Yes?'

'As I'm going to be taking over the distillery one day I'd like to spend time there. Get to know how everything works.'

Andrew stared at his son in astonishment. 'But you're only eleven.'

'I know that. But you're never too young to learn, you've said so yourself.'

Andrew laughed. He had indeed. 'Rose?'

'Anything to stop him trailing around after me and continually getting under my feet.'

Andrew couldn't think what he could possibly find for Drew to do at the distillery, but no doubt he'd come up with something. And if he didn't, someone else would.

It pleased him, no, it delighted him, that the lad was showing an interest in his inheritance. No more talk about possibly doing something else when he was older. What a relief that was.

'Right then,' he stated. 'You can come with me in the morning. How's that?'

'Does that make you happy, Mummy?'

The question startled Rose. 'Yes, of course it does if it means I won't have you plaguing me for a while.'

Drew beamed, first at her then at his father.

'What are you up to?' It was early evening and Andrew had found Rose sitting in the garden.

'Just enjoying the sun,' she replied dreamily.

'Well, don't take too much of it. I don't want you spoiling that gorgeous complexion of yours.'

Her laugh was a bright tinkle. 'We hardly get enough sun in this part of the world for it to do that.'

'Even though. I don't want you even beginning to go brown. I prefer you the way you are.'

He could be so sweet, she thought. It was lovely.

'We're interviewing tomorrow,' she said. 'Or at least I am. There's no need for you to be involved unless you insist.'

'Aah, the new cook.'

'There are three applicants. On paper all of them are suitable. I suppose it's down to the one I consider will fit in best.'

Andrew sat on the bench beside her. 'I've been thinking about what Mrs Moffat said. Perhaps we should get a housekeeper.'

Rose's mood instantly changed. 'Are you also saying I'm not up to it any more?'

'No, I'm saying it might be too much for you right now. You have been through a lot recently, darling. You should be taking things easy. The housekeeping is a full-time job after all. I just don't want you tiring yourself out.'

That mollified Rose a little. 'I'm quite capable, Andrew. Honestly.'

'I've never doubted that for a moment, Rose. But I do think we should consider the matter. Even if it's only a temporary arrangement.'

Maybe she should agree, she reflected. Truth was, though she'd never admit it after what had happened with Mrs Moffat, she'd begun to find the housekeeping not tiring but boring, irksome. There were occasions, which didn't use to be the case, when she'd been going about those duties when she'd much rather have been doing something else. Riding, for example.

'I'll think about it,' she prevaricated.

'Good, Rose.'

'But only think, mind. I'm not agreeing to anything yet.'

'I'm sure your decision, whatever it is, will be the right one.' He paused, then said, 'There's something else I've been meaning to speak to you about.'

'Oh?'

'Why don't you and I go away for a holiday. Just the pair of us.'

Alarm flared in her. That would be awful. The two of them together morning, noon and – most importantly of all – night. Nights during which he'd undoubtedly want to share a bed.

She saw this for what it was. A ploy for them to resume regular lovemaking. The very thought made her wince inside.

'To where?' she asked.

'Anywhere you like. Abroad if you wish. It's entirely up to you.'

Rose took a deep breath. A holiday would be wonderful, but not under these conditions. Despair filled her. She did love Andrew, loved him dearly. But she didn't want him in her bed or to be with him all day long. The prospect was a nightmare.

'What about the distillery?' she queried, knowing how loath he was to leave it for any length of time.

'I'll sort matters out so that it'll run smoothly while we're gone. Kelly will manage just fine. It'll all be tickety-boo.'

Rose hung her head, horribly aware this had been proposed entirely for her benefit. 'I'd rather not if you don't mind, Andrew,' she said quietly.

'I see.'

'I . . .' She was frantically trying to come up with an acceptable excuse. 'I don't feel up to that yet. Perhaps next year.'

'Of course, darling.'

'I'm sorry.'

He reached over and took her hand in his. 'Don't worry about it. It was only a suggestion, that's all.'

'And a kind one too. I appreciate it.'

'But if you don't want to go then we won't. I fully understand.'

He was smiling, but she didn't miss the hurt in his eyes.

'I need some fags,' Irene announced, as she and Bell made their way home from work.

'And I want to buy a packet of kirbys. I keep losing the damn things.'

'I know what you mean. I'm just the same.'

Bell yawned. She was tired. Every day at the distillery was long but this one, for some reason, had seemed even longer. She'd wash her hair after tea and then have an early night. She smiled in anticipation.

When they reached the village shop they went inside, Bell collecting a packet of grips and joining the end of the waiting queue.

'That's her being served,' Irene whispered conspiratorially.

Bell was mystified. 'Who?'

'Barbara McTaggart, the lassie Tommy's been seeing.'

All Bell could make out was the back of a head and the top part of what looked like a rather expensive dress. 'Are you sure?'

'Oh, aye.'

'I thought you didn't know her?'

'Only by sight. That's her all right.'

Come on, Bell mentally urged. Turn round. She wanted a good look at the face.

'Thank you,' Babs said, picking up her change.

Mrs Wilson, who ran the shop with her husband, muttered something in reply.

Babs left the queue, halting to put the coins into her purse.

Well, she was no raving beauty, Bell thought with satisfaction. Not nearly as pretty as she'd been led to believe by Irene. But she was no gargoyle either. You could never say that about her.

Babs walked past them and straight out of the shop.

'What do you think?' Irene queried.

Bell shrugged.

'A wee bit jealous perhaps?'

Bell could have smacked her friend, for Irene was right. She was jealous. 'Of that? You must be joking.'

'It was a lovely dress she had on.'

'I never really noticed,' Bell lied.

'Classy. I bet that cost a bob or two.'

'It didn't suit her in my opinion. Wrong colour.'

'Ooh, I wouldn't say so.'

'Well I would,' Bell snapped.

Irene smiled. 'You *are* jealous.'

'I am nothing of the sort. Jealousy doesn't enter into it. If that's what Tommy fancies then good luck to him.'

'Well, I will say this for you, Master Drummond, you're not shy of work.'

Drew beamed at Ramsay Dodds whose job it was to fuel the peat furnaces. 'This isn't work, it's fun. I'm thoroughly enjoying myself.'

Ramsay laughed. It was hard graft as far as he was concerned, but then he had to do it day in day out.

Drew gazed into the flames dancing before him. What a strange mystical land this all was, he thought, one he found fascinating. It was a pity he'd have to go back to school at the end of the summer. He'd happily have continued on at the distillery.

How could he have considered doing anything else? he wondered. What a mistake that would have been. He knew with utter certainty that he'd been born to be a distiller, the latest in a long line of them.

It was as though . . . he'd somehow come home.

'Ah, Tommy, it's you. Come in.'

Andrew laid aside the pen he'd been using and smiled at Tommy now standing at his desk. 'How are you getting on then?'

'Fine, thank you very much.'

Andrew nodded his approval. 'The reason I've asked you here is that I want you to take a correspondence course.'

Tommy frowned. 'Correspondence course?'

'That's right. It's about distilling, of course, theory and practice, that sort of thing. I did the same course myself years ago and loved every minute of it. Found it most rewarding as I'm sure you will. I'll pay the fees naturally, so it won't cost you anything. Now, what do you say?'

'Yes please,' Tommy replied enthusiastically.

Andrew passed over a slip of paper. 'That's the name and address of the firm that runs the course. Write to them for an application form. When it's time to return the form come back and see me again and I'll give you a cheque to accompany it. All right?'

'I'll write this evening.'

'Good. The very dab.'

'I'll get on about my business then.'

Tommy was continuing to do well, Andrew reflected as the door snicked shut. He must mention it to Jack when they next met up.

* * *

'Why are you so restless?' Hettie queried of Jack, who was silently drumming his fingers on the arm of his chair.

'I look forward to my Friday night visits to the pub with Andrew. Only he's away for a few days and I don't like going on my own.' He didn't suggest Hettie accompany him; women of her age and standing in the village simply didn't enter pubs.

'I'll go with you, Dad, if you like,' Tommy volunteered.

'You!' Hettie exclaimed in surprise.

'Why not? If Dad wants company.'

'They wouldn't serve you.'

'Oh yes they will, as long as I behave myself and don't go daft.'

'And how do you know that?'

'I've heard, Mum.'

'Just heard?' she queried pointedly.

'Just heard. Now how about it, Dad?'

Jack came to his feet, thrilled at the idea of visiting the pub with his son. 'Let's get a move on then.'

Hettie sighed. Another sign of how grown up Tommy was becoming. She and Jack had been talking about that only the other night. He'd come on a great deal since starting at Drummond's, something of which they both heartily approved.

But the pub? She wasn't so sure about that.

'There you are, Dad,' Tommy said, placing a pint and chaser in front of Jack. He then returned to the bar for his own pint.

'It's crowded tonight,' Jack commented when Tommy rejoined him.

Tommy glanced around. The pub was rather full, though he couldn't have said whether that was normally the case or not. There were quite a few people he recognised.

There hadn't been any problem at the bar. He'd merely given his order then paid for it when it arrived. Nothing untoward had been said.

'*Slainthe!*' Jack muttered, tasting his whisky.

'*Slainthe*,' Tommy responded.

Jack cleared his throat. 'Well, this is a new experience for you, eh?'

'It is indeed, Dad.'

'So what do you think?'

Tommy grinned. 'I like it.'

'Aye well, just don't make a habit of coming, that's all. Apart from anything else pubs are expensive. You can't afford them.'

Not on a regular basis anyway, Tommy thought. But once in a while wouldn't do any harm. Especially as there wasn't any objection to his being served. It was just as Bell had said.

Tommy had no sooner thought of her than she appeared with her friend Irene, the pair of them all dolled up. Tommy hadn't realised it was dance night which was where Bell and Irene were ultimately headed.

'There's Isa and Ronnie,' Irene gestured. They made their way over.

'You've gone quiet all of a sudden,' Jack commented to Tommy.

'Sorry.'

'Seen someone you know?'

'There are a few people from the distillery here.'

'Oh aye?'

'No one in particular,' he lied. He certainly wasn't going to mention Bell who he thought was looking rather stunning.

'David, this is Bell and Irene,' Ronnie declared, introducing the chap with him and Isa.

'How do you do,' David smiled.

'David comes from Auchgloan. He's my cousin.' Auchgloan was a village about ten miles away.

'I can see the family resemblance,' Irene said.

'Aye, there is a likeness,' David acknowledged, thinking that Bell was a cracker. He'd fallen on his feet here.

Bell was staring over David's shoulder at Tommy. With his father, she saw. Barbara McTaggart nowhere in evidence. There again, you would hardly expect the likes of Barbara McTaggart to come into a common pub. A madam like her wouldn't be seen dead in one.

'So what are you ladies having?' David queried, eyes fixed firmly on Bell.

'Mine's a gin and orange,' Irene replied.

'And you, Bell?'

She brought her attention back to him. 'The same please. That's very kind of you.'

'Not at all. The pleasure's all mine.'

Isa winked at Bell when David went up to the bar, having noticed the interest he had in her. 'It should be a good dance tonight, eh?'

'He fancies you,' Irene whispered to Bell, disappointed, for she'd fancied him.

'I'll give David a hand,' Ronnie declared, and left the three of them together.

Bell was aware of Tommy watching her and wondered what he was thinking. Well, he wasn't the only one who could get a click. By God and he wasn't. She'd show him all right.

'What does David do?' Irene inquired of Isa.

'He's a postman.'

'A postman!' Irene exclaimed. 'He doesn't look like one.'

'And what exactly does a postman look like,' Bell said sarcastically. 'Is there a type?'

'He gets paid good money,' Isa informed them.

'Is that a fact,' nodded Bell.

'More than Ronnie gets at the distillery. Quite a bit more.'

'And he's free I take it?' That was Irene.

'He was going out with someone but that's finished. He's been down in the dumps which is why Ronnie invited him here tonight.'

David turned from the bar and smiled directly at Bell. There was no mistaking he was keen.

'Jammy sod,' Irene muttered, meaning Bell.

He was attractive, Bell thought. And seemed pleasant enough. A surreptitious sideways glance told her Tommy was still watching.

'Here we are then,' David said, appearing beside them holding two glasses. He handed the first to Bell.

Bell made up her mind. A click was on offer and a click it would be. To hell with Tommy Riach and his stuck-up fancy piece. He could go and take a running jump as far as she was concerned.

'Thank you very much,' Bell murmured coyly.

'As I said, the pleasure's all mine.'

Bell gave him a winsome smile. This was a fish that wouldn't take much landing. She'd have him firmly netted before they even left for the dance.

*   *   *

'Another?' Jack asked Tommy.

'If you're having one.'

Jack chuckled. 'Damned right I am.' He groped for his wallet. 'Will you go up or shall I?'

'I'll go again, Dad. It's a bit of a scrum over there.'

'There's a quid then. And don't forget my dram.'

When Tommy returned to the table it was to note that the chap Bell was talking to had his arm round her waist.

He forced himself to concentrate on what his father was saying.

Chapter 14

'I'm not interrupting, am I?'

'Not at all, Andrew,' Jack replied enthusiastically. 'Have a pew.'

Andrew handed Hettie the bottle of Drummond he'd brought with him. 'As you can see, I've come bearing gifts.'

Hettie laughed. 'There was no need for this, Andrew. We always have some in the house.'

'What's that?' Jack queried.

Hettie explained.

Jack rubbed his hands together. 'Just the thing. Get pouring, woman. And make them large ones.'

'Mine too,' Tommy chipped in, knowing there was little likelihood of that.

'You'll take what you're given and be thankful,' Hettie admonished him.

Andrew sighed. He was weary and troubled. He'd tried to talk to Rose but she'd been in one of her unreceptive moods so in the end he'd given up and come to Jack's.

'Is there anything special on your mind?' Jack asked softly.

'It's going to be war, Jack. There's no doubt about it.'

Jack's expression became grim in the extreme. 'I agree, if the papers are anything to go by. Not to mention the news broadcasts. This nonsense in Danzig is going to be the spark that'll light the whole bag of fireworks.'

A wide-eyed Tommy sat listening to this. War!

'Hitler's a bloody maniac,' Andrew went on. 'Has he forgotten what it was like the last time? The damned man was in it, after all.'

Andrew accepted the glass Hettie gave him, noting that she had indeed poured large ones.

'Well, I won't be fighting this time,' Jack said gravely. Then, with a bitter laugh, 'I don't suppose they'll have any use for blind folk.'

'You've done your bit. And paid the price,' Hettie declared. 'And a high price it was too.'

'Aye, it was that,' Jack murmured.

'The crass stupidity of it all!' Andrew suddenly exploded. 'It makes my blood boil.'

Jack had a swallow of whisky, and shuddered. The shudder had nothing to do with alcohol. So many lives had already been lost, thrown away, and for what? So it could be done all over again it would seem.

Hettie placed a weak drink beside Tommy, trying not to think of his being caught up in all this. The thought made her feel sick inside, and scared. Not for herself of course, but for Tommy.

'What about you? What will you do?' Jack queried of Andrew.

'If they want me they can have me. Though I doubt they will. They'll wish me to stay put and run the distillery. I will lose men though, that's what happened in the last show. Some are bound to join up which will cause me problems. Still, we managed before and no doubt will do so again.'

'War,' Jack breathed. It seemed incredible.

'It still might not happen,' Hettie said tremulously. 'It's all supposition so far.'

'Anything's possible,' Jack demurred. 'Even miracles. And that's what it's going to take for war to be avoided.'

A thrill of excitement ran through Tommy. This could be the biggest adventure of all. 'How long will it last for, do you think?'

'Till it's finished, lad,' Jack replied heavily.

'Could we possibly lose?' Hettie queried.

Neither Jack nor Andrew replied. The possibility of that was horrendous. Life under the German jackboot would be intolerable.

'Well?' Hettie prompted.

'No,' Jack growled. 'By God and all his Angels we won't.'

Andrew wished he could be so certain about that.

'This is Miss Campbell, the new housekeeper,' Rose declared.

Andrew gave her a slight nod of recognition. 'Miss Campbell.'

'Pleased to meet you, sir.'

'And you, Miss Campbell.'

She wasn't at all what Andrew had expected. She was a lot younger for a start, and rather pretty in a bony-faced way. How old? He judged her to be in her early thirties.

She had raven-black hair cut just above shoulder length and was well breasted, her bosom amply filling the top of the black uniform she wore. Her hands were long and graceful, ivory coloured as opposed to pink. They rather fascinated Andrew.

'I hope you'll enjoy life here,' Andrew said.

'I'm sure I will, sir.'

'And where were you before?'

She told him, naming a place he'd never heard of, which she said was in Fyfe. Andrew wondered why she'd left there. He'd ask Rose later when they were alone.

'Well, what did you think?'

'She's fine. Though I have to say rather young in my opinion,' Andrew replied.

'She is young I admit, though I fail to see why that should stand against her. All I care about is her being up to the job, which I'm certain she will be.'

'Why did she leave her previous position?'

'She wanted a change, that was all. She fully understands the post is only temporary which she said suits her for the time being. We were fortunate to get her actually. The applications weren't exactly thick on the ground. Because the post is only temporary, I suppose.'

'I really am pleased you've hired someone, Rose. I'm sure it's the right thing to do.'

Rose had thought long and hard before making her mind up on the subject, but once decided had felt a lot better for it. For the present anyway she didn't have any housekeeping worries to contend with which was an enormous relief.

'I'm considering taking up painting,' she announced.

That surprised Andrew. Rose had never shown any artistic leanings in the past. 'Painting, eh?'

'Landscapes in watercolour. I think I'll rather like that.'

'Whatever, Rose, if it makes you happy then it does me. When do you intend starting?'

'I've already written to a shop in Edinburgh telling them my requirements which they will be forwarding on.'

'You *are* organised.' Andrew smiled, still bemused by this. But he certainly approved of her new project and wondered what standard of paintings she'd produce.

'I'll tell you what,' he enthused. 'If you're good we can perhaps arrange to have them shown in a gallery.'

Rose blushed. 'Don't get carried away, Andrew. Displayed indeed! I doubt it'll come to that.'

'You never know, Rose. You never know.'

Rose laughed, and for the space of a few moments it was like old times between them.

Moments that Andrew brought to a halt when he reached out to touch her and she flinched away.

It was nine o'clock on a Wednesday evening, bath night for Nancy. Something she always looked forward to.

She locked the door of the staff bathroom carefully behind her and then set down the towel and other things she'd brought along.

The bath itself was a huge, ornate affair which she now began filling. Clouds of steam billowed upwards as water cascaded from the silver-coloured taps.

There was an ancient wicker chair which Nancy threw her dressing gown over leaving her standing in her nightdress. As it was already warm in the room, thanks to heating pipes that ran along one of the walls, and getting warmer by the second, the nightdress swiftly followed the dressing gown.

Naked, she lifted her arms above her head and stretched. Smiling in anticipation of the long soak that lay ahead.

Crossing back to the bath she tested the water, judging the mix just right. She was standing upright again when she paused, thinking she'd heard a noise.

Nancy frowned. If she had heard something it certainly hadn't come from the bathroom as she was quite alone. Imagination, she mentally shrugged. Unless the noise had come from out in the corridor.

She started to hum, a folk tune she'd known for years and was a favourite of hers.

She laid her soap on the edge of the bath, and her flannel alongside. Then she scratched her bottom as the bath continued to fill.

There it was again! The same sound as before. Like . . . she wasn't sure.

Panic suddenly flared in her causing her to gasp. Surely there weren't mice in the bathroom. Or worse still, rats. Despite her country upbringing she'd always had a horror and fear of both, particularly the latter.

Quickly she looked under the bath but there was no sign there of either. She then scanned the rest of the room.

Nancy shivered, recalling a bondager friend of hers who'd once been bitten by a rat. A monstrous black brute who'd torn a chunk out of the lassie's leg before being dispatched by one of the men present at the time.

That had been horrible. It had taken them ages to calm the hysterical lassie down. Luckily the wound had healed without becoming infected. The bite from a rat could prove fatal.

There it was again! Coming from the nearer of the two old disused metal lockers standing against the rear wall. She grabbed her dressing gown and hastily put it on.

What to do? Call for help or investigate herself? She decided to investigate.

She glanced around for a weapon but there wasn't one. This was daft, she thought as she slowly approached the lockers. What if there *was* a bloody rat!

She stopped in front of the locker in question and listened. If she heard a scurrying from inside, or that of claws on metal, then she was off. Out of there like a flash.

What she did hear surprised her. Surely it couldn't be. But it damn well was. Heavy breathing.

'Right,' she muttered, angry now. Grabbing the locker handle she turned it and yanked the door open.

'Master Drew!'

He blinked at her, clearly terrified at having been found out.

'What are you doing in there?'

'I . . . I . . .' He swallowed hard.

It was blindingly obvious why he'd hidden in the locker which had a series of small holes three quarters of the way up the door. 'You were spying, you little swine,' she hissed.

'Please, Nancy, don't tell Dad. *Please.*' Tears welled in his eyes to fall tumbling down his cheeks.

'Get out of there while I decide what to do with you.'

He emerged from the locker and backed away from her. 'I'm sorry, Nancy. Really I am. Please don't tell Dad.'

She pulled the dressing gown more tightly about her. To think he'd been watching while she'd been standing there without a stitch on. Getting a right eyeful.

'I've . . . I've . . .' He gulped. 'I've never seen a naked woman before.'

Her face softened. It was quite funny really. Though unforgivable too.

'And I so wanted to see you, Nancy. You're so beautiful.'

'With or without my clothes on?' she replied tartly.

'Both, Nancy. I think you're wonderful.'

She wagged a finger at him. 'Spying like that. It's . . . disgusting.'

'I'm sorry.'

'No you're not. I can see it in your face. The only thing you're sorry about is being caught.'

He hung his head in shame.

Nancy took a deep breath. If she reported this God knew what his father would do to him. And it was innocent enough when you thought about it. A young boy's curiosity, that's all.

'And you are beautiful,' he insisted, head still hung.

'Am I indeed?'

'Oh yes. None of the other maids is nearly so pretty.'

She should be flattered, she thought, for him to have taken such a risk on her account. She was strangely moved.

'Do you forgive me, Nancy?'

'I don't know,' she replied hesitantly.

'Please do. And please don't tell Dad. I'd be so ashamed.'

'With a sore backside into the bargain no doubt.'

'Yours was gorgeous.'

She couldn't believe he'd said that. 'What!'

He looked up at her, mischief and lust in his eyes, the tears now gone. He was his father's son after all. 'Your bottom, Nancy. It was gorgeous.'

She opened her mouth to speak, but couldn't think of a thing to say.

'I'm going to marry you when I grow up.'

Nancy burst out laughing. This was getting ridiculous. 'Don't be soft, Drew. Your sort don't marry the likes of me.'

'But I will,' he stated stubbornly. 'I decided so weeks ago.'

The bath! She'd forgotten about that. Whirling, she hurried back to it and turned off the taps. Fortunately it hadn't overflowed.

'Nancy?'

She turned to find him behind her. 'What?'

'Can I have another look?'

His gall was amazing. Imagine him asking that? 'No you can't,' she snapped.

'You're not that much older than me you know. Only a few years.'

True enough, she reflected, somewhat in surprise. Well, it may only be a few years but there was a world of difference between them. She was a fully mature woman who'd lived with a man, while Drew was no more than a schoolboy.

She stared in astonishment when he reached out and covered her breast. He gently squeezed before she shrugged his hand away.

'You'd better go,' she said.

'You won't tell anyone, will you?'

She shook her head.

'Let me see you again, Nancy. I beg you.'

Beg! No one had ever begged her for anything in her life. Up until now that was. It was rather nice to be begged.

She didn't know why she did it, sheer madness she thought. Slowly she undid her dressing gown and held it open.

Drew sucked in a breath as he stared at her nakedness.

Then the vision was gone, Nancy's dressing gown firmly wrapped round her again.

'Now go,' she said.

At the door he turned to smile beguilingly at her. 'I will marry you, Nancy Thompson. I will.'

When he'd left she relocked the door and leant against it. She was trembling she noted. Excited too.

What to make of all this? she wondered. What indeed.

For Drew the episode with Nancy was a watershed. Childhood was gone, adulthood beckoned. Overnight he'd acquired a maturity that belied his years. He might still be only eleven, but he was a very different eleven to the one who'd climbed into the locker.

Nor had he lied to Nancy about wanting to marry her. He fully intended that he would one day.

It was only a matter of time and patience.

Tommy wiped sweaty palms on the back of his jacket, nervous as all get out at the prospect of having afternoon tea with the McTaggarts.

He cleared his throat, adjusted his tie, and then knocked. He could only pray he was going to pass muster and that they approved of him. This was a test, as he was well aware.

It was Babs herself who answered. 'Hello, Tommy,' she smiled.

'Hello, Babs. I hope I'm not late.'

'You're . . . right on the dot.'

They both laughed which made Tommy relax a little. 'Come on through then.'

He carefully wiped his shoes before stepping inside.

*   *   *

Barney McTaggart was younger than his own father, and rapidly balding. He was a tall, slim man with a fierce gaze and ruddy complexion. Tommy found him extremely daunting.

'A sandwich, Tommy?' The speaker was Anne McTaggart, slim like her husband and wearing spectacles. Despite the latter it was clear where Babs got her good looks from, and it wasn't Barney!

'Please, Mrs McTaggart.'

'Cucumber and cress or egg?'

'Cucumber and cress would be lovely.'

Tommy was horribly aware that Mr McTaggart had been studying him keenly ever since his arrival. He wished the damned man wouldn't be so blatant about it. It was most off-putting, making him feel like a specimen under a microscope.

'We grow the cucumber ourselves in our vegetable garden,' Mrs McTaggart informed Tommy, handing him a plate. Tea had already been poured, Tommy electing Indian rather than the China also on offer.

'Are you interested in gardening?' Mr McTaggart inquired.

'I'm afraid not, sir.'

'Hmmh, maybe later on in life. It's a wonderful hobby which Anne and I both thoroughly enjoy.'

'Delicious,' Tommy commented after tasting the sandwich.

Mrs McTaggart beamed.

'Tommy and I are going for a walk after tea,' Babs announced.

Mr McTaggart raised an eyebrow but didn't comment.

'That's nice, dear,' Mrs McTaggart said instead.

Tommy couldn't wait for the walk and to escape from the house. This was awful.

'And how do you like being at Drummond's?' Mr McTaggart inquired.

'Just fine, sir.'

'You're going eventually to be a traveller I understand.'

'That's right, sir.'

Mr McTaggart grunted, a neutral sound that was neither approval nor disapproval. Or if it was either that much wasn't apparent to Tommy.

'You're also a Sunday school teacher,' Mr McTaggart went on.

'Still learning to be one, sir.'

'Most commendable.'

'Thank you.'

Babs sipped her tea, eyes sparkling across the room at Tommy. They'd be going to their favourite spot for more kisses and cuddles. She was looking forward to that and had been since the previous week and their last visit there.

Like wading through mud, Tommy was thinking. He wasn't finding this easy at all.

The next moment a door banged shut. 'My brother Gerald,' Babs explained. 'He always does that. Bang the outside door I mean.'

'Terrible habit,' Mr McTaggart muttered. 'Never been able to break him of it.'

It was news to Tommy that Babs had a brother. She'd never mentioned him.

The chap who breezed into the room was in his early twenties and dressed in the uniform of the RAF. 'Ah, just in time for tiffin I see,' he declared, rubbing his hands vigorously together. 'I hope there are crumpets and strawberry jam, Mater. That would be just the ticket.'

'Of course there are, Gerald,' Mrs McTaggart replied. 'Let me introduce you to Tommy Riach, Barbara's friend.'

Tommy laid his plate aside, stood up and shook Gerald's hand. 'Are you a flying officer?' he asked, almost overcome with awe.

'That's right, Hurricanes. I'm on a spot of leave.'

Shaking hands and talking to a real live pilot. Tommy was stunned. He was remembering the Spitfire he'd once watched, what a beauty that had been.

'Wouldn't you prefer Spits?' he queried.

Gerald laughed. 'Damned fine machines, best in the world at what they do. But give me Hurrys any day.'

'Aren't they slower?'

'I hope we're not going to talk air force,' Mr McTaggart said. Then, to Tommy, 'That's all we have morning, noon and night when Gerald's home.'

'Sorry, Pater,' Gerald apologised.

Tommy's face had fallen. There was nothing he'd have liked better than to talk air force, as Mr McTaggart had put it.

'I'd love to be a flyer myself,' he stuttered.

'Really?'

'Oh yes. It must be marvellous.'

Babs thought of teasing him by saying she'd understood he wanted to be an African explorer and big-game hunter, but decided that might be too embarrassing for him. She certainly knew how her father would react. He'd think Tommy was off his chump and she didn't wish that.

Gerald glanced at his father, then turned his attention again to Tommy. 'I have some pictures up in my room. Would you care to see them?'

'Oh, yes please.'

'Spiffing. Just let me grab some tea and eats and then

up we'll jolly well go. I've not only pictures taken round the various 'dromes I've been at but also models that might interest you.'

'They would indeed,' Tommy answered enthusiastically.

As far as he was concerned what had been a rather dismal and uncomfortable occasion had suddenly become transformed.

'Your brother's a smashing bloke. I liked him enormously,' Tommy said to Babs as they were leaving the house.

'You were certainly up in his room long enough. I was beginning to think you'd forgotten all about our walk.'

Their walk had been the furthest thing from his mind when he'd been with Gerald, Tommy reflected. Though he wasn't about to admit that. He'd only remembered about it again when they'd eventually rejoined the others.

'Not me,' he lied. 'But your brother was jolly interesting.'

Babs glanced sideways at him. 'Up in the wild blue yonder were you?' she teased.

'Something like that,' Tommy admitted sheepishly.

She hooked an arm round his. 'You really are adorable, Tommy Riach. Quite scrummy.'

'You're fairly scrummy yourself, Babs.'

'Am I really?' she queried coyly.

'As scrummy as they come.'

'Go on, you're just saying that.'

'I am nothing of the sort! Cross my heart and hope to die.'

That filled her with the most wonderful warm glow. She pulled herself even closer to him. 'My parents took to you.'

That mildly surprised him, remembering Mr McTaggart's unrelenting fierce gaze. 'Did they?'

'Very much so. Believe me, I can read the signs. They took to you all right. Mind you, in all honesty, being the son of a rich and famous author helps.'

She laughed at the expression on his face. 'I only said it helps, Tommy. Not that it was the be all and end all. If they hadn't found you personable and acceptable I'd have picked it up. Especially from my dad, he'd probably just have upped and left us to it.'

Tommy closed his eyes for a brief moment, visualising the Spitfire he'd seen.

He decided he must read up more about Hurricanes. Fantastic planes, according to Gerald.

The flesh pressed against his was hot and burning, the hand caressing him promising delights to come.

Andrew smiled in his sleep. This was wonderful, so real it could have actually been happening.

Now a voice was crooning in his ear, whispering his name over and over. A tongue flickered in the same ear, darting sensuously in and out.

He shivered, feeling himself respond. 'Rose,' he heard himself whisper. 'Oh Rose.'

'Wake up, Andrew. Wake up.'

He didn't want to do that and lose this erotic angel. And yet still the voice was urging him to do so.

'Andrew.'

There was a little nip which made him jerk and his eyes flew open. The face peering into his was no fantasy, no figment of the imagination. He hadn't been dreaming at all.

'Rose?'

She was breathing heavily and even though it was dark in his bedroom he could make out that her eyes were dilated, nostrils flared.

'Oh, my darling Andrew.'

His hands were moving now, touching a breast, rubbing a nipple, the urgency in him growing with every passing second.

'Now,' she commanded in a rasping tone. 'Now!'

He twisted her on to her back, moved on top of her and thrust hard.

Rose screamed in ecstasy.

As had happened before, she was gone when he awoke in the morning. And, as before, all that remained was the sweet smell of her scent.

'Christ,' he muttered. Talk about wild abandon, she'd been positively demonic in her demands. How long had it gone on for? Must have been hours. Hours and hours.

He moved and winced, then remembered the fingernails slicing their way down his back. Not once, but over and over. His buttocks were also lacerated.

The previous visitation had been unbelievable, but last night surpassed even that. Vastly experienced as he was he'd never known anything like it.

Just what in hell was going on? he asked himself. Time after time it was the cold shoulder, not wanting to know. And then suddenly, out of nowhere, two visitations that were extraordinary to say the least.

How often had she told him she loved him? Again and again. And yet he'd be willing to bet if he met her over breakfast she'd be as distant as usual. Polite, pleasant, but distant.

The contrast between that Rose and the one who'd

shared his bed was incredible. It was as if they were two different women entirely. Jekyll and Hyde.

Yes, he thought. That was exactly it. A female Jekyll and Hyde.

He didn't know what to make of all this. He didn't at all. He was completely and utterly lost.

He'd speak to Lesley again. Well, he'd been going to visit the doctor anyway as his indigestion had returned even more severely than before.

But for now, for the moment, he was just going to lie there and savour the memories.

And what delicious memories they were.

Delicious, yet somewhat frightening too.

Chapter 15

'Here's the breakfast tray you asked for, Mrs Drummond.'

'Thank you, Nancy. Just put it on the bed and I'll have it shortly.'

Rose peered into the mirror of her vanity table and frowned. What was wrong with her today, she was all fingers and thumbs. She sighed in exasperation.

'Will there be anything else, Mrs Drummond?'

Rose swivelled round to stare at Nancy. 'Are you any good with hair?'

Nancy blinked. 'I beg your pardon?'

'I said, are you any good with hair?'

'I don't know. I mean . . . I just do my own, that's all.'

Rose decided she wanted company, and Nancy's was always pleasant. Nancy . . . somehow brought her comfort. Eased the terrible pain that gnawed at her day and night. Nancy whom she sometimes thought of as . . .

'Well come over here and see what you can do with mine.'

Nancy gulped. 'Oh I couldn't do that, Mrs Drummond. I'd be too scared to even try.'

That amused Rose. 'Brave heart, Nancy, brave heart. Have a go.'

Nancy was still hesitant. Rose had such beautiful hair which was usually immaculate. For her to put her mitts on it seemed a sacrilege.

'Come on, I won't bite.'

Nancy moved to a position directly behind Rose who handed her a large tortoiseshell comb.

'Pins, brushes, everything's here.' Rose smiled into the mirror. 'The rest is up to you.'

Twenty minutes later Nancy inserted the final pin. She didn't know the name of what she'd done to Rose but had tried to copy a style she'd admired in a magazine. It was a French pleat.

A little rough and ready, Rose was thinking, but excellent all the same. Certainly better than any of her morning's efforts.

'That's it, Mrs Drummond,' Nancy stated quietly.

Rose turned her head first to one side, then the other. There was talent here, definitely so. What had started out as a whim on her part had borne unexpected fruit.

'You're pulling my leg, Nancy, you *have* done hair before.'

'No, ma'am.'

'Are you certain about that?'

'Oh yes, ma'am. As I said, only my own.'

Rose patted down a few stray strands. 'Then you're to be commended. It's a fine effort. A very fine effort indeed. I'm impressed.'

Nancy blushed at this praise.

'Don't blush. I mean what I say otherwise I wouldn't say it.'

'Thank you, Mrs Drummond.'

Rose had another thought. 'Now you've done my hair why don't you help me get dressed?'

Nancy bit her lip. 'Miss Campbell will be wondering where I am.'

'Let her wonder. I want you here and that's an end of it.'

Rose got up from her stool feeling strangely buoyant and elated, though she didn't know why. She was enjoying this.

'Let's get started then, shall we?'

'In my opinion she's merely readjusting, Mr Drummond. As I mentioned previously, she needs time for matters to correct themselves.'

Andrew was deeply embarrassed, having related, though not in detail, what had happened when Rose had come to his bed a second time.

'It's early days yet, Mr Drummond,' Lesley went on. 'Believe me.'

What else could he do but take the doctor's word for it. He was the expert after all. 'I just thought I should bring it to your attention, put you in the picture.'

'Which was the right thing to do.'

'I was coming to see you anyway, doctor. It's my indigestion, it's back with a vengeance.'

Lesley frowned. 'Describe these pains precisely if you can,' he said slowly.

He listened intently as Andrew spoke. 'Hmmh,' he murmured when Andrew was finished.

Lesley rocked back in his chair and made a pyramid with his hands. 'I think maybe an examination is in order,' he declared eventually.

'An examination?'

'If you'll just slip behind the screen, Mr Drummond, and strip to the waist. Let me know when you're ready.'

That flustered Andrew who hadn't been expecting such a request. 'Certainly,' he replied.

A few minutes later Lesley joined Andrew behind the screen, instructing him to lie down on the black leather couch there.

Andrew emerged from behind the screen to find Lesley writing on a sheet of headed paper. 'So what's the verdict?' he asked.

Lesley finished what he was writing, capped his pen, a beautiful Mont Blanc Andrew noted, and regarded Andrew thoughtfully. 'I'm making an appointment for you at Perth Hospital. There's a good man there called Creighton whom I want to see you.'

Alarm flared in Andrew. 'Isn't it indigestion then?'

'It might well be. Certainly the symptoms would fit in with that. And yet . . . To put it bluntly my suspicions are that you have an ulcer.'

'An ulcer?'

'Worry, Mr Drummond, all manner of things bring them on. And nasty blighters stomach ulcers can be too if not treated properly.'

'Does that mean an operation?'

Lesley smiled disarmingly. 'I said I only suspect you might have one. Let's establish exactly what's what before we start worrying about operations, eh? In other words, let's not cross bridges before we come to them. I may be entirely wrong about this. But it's better to be safe than sorry. Don't you agree?'

Andrew nodded.

'I'll send this letter off today and will contact you when I hear from Creighton. I take it there won't be any problem in going to Perth?'

'None at all, doctor.'

'Fine then.'

Lesley rose and escorted Andrew to the door. 'I shall be in touch in probably about a week. I'll ring you either at home or the distillery to give you a time and date.'

An ulcer? Andrew reflected once outside the surgery. Lesley had said he might be wrong which must be the case.

He was quite convinced of that.

Andrew was restless, unable to concentrate, which was most unlike him while at work. Rose, the visit to Perth, what the latter might lead to should the ulcer theory prove correct, all kept churning round and round in his mind. He considered having a drink to try to settle himself, and decided against it. In his present agitated mood he'd probably drink the whole bloody bottle.

Maud, one of the typists, stuck her head round his office door. 'Tommy Riach is here asking if he can see you, sir.'

'Send him in.'

'Yes, sir.'

'And, Maud!'

'Yes, sir?'

'I'd like some coffee.'

'I'll make you some, sir.'

He'd settle for that, he thought ruefully. Though, in truth, he'd much have preferred whisky.

'Ah, Tommy!' he exclaimed when the lad entered.

'You said to come back when I'd filled out the application form for the correspondence course and here I am.'

'You'll be wanting a cheque then.'

'Yes please.'

Andrew opened a drawer in his desk, extracted a cheque book and placed it before him. 'How much are the fees?'

Tommy told him.

Andrew pulled a face. 'They've gone up since my day. But then, hasn't everything.'

When the cheque was completed he detached it and handed it over. 'There you are, send it off.'

'Thank you very much.'

'Start in September?'

'That's right.'

'It isn't so hard really. A chap of your intelligence will probably find it a doddle.'

Tommy flushed with pleasure. A chap of his intelligence! He liked that and would repeat it to Babs when they next met up.

'Any problems with the course, which I doubt you'll have, feel free to consult me. I'll be only too happy to give you any help I can.'

'Thank you again.'

Andrew suddenly wanted out of the office, to do something else that might take his mind off his worries. Being unable to concentrate was most unlike him, and another cause for concern itself.

'You don't drive, do you?'

Tommy shook his head.

'Ever been behind a wheel?'

'I'm afraid not. As you know Dad doesn't own a car.'

'How do you fancy a lesson then? Your first.'

Tommy gawped at Andrew. 'Do you mean that?'

'You'll have to learn to drive at some stage, it's going to be a huge part of your life when you go on the road. So why don't I get you started now?'

Andrew laughed at Tommy's stunned expression. 'Not scared are you?' he teased.

'Not in the least. There's nothing I'd like more.'

'Right then,' Andrew declared, coming to his feet. 'Let's go.'

En route he told Maud to cancel the coffee.

'That was kind of Andrew!' Hettie exclaimed after Tommy had told them about his lesson.

Tommy's eyes were burning with enthusiasm. 'It was wonderful. Absolutely wonderful.'

'How far did you go?' Jack asked quietly.

'Miles, Dad. Miles and miles. We did a big loop that eventually brought us back to the distillery.'

'And did Andrew comment afterwards?'

'He said I had natural ability as a driver. That I could pick it up properly in no time at all.'

'Well well,' Hettie smiled, proud as punch.

'He's going to take me out again fairly soon. He promised.'

'Well, if he promised he will. Andrew doesn't break his word,' Hettie declared.

'*Baroom baroom!*' Tommy growled, pretending to be turning a steering wheel. '*Baroom baroom baroom!*'

'And he took you out in his own car?' Hettie asked.

'The Austin. Pity it hadn't been that Rolls he used to own. I'd love to have had a go at that.'

'I doubt he'd have let you drive the Rolls,' Hettie

laughed. 'Far too expensive and precious a car for a beginner. It would cost a mint if you damaged it.'

'You're being awfully quiet, Dad. Aren't you pleased for me?' Tommy frowned.

'Of course I am.'

'You don't sound it.'

'Well, I am. Now when's tea being served, I'm starving.'

'Don't you want to hear more?'

Jack sighed. 'I suppose I'm going to have to.'

As Tommy launched into a blow-by-blow account of his lesson Jack was quietly reflecting how jealous he was of Andrew. In normal circumstances it should have been he, Tommy's father, who taught the boy to drive. But the circumstances, he being blind, were far from normal. Blind men didn't drive, far less teach others.

He'd long since come to terms with his disability but there were still occasions, this being one, when he cursed what had happened to him in the war.

He'd missed a great deal in Tommy's upbringing, things a sighted father would have done that he simply couldn't. And that hurt.

He'd never played football with Tommy, never taught him to ride, which had been a great passion of his before the war, never . . . oh the list went on and on.

And now this, driving.

Yes, he was jealous of Andrew, but in the nicest way. There was no animosity or rancour involved, Andrew was his dear friend after all.

If he'd been able to cry he just might have done so at that point.

'Oh Christ, you're lovely,' David gasped, having emerged

from a deep clinch with Bell. They'd been out to the pub and were now round the back of her house saying goodnight.

David had asked to see Bell again after the dance and kept on seeing her. They were now regarded as a courting couple.

A brief image of Tommy Riach flickered through Bell's mind, an image she swiftly banished. It was daft to dwell on what might have been and now never would. David was her beau, which was fine by her. More than fine for he was a helluva nice lad. She could certainly do a lot worse.

'Oh Bell,' he whispered, his hand rubbing her breast. He then began worming it inside her blouse.

They'd done this before, many times, so there was nothing new about it. She'd allow him to go so far, and no more. Up until then she'd steadfastly refused to go all the way.

She could feel his hardness pressing into her which excited her. She shivered, and broke out in goose bumps. Men never believed that women had the same intensity of urges they themselves had, but then most men didn't understand women one little bit.

His free hand fumbled with her skirt, rucking it upwards. Eager fingers tugged at the elastic of her knickers.

The breath caught in her throat when he found what he was after. She squirmed her hips, relishing the sensations coursing through her.

'I want to fuck you so much,' David moaned. 'You don't know how much.'

But she did, only too well. For she felt exactly the same about him. She'd often wondered, tried to imagine ... Was it as good as they said? Did the earth really move? She doubted the latter. But good it surely must be.

'Baby, baby,' he further moaned.

Both hands were now up her skirt, one at the front, the other kneading and stroking her rear.

'Bell, please. Please!' he pleaded.

'*No.*'

He groaned.

For the first time her resolve began to melt, the urgency in her almost overwhelming. She touched him which made him groan again.

Despite the writhing and squirming, part of her mind was detached, clinical almost. It was that part which came to a decision. 'Have you got a johnny?'

'In my wallet.'

'Came prepared did you?'

'Don't, Bell. Don't. That's not fair.'

She'd have preferred the comfort of a bed, but that luxury was highly unlikely before marriage. And marriage it would be.

'Why don't we get engaged?' she whispered.

He immediately stopped what he was doing. 'Are you serious?'

'Never more so. Do you love me?'

'I . . .' He halted, aware of the commitment he was being asked to make.

'You've never said.'

'That's jessie.'

'No it's not. I love *you.*'

His face broke into a beaming smile. 'Do you?'

'Yes, David, I do.'

He swallowed hard, and with that swallow he too made a decision. Why the hell not? he thought. Why the hell not! He certainly didn't want to lose her. That would have been awful. 'And I love you, Bell,' he declared in a rush of words.

'Are you sure about that?'

'Oh aye. Sure as sure. Just don't ask me to keep repeating it all the time, that's all.'

He may or he may not, but he would before she was through with him. He caught his breath as she began undoing his flies.

'The johnny,' she said. 'We have to use a johnny.'

Later she reflected that the earth hadn't moved. But it had been good. Oh yes, it had been that all right.

He'd sworn he'd bring a ring the following week.

'Engaged!' Irene squealed. 'Congratulations, Bell. When did this happen?'

'Saturday night. But you're not to say anything until I have a ring on my finger. Promise?'

Irene nodded vigorously. 'I promise.'

'Cross your heart and hope to die?'

'Cross my heart and hope to die.'

'Your word of honour?'

'My word of bloody honour. Now tell me all about it. I want to know every last detail.'

Bell glanced about her. It was Monday morning and they were on their way to work. After David had left her she'd gone inside and straight to a mirror to see if she looked any different. She hadn't. The Bell who'd stared back at her was the same Bell who'd stared back earlier when she was getting ready to go out. Yet she did feel different. A little piece of magic had been wrought and she'd never be the same again.

'I let him shag me.'

Irene stopped dead in her tracks and stared in astonishment. 'You what?'

'I let him shag me,' Bell repeated nonchalantly. 'But only after I decided we were going to get married.'

'You decided?'

'Damn right I did. There and then. There's no one better likely to come along so I'll settle for David, thank you very much.'

Irene was still trying to digest this as they resumed walking. 'What was it like?'

'What was what like?' Bell queried innocently. She was enjoying this.

'The shag, you eejit.'

Bell wanted to laugh at the way Irene's eyes were almost popping out of her head. 'Very nice.'

'Is that all you can say, *very nice*!'

Now she did laugh. 'It's difficult to describe. You know when you . . . eh . . . ?' She winked knowingly.

Irene coloured. 'Go on.'

'Well, it's something similar only a hundred times better.'

Irene was astounded. 'A hundred times?'

She nodded.

'Bloody hell.'

'You should have heard the noise I made. I'm surprised someone didn't come to find out what was going on.'

'Was it . . . his . . . big?'

'Huge.'

'Huge?'

'Ginormous.'

Irene gulped. 'Did he . . . have trouble getting it in?'

'He managed in the end. Though it was a tight fit. But that makes it all the better.'

'So I've heard,' Irene muttered.

'Well, it's true.'

Irene's mind was whirling. God, how she envied Bell. First a regular boyfriend, now a fiancé, and not only a fiancé but a shag into the bargain. She was green.

'I wouldn't have done it of course unless he'd agreed to us getting engaged.'

'Naturally.'

'I'll have the ring next week.'

'Oh Bell, I can't wait to see it.'

Me neither, Bell thought with enormous satisfaction.

'How long till the wedding?'

'We'll have to discuss that. But I would imagine next year. Well, I mean, once your mind is made up there's no use hanging around.'

'True enough. You'd just better make sure you don't get up the duff in the meantime.'

'There'll be no worry about that, Irene. I'll insist he always uses a johnny. I'm not walking up the aisle with a bun in the oven. No fears.'

'Can I be your bridesmaid, Bell?'

'I was going to ask you anyway.'

That delighted Irene. She'd never been a bridesmaid. It was something to look forward to.

They were fast approaching Drummond's. 'Not a word mind,' Bell cautioned. 'Not even a hint. I want the ring first before I let on.'

Irene giggled. 'I think it's tremendous so I do.' Then, soberly, 'Was it really ginormous?'

'I swear it.'

'Just like Tommy Riach's?'

Bell's good humour abruptly vanished. She wished Irene hadn't brought Tommy's name up. 'We don't know he's got a big one. That was only a joke, remember?'

'Oh aye, so it was. I'd forgotten.'

But what had gone up between her legs was no joke, Bell recalled with a smile. It had been nothing to laugh about. Shout about yes, but not laugh.

She mustn't make so much noise in future, she told herself. It would be awful if someone did get nosy and they were discovered 'at it'.

Particularly if it was either her mother or father. How humiliating, a real red-faced situation.

Oh, but she was pleased with herself. Pleased as could be. Things couldn't have worked out better. Especially as David earnt such a good wage.

'Christ, that was quick!' Sandy McAlpine declared enviously, staring at the engagement ring Bell was swanking to all and sundry, moving her hand so that the diamonds flashed and sparkled. 'You've only known each other five minutes.'

'It was love at first sight so it was,' Bell replied solemnly.

'The ring's a smasher,' Hannah McIlroy enthused. 'I couldn't be more pleased for you, Bell.'

They were all in the cloakroom prior to going on shift. It was the following Monday morning and that Saturday David had been as good as his word, presenting Bell with a little blue box containing the ring nestling in matching velvet.

To Bell's delight the ring had fitted perfectly so there was no need for her to go to the jeweller's in Pitlochry, where it had been bought, to have the band resized.

It was a smasher too, Bell thought proudly. Small

perhaps, a single stone surrounded by chips, but what else did she expect from a working man. The Koh-i-noor?

If her workmates were pleased for her it was more than her mother and father had been. They'd both hit the roof, her father most of all. His reaction was purely selfish, as was her mother's. Engagement meant marriage and marriage meant losing her weekly pay packet. No wonder they'd been put out. Tough shite, she'd thought at the time.

'What's his surname again?' Sandy demanded.

'Nelson.'

'So you'll be Mrs David Nelson.'

'That's right.'

'I'm to be a bridesmaid,' Irene informed the others.

'Are you indeed,' Isa commented caustically. She was jealous of Bell and thought she must cajole Ronnie into popping the question. The fact that his cousin David had done so might be an incentive.

'When are you seeing him again?' That was Hannah.

'Wednesday night.'

'Have your folks met him yet?' Sandy asked.

Bell's face clouded. That was something she was dreading and which she'd put off for as long as she could. 'Not yet,' she replied airily. 'But they will. All in good time.'

'Aye, well you know best.'

Bell glanced at Irene whom she'd confided in about her parents' reaction. Irene's response was to raise her eyebrows.

'I still think you're awfully quick off the mark,' Sandy went on. 'I hope you aren't going to regret this.'

'Never,' Bell stated emphatically. 'As I said, it was love at first sight. There's no doubt in either of our minds.'

'Come on you, lot.' Mrs Reid, one of the older members of staff, intervened. 'Engagement or not, we have to get to work or else Balfour will be hammering on the door.'

That had gone well, Bell thought with satisfaction as they all trooped from the cloakroom. As pointed out it had been a short courtship but there was nothing wrong with that.

Nothing whatsoever in her opinion.

Nancy was about to climb into the bath when there was a tap on the door. 'Who is it?' she called out.

'Drew,' came the whispered reply. 'Let me in.'

Of all the cheek! 'Go away.'

'Oh, Nancy, let me in.'

'Get lost!'

'I'm going back to school in a couple of days and want to see you before I go.'

See being the operative word, she thought. Well, she was having none of it. 'I said, get lost, and mean it.'

'Nancy, it'll be months before I'm home again.'

'That's your lookout.'

She slid into the steaming water, sighing with pleasure as it closed over her body. On several occasions since the last incident she'd caught Drew eyeing her, the look on his face clearly reflecting what he was thinking, or remembering to be more precise.

'Nancy?'

She didn't reply.

'Oh come on, Nancy. This is my last chance.'

She should take it as a compliment, she thought. Even if he was so young.

'Nancy?'

Marry her one day, he'd promised. She almost laughed. Aye, cows would fly first.

'Nancy, please?'

After a while the pleadings stopped.

Chapter 16

A wild-eyed Kelly burst into Andrew's office without knocking. Albeit a Sunday, the entire distillery was working that weekend due to the pressure of orders. Andrew glanced up at him in astonishment.

'War's been declared,' Kelly stated abruptly.

The two men stared at one another. Neither was surprised as the news had been expected, but both felt sick to the pits of their stomachs that it had actually happened.

'The PM announced it on the wireless at eleven o'clock,' Kelly added.

Andrew let out a long drawn-out sigh and then ran a hand over his face. There it was, they were going to go through the whole damn thing again. The words Kelly had just uttered were a death knell for God knows how many millions.

Kelly slowly shook his head. 'I can't believe it. I really can't.'

Nor Andrew. But it was apparently fact. 'Get a bottle and glasses,' he instructed. If this didn't call for a drink nothing did.

Thank the Lord Drew was only eleven and well out of it. Surely the forthcoming conflict wouldn't last until he was eligible for the Forces. That was a ridiculous scenario.

But there were countless men who wouldn't be so fortunate. Tommy Riach for one. He thought of Jack and Hettie, how were they taking this? He dreaded to think.

Kelly placed the glasses on the desk and poured, Andrew noting that Kelly's hand was trembling. He could well understand that.

'I lost a brother in the last lot,' Kelly said quietly.

'Me too.'

'Yes, I know. I've heard.'

Andrew picked up his glass and stood. 'What shall we toast, Mr Kelly?'

'Victory I suppose. What else?'

'Yes,' Andrew replied bitterly. 'What else indeed. Do the workforce know?'

'The word's going round like wildfire.'

Andrew nodded, wondering if he should call a meeting and address them. He decided against that.

He crossed to the window and stared out. It seemed just an ordinary September day. Nothing special about it at all. But it *was* different. Oh yes, it was most certainly that.

When Andrew turned round again he found Kelly standing there, lost in thought, with tears in his eyes.

'I'm sorry, Mr Drummond,' Kelly mumbled, groping for a handkerchief.

'Don't be. There's no shame in it. As far as I'm concerned the whole bloody country should be weeping.'

'Aye,' Kelly agreed softly.

'All I can say is, no matter what happens, I hope that bastard Hitler and his cohorts roast in hell for ever more.'

'Amen,' Kelly nodded.

Andrew finished his drink. 'Another?'

Kelly considered that. 'You know, I think I will.'

Andrew and Rose were in the middle of dinner, neither having spoken much, the atmosphere funereal, when Pattie Williams appeared.

'Sorry to disturb you, sir, but Mr Riach is on the telephone.'

He'd been going to ring Jack after the meal, this saved him the trouble. He pushed his plate away, not having an appetite anyway. 'I'll take the call.'

'Yes, sir.'

'I'll only be a few minutes,' he said to Rose, and departed from the room.

'It's Tommy, isn't it?' Andrew said softly, he and Jack having met up in the pub at Jack's request.

'Yes,' Jack croaked in reply.

'He's seventeen, hopefully too young yet.'

Jack laughed mirthlessly. 'I served alongside many lads that age on the Western Front. Good lads all, most of them now . . .' He trailed off, and shook his head.

'How's Hettie?'

'Crying her eyes out. She'd recovered before I left but knowing her she probably started up again as soon as I was out of the house.'

'And Tommy?'

Jack's hand crunched into a tight fist. 'The idiot thinks it's wonderful. Imagine, wonderful! No doubt he sees himself winning a VC and becoming a hero.'

'*If* he's called up, Jack, it won't be for a while.'

'We hope.'

'Yes,' Andrew said quietly. 'We hope.'

'I can't bear the thought of him going through what I did, Andrew. The sheer horror, the total nightmare of that.'

He'd been lucky, Andrew reflected. Ireland had been a doddle compared to France and Belgium. There had been no comparison.

Another customer in the pub laughed loudly and shrilly causing Andrew to frown in irritation. Then he saw the chap's face and realised the laugh was no doubt a nervous reaction to the day's events.

'I prayed this wouldn't come about,' Jack went on. 'Night after night I prayed that someone, somewhere, would see sense. Fat lot of good that did.'

'I wonder what will happen next,' Andrew mused. 'I mean, in the immediate future.'

'The first thing they want to do is get rid of Chamberlain. He's worse than useless.'

Andrew nodded his agreement.

'Churchill should lead the country in my opinion. He's the man for the job.'

'But will he get it? That's the question.'

There was a pause, then Jack said softly, 'Do you know one of the worst things about being blind, Andrew?'

'What?'

Jack took a deep swallow of whisky and carefully replaced the now empty glass on the table between them. 'Having children and not knowing what they look like. Oh, I've had Tommy described to me often enough but it's hardly the same thing. I know what you look like, and Hettie, because I'd seen you both before I lost my eyes.

And it's easy to imagine the pair of you grown older. But Tommy? He's a complete mystery.'

Andrew didn't know what to reply to that, thinking of Drew, picturing his son in his mind. It was amazing the everyday things you took for granted, he reflected. Things denied to others.

'It might not last long,' Andrew said hopefully.

Jack laughed. 'All over by Christmas? That sort of guff. That's what they said the last time and it took four long hellish years for it to finish. Well, this won't be any shorter. Anyone who thinks differently is kidding themselves.'

Andrew was sure that was right. Four years, maybe more. And what if the Germans did win? He went icy cold all over at the thought.

'Do you fancy getting pissed tonight, Andrew? Really pissed. The falling-down kind.'

That appealed. 'It's not every day war is declared after all.'

'No, it isn't.'

The same customer as before laughed again, this time even more loudly and shrilly. He was in his early twenties, Andrew noted. Prime fighting material. The poor bugger was probably shitting bricks.

'Let's do that,' Andrew said.

'Pissed as farts.'

'Rat-arsed.'

'Deid mockit.'

'Boaking drunk.'

A few seconds' silence passed between them after that exchange. 'I'll get them in,' Andrew declared, and headed for the bar.

Jack sat still as a stone statue thinking about Tommy, fearing what might lie ahead for his son.

* * *

Andrew had slept a little then woken with the most fearful stomach ache. It was the whisky of course, he and Jack having consumed copious quantities, first at the pub then back at Jack's house. The strange thing was, although they'd set out to get drunk neither had actually become so.

Andrew groaned, and rubbed his belly. This was awful. If it kept up he wouldn't get another wink of sleep that night which meant going to work like a wrung-out old rag.

He tossed and turned for a while longer, but the pain remained. He'd go down to the kitchen and get some bicarb he finally decided. That should help.

He halted briefly at Rose's door, imagining her inside all tucked up. With a shrug he continued on his way.

He stopped again when he came in sight of the kitchen, wondering why the light was on. He found Miss Campbell sitting at the table hunched over a cup and saucer.

'Mr Drummond!' she exclaimed, blushing. 'What are you doing here at this hour?'

'I might ask the same thing, Miss Campbell.'

The housekeeper self-consciously pulled her dark-blue velour dressing gown more tightly about her. 'I have a confession to make. I'm something of an insomniac and often come down for cocoa about this time. I hope it's all right?'

'Of course, Miss Campbell. Feel free to do whatever you wish.'

He tried not to stare at the deep cleft between her breasts, one of which had a tiny mole on it. She really was well bosomed, he thought, not for the first time.

'I'm looking for the bicarb,' he explained.

'Stomach trouble?'

He nodded. 'Jack Riach and I rather overdid it earlier and now I'm paying the price.'

She rose. 'You sit down, Mr Drummond, and I'll fetch the bicarb for you.'

'Don't let me disturb you, Miss Campbell.'

'You're hardly doing that.'

Lovely backside too, he thought as she moved away from him, the material of her dressing gown accentuating its curves.

'What do you think of today's news?' he asked, sitting as instructed.

'It's dreadful.'

'Aye, it is that.'

'It's been coming for a while, mind. But it's still a shock now that it's actually arrived.'

'I agree.'

He watched her spoon bicarb into a glass of water and swirl the contents.

'That should do the trick,' she declared, placing the glass in front of him. 'Now drink it all down at once.'

'Bossy boots,' he smiled.

She blushed again. 'Sorry. I didn't mean it to sound like that.'

It tasted foul, but he managed to swallow it in one go. 'Horrible,' he grimaced.

'Quite disgusting, I agree. But if it helps that's all that matters.'

Definitely a handsome woman, he thought. There was a basic honesty and openness about her face which he liked. She seemed the sort of person you could easily confide in.

'We haven't really had a talk, you and I,' he said.

'No.'

He glanced around. 'It's a bit spooky here this time of night. I hadn't realised.'

'I can't say it bothers me. But I can see what you mean.'

They smiled at one another. 'How are you settling in, Miss . . .' He broke off. 'I can't keep calling you Miss Campbell. Not in a situation like this. What's your Christian name?'

'Elspeth.'

'Elspeth,' he repeated. 'It suits you. And I'm Andrew.'

She'd thought him rather austere up until then, but could see now that wasn't really the case. There was a warmth there she hadn't experienced before.

'The answer to your question is I'm settling in fine. I'm enjoying it here,' she replied.

'Good. It's a pity the position isn't a permanent one. Though, just between you and me, I suspect Mrs Drummond won't take over the housekeeping duties again.'

'No?'

'It's only a guess, but that's what I think will happen. So it may be you'll be here longer than you anticipated. If you wish to stay on that is.'

Elspeth frowned. 'I'll have to think about that.'

'Of course.'

She had a sip of cocoa.

'Have you always suffered from insomnia?'

'Ever since I was a child. I've no idea what causes it. Just the way I am I suppose.' She shrugged. 'One of these things.'

He should leave her now, he thought, and found himself reluctant to do so. He was enjoying their conversation, and her company. She was relaxing to be with. Such a change from Rose since the miscarriage.

'Would you mind if I smoke?'

'No, go ahead. I didn't know you did.'

She smiled conspiratorially. 'Only a few per day. And I really shouldn't in the kitchen of all places.'

'Well, I won't tell Cook on you. That's a promise.'

He watched her light up, thinking again how fascinating her hands were. Long, elegant and ivory coloured. He could just imagine . . .

He coughed, putting that straight out of his mind. 'My stomach seems to be settling a bit.'

She exhaled, sending a stream of white smoke spiralling towards the ceiling. 'Give it a little while longer and it should hopefully be gone altogether.'

'I've had a lot of trouble with my stomach recently,' he confessed.

'Oh?'

'I thought it was indigestion but Dr Lesley has other opinions. He believes it might be an ulcer.'

Her face immediately clouded with genuine concern. 'How awful if it is.'

'I'm seeing a specialist in Perth next week which I'm not looking forward to at all. If it is an ulcer that could lead to an operation and being away from the distillery for a time, recuperating and all that.'

'Does that worry you?'

He contemplated his reply. 'If you imagine a ship. Well I'm the captain who doesn't like being away from his bridge for too long.'

'I see,' she murmured, thinking how conscientious and responsible he was. They were admirable traits, ones she admired.

'Still, health comes first,' she said.

'I suppose so.'

'Work is only work after all, even if you do own your own business. Anyway, a distillery isn't a ship. A distillery won't founder if you're off for a few weeks.' Then, teasingly, 'I shouldn't think there are many unexpected icebergs in Dalneil.'

He laughed at the absurdity of that. 'Heaven forbid.'

'Drummond's hardly the *Titanic*.'

Andrew was lonely, she realised. She could read it in his eyes. Lonely and . . . sad. Somewhat lost even. That surprised her.

'Can I ask a personal question, Elspeth?'

'If it's too personal I don't guarantee I'll answer.'

He fiddled with his empty glass, thinking this was embarrassing. But he was curious. 'How come a good-looking lassie like yourself isn't married?'

She sucked in a breath, and turned her head away. Where she'd blushed before she now went a deep shade of red.

'Perhaps you haven't found the right man?'

'It isn't that,' she replied slowly. 'I did. Once.'

He didn't speak, waiting for her to go on.

All the old hurt and humiliation came welling back. Black memories, terrible ones. She flicked ash into her saucer.

'Sorry, I obviously shouldn't have asked. It was rude of me.'

'So why did you?'

'Curiosity,' he confessed.

Elspeth inhaled deeply, then ground out what remained of her cigarette. 'We were supposed to be married, except he jilted me.'

'At the . . .'

'Yes,' she interjected quickly. 'At the altar. He took fright, I was told afterwards, and ran for it. Last I heard he was somewhere in New Zealand.'

'I'm sorry.'

Elspeth hung her head. 'It was a long time ago now. I try not to think of it. Remember. That's why I went into service, to get away from the wagging tongues and whispers behind my back. Everyone was very sympathetic and yet . . .' She trailed off.

'And yet what?' he prompted gently.

'I got the distinct impression they blamed me. Thought there was something wrong with me that had made Stuart take fright. Oh, you know what village people are like, Andrew. The gossip, the speculation, the downright lies that are circulated. It was just too hurtful for me to stay there and so I also left. Better that way.'

'I shouldn't have been so nosy,' Andrew apologised. 'I had no idea.' He felt for the woman, he really did. What an appalling thing to have happened.

'I was so ashamed,' she choked.

'But the fault wasn't yours. Was it?'

She shook her head.

'There then. As you say, the young chap simply took fright. It affects some people that way. Marriage is a huge step after all.'

Pull yourself together, Elspeth berated herself. She couldn't imagine why she'd confided in Andrew. It was a piece of her past she rarely divulged.

'You mustn't let it put you off men for life,' Andrew advised. 'They're not all like that. You mark my words, someone else will come along in time. You'll see.'

She managed to smile. 'Perhaps.'

'No doubt about it. So there.'

Elspeth stared him straight in the eyes. 'Please don't let on to anyone else in the house?'

'I won't. You have my oath on that.'

'Thank you.'

He wanted to go to her, put an arm round her shoulders and give her a comforting squeeze. But that would hardly be right. Up until a few minutes ago they'd been relative strangers after all.

'How's your stomach now?'

His eyebrows shot up. 'I do believe it's better, thank God.'

'The pain's gone?'

'Completely.'

There were a few seconds during which they gazed at one another, then he rose from his chair. 'I'd better get back to bed.'

'And I'll clear up here.'

'Thanks for talking to me, Elspeth.'

'I'm not usually so forthcoming. Maybe it's the lateness of the hour, my mood.'

'Whatever, your story's safe with me.'

She flashed him a smile of gratitude. 'And someday you must tell me yours.'

That jolted him. 'Mine?'

'Oh, I think there's one to tell. I can sense it.'

At the kitchen door he stopped and turned again. 'I'm glad you've joined the household, Elspeth Campbell. I approve of you.'

He was gone before she could reply, even if she could think how to respond.

*   *   *

'We had a letter from Gerald yesterday,' Babs stated quietly. 'He says he's going to be in the thick of it.'

Tommy's eyes gleamed. 'Lucky blighter.'

That angered Babs. 'Don't be so stupid! He could get killed. My brother could get killed.'

Tommy was instantly contrite. 'I didn't mean that the way it sounded.'

'Oh yes, you did. You're just like him. All gung ho and charge! What neither of you seems to appreciate is this is for real. It's not a story out of the *Wizard* or *Hotspur* you know. But *real.*'

Tommy glanced about him. They were in their favourite spot where they always came for kissing and cuddling. So far there had been none of that.

He picked a blade of grass and rubbed it between two fingers. Women, he thought. They always overdramatised everything. His mother was just the same. Ever since war had been declared she merely had to look at him and tears came into her eyes.

'At least you're safe for the time being,' Babs went on. 'Until you're eighteen anyway.' Compulsory military service had been announced for all men in Britain between the ages of eighteen and forty-one.

Tommy didn't reply to that.

'I couldn't bear it if you had to go off as well. Have two of you in the firing line, so to speak.'

Tommy was aching to 'go off', as she put it, but had more sense than to say so. He could well imagine the reaction if he did. From Babs and his mother.

Silence fell between them.

'What are you thinking about, Tommy?'

'Nothing,' he lied.

'I keep wondering . . .' She shuddered.

'What?'

'If I'll ever see Gerald again.'

'Of course you will,' Tommy replied scornfully.

'But I might not.'

'You will.'

'I wish I could believe that,' she muttered.

This was rapidly becoming a bore, Tommy thought. He wanted to talk about the war, but not like this. Didn't she understand how exciting the whole thing was? As for Gerald, he *was* a lucky blighter. He'd have given anything to be in Gerald's shoes. Shoes *and* Hurricane.

Tommy briefly closed his eyes, picturing himself at a plane's controls, zooming through the sky, a Hun squarely in his sights. *Rat a tat tat tat!*

Got you! The Hun blew up in a glorious ball of flame. Another miniature swastika to slap on to his fuselage.

'Why are you smiling?'

The smile abruptly vanished. 'Am I?'

'Like a Cheshire cat.'

'I wasn't aware.'

She regarded him suspiciously. 'You wouldn't suit a uniform anyway.'

That she'd more or less read his mind startled him. 'Why not?'

'Wrong shape. You'd look daft.'

He bristled. 'I wouldn't.'

'Oh yes you would.'

'Wrong shape?' he mumbled with a frown.

'As I said, you'd look daft.'

It simply wasn't true, he told himself. Babs was only trying to put him off any thoughts in that direction. Well she hadn't succeeded. Not by a long chalk.

'I think we'd better get back,' he declared.

She stared at him in surprise. 'If you wish.'

'It's getting late.'

'Not too late though,' she replied hesitantly. When she tried to catch his gaze he glanced away.

'Let's go then,' she said.

They usually held hands when they walked home, but didn't on this occasion. Their conversation was sparse and stilted.

At her door Tommy kissed her quickly on the lips. 'See you during the week.'

Her smile was stretched and strained. 'Yes.'

Babs bit her lip as she went inside. It was the first time things hadn't gone well between them.

McFarlane was rubbing down Moonbeam when a dishevelled Rose appeared before him. It was clear she'd taken a tumble.

'Mrs Drummond, are you all right?' he asked anxiously.

'Strumpet's dead,' she answered in a cracked voice.

'Dead?'

'We were galloping when she collapsed.'

McFarlane knew with certainty that Rose had pushed the mare too hard. It was something he'd been half expecting, dreading. 'Where is she now?'

Rose told him.

'Right, leave it to me. I'll attend to matters.'

'Thank you, McFarlane.'

He hesitated, unsure of Rose's reaction to the next question. 'Did she . . . suffer at all?'

Rose glanced down at the straw-covered floor, the memory of those terrifying few moments clear in her head. Luckily she'd cleared her stirrups otherwise she could have become entangled with the horse with who knows what result.

It had been madness, sheer madness. But at the time the thrill had been almost ecstatic. Urging Strumpet on, trying to go faster, faster. And then . . . suddenly . . .

Rose shook herself. 'I don't believe so, McFarlane. I'm sure she was already dead when she hit the ground.'

'Well, that's a mercy at least.'

'Yes,' Rose agreed.

'And you didn't hurt yourself?' He almost wished she had, the callous, cruel bitch. If she'd been his wife he'd literally have knocked her from pillar to post for what she'd done.

'I'm shaken, that's all.'

'You'd still better go to the doctor and have yourself checked over.'

'Yes,' she muttered, having absolutely no intention of doing so. She'd be fine after a long hot bath and rest.

McFarlane couldn't help himself. 'Strumpet was a bonny mare. A right willing beast.'

Rose didn't reply to that.

Without uttering a further word she left the stables.

This was it, Andrew thought, staring up at the grey hospital building. His appointment with Mr Creighton was in ten minutes' time.

He unconsciously touched his stomach which hadn't bothered him since the night he'd chatted with Elspeth Campbell, and that upset had been brought on by overindulgence, nothing else.

Rose knew nothing about this visit, just as she didn't know about his visits to Lesley. As far as she was concerned he was off on a business trip, nothing more.

He'd been nervous since waking that morning, which was perfectly natural after all. Ulcers could be nasty, as Lesley had warned him.

Not that he believed he had one. He didn't, convinced it was indigestion that had been plaguing him. Still, it was best to have that confirmed.

You're wasting time, he told himself. Dawdling, putting off the evil moment.

He took a deep breath, squared his shoulders and began mounting the steps that led to the main entrance.

Chapter 17

'I've been thinking,' Rose said to Andrew, who was sitting opposite. 'How would you feel about making Nancy my personal lady's maid?'

Andrew, engrossed in the newspaper full of the latest war news, glanced across at her in surprise. 'I beg your pardon?'

'How would you feel about making Nancy my personal lady's maid?'

He frowned. 'Do you need one? You haven't up until now.'

'It would be a tremendous help. I've discovered Nancy is terribly clever with hair and extremely useful when I'm getting dressed.'

'I see,' Andrew murmured, wondering what had brought this on.

'Besides, she's marvellous company. The pair of us chatter away for hours at times. She's ever such fun.'

'Isn't it . . . Well the idea of a lady's maid, isn't it just a wee bit pretentious nowadays?'

Rose scowled. 'Not at all.'

'It might be construed as such.'

'I don't give a fig how it's construed. Other people's opinions don't bother me one whit.'

Andrew sighed. 'I'll have to speak to Miss Campbell.'

'Don't speak to her, *tell* her,' Rose snapped. 'She's only another employee when all's said and done.'

'Still, it would only be polite to consult her.'

Rose snorted in irritation. 'Honestly, Andrew, you can be so damned weak on occasion. I despair.'

'Weak?' he repeated. He knew he had many faults but didn't consider weakness to be one of them. Quite the contrary.

'That's right, weak!'

This could very easily get out of hand, he thought. If he wasn't careful it could blow up into a major row.

'It would mean taking on another maid, a replacement for the duties Nancy does now.'

'Are you trying to say we can't afford another maid? Have you become mean as well as weak?'

Rose really had her heart set on this, that was obvious. But there was no need for her to be so disagreeable about it. As for name calling, that was most unlike her. Or at least, he reminded himself, *had* been unlike her. So many things about Rose had changed since the miscarriage.

'I am neither weak nor mean,' he stated levelly, becoming ever so slightly angry.

'Then prove it.'

He laughed. 'I don't have to prove anything, Rose. Not to you or anyone else.'

'See!'

See what? He wasn't sure. 'I'll consider the matter. How's that?'

Rose glared at him.

'Well?'

'I *want* her as a lady's maid, Andrew. Understand?'

Now he was angry. A request was one thing, being dictated to quite another. Even by Rose. 'We don't always get what we want you know.'

The glare had become venomous. 'And what if I insist?'

He shrugged. 'Won't alter things. I said I'd consider the matter and that's final.' He was damned if he was going to be bulldozed into anything. He would probably have readily consented if she'd gone about this differently.

'I'm going to bed,' Rose announced abruptly.

'Goodnight then.'

Rising, she flounced from the room.

Bitch, he thought. Which surprised him. He'd never thought of his wife that way before.

He doubted he'd be having a visitation that night.

On the other hand, and he smiled, it might just be that he would, Rose trying to persuade him where she considered him most vulnerable.

But it wouldn't make a blind bit of difference, no matter how great the temptation. If it was blackmail then she could go whistle Dixie.

Nancy was *en route* to the village shop to buy some kirby grips for Rose when she came across a group of lassies playing 'ropes'.

She halted to stare at them, observing how much they were enjoying themselves. Two of the girls each had an end of the rope, a length of washing line, which they were cawing, as the expression went. Whirling it round in an arc, the girl in the middle having to jump over it when it hit the ground. All the while they were singing a ditty that went with the game.

Nancy smiled wistfully to see the fun. How unlike her own childhood where fun was almost unknown, life simply too hard for levity. Even as a tiny child all she could remember was work of some description.

Sadness filled her at what she'd missed. Envy too watching these girls.

It suddenly struck her that several of the taller lassies were only a few years younger than herself. How old she felt by comparison, but then that was only natural after what she'd been through, not least living with, and being used by, Bill McCabe.

She moved closer, letting the happiness from the group wash over her. Beginning to feel as carefree as they, as innocent – if that was possible – as they.

She could almost imagine there had never been a Bill McCabe in her life, and that she'd never been a bondager and all that entailed. The sheer slavery of it.

A roar of laughter combined with jeers went up when the lassie in the middle mistimed her jump and fouled the rope. Now it was her turn to caw.

Nancy glanced about her. There was no one else in sight, just this group.

She moved even closer. 'Can I join in?'

The girl she'd addressed turned to look at her. 'Aye, if you wish.'

'You won't mind?'

'Can she have a play, Effie?'

One of the older girls nodded. 'She can start in the middle.'

Nancy eagerly hurried forward, thinking this wonderful. A real treat.

'One, two, three a leerie . . .' the group started to sing as the rope spun into action.

Nancy didn't last long, but no matter that. She was humming jauntily and beaming broadly when she continued on her way.

For a few minutes there she'd been a child again. A child experiencing a normal childhood.

'David!' Bell exclaimed, having answered a knock at the door.

'Do you fancy a trip to the pub? I have to talk to you.'

David's appearance had thrown Bell into a tizzy, it being completely unexpected. There hadn't been an arrangement.

'Who is it, Bell?' her father called out from the sitting room.

That alarmed Bell. The last thing she wanted to do was invite David in to meet her parents. Not there and then. That meeting was still in the future. God knows what he'd make of her father sitting unshaven and stinking, her mother rattling around like a female scarecrow.

'The pub?' she repeated.

David regarded her anxiously. 'Aye, that's right. We have to talk.'

Bell's hand went to her hair. She too was something of a mess; she certainly couldn't go out in public as she was. 'Can I meet you there in about fifteen minutes? Let me tidy myself and put on some fresh make-up.'

'I'll be waiting then,' David smiled.

Having closed the door again Bell flew up to her room. Now what was this all about?

*   *   *

'I got you a gin and orange,' David said as Bell joined him at the corner table he'd selected.

Bell hadn't liked coming into the pub on her own. It wasn't proper. But she was meeting someone and that made all the difference. She quickly sat. 'Is something wrong, David?'

He picked up his pint and had a long swallow, feeling totally and utterly wretched. 'Aye, it is.'

'To do with us?' My God, she suddenly thought, he was going to break off their engagement. How could she face the lassies at work if he did?

'I had a letter this morning,' he stated slowly.

'And?'

'Well, more of an official form actually. It came as quite a shock.'

He didn't seem to be breaking off the engagement, Bell thought with relief. But why was he looking so miserable?

'What sort of form?'

'You must have heard or read in the papers about the compulsory military service. Hundreds of thousands have been called up.'

She went cold all over.

He nodded. 'That's right. I'm one of them.'

The gin and orange vanished down her throat. 'Can I have another?' she croaked.

'Of course.'

Called up! It had never crossed her mind that might happen to David. Only to others, people she didn't know.

She stared at him standing at the bar. This would put the cat amongst the pigeons where their marriage was concerned. It had all seemed so cut and dried before. Now this bombshell.

'I made it a large one this time,' David said, sitting down again.

'When?'

'Do I have to go away?'

'Aye.'

'It doesn't say. It merely informs me that I'm to be drafted and to await further communication.'

Well that was something at least. A little respite.

'But it'll be soon, Bell. A couple of weeks probably.'

'You don't know that for certain.'

'No,' he admitted reluctantly. 'But it's my guess. Mobilisation is moving swiftly by all accounts. They're hardly likely to keep me and others hanging around. They'll want us in the army and square-bashing as fast as possible. It stands to reason.'

'Oh David,' Bell whispered, a hint of tears in her eyes. 'This certainly puts the kibosh on things.'

He nodded.

'So what are we going to do?'

'Well, I can't be exempted and it's highly unlikely I'll fail the medical.'

'And what about us getting married?'

He pulled a face. 'That'll just have to wait, I suppose. There's nothing else for it.'

Reaching out she took his hand and squeezed it. 'No wonder you were looking so miserable.'

'I so desperately want you to be my wife, Bell. For the pair of us to set up home together.'

'Me too.'

'For the pair of us to share a bed night after night and forget about going round the back of your place.'

She smiled. 'It would certainly have its advantages. There's no denying that.'

'Besides, I want to wake up in the morning with you lying beside me. There's a lot more to it than just the nookie side of things.'

'Yes,' she agreed softly, thinking him ever so romantic. What a lovely thing to have said.

'And children. Our children, Bell.' He took a deep breath. 'We can still have all that, it's simply that we're going to have to wait longer than expected.'

What if he didn't come back from the war. What if . . . ? Fear gripped her, that and a terrible sense of foreboding.

She was letting her imagination run away with her, she berated herself. Of course he'd come back. Safe in life and limb.

But what if he didn't? Oh God, what if he didn't?

Dr Lesley stared at Andrew across his desk. 'I have here your report from Mr Creighton in Perth, and I'm happy to tell you that the tests were negative. There's no sign whatsoever of an ulcer.'

Relief flooded through Andrew, followed almost instantly by a surge of triumph. He was in the clear, just as he'd known he'd be. If it hadn't been undignified he'd have let out a whoop.

'I'm delighted for you, Mr Drummond.'

'Not half as delighted as I am,' Andrew beamed. 'That's a real worry off my back. Though, I have to say, I never really believed I had an ulcer.'

Lesley didn't comment on that. 'Which leaves us with the ongoing problem of indigestion.'

'That hasn't been so bad recently,' Andrew replied jauntily. 'I haven't had an attack since I went to Perth.'

'Good. How do you feel generally?'

'Right as rain, doctor. Never better. Though I do find

I have a slight loss of energy now and again. But I put that down to advancing age.'

Lesley smiled. 'I'm afraid that's something no doctor can cure. Advancing age I mean.' Then, drily, 'We even suffer from it ourselves.'

Andrew laughed.

'So that's that then. A clean bill of health.'

Andrew rose from his chair feeling buoyed in the extreme. 'All that's left for me to do is thank you for your trouble.'

Lesley also rose, intending to see Andrew to the door. 'How's Mrs Drummond?'

Andrew frowned. 'The same.'

'Still sleeping apart?'

'Yes, sad to say. She continues to insist on it.'

'As I said before, Mr Drummond, time. Just give her time.'

Andrew had begun to wonder about that. Perhaps Rose had changed for ever. If that proved to be the case . . .

It was an appalling thought, one he mustn't dwell on.

'I wondered if I'd find you here,' Andrew smiled.

Elspeth Campbell, hunched over cocoa and smoking, smiled in return. 'You obviously can't sleep either.'

He came and sat facing her. 'Not a wink. I got fed up staring at the ceiling, so here I am.'

'The insomniacs' club,' she joked.

'Apparently. At least this time there's no stomach upset I'm pleased to report.'

'Can I get you something?'

'A cup of tea would be nice.'

Elspeth ground out the remains of her cigarette. 'That won't take long.'

He stared admiringly at her as she busied herself with the kettle. Beautiful backside, he noted again. He tried to visualise her naked, and the picture he conjured up made the breath catch in his throat.

Down, boy, he warned himself. Down. He mustn't get any ideas in that direction. It would be quite out of order.

Damn Rose, he thought bitterly. A man of his nature shouldn't be going without, it wasn't natural. To do so was sheer, and continued, torture.

For a wild moment he contemplated simply bursting into Rose's bedroom to have her there and then, whether or not she objected. It was his right after all. She was his bloody wife, for Christ's sake!

But that would be an awful mistake, no doubt about it. Rose would never forgive him for forcing himself on her. It could literally, in all but name, be the end of their marriage.

'Sugar, Andrew?'

'Please.'

A few minutes later she returned to the table and placed a cup of tea in front of him.

'I hope your cocoa hasn't gone cold,' he said.

'I doubt that, I'd only just made it.'

'I had my report from Perth yesterday,' he informed her.

'And?'

'I don't have an ulcer.'

'Wonderful!' she exclaimed.

'As you know it was taking time off work which was causing me the most anxiety. Now I can forget that. And any possible operation.'

'You must be thrilled.'

'Oh, I am, Elspeth. There's still the indigestion of course. But hopefully it'll simply disappear in time.' He cleared his throat. 'I've been meaning to talk to you.'

'Oh?'

'My wife wants Nancy as a personal lady's maid. How do you feel about the possibility?' He'd purposefully kept Rose waiting for a decision on this, a small punishment for her rudeness.

'I've no objections,' Elspeth replied slowly, thinking this rather grandiose of Rose. But then who knew what went on in that woman's mind? Certainly not her.

'I have to admit it took me somewhat by surprise,' Andrew confessed. 'She's never had a personal maid before. Anyway, as far as I'm aware, lady's maids went out of fashion years ago, except in the largest and wealthiest of households that is.'

'And she particularly wishes Nancy?'

'She was quite specific about that.'

'I see.'

Andrew had a sip of tea while Elspeth lit up another cigarette. 'They seem to get on very well together,' he explained. 'Rose is quite taken with her.'

'It'll mean employing someone else.'

'I realise that. Can I leave the arrangements to you?'

Elspeth nodded. 'I'll start inquiries straight away.'

Andrew had the sudden insight – it might have been something in Elspeth's tone, or her expression – that the housekeeper didn't like Rose. Well he could hardly blame her for that. Nowadays Rose was difficult, to say the least. As he well knew.

He stayed for over half an hour before excusing himself, the pair of them chatting away about all sorts of things. When he did finally leave it was with a sense of regret.

As she'd done on the previous occasion Elspeth remained behind to clear up.

Tommy's temper snapped. 'That's it, I've had enough. As far as I'm concerned, Mr Kelly, you can go jump off a cliff for all I care.'

Kelly stared at him in astonishment.

'You're never off my back, forever getting at me. Whatever I do is wrong and I'm sick to the back teeth with it!' a red-faced Tommy raged on.

'Don't talk to me like that,' Kelly barked.

'I'll talk to you any way I wish from now on. Because I'm leaving. I can't stand working here one moment longer. Not with you around I can't.'

Tommy was close to tears, amazed at his own audacity. But this had been building for months and the latest sarcastic criticism had been the last straw.

He didn't care that he was putting himself out of a job, or any of the consequences of this. He just couldn't take any more.

'You're a tin-pot despot, Mr Kelly, and a bully with it. You've had it in for me since the moment I arrived. Had it in for me in spades. I don't know why. I've tried to do my best and all I get from you are snide remarks. Well, up yours, Mr Kelly. Right up yours!!'

And with that Tommy crashed from the room, knocking a chair over in the process.

Kelly was left gazing grimly and angrily after him.

Tommy picked a blade of grass and rubbed it between two fingers. He'd come to his and Babs' favourite spot to cool off.

He was damned if he was going back to Drummond's.

He was finished there for good. No matter what, he was determined about that. He simply couldn't face another single day with Kelly.

What would Mum and Dad say? he wondered. Well, they wouldn't be best pleased, that was certain. And what about Andrew? He'd let him down.

No, he hadn't, he told himself. He hadn't at all. If anyone had let Andrew down it was Kelly. Kelly the tormentor. Kelly whom he'd come to hate with an unbridled passion. Kelly whom he could happily have seen boiled in oil.

The big question was, what next? Where did he go from here?

He brought the blade of grass to his mouth and blew on it to produce a whistling sound. He smiled. It was years since he'd done that. Somehow he found it strangely consoling.

Then there was Babs. What was her reaction going to be when he told her? She'd probably call him a fool. An idiot. But she hadn't had to put up with Kelly. She hadn't had to endure the daily agonies of being continually belittled and sneered at.

Tommy sighed. What a mess. What an awful mess. Thankfully he hadn't punched Kelly as he'd so wanted to. That would only have made matters a whole lot worse. But part of him wished he had for the pure satisfaction of it.

He tossed the blade of grass aside thinking he couldn't stay where he was for ever. He was going to have to go home and face his parents, explain what he'd done. And more importantly, why. He could only hope there would be some sympathy for him.

Kelly, how he loathed and detested the man. The beady-eyed, bushy-eyebrowed little runt. It was too much to hope that Andrew would sack Kelly over this. Knowing Kelly he'd give a distorted explanation of what had happened, with himself totally in the clear. What would his word count against that of the book-keeper? Not a lot. Kelly was a senior member of staff after all, he a trainee. No better than an apprentice.

And then he had it. The perfect answer to all this. The only one.

'Oh cheer up, it's not the end of the world,' Irene said to Bell. The pair of them were in Irene's bedroom where they'd gone to chat away from the rest of the family.

'Like hell it isn't.'

Irene crossed over and sat on the bed beside her friend. 'Look at it this way, it just means you're going to have a long engagement instead of a short one.'

'Long!' Bell snorted. 'It could be years.'

'Aye, well, it's not within your control. There's nothing you can do about it.'

'No,' Bell agreed morosely. There wasn't.

'Besides, I think it's all rather exciting.'

Bell stared at Irene in disbelief. 'What's exciting about it?'

'You know . . . war and all that. David being called up. Off fighting for King and Country.'

Bell gave a small hysterical laugh. 'He could get his fucking head blown off. What's exciting about that for God's sake?'

'He won't.'

'What are you, an oracle? Can you see into the future?'

'Don't be daft.'

'Then don't talk such nonsense.'

Irene hung her head. 'I'm sorry. I was only trying to help. Be a pal and that.'

Bell took a deep breath. All this meant she was going to have to continue living with her parents instead of having a house of her own which she'd been so looking forward to. It was as though she'd been released from prison only to be suddenly dragged back in again.

'Are you going to see him off?'

Bell nodded. 'I had a word with Balfour and he's agreed. He was very understanding about it.'

'Aye, he's no' a bad old stick Balfour. There are a lot worse.'

'A week this Saturday,' Bell mumbled. 'The ten o'clock train from Pitlochry.'

Ten days, Irene thought. They'd fly by. At least she didn't have to worry about a fiancé being called up. She didn't have one, not even a boyfriend. And now with the war there were bound to be fewer men around, less chance of finding a chap at all. It was a sickening prospect.

'What do you think of this Tommy Riach business?' Irene asked.

They fell to discussing that.

'Where have you been?' Hettie demanded indignantly as Tommy strode into the room.

Jack immediately came to his feet. 'Is that you, lad?'

'That's right, Dad.'

'We've been out of our minds with worry. Your mum was beginning to think you'd run away.'

'We've been up all night,' Hettie declared. 'So where were you?'

'Have you heard?'

'If you mean about Drummond's, yes. Andrew called in yesterday evening to speak to you. But of course you weren't here.'

'I went to Perth. I stayed in a boarding house.'

'Perth!' Hettie exclaimed. 'What on earth were you doing there?'

'I couldn't bear Kelly any longer. I just couldn't.'

'But why Perth?' Hettie persisted.

'I'm never going back to Drummond's. So I've joined the RAF.'

There was a stunned silence. 'You've what!' Jack choked.

'Joined the RAF. I'm going to be a pilot.'

'Oh my God,' Hettie breathed, thinking she might faint.

For Jack his worst nightmare had become reality.

'I'll have to go into the Forces eventually anyway. So why not sooner rather than later?'

Tommy gave them a broad smile that was entirely forced. This was turning out as bad as he'd feared.

'Your age . . .' Hettie started to say.

'There wasn't any problem about that,' Tommy interjected. In fact he'd lied about his age just in case there might be.

'You stupid bastard,' Jack hissed. 'You don't know what you've done.'

'Yes I do, Dad.'

'*No you don't!*' Jack shouted. Stumbling backwards he fell into his chair. Tommy in the RAF, right at the sharp end. In the Great War the average lifespan of a pilot had been three weeks. Three weeks! Many a time he'd watched a plane tumble from the sky, pitying the poor sod trapped inside. Some ablaze, others trailing smoke. It didn't matter. They all ended up dead.

'It'll be an awfully big adventure,' Tommy whispered, stricken by his parents' distress.

He reeled, crying out when Hettie slapped him hard across the face.

Then Hettie burst into floods of tears.

'So what's up then?' Babs asked as they came to a halt on a stone bridge below which a broad burn murmured gently on its way.

Tommy took a deep breath.

And told her.

'That was the best yet,' Bell sighed. She and David were round the back of her house for the last time before he went off.

'Yes. It was quite something.'

'You can say that again.'

'Oh Bell,' he whispered. 'I don't want to go. It's the last thing I want to do.'

'I know.'

'You will write?'

'Of course.'

'And so will I when I get the chance.'

She couldn't help herself. Throwing her arms round him she pulled him tightly against her and sobbed her heart out.

'Here's the train,' Andrew said. He'd brought them to the station and would be taking Jack and Hettie home again.

There were quite a few people waiting, a number of them young chaps who were obviously off into the Forces. Further down the platform were Bell and David whom Tommy had spotted earlier, correctly assuming

David to be the young man he'd heard Bell had got engaged to.

He thought of Babs who'd declined to join them which had disappointed him no end. But she'd been adamant. They'd said their goodbyes several days previously. And a cold parting it had been. He'd been left with the definite impression it was all over between them. Babs hadn't been amused by his joining up.

Bell suddenly glanced in his direction and their eyes met. He smiled and she smiled back. For a few brief seconds their gaze held, then she broke contact to say something to her young man.

'All the luck in the world, Tommy. We'll be thinking of you,' Andrew declared, holding out a hand.

Tommy shook with him. 'It was kind of you to drive us here today.'

'Not at all. The least I could do.'

'Well, son,' Jack said, also holding out a hand. 'This is it.'

Tommy suddenly realised with a shock how much his father had aged in the past few days. He'd become stooped and somehow a lot thinner. There were lines on the scarred face that hadn't been there before. Or if they had, Tommy couldn't remember them.

'Goodbye, Dad.'

'Goodbye, son.' Jack swallowed hard, not trusting himself to speak further without embarrassment.

'Now come on, Mum, you promised you wouldn't break down,' Tommy smiled as the train drew alongside.

'I won't.'

He gave her a hug and kiss on the cheek. He could feel her trembling in his arms.

A few minutes later he was ensconced in a first-class

carriage, leaning out of the window. He was bitter about the fact Babs hadn't come.

The last door slammed shut and the guard waved his flag. Jack half raised a hand in farewell, while Hettie desperately clung on to his other arm.

The train juddered, and then moved off in a great exhalation of steam.

'Good luck, Tommy,' he distinctly heard Bell call out as he passed her.

He watched the station and Pitlochry recede until they finally vanished round a bend.

Settling back in a seat he smiled. The big adventure had begun at long, long last.

Regrets? Yes, he had those. But above all he was feeling a sense of excited anticipation at what lay ahead.

Chapter 18

'Tommy Riach got away safely,' Andrew announced on finding Rose sitting painting by the drawing-room window. He frowned when he saw Nancy there as well.

'That's good,' Rose muttered in reply, concentrating on her brush.

'Have you nothing else to do, Nancy?'

The brush paused in mid-stroke. 'I want her here with me, Andrew. All right?'

That irritated Andrew. The lass should have been busy, not idling her time away. 'If you wish.'

'I do.' That was stated emphatically.

Andrew crossed over and poured himself a whisky from the decanter. 'How's the painting coming along?'

'Fine.'

'Can I have a look?'

Now it was Rose's turn to be irritated. 'I've told you before, not until I'm finished.'

He shrugged. 'I'm just dying to see it, that's all.'

'When it's ready, Andrew, and not till then.'

This was Rose's first attempt at a picture which she'd been labouring over for several weeks now. She'd started it outside but had come in when the weather had turned colder. Her easel was surrounded by cloths to avoid getting paint on the carpet.

'How are Jack and Hettie?' Rose inquired.

'Not too bad, considering. I might drop by later to try and cheer them up. Want to come?'

Rose shook her head.

'I'm sure they'd appreciate you calling.'

'I've got far too much to do.'

That was a lie. She had precious little to do round the house now that Elspeth Campbell was in residence. She clearly just didn't want to go.

'Can I get you a drink, darling?'

'No thank you.'

Her tone was dismissive, he thought. It was obvious she didn't want him there.

'How long before you do finish?'

Rose paused in what she was doing and gave a long, drawn-out sigh. 'I really have no idea. But the more you keep interrupting me the longer it will be.'

'I'm sorry.'

She didn't reply to that.

Andrew could see that Nancy was embarrassed by this exchange which, under normal circumstances, would never have taken place in her presence. He wondered what the girl was making of her new role as lady's maid – and now companion it would seem. For more and more that's what Nancy was becoming. Rose's companion and shadow.

He found himself at a loss as to what to do with the rest of the afternoon stretching ahead of him. He could always go to the distillery of course, immerse himself in paperwork. But for once that didn't appeal.

'Will you stop fidgeting, you're distracting me,' Rose snapped angrily.

'I wasn't aware I was.'

'Well you are. It's hard enough to concentrate as it is without that.'

'I presume you prefer to be left alone,' he commented drily.

'It does help.'

Alone meant with only Nancy in attendance. 'You've done a lovely job with Mrs Drummond's hair today.' He smiled at the girl.

'Thank you, sir.'

'Is it a particular style?'

'No, just one I made up.'

'It certainly suits her.'

Nancy flushed.

'Andrew,' Rose murmured threateningly.

He drained his glass. 'I'm off then.'

Again Rose didn't reply.

He left the room, closing the door firmly behind him.

'Hello, McFarlane.'

The groom touched his forelock. 'Good day to you, sir. I haven't had you in here for a while.'

'No,' Andrew agreed. 'I haven't been in the mood for riding recently. How's Moonbeam?'

'In the pink, sir. In the pink.'

'I hope you've been exercising her regularly.'

McFarlane looked pained. 'Naturally, sir.' What he didn't say was that Rose had been riding the animal presuming, correctly, that Andrew knew nothing about that.

Andrew went to the horse who whinnied at his approach, trying to nuzzle into Andrew's hand when his nose was rubbed.

'It was a great shame about Strumpet,' Andrew said over his shoulder.

McFarlane's face clouded. 'Indeed, sir.'

'She was a good mare that.'

It was on the tip of McFarlane's tongue to tell Andrew what had really happened, but knew it would cost him his position if he did. Mrs Drummond would ensure that.

'Just dropped dead, eh?'

'That's correct, sir.'

'Terrible shame. Still, we should have a replacement soon. I know Mrs Drummond is trying to find one.'

Poor beast, McFarlane thought. He'd been asked by Rose to keep an ear to the ground and let her know if he heard of a suitable horse for sale. Well he hadn't, and even if he had, or did, he wouldn't be passing the information on. He loved animals too much to have that on his conscience.

Andrew was tempted to take Moonbeam out, but wasn't dressed to do so. Nor did he fancy returning to the house and getting changed.

'Do you have an apple, McFarlane?'

McFarlane smiled. 'Of course, sir. A right sweet and juicy one too. A proper treat.'

Moonbeam snickered as though he understood.

A proper gentleman, McFarlane thought as he went to fetch the apple. A joy to work for.

Unlike some he could name.

'I think I'll give the book a miss today,' Jack said as Hettie was clearing away the breakfast things.

She stopped and stared at him in astonishment. 'Are you feeling ill, Jack?'

He shook his head.

'Then what's wrong? Monday to Friday, you never take a day off once you start a project.'

'There's always the exception to the rule,' Jack replied softly.

'Are you stuck?'

'No.'

'What then?'

'I just don't want to write. I don't feel like it.'

Hettie replaced the dishes she was holding on the table. 'It's Tommy, isn't it?'

There was a long silence. 'Yes,' Jack finally admitted.

Hettie's shoulders sagged. 'I'm worried sick too, Jack. But we can't let it get on top of us. Life goes on regardless.'

Oh no it didn't, he thought. There were many in this war for whom it would cease abruptly. And Tommy, God help him, might be amongst them. But he knew that she meant life in general, not in particular.

Jack was in that state halfway between sleep and consciousness. Perhaps that was why it was all so vivid and real. Not just re-running memories, but as if he was actually back there.

It was a bright day somewhere on the Somme, and a dogfight was taking place high overhead.

He was drained, emotionally and physically. He'd slept after the previous night's foray into no-man's-land, but felt as though he hadn't. He'd have sold his soul for a shave, hot bath and, equally, a hot meal. As for a nice cosy bed with fresh linen, he'd have sold ten souls for that.

He stood with his back against the trench wall, watching the dogfight. The British planes were outnumbered, their German counterparts creating havoc.

A Nieuport exploded, he could clearly see bits of debris flying in all directions. Another boy lost. The German assailant sped off, seeking further victims.

Another British plane, a Sopwith this time, was hit, turning turtle and diving earthwards trailing a thick pall of black smoke in its wake.

A figure tumbled from the cockpit, the pilot. Enveloped in flames he frantically flapped his arms as he plummeted through the air. It was sickening to witness. Was the lad flapping to try to extinguish the flames or in a bid to fly himself? Who knew?

And then he heard it. Real or his imagination? He wasn't sure. A death scream of pure agony that made his flesh crawl and his breath catch in his throat.

How slowly the human ball of flame seemed to fall, and all the while the lad was still flapping.

It was an horrific, stomach-churning sight that made him want to vomit. Truly, a *danse macabre.*

Then the ball of flame vanished from sight, cut off by the top of the opposite trench wall. He slowly counted to three, by which time it must have been all over.

He stumbled into the dugout and sprawled on to his cot. Please God his own end wasn't like that, but clean and quick.

Please God.

'By the way, Nancy, I have a letter for you.' Elspeth had been waiting to catch Nancy alone, away from Rose for a change. This was because she'd recognised the handwriting. If Nancy elected to inform Mrs Drummond then that was her affair.

Nancy stared at the housekeeper. 'A letter for *me*?'

'That's right.' Elspeth fished in her pocket. 'Here you are.'

Nancy gazed at the letter in wonderment. Who on earth could be sending her a letter? She hadn't the foggiest. It was a mystery. 'Thank you.'

Elspeth went on her way while Nancy continued down the corridor to her room.

The trouble was, she couldn't really read. Bits and pieces, odd words, yes. But not read properly.

The signature was large, and bold, followed by crosses which she knew signified kisses.

D, she deciphered. Then R.

Nancy smiled. The letter was from Drew, her admirer. Had to be. Drew who'd sworn that one day he'd marry her. It was laughable really, he was only a boy. And yet, as he'd rightly pointed out, he was only a few years younger than herself.

She did her best, but couldn't make head nor tail of the letter's contents. The only way she was going to know what it said was to have it read for her. And she couldn't do that.

Still, and a warm glow filled her, it was nice to know he'd written. That he'd taken the trouble.

She recalled the night in the bathroom when he'd asked to see her naked and she, for some reason, had revealed herself. It made her shiver ever so slightly.

He'd be home again soon, she thought. The Christmas holidays weren't that far away.

He was going to be disappointed if he imagined he was going to get a reply. Even if she'd wanted to write, she couldn't.

She hid the letter amongst her belongings.

'What do you *do* all day long?' Pattie Williams asked Nancy, the pair of them sitting alongside one another at the evening meal.

Nancy glanced up the table at Mrs Owen, the new cook, a Welsh woman. Mrs Owen wasn't nearly as popular with the staff as Mrs Moffat had been. Nor was she as good a cook. In fact some of the dishes she produced were pretty unpalatable.

'This and that,' Nancy prevaricated. She didn't really want to talk about it, aware that some jealousy had grown up over her new status.

'But what exactly is this and that?' Pattie persisted.

Nancy wasn't enjoying the beef stew on her plate. The meat was tough, not nearly done long enough. But the vegetables were nice, if a trifle soggy. How she wished Mrs Moffat was back in the kitchen. You could never find fault with her.

'I do Mrs Drummond's hair,' Nancy said.

'And?'

'Help her dress.'

'And?'

'Oh, all manner of things, Pattie. I iron for her, of course, she's a stickler about that. I look after her wardrobe. Lay out clothes, put others away. Keep her company.'

Pattie shook her head. 'That's right jammy, so it is.'

It was too, Nancy reflected. Though she wasn't entirely happy with the situation. There was something very peculiar about Rose Drummond. A grown woman playing with dolls and a doll's house for example. Who'd ever heard the like? In many ways she wished she was back doing her old duties.

'I never asked to become a lady's maid,' Nancy reminded Pattie. 'It was offered. And don't tell me you'd have turned it down. I won't believe that.'

Pattie sighed. 'You're right. I'd have grabbed the chance.'

'So don't criticise.'

'I'm not criticising, Nancy.'

'Then stop being jealous.'

Pattie glared at Nancy. Then her expression softened. 'I suppose that's what I am.'

'It can be boring at times,' Nancy went on. 'Especially when she's painting. I have to sit there for hours on end, only replying when spoken to.' She smiled. 'It can give you a sore bum, sitting still for ages.'

Pattie laughed. 'I can imagine.'

'Tell me, can you read?'

Pattie blinked at this sudden change of subject. 'I'm not brilliant, but yes I can. Why?'

No, she daren't risk it, Nancy decided. If Pattie opened her yap it could get back to the mistress and who knew what the outcome of *that* would be. A son of the house simply didn't write to a maid, even a lady's maid. It just wasn't done. If Rose found out it would get them both in trouble, maybe for her even the sack.

'Oh, no reason,' Nancy shrugged. 'I just wondered.'

'Can't you?'

'I never really learnt. Didn't have the chance.'

'Well, perhaps some day.'

'Some day,' Nancy repeated wistfully. She doubted it.

*   *   *

'I've decided to spend a few days with Pa and Georgina,' Rose announced. 'Naturally I shall take Nancy with me.'

Andrew noted he hadn't been included. Not that he'd have gone, the present pressure at work was too great. But it would have been nice to be asked.

'Any particular reason?' he inquired casually.

'Should there be?'

Andrew sighed in exasperation. Why was she so often defensive. It wasn't as though he was trying to pry. Suddenly he wanted to be out of the room, away from Rose. It was becoming more and more difficult to be alone in her company. Truth was, he'd welcome a short respite from having her around and the strain it had become.

'I don't suppose so,' he muttered neutrally in reply.

Rose snorted. 'That's settled then.'

'When will you go?'

'Does it matter?'

He closed his eyes, took a deep breath, then slowly opened them again. 'Not in the least, darling.' He couldn't help the trace of sarcasm that tinged his voice when he spoke that last word.

'Shall we say Friday? Does that suit?'

'Perfectly.'

'And I shall probably return midway through the following week.'

He glanced at the mantelpiece clock. Too early yet to go to bed. He'd have another drink instead, he decided, his promise to Lesley about cutting down his intake long forgotten. He hadn't had a twinge of indigestion since going to Perth. He smiled ruefully to himself. Maybe the fright of possibly having an ulcer had scared it out of him.

'What are you grinning at? You look like a demented cat.'

'Was I grinning? I wasn't aware.'

'You were grinning, I assure you.'

He shrugged and continued reading his newspaper.

'Well?' That was said shrilly.

'Nothing, Rose, I told you, I didn't know I was grinning.'

She snorted again, this time in disbelief.

He glanced at her through half-lowered lids. There were occasions when Rose could appear quite ugly, and this was one of them. It was somehow the way she contrived to contort her features.

'I hope you'll give Willie and Georgina my regards,' he said.

'Of course.'

'And you might invite them for Christmas, should they care to come. Do you approve?'

Rose considered that. 'I'll decide towards the end of my stay there. It depends how that goes.'

'Well, it's entirely up to you.'

Rose knew she was being beastly, which upset her. One moment she could be happy as larry, the next . . . quite awful, wretched inside. And when like that she wanted to vent her spleen.

'It's a pity Drew isn't here,' Andrew went on. 'He could have gone along.'

'Yes, he and James are great friends.'

Andrew ran a hand over his forehead. He felt incredibly weary. Not tired, but weary. He was working too hard, he decided. He must do something about that.

Getting up from his chair he crossed to the decanter, pouring himself an extra large one. 'You, Rose?'

'No thank you.'

For a moment his head spun, then it was gone. How strange, he thought. He really was working too hard. 'I lost Duncan Sims today,' he stated.

'Duncan Sims?'

'One of the chaps at the distillery. He's been called up.'

'That's the second, isn't it?'

Andrew turned to face her and nodded. 'I'm going to be in a right pickle if there's any more. You can't just replace a skilled man as easily as that.'

'No,' Rose agreed.

'Still, I'll manage somehow. Dad did during the Great War and I will during this lot. Though it won't be easy.'

He downed his drink and poured himself another, instantly feeling better as the alcohol hit home. He contemplated going into the village and calling on Jack, then decided he wouldn't. He and Jack could have a few consecutive nights at the pub while Rose was away, if Hettie didn't object, that is. The prospect cheered him considerably.

Rose got up from where she was sitting. 'I'm off upstairs.'

He found that a relief. 'Have a good night's sleep.'

'I shall, thank you very much.' She hesitated, then added, 'And you.'

When she was gone Andrew slumped back into his chair. What a sorry state of affairs, he reflected. Not even a goodnight kiss, not that there had been for a while now. No sign of affection whatsoever. Strangers to each other they'd become, and strangers they remained.

It was enough to make an angel weep.

*   *   *

Some time later he paused outside her bedroom door. How often had he done that now? he wondered. Too often.

Should he make another effort or not? Try for a reconciliation between them. See if he could win his way back into her bed. *Their* bed.

God, how he ached with longing. It had been months now. His entire body was screaming for release.

She was being downright cruel in denying him, he thought in self-pity. Rose knew only too well what he was like. How much he needed the physical pleasures of life.

It would serve her right if he went elsewhere. She would only have herself to blame after all. Even if she didn't enjoy it, the least she could do, for his sake, was her wifely duty.

He turned away, stopped, and turned back again. The very thought of joining his body with hers had already roused him and caused him to break out in a cold sweat.

Taking a deep breath he tapped her door. 'Rose?'

There was no reply.

He tapped again, this time slightly louder. 'Rose, can I come in?'

Again there was no reply.

He bit his lip. As her light was off it could be she was fast asleep and just not hearing him. He tapped a third time, more a rap than a tap. 'Rose?'

Still no reply.

He sighed. What was he, man or mouse? Reaching out he grasped the door handle and twisted it.

The damn door was locked, he inwardly raged. Now where had she found the key for the lock, he hadn't seen it in years. He twisted again. No doubt about it, the door was firmly locked.

'Go away!'

Rose's voice was cold, commanding and had an authoritative ring about it that immediately took away all desire.

She wasn't sleeping after all, but wide awake. 'Bitch,' he muttered to himself. 'Bloody bitch.'

'The End,' Jack announced, and let out a long, heartfelt sigh.

Hettie glanced up at him, eyes glowing.

'That's it then,' he smiled. 'All finished. What do you think?'

'It's wonderful, Jack.'

'You wouldn't lie to me?'

She laughed. 'No, I wouldn't lie. It is wonderful. And if I may say, my heart's in my mouth.'

Now Jack laughed. 'Good. That's what I intended.'

Hettie shook her head. 'The twist in the final few pages caught me completely by surprise. I never saw it coming. And yet it's so right somehow.'

'I feel . . . liberated. Yes, that's it. Liberated. As though I've finally broken an extended bout of constipation.'

'Jack, that's awful!'

'But precisely how I feel. And a fabulous feeling it is.'

Hettie laid the dictation aside. 'I'll type this up later.'

'And in the meanwhile, why don't we celebrate?'

'In what way?'

'Upstairs.'

Hettie smiled. 'I can't think of anything I'd like better.'

'Me neither. Now come here, woman.'

She crossed to him, sitting on his lap when he patted it. He put an arm round her and drew her close. 'What would I ever have done without you, Hettie?' he said, a sudden husk in his throat.

'Or I you?'

'We were made for one another.'

'That's what I've always believed.'

'If only . . .' His expression darkened.

'If only what, Jack?'

'Tommy,' he whispered.

The happiness oozed out of her. The cloud that had descended over Jack now extended to her. 'Yes.'

'I worry so much about him, Hettie.'

'I know. As do I.'

He shuddered, his nightmares returning. Nightmares that were haunting him night after night. He wondered what Tommy was doing at that moment. Training, he presumed. Had to be. His letters said he was thoroughly enjoying himself. Revelling in it.

But it was early days yet. The real horrors of war were still to come. Lurking over the horizon.

'Let's go for a walk first,' Jack suggested.

'Good idea.'

'Get a breath of fresh air. Blow the cobwebs away.'

'Whatever you wish.'

Neither of them mentioned Tommy again that day.

Andrew had dined alone, Rose having departed for The Haven earlier, and was now off to meet Jack in the pub. With Rose away, and Jack having finished his book, no doubt it would be an extended session with the pair of them probably ending up back at Jack's. But first he wanted to stop in at his study to jot down a work reminder, something he often did in the evenings.

In a good mood, he was humming as he snapped on the overhead study light. He smiled in remembrance of how fond his father Murdo had been of this particular room. It had been his sanctuary, the holy of holies, no one normally being allowed inside except Murdo himself.

Andrew started for his desk, then came up short when he saw what was propped up on it. A watercolour painting.

Rose's, he guessed correctly. She'd finally completed it and left it on his desk as a surprise. He thought that rather touching.

Swiftly he crossed over to study the painting up close. Not bad at all, he mused. He'd certainly seen a lot worse in his time.

He recognised the scene, there was no mistaking it, though Rose had added certain bushes, trees and shrubs that weren't actually there. Why she'd done that he had no idea. Artistic licence, he supposed.

The painting certainly merited being framed and he wondered where they might hang it. In the study perhaps? That was a possibility. But he'd leave the final choice of place to Rose.

She must be pleased with it, he thought. She'd hardly have left it on his desk otherwise. And she had every right to be.

And then he saw it. A tiny figure, almost obscured by bushes. It was that of a young child, a girl, staring out. A girl whose face was a combination of his own and Rose's.

'Mary,' he whispered. That must be who the child represented. Who else? The wee lassie Rose had lost.

Not only his face and Rose's, it suddenly dawned on him, but that of another person as well. Yes, quite definitely, that of another person. But who?

An icy coldness gripped him, his skin prickling with gooseflesh.

He felt sick inside.

Chapter 19

'So what do you think?' Willie Seaton queried.

The mare was similar to Strumpet in many ways, the same colour but with slightly different markings. A friendly beast, she nuzzled into Rose's hand.

'She's beautiful, Pa.'

'I thought you'd like her. She's yours. A present from me.'

'Oh Pa!' Rose exclaimed excitedly. 'What's her name?'

'Gypsy.'

'Gypsy,' Rose repeated in a murmur. 'You and I are going to be great pals.'

Gypsy snickered her pleasure.

'I'll arrange to have her taken to Drummond House so you've no worries on that account.'

'How old is she?'

'Three.'

Rose wanted to ride her there and then, and promised herself she'd do so at the earliest opportunity. 'I'm so thrilled, Pa. Thank you.'

'Do I get a kiss from my girl?'

'Of course.'

Willie beamed as he was pecked on the cheek.

'She's a perfect woman's horse,' Willie went on. 'Spirited, but not fiery. Easily managed. You shouldn't have any trouble with her.'

They stayed in the stables for a few more minutes, then emerged again into cold winter sunshine. Willie coughed. 'I haven't had a chance to speak to you alone yet. Are you fully recovered?'

She stared blankly at him.

'From what happened. The, eh . . . baby.'

'Oh, that! More or less.'

He frowned. 'What does more or less mean?'

'It's not something you ever fully get over, Pa. It'll always be with me.'

'Aye,' he sympathised. 'I can understand that.'

'It's like losing part of yourself. Which of course a baby is. It's terribly hard to explain.'

Willie thought of his first wife Mary who'd died from influenza and the pain that had caused him. He was no stranger to loss and grief.

'You'll be trying again, I take it?'

'For another child?'

He nodded.

'That's not entirely in our hands, Pa. We had to wait long enough the last time, who knows what'll happen in the future.' She smiled inwardly at her prevarication. She'd managed to answer the question without answering it.

Willie cleared his throat. 'Yes, quite so.'

They walked a little way in silence. 'Is Andrew well?'

'Couldn't be better. Working extremely hard mind you, thanks to the war. Demand has risen due to exports. In fact not only risen but is positively booming. There are times when Andrew says he doesn't know whether he's coming or going.'

'Booming, eh?' Willie chuckled. 'Well, that's no bad thing. More demand means more profits, a very satisfactory state of affairs. Pity it's due to war though.'

'Yes,' she agreed.

Rose slipped an arm round her father's. 'It's good to be back, Pa. To see you and The Haven again.'

'You should visit more often.'

'Perhaps I will,' she smiled. 'And thank you again for Gypsy. She's a lovely present.'

'There's absolutely nothing wrong with Rose,' Willie declared to Georgina later that day as they were dressing for dinner. 'I had a long chat with her earlier and there was no sign whatsoever of anything untowards. So I was right, we needn't have worried after all.'

'You must admit what happened in Edinburgh when she and I were there *was* strange, Willie. Rose looking at baby clothes and toys. Bizarre in the circumstances.'

Willie shrugged. 'If there was anything wrong, something playing on her mind, it's gone now. She's right as rain. I don't think I've ever seen her looking better.'

Georgina remained unconvinced. There was something about Rose that was eluding her, something she couldn't quite put her finger on. There again, as Willie had originally said, it might simply be her imagination.

'She was delighted with the horse,' Willie went on. 'Thrilled was the word she used.'

'It was very kind of you to give it to her.'

'Not in the least. She may be a married woman but

she's still my daughter. Anyway, I got as much pleasure out of giving it to her as she did receiving it.'

What a good man Willie was, Georgina reflected, not for the first time. One of the best. A real gem. She doubted there was a mean bone in his body.

It shamed her to remember how she'd once betrayed him with Andrew Drummond, and that James was Andrew's son. Still, all that was in the past, buried if not entirely forgotten. Willie would never find out. She'd never say anything, and neither would Andrew. Her secret was safe, thank the Lord.

'They've invited us there for Christmas and Hogmanay,' Willie announced.

'Oh?'

'I said we'd go.' He rounded on Georgina. 'That's all right I take it. Perhaps I should have spoken to you before accepting?'

'It's absolutely fine by me, Willie. I'll enjoy myself. And I'm sure James will.'

'That's what I thought. It'll be a nice break for the pair of us.'

He was fiddling with a gold cuff-link, one of a pair Georgina had given him. 'Damn thing,' he muttered.

She smiled. 'Here, let me.'

'She's all saddled up and ready to go,' the groom declared to Rose who'd arrived in the stables to take Gypsy out.

What a handsome creature, Rose thought. Dark swarthy looks, strong face, broad shoulders, narrow waist. He might have stepped straight from the pages of a romantic novel.

'What's your name?' she asked in a voice suddenly grown husky.

'Andy, ma'am. Andy Somerville.'

She was staring at him. He exuded raw masculinity and charisma. Rose was mesmerised by the oozing magnetism of the man.

Rose accepted Gypsy's reins when Andy handed them to her. 'And how long have you been at The Haven?' she inquired.

'Just over a year now. I was on the land before that but always fancied working with horses. When I heard this job was going I applied and was lucky enough to be taken on.'

'And which cottage are you in, Andy?' It was bound to be on the estate.

'Rose Cottage, ma'am.'

That made her smile. 'I know it. Tell me, are you married, Andy?'

'Oh no, ma'am. There's plenty of time for that. I intends remaining a bachelor for some while yet.'

Now that was interesting. 'I'll bet you have lots of lady friends?'

He regarded her curiously, wondering why she'd asked that. 'They come and they go, Mrs Drummond. Nothing serious, which is how I wants it.'

'I see.' She wanted to stay longer, but couldn't think of a reason for doing so.

'Is there anything else, Mrs Drummond? If not I'll get on.'

'That's all for now, Andy. Thank you.'

She led Gypsy outside and mounted, glancing back into the stables before she moved off. Her last glimpse of Andy Somerville was him bending over, backside pointing in her direction.

A wave of pure lust flamed inside her.

*   *   *

'Can I have a word, Mr Drummond?'

Andrew, sitting in front of the fire after his evening meal, instantly roused himself. He'd been lost in thought.

'Please do.'

Elspeth Campbell carefully closed the door behind her and came closer to Andrew.

He was smiling, pleased to see the housekeeper. 'Now what's bothering you?'

Elspeth folded her hands in front of her. 'It's a delicate matter.'

'Oh?'

'I believe Mrs Owen has been taking wine from the cellar.'

Andrew leant forward fractionally. This was serious. 'Are you sure?'

'Only she and I have keys and a number of bottles are missing. A dozen, maybe more.'

'It's a large cellar, Elspeth, even I couldn't say what's down there.'

Her face hardened. 'I know what I've removed on instruction and what I haven't. Bottles have disappeared that should still be there.'

'Well well,' Andrew mused. He was surprised to say the least. He'd never have guessed from Mrs Owen's prim and proper manner that she had a taste for alcohol. 'Have you found any empties?'

Elspeth shook her head. 'I took the liberty of looking in her room and there wasn't any trace. So wherever she's put them it isn't there.'

Andrew gestured to the chair opposite. 'Come and sit down, Elspeth. I could use some company.'

She blushed. 'I couldn't possibly do that. I'm on duty and . . . well it just wouldn't be right.'

Andrew rose from his chair. 'At least join me in a drink. In fact, I insist.'

That flustered Elspeth. 'I said, I'm on duty.'

'I heard you, and I still insist. One drink isn't going to do any harm.'

She relented, thinking she'd enjoy a drink with Andrew. 'What if someone comes in?'

He laughed. 'I'm the employer, Elspeth, don't forget that. If I wish to have a dram with my housekeeper then who's to criticise.' He added, ominously, 'They'd just better not, that's all.'

'In which case I'll have a sherry please.'

As Andrew was pouring he had a sudden thought, one that brought a smile to his face. He had the address somewhere and would write before going to bed that night. As for Mrs Owen, she was a rotten cook anyway.

Elspeth stayed for nearly half an hour before Andrew would let her go.

A half hour that gave them both great pleasure.

'I'm missing David so much,' Bell said to Irene, as they neared the end of the day's shift.

'Is he still writing?'

'Oh aye. Though not as often as I write to him.'

Their hands were moving deftly as they spoke. They'd been doing the job for so long it didn't need any concentration.

'Where is he again?'

Bell reminded Irene. 'He says it's a bleak place with none of the comforts of home.'

Irene pulled a sympathetic face. 'Any news of leave yet?'

'None. He was hoping to get back for new year's but that's not on apparently.'

'Pity.'

Bell thought of their sessions behind her house. She missed those as well, dreadfully. She wondered what she missed most, David or that? A combination of both, she decided.

'I heard on the wireless there's been some air raids on the south coast,' Irene stated.

'I heard that as well.'

'It'll be London next. You wait and see.'

'I've always wanted to go there.'

'London!'

'Just for a few days like. It must be wonderful.'

'Certainly different to Dalneil,' Irene replied drily.

They both laughed.

'Just a bit.'

'You could always go on your honeymoon there,' Irene suggested.

Bell had never thought of that. 'So we could. Mind you, it can't be that much fun at the moment, what with the blackout and all.'

'It must still be London. There might not be as much going on as before the war, but there again, possibly there is. Anyway, it couldn't fail to be a great experience for you.'

Bell decided she'd mention it to David in her next letter.

A honeymoon in London! That would be something to remember for the rest of her life.

Rose strode into the stables, her face bright with exhilaration. Steam was coming off Gypsy in clouds.

Andy paused in forking hay. 'You look as though you've enjoyed yourself.'

It was the third time Rose had taken Gypsy out, and she had thoroughly enjoyed herself. She hadn't pushed Gypsy too hard though. Partly because of what had happened to Strumpet, and partly because there were far more eyes on the estate than at home.

'I did, I can assure you.'

His shirt was sodden with sweat and consequently sticking to him, she noted. It threw his chest and shoulders into sharp relief.

What an Adonis, she thought yet again. The sort of man to make a maiden's heart melt. Well, she was no maiden, she reminded herself. Far from it. But she was affected nonetheless.

Andy crossed to her and held out his hands for the reins.

'No, I'll rub her down and feed her myself,' Rose smiled. That was simply an excuse to remain with Andy.

'If you like.'

'Is there any tea going?'

'I can brew up a cup if you wish.'

'Then let's have some. I'm parched.'

She could suddenly smell him which made her go weak at the knees. She fought back the mad, insane impulse to leap on him and rip the clothes from his body.

This was ridiculous, she thought. What on earth was making her think in such an outrageous way? It didn't make sense.

She stared hungrily at him as he moved off to where the kettle was kept.

'Jack!'

'Is that you, John?'

The Reverend John McLean, Andrew's brother-in-law,

hurried over to Jack standing just inside the church doorway. 'I've never seen you in here during the week before.'

A wry expression creased Jack's face. 'I felt the need to come. I hope that's all right?'

'Of course. It's God's house, open to all. You're more than welcome any time you wish.'

Jack took a deep breath. 'It's always so peaceful in here. That and . . . somehow reassuring.'

John nodded his understanding. 'A haven of tranquillity from the troubled world outside.'

'And troubled it surely is.'

'Aye,' John said softly. 'And it's going to get a lot more troubled before it gets better.'

'I wish I could disagree with you, but I can't.' Jack smiled. 'Are we alone?'

'Quite.'

'Am I disturbing you?'

'Not in the least. I wasn't doing anything I can't do later.' John hesitated. 'Is there something special brings you today?'

'Only to pray.'

'I understand. There are many have been coming to do that lately.' He hesitated again. 'It's Tommy, isn't it?'

'Yes,' Jack admitted quietly.

'A good lad.'

'He's joined the RAF you know.'

'Yes, I know.'

'They'll be at the sharp end. And not before too long I shouldn't imagine. I . . .' Jack trailed off as emotion welled within him. He couldn't bear the thought of losing Tommy. Or worse still, and there were many such scenarios. Some just too horrendous to contemplate.

'Would you like me to pray with you, Jack?'

'Would you?'

'Of course. Now where would you care to sit?'

'Not my usual pew, but right at the front.'

'Do you wish me to help or can you manage by yourself?'

'If you'll take my arm.'

When they reached the pew, instead of sitting Jack knelt on the floor and bowed his head. John did likewise.

'Let us pray,' John began.

Andrew hung up the telephone. That had been Rose to say she intended stopping off in Edinburgh *en route* to do some shopping. She'd stay overnight and then resume her journey on a mid-morning train.

She'd been distant during the call and that had been nothing to do with the line either. Cold, aloof almost. Not a trace of warmth or affection in her voice.

He'd made a joke about not going overboard and spending too much, which had gone down like the proverbial lead balloon. When he'd inquired how things were going she'd replied fine and not elaborated. Her goodbye had been almost curt.

Andrew sighed, ran a hand over his face, and thought how weary he was. Bone weary.

He'd have an early night, he decided.

'Where's Andy?' Rose demanded of Jenkins, the senior groom who was an old man teetering on retirement.

'Gone home, Mrs Drummond.'

'Home?' Andy had been there when she'd taken Gypsy out for a ride. 'Is something wrong?'

'No, Mrs Drummond. It's his half-day.'

'I see,' she murmured, bitterly disappointed. She'd been going to attend to Gypsy herself but now Jenkins could do that.

She left the stables in a right old temper.

'Are you all right, Rose?' Georgina inquired across the dinner table.

Rose started. 'Yes. Yes of course.'

'You've hardly touched your food,' Willie commented with a frown.

'I'm not really that hungry for some reason.'

The reason was Andy Sommerville; she just couldn't get him out of her mind. A mind running riot with lecherous thoughts which, on the one hand, were inflaming her, on the other, making her feel deeply ashamed.

She'd only ever been to bed with Andrew and couldn't help wondering what it would be like with another man. Andy Somerville in particular. A picture conjured up in her mind made her shiver.

'You're not ill, are you?' Willie asked anxiously.

'No, Pa. I've just lost my appetite tonight, that's all.'

Rose glanced at Georgina. She hadn't mentioned her intended stop-off in Edinburgh to either her or Willie in case Georgina suggested accompanying her. She didn't want her stepmother along this time.

Later she was aware of Georgina watching her keenly, which both annoyed and alarmed her.

It was as if Georgina knew what she was thinking.

The clock on the mantelpiece chimed midnight. Rose was sitting by her bedroom window staring out, a fire burning brightly in the small grate giving the room its only illumination. Ghostly shadows were dancing on the wall opposite the fire.

Rose was in her night-things including a heavy quilted dressing gown of a Far Eastern style. Despite the hour she didn't feel the least bit tired.

There was a fever in her that was keeping her awake. A red-hot fever of longing and desire.

She had to do something about this, she thought. She just *had* to. But what?

She couldn't just throw herself at Andy. Think of the humiliation if he rejected her.

But he wouldn't. She was almost certain of that. The previous afternoon she'd caught him staring at her out of the corner of his eye in a way that left no doubt he was attracted to her.

'Oh God,' she moaned, shifting in her chair. If she was on fire inside then it was a veritable furnace down there. A furnace clamouring to be attended to.

'Rose Cottage,' she said, and smiled. How apt. How very apt. An omen you could say. Of all the cottages on the estate Andy had to live in that one.

The mantelpiece clock ticked relentlessly on.

The house was deathly quiet, everyone, with the exception of her, abed when Rose slipped outside.

She shivered with cold, hastily pulling her coat more tightly about herself. It was pitch black, but that didn't hinder her. She knew exactly where she was going.

The cottage was in darkness as she'd expected it to be. There was a gentle wind causing the branches of some nearby trees to rustle spookily.

Rose stopped in front of the door and stared at it. What if Andy had someone with him? It was possible as he did have lady friends from time to time, though nothing serious he'd assured her.

She shook her head, aware of her heart thumping nineteen to the dozen. Turn back, she counselled herself. Turn back before it's too late!

But her body wouldn't allow her to do that. It was insistent, demanding gratification. Crying out for it.

She knocked and waited.

No reply.

Rose swore, and knocked a second time.

What if he wasn't in? What if he was elsewhere?

'Andy?' she heard herself call out. 'Andy!'

There were sounds from within, those of cautious movement. A light blossomed in the window only feet away.

'Who is it?'

'Rose Drummond.'

There was a pause, broken by the scrape of bolts being retracted. The door was thrown open to reveal Andy, clad only in a shirt that came almost to his knees, holding a paraffin lamp.

'Holy God,' he whispered. 'What are you doing here?'

She brushed past him. 'Shut that quickly,' she breathed.

The room she found herself in was relatively warm with the remains of a fire glowing cherry red in the grate. A glance round confirmed it to be a typical single man's domicile, messy with dishes piled in the sink. There were no feminine touches anywhere.

He came to stand beside her, his expression a combination of puzzlement and concern.

'Mrs Drummond?'

'You know why I've come.'

He studied her hard. 'Do I?'

'Don't play the innocent with me, Andy Somerville. You know precisely why.'

He visibly relaxed, his eyes twinkling. 'I reckon I does.'

She undid her coat, shrugged her shoulders and allowed the coat to drop to the floor. All she was wearing underneath was her nightdress.

'I reckon I does,' Andy repeated softly.

There was no reneging now; she was committed. 'Well?' She was amazed by her boldness.

Andy reached out and ran a calloused hand over her breast. Rose moaned in response.

Now using both hands he grasped hold of the front of her nightie and, in one violent movement, ripped it apart and from her, leaving Rose standing totally naked.

'Beautiful,' he whispered. 'You're a real beauty, Mrs Drummond. My oath and you are.'

And so was he, she thought. So was he. She trembled all over.

Taking her by the wrist he hurried her through to the bedroom.

Rose sat bolt upright. Had it been a dream? Had she imagined it? No, it had been real. She'd gone to Andy's cottage, returning to The Haven as dawn was breaking.

What had she done! screamed in her head. And yet she had done it. In the most wanton fashion.

She closed her eyes, remembering all that had occurred. How he'd . . .

Shame filled her, that and remorse. Guilt above all. How could she do such a thing when she loved Andrew?

For the first time it dawned on her they both had the

same Christian name. Andrew, Andy. Somehow that made it even worse.

And then a terrifying thought struck her. What if . . . what if . . . She swallowed hard. What if Andy had made her pregnant? How could she possibly explain a pregnancy to Andrew whom she hadn't slept with in months?

It was unlikely, true. But possible all the same. Who was to say the trouble she'd had conceiving in the past wasn't Andrew's fault? If that was so then it could be oh so different with Andy.

Fear gripped her, the fear of producing a bastard, the fear of losing Andrew, of divorce.

For she loved Andrew. When all was said and done she loved her husband. Incredible as that might seem after what had happened the previous night.

There was only one thing for it, she decided. As soon as she was home she and Andrew had to make love. That way there wouldn't be any discrepancy in dates, should she be pregnant, though God forbid!

Yes, that was it. Had to be.

Rose hung her head and began to cry. What had possessed her? What!

Chapter 20

'Is something wrong, Mr Drummond?'
   'Just tired, that's all, Kelly.'
   The book-keeper thought how pale and drawn Andrew had looked recently. The man was clearly overdoing it. 'Would you like a dram, sir?'
   Andrew considered that. 'You know, I believe I would.'
   'I'll pour it for you, sir.'
   'Will you join me, Kelly?'
   'No thank you, if you don't mind.'
   Andrew rubbed his eyes which were painful. That was another thing, he was having trouble with his sight of late. A visit to the optician would be in order he decided, smiling at a vision of himself wearing glasses. Still, he couldn't really complain. Many men wore spectacles at his age.
   He recalled the dashing young blade he'd once been, his sight had been perfect then. As had his figure which had now expanded somewhat over the past few years. Not too much, mind, but certainly a bit.

'There you are,' Kelly declared, placing a glass in front of Andrew.

Weary, God he was weary. Normally he would have considered a holiday, but he could hardly do that in wartime. It didn't seem right somehow.

Andrew glanced up at the attentive Kelly, another well past fighting age. 'Why were you so hard on Tommy Riach?' he asked softly.

Kelly blinked, having been caught off guard. 'I wasn't particularly aware I was.'

'Yet he said you were.'

Kelly's brow furrowed. 'If anything I was trying to teach him discipline, towards his work that is. He could be very lackadaisical.'

Andrew smiled. How often had his father Murdo accused him of that? He hated to think. But it had all come right in the end, time and maturity had seen to that.

'Your problem, Mr Kelly, is you don't have any children.'

Kelly frowned. 'Pardon?'

'You've never learnt to make allowances for youth. You have to when you're a parent.'

'There was never anything personal in it,' Kelly replied hurriedly.

'I believe that. But Tommy thought there was. He told Jack he disliked you as much as you disliked him.'

Kelly was appalled. 'I never disliked the lad, it simply isn't true. He irritated me, I can't deny that. And occasionally it went beyond irritation. But I certainly never disliked him. On the contrary, I thought he had the makings of a fine traveller. The potential was there.'

'Did you ever tell him that?'

'Of course not,' Kelly spluttered.

'Perhaps you should have done, eh?'

Kelly took a deep breath. 'Are you blaming me for his leaving, sir?'

'No, not really. I know he flounced off in the huff but I think he'd have come back again after I'd had a word with him and sorted things out. But he'd have eventually gone off to war anyway and been lost to us. At least for the duration.'

Andrew had a sip of whisky, closing his eyes in appreciation as it rolled smoothly down his throat. He'd put his single malt up against any distilled in Scotland. If it wasn't the best it certainly ranked high amongst them. A tribute to the skills of his forebears.

'I hope he returns safe and sound when it's all over,' Kelly said. 'I'd hate the idea of anything happening to him.'

'Amen,' Andrew murmured, thinking of Jack and Hettie.

'Amen,' he repeated.

The atmosphere during dinner had been frosty. In fact it had been more than that, it had been downright glacial. Now they were alone Andrew knew what was coming, and it amused him.

'So, why did you get rid of Mrs Owen?' Rose demanded in a steely voice. Her intention had been to be all sweetness and light towards Andrew but that had swiftly evaporated when she'd discovered what had occurred in her absence.

'She was stealing and I can't have that.'

'What did she steal?'

'Wine from the cellar. Miss Campbell noticed the missing bottles and as only she and Mrs Owen, plus me of course, had the keys then it had to be her.'

Rose harumphed. 'Is Miss Campbell certain about that?'

'Yes, she is.'

'There wasn't any mistake?'

'None.'

Rose was angry, seeing this as a direct challenge to her authority.

'Besides,' Andrew went on slowly, 'she wasn't much of a cook. Not a patch on Mrs Moffat.'

'Which is why you re-hired Mrs Moffat I suppose?'

'We were lucky there. I wrote to her sister in Stirling asking what had happened to her and surprisingly she was still available, not having found any other suitable employment in the meantime. I re-engaged her by telephone and, happily, back she came.'

Andrew smiled, not having told Rose that he'd had to be most persuasive for Mrs Moffat to agree. Nor that he'd upped Mrs Moffat's salary.

Rose's lips became a thin slash of disapproval. 'I find what you've done quite unacceptable, Andrew.'

'Oh?'

'Have you forgotten why she was dismissed in the first place?'

'Not at all. But she wasn't dismissed, she resigned. More or less forced to by you. Anyway, let bygones be bygones, Mrs Moffat belongs here. It's almost as much her home as it is ours.'

Rose stared balefully at Andrew, furious now. 'What you did was strictly against my wishes.'

He raised an eyebrow which infuriated her even further.

'I will not have her here,' Rose snapped.

'She stays, and that's that. What's more, you will stop

interfering in the kitchen now that you're not responsible for the housekeeping duties any more. Understand?'

Rose coloured. She wasn't used to being spoken to this way, by Andrew or anyone else.

'Understand?' Andrew repeated ominously.

'I want her sacked.'

'She stays.'

'I . . .'

'It's what *I* want in this case, Rose,' he interjected. 'She stays, and that's that.'

'I won't . . .'

'You'll do as you're bloody well told,' he cut in.

Rose scrambled to her feet and, looking straight ahead, without another word swept from the room.

Andrew waited till she'd gone before laughing softly. He'd enjoyed that. The trouble was he'd indulged Rose too much in the past. Well that was over.

And about time too.

How could she go to him tonight? It was now impossible. Out of the question after how he'd spoken to her downstairs. Damn that Mrs Owen for a thief. Stupid woman.

Rose was still seething inside. Positively livid. Well, a few nights either way wouldn't make any difference, she assured herself. Months yes, but hardly nights.

She'd go to Andrew when she was ready. But it had to be soon.

Just in case.

Dog tired as he was, Andrew had been unable to sleep. His mind had kept whizzing round and round. A jumble of memories from the past, matters concerning work, Rose.

In the end he'd decided to get up and seek out Elspeth

Campbell, hoping to find her in the kitchen. He only wanted to talk, have some company, perhaps get a little sympathy.

He stopped when he came in sight of the kitchen to see that the light wasn't on. 'Damn,' he swore, disappointed.

Go into the kitchen anyway and make a cup of tea, or return to bed? Elspeth might well turn up shortly after all. There was always that possibility.

Nearly an hour, and several cups of tea later, he gave it up as a bad job and went back to his room.

It was the following morning that Andrew ran into Nancy in the corridor. He came up short to stare at her in astonishment for she was wearing a tailored dress, an expensive one too from the look of it, instead of her usual uniform.

The dress had a neat, bloused top with pocket-like tabs. There was a swoopy skirt and set-in belt which gave it a smooth waistline, with half-sash ties at the front. The sleeves were long, the colour dark cadet blue.

These niceties were quite lost on Andrew who saw only a dress. 'Nancy?'

'Good morning, Mr Drummond.'

'Good morning to you.' He cleared his throat. 'That's a pretty outfit.'

She flushed. 'Thank you, sir.'

'But shouldn't you be wearing your uniform?'

'Mrs Drummond doesn't want me in a uniform any more, sir. She bought me this and other clothing in Edinburgh. Her instructions are that I'm to wear them now.'

Andrew recalled the painting Rose had left in his study as it suddenly struck him who the other face, apart from his and Rose's, had been reflected in that of the child. He could see now that it was Nancy's.

'I see,' he murmured. 'Most unusual I must say.'

'Those are her instructions, sir.'

'Then you must carry them out.'

'Yes, sir. Can I be excused, sir? Mrs Drummond is waiting for me.'

'Of course. On you go.'

He watched her hurry away with a chill of some nameless fear running through him.

'I haven't had a chance to say yet, but I liked your painting,' Andrew commented that evening.

Rose glanced across at him. 'I'm pleased.'

'It's very good. I thought I might hang it in my study, unless you have another preference?'

She shook her head. 'Your study will be fine.'

'When will you start the next one?'

'Not till the new year sometime. The holidays are almost upon us and Drew will shortly be home. And of course we have Pa and the family coming. So I think I'll leave it till the new year.'

'Yes, it was very interesting,' he said slowly.

He sensed her suddenly become wary, though it didn't show. Ask about the child, or not? He decided not.

A silence fell between them.

Andrew had never stopped halfway through making love before, far less with Rose, but he did now. Extricating himself he rolled over on to his back.

'Andrew?'

'What?'

'Is something wrong?'

'Only that I may as well be making love to a corpse. It's most offputting to say the least.'

Rose turned her head away. 'I'm sorry.'

'I can't think why you came if you're not really interested.'

She didn't reply to that.

He remembered the last time she'd been, and the time before. There was no comparison between that Rose and this. Then she'd been wild in the extreme, abandoned, passionate almost beyond belief. Now . . . nothing. No response whatsoever. As he'd said, it was most offputting. Eerie.

'I'm sorry,' Rose repeated.

'Is it ever again going to be as it once was between us?' he asked sadly.

Again Rose didn't reply.

Time, Lesley had told him. Time. But God, it was hard to bear. It was an ongoing torture. And now this which was even worse than her not coming to him at all.

Pity welled in Rose. For Andrew, for herself. How her entire world had changed in a relatively short while. She hardly recognised herself as the Rose who'd gone to Glasgow with Andrew.

'Was it a sense of duty? Or guilt perhaps?' Andrew queried, again sadly.

It had been neither of course, but the necessity to ensure she was covered where Andy Somerville was concerned. How she regretted that incident.

'Can we try again?'

There was no response from Andrew.

'Please?'

He twisted round to look at her. 'Is there any point?'

'Yes,' she murmured.

He'd completely lost the notion, which was extremely unusual for him. Unheard of even. He'd always had the notion where women were concerned.

'Please, Andrew?' Rose repeated, a sting of tears in her eyes.

Reaching out he drew her to him, she snuggling up against his chest. 'That's nice,' she whispered.

He stroked her hair, and she closed her eyes while he did.

After a while the hand moved from her hair to her shoulders, and then to her breasts which he gently caressed.

Rose thought of Andy Somerville. Up until then she hadn't realised how expert Andrew was in the art of lovemaking. Or that he was gifted with a stamina many men weren't.

With Andy it had been rough, he using her, plundering her body for his own satisfaction with no real thought to her needs. True, it had been exciting, but only up to a point.

It was so different with Andrew. He played her the way a master musician does an instrument, extracting sweet music of the very highest degree.

Rose sighed, feeling herself begin to respond to his touch. 'Oh, Andrew,' she whispered.

His own desire returned.

As had happened previously, when he awoke in the morning she was gone, leaving just a lingering hint of her scent.

Rose gathered Drew into her arms. 'Welcome home, son.'

He wanted to be with her, desperately so, and yet at the same time was uncomfortable. He'd never forget it was because of him that she'd lost the baby.

Rose held him at arms' length. 'Now what do you want to do?'

'Go over to the distillery and see Dad. I shall work there during the holidays.'

Rose raised an eyebrow. 'Really?'

He broke away from her. 'I enjoy it, Mum. There's so much to learn and do.'

'And what about when James comes?'

Drew shrugged. 'There will be the evenings and days off. We can be together then.'

'I'm not so sure I approve of this.' Rose frowned.

'Approve of what?'

'Your working at the distillery. During the summer's fine, it keeps you occupied. But Christmas and new year?'

His expression became stubborn. 'The distillery will be mine one day, Mum. I want to know everything about it there is. So why not start my education early?'

A Drummond through and through, she thought. There was a lot of Andrew in him. And Murdo, his grandfather. Perhaps even more of the latter from what she'd heard, never actually having met the man.

Drew wondered where Nancy was, at which point, as though on cue, she entered the room. He took in the fact she wasn't in uniform.

'Hello, Master Drew.' Nancy smiled. She'd been a little worried about his homecoming, but now realised she was pleased to see him. He'd changed a bit, she thought. He was somehow more mature.

Drew's eyes sparkled. 'Hello, Nancy.'

'When did you get in?'

'Just now. Only a few minutes ago.'

'Pleased to be back?'

He pulled a face. 'Anything's better than school.'

She laughed, thinking him lucky to be going to school in the first place. But she didn't say so.

'Nancy and I are off out shortly, a women's meeting,' Rose said to Drew. 'To do with the war effort.'

'Then I'll just get on up to the distillery.'

'Would you like something to eat before you go?'

He shook his head. 'Not till later, Mum, thank you.'

During his walk to the distillery all he could think of was how nice Nancy had looked. He'd somehow contrive to speak to her alone later.

Bell burst into the room where her two brothers, as usual, were squabbling. 'Will the pair of you shut the fuck up!' she screamed.

They stopped and stared at her in amazement.

'It's like bedlam in this bloody house. There's never any peace and most of that's down to you.'

Not waiting for a reply she went out again, slamming the door behind her.

Her father was in the living room sitting slumped in front of the fire still filled with ashes from the previous night. He was fast asleep and snoring, drunk, judging by the empty bottles strewn by the side of his chair.

'Jesus Christ,' she muttered, shaking her head. What a family. God alone knew where her mother had got to. And what a tip the place was!

She thought in despair of David, and the home they'd planned together, for the time being cruelly snatched from her because of this stupid war.

There was no tea, unless she made something herself, and she couldn't be bothered to do that. She'd eat later.

She'd go to Irene's, she decided. Have a natter with her. Anything was better than staying in this hellhole.

Her father, true to form, lifted a buttock just then and farted loudly.

Bell fled.

'She's a cracker right enough,' McFarlane declared to Rose, rubbing Gypsy's muzzle.

Willie and Georgina, who'd brought the horse with them, were also present.

'She's to have Strumpet's old stall,' Rose instructed McFarlane.

'Yes, Mrs Drummond,' he replied, touching a forelock.

'I'll be taking her out first thing in the morning. Make sure she's ready.'

McFarlane nodded that he understood.

'Let's have tea then,' Rose tinkled to Willie and Georgina. Talking together the three of them started back for the house.

McFarlane stared sympathetically at Gypsy, thinking what a fine beast she was. Well cared for too, that was obvious. Mr Seaton's groom clearly knew his business.

'Well, Gypsy,' he murmured, patting the horse's flank. 'I only hope that bitch doesn't ride you into the ground as she did Strumpet. But we'll have to wait and see about that.'

Shaking his head he led Gypsy towards her new stall.

Nancy yawned as she headed for her room. It was Christmas day, and a long one it had been. She couldn't wait to be tucked up.

There had been a drink in the kitchen earlier, Mrs Moffat and Miss Campbell dispensing sherry and cake.

They'd had their own Christmas dinner after the family had retired from theirs. And sumptuous it had been too. Mrs Moffat had done them all proud.

Good old Mrs Moffat, how pleased everyone had been to have her back. Not only to have her back but also to be rid of that sour-faced Mrs Owen whom nobody had liked.

Nancy had started to undress before she noticed the small tissue-wrapped parcel on her bed. Frowning, she crossed over and picked it up.

It was a slender gold chain that caused her to gasp with pleasure. There wasn't a card to go with it but she knew who it was from. Drew, of course. Who else?

She was deeply touched, and for the space of a few moments held it to her bosom.

She'd thank him when they were next alone together.

'Drew isn't fun any more,' James Seaton said to his mother Georgina.

'Oh?'

'He won't play like we used to. And he's always over at the distillery. I hardly ever see him.'

Georgina too had noticed the change in Drew. The lad was growing up fast. A little too fast possibly.

'Everything changes,' she smiled at James. 'That's the way life is. Nothing stands still. Or lasts for ever.'

She gave him a sympathetic cuddle.

'Nancy!'

She turned to find Drew hurrying after her. 'I hoped I might run into you,' he said.

'I'm off on an errand for your mother.'

'You're so hard to speak to nowadays. You're always by her side.'

'I'm afraid so.'

'What about during the party tonight?' he asked eagerly.

'I shan't be with her then. I'm not required, for once.'

He was drinking her in, thinking how lovely she was. 'So what are you going to do instead?'

'Nothing I suppose. I'll probably stay in my room.'

'Can I come and see you there?'

'Definitely not,' she laughed.

'Oh, Nancy. Please!'

'No,' she stated emphatically. Her hand went to the high collar of the dress she had on, underneath which she was wearing his chain. She still found it hard to believe it was real gold and that he'd bought it for her having saved up his weekly allowance. She remembered how the pair of them had laughed when he'd asked why she hadn't replied to his letters and she'd told him she could neither read nor write. He'd confessed he'd never thought of that.

'Can I have a hogmanay kiss then?'

'Drew, behave yourself,' she admonished.

'No one's about.'

'That's not the point.'

'Don't you want to kiss me, Nancy? I want to kiss you.'

Her good humour vanished, replaced by a more serious mood. She studied him, noting the changes in his features, particularly a new firmness that hadn't been there during the summer.

'Please, Nancy?' he repeated.

'You'll get me the sack.'

'No I won't. Mother adores you. Thinks the sun shines out that gorgeous bum of yours.'

'Drew!' she exclaimed, shocked. 'What a thing to say.'

'But it's true.'

She realised they were standing outside a large walk-in linen cupboard. Why shouldn't she indulge in a little flirtation and affection, even if it was with someone so young?

'Come here then,' she said, and crossed swiftly to the cupboard. Seconds later they were both inside, the only light being that coming through the crack at the bottom of the door.

'Oh, Nancy,' he whispered, taking her into his arms.

'Just one now.'

'Just one,' he promised.

A promise he broke. Nor did Nancy pull away or rebuke him, finding it a very pleasant experience, passionate too.

Afterwards she wondered how he'd learnt to kiss so expertly. If she'd asked him he'd have truthfully told her it just came naturally.

He was his father's son after all.

'Are you all right?'

Andrew started, not having heard Elspeth Campbell's approach. He smiled at her. 'I'm fine. I just came out for a breath of fresh air. It's rather fuggy in there with so many smokers present.'

'It is rather. I saw you leave and wondered if something was the matter.'

He shook his head. 'Just needed the fresh air, that's all.'

He'd drunk quite a bit that evening, but it was one of those occasions when it had little or no effect on him.

'I'll get back in then,' she said.

'Elspeth?'

She hesitated.

'Keep me company for a few minutes. Unless it's too cold for you that is.'

It was cold, but not unbearably so. She could manage a few minutes of it.

'I've got some news for you,' he declared.

'Oh?'

'Mrs Drummond has agreed for you to stay on full-time. If you wish that is.'

She'd been hoping for this, while at the same time wondering if it was such a good idea.

'Well, Elspeth?'

'I'd be delighted to accept.'

'That's settled then,' he beamed.

'You haven't been down to the kitchen at nights for a while,' she said slowly.

'No, I've been sleeping better of late.'

'That's good.'

He glanced round at the house. 'It's strange seeing all the windows blacked out. I find that quite disturbing.'

She didn't know what to reply to that, so remained silent.

'They'll all be up for hours yet. The usual hogmanay,' he smiled.

'I've never really liked hogmanay myself. The end of one year, the start of another. A sort of nothing time really. At least that's how I see it.'

'I understand what you mean.'

There was a silence between them during which neither felt ill at ease.

'I must get back,' she said eventually.

'Me too. You'd better go first.'

It wasn't lost on her he'd said that as though they'd conspired to meet up, a rendezvous.

'I was just concerned about you, that's all.'

'Thank you, Elspeth, and happy new year.'

'Happy new year to you, Andrew.'

She moved away, silent as a shadow, leaving a thoughtful Andrew behind.

Chapter 21

'Any news yet?'

It was September 1940, and the Battle of Britain was at its height. Tommy shook his head in reply. 'Not a sausage.'

Mavis Giddings, barmaid at the Lamb and Flag, gave him a sympathetic smile. 'Don't worry, you'll be made operational before long.'

'I hope you're right.'

Tommy and the rest of his training squadron were itching to get into the fight, hating kicking their heels while others got on with it. Normally their training would have extended well into the following year. But these were desperate times calling for desperate measures.

'The usual?'

'Please, Mavis.'

Tommy had struck up a friendship with Mavis, though, so far, that's all it was. He enjoyed her earthy humour. In many ways she reminded him of Bell Mathieson.

Dingo Roberts, an Australian also in the squadron, slid on to the stool beside Tommy. 'How are you going, mate?'

'Not too bad. You?'

Dingo shrugged. 'Anxious to get at the Jerries like everyone else. I've heard the Poles have been made operational now.'

'The Poles!'

'That's what I heard. If it's true then we can't be far behind.'

Mavis placed a half of bitter in front of Tommy. 'You, Dingo?' she asked.

'Make mine a pint. I'm dry as the Nullarbor Plain.'

'How are you getting on?' Dingo asked in a whisper after Mavis had gone back to the pumps.

'What do you mean?'

'With the fair Mavis there. Everyone's after her but she's only got goo goo eyes for you.'

Tommy blushed.

'Well, sport?'

'Mind your own business, Dingo.'

'Aha! Do I detect progress at last?'

'No, you do not. Now be a good aborigine and shut up.'

Dingo laughed. With his red hair and freckles he couldn't have looked less like an abo.

Others from the squadron sauntered in. All of them, including Dingo, were older than Tommy.

'Let's have a tune on the old ivories, Fitz,' Dingo called out to one of the newcomers.

Justin FitzHugh waved back. 'Let me wet my whistle first.'

More men from the squadron arrived, the small pub rapidly filling up.

'Come on, Fitz, get a move on, you lazy sod. We want entertaining,' Paul Wyborn shouted from the corner where he was ensconced with a girl from the village.

'I think it's going to be one of those nights, mate,' Dingo grinned at Tommy.

'Isn't it always,' Tommy replied drily.

'Can I have a word with you during the dinner break, Mr Balfour?' Irene asked him as he was walking by.

The gaffer stopped to stare at her. 'What about, Irene?'

'Private, sir.'

'Oh, all right,' he shrugged. 'Come to my cubbyhole.'

'Thank you, Mr Balfour.'

He moved off again.

'What was that all about?' a curious Bell queried.

'I'll explain after work.'

Bell didn't press as Irene clearly didn't want to discuss the matter further, guessing correctly it was because of others listening in.

'Well?' Bell demanded as they were leaving the distillery on completion of their shift.

'I've handed in my notice.'

Bell came up short to stare incredulously at her friend. 'You've what!'

'Handed in my notice. I go in a fortnight.'

Bell was stunned. 'But why?'

'Because I've joined up.'

Bell's mouth opened, then shut again. 'You've joined up?' she managed to say after a few seconds.

'The ATS. Auxiliary Territorial Service. They're going to train me as an ambulance driver. At least, that's what they promised.'

The pair of them continued on their way. 'You never said anything?' Bell complained.

'I didn't want to let on until I'd been accepted. The letter I've been waiting for came this morning.'

'But why, Irene?'

Her friend chuckled. 'Apart from the obvious reasons, helping with the war effort et cetera, it's a perfect opportunity to meet new men.'

Bell laughed. So that was it! 'You sly old thing.'

'There's no one round here seems interested in me. And I don't want to end up an old maid. By joining the ATS I might meet someone nice.'

Bell was jealous, but reminded herself she had David. Nonetheless, she too would have liked to join something like the ATS. It sounded tremendously exciting.

'Do you know where they're sending you?'

Irene shook her head. 'Haven't a clue. All I know is I've to report to a place in Glasgow. After that, who knows?'

Bell's eyes gleamed. 'Driving an ambulance sounds fun.'

'That's what I think. I should have a rare old time.'

Bell hooked an arm round Irene's. 'I'm dead pleased for you, so I am. But I'll miss you, mind. Oh aye, I will that.'

'And I'll miss you, Bell. But look on the bright side, think of all those gorgeous men I might meet. With a bit of luck there'll be a husband among them.'

They both laughed.

Their new CO strode into the operations room where Tommy and the rest of the squadron were waiting. They all rose to their feet.

'Please sit, chaps,' the CO said.

With a shock Tommy recognised him. He was older than he remembered, or at least looked older. He'd lost weight and there was an air of authority about him that hadn't been there before. That and something else Tommy couldn't put his finger on. Their new CO was Gerald McTaggart, Babs' brother.

Gerald introduced himself, then stared grimly at the assembly. 'You'll be pleased to know that as from midnight tonight the squadron becomes operational. Well done.'

A great cheer went up. It had happened at long last.

Gerald's smile was razor-thin, a smile that belied the look in his eyes.

It was a look Tommy was to encounter many times in the coming months.

'Top Hat, I have trade for you. Bandits at Angels 4000.'

Tommy glanced up through his canopy, quickly scanning the sky. There they were, Me109s. About a dozen of them.

'Here we go, chaps,' Gerald's voice came crisply over the R/T. 'Good luck.'

'Yoicks and tally ho!' someone added.

Tommy smiled, recognising Dingo's voice. His assumed English accent was diabolical.

The pub was muted when Tommy went into it later that evening. A sympathetic Mavis greeted him at the bar.

'I heard about Fitz,' she said.

Tommy's face was ashen, completely devoid of colour. 'I saw it happen,' he croaked. 'Fitz just . . . blew up.'

They both glanced over at the piano standing silent, both recalling uproarious nights when Fitz had played. Tommy knew it to be his imagination, but the piano seemed to have a dejected air about it. As though it was in mourning.

'The usual?'

Tommy took a deep breath, and nodded. 'Add a chaser as well, Mavis. I need one.'

'The CO wants to see you.'

'Thank you,' Tommy replied to Sergeant O'Dowd, a Liverpudlian of Irish descent.

Now what did Gerald want him for? he wondered as he headed for his office. So far they hadn't spoken together since Gerald had taken over.

'Hello, Tommy.' Gerald smiled as he closed the door behind him.

'Hello, sir.'

Gerald waved to a seat. 'I thought I recognised the face but couldn't place you to begin with. Then I looked up your file.' He paused, then said, 'A long way from Dalneil.'

'Yes, sir.'

'Call me Gerald when we're alone. But only then.'

'Right, Gerald.'

Gerald rocked back in his chair and studied Tommy. 'Well well, it was quite a surprise finding you here.'

'And I suppose for you to turn up.'

'A lot has happened since we met,' Gerald mused darkly.

'Indeed.'

Gerald's eyes took on a faraway look and became pained. He shook himself out of his reverie. 'Are you still in touch with my sister?'

'No, she didn't approve of me joining up.'

Gerald grunted, and a flash of disappointment and anger crossed his face. 'I see.'

'Maybe she did the right thing. I can't say.'

Gerald didn't answer that. Instead he got up and crossed to a window to stare out. He was about to speak when the klaxon sounded. Both men were galvanised into action.

'Heinkels, swarms of the bloody things,' Billy Moore commented over the R/T.

There were too, Tommy observed. And no fighter cover as far as he could make out. It would be like shooting ducks in a barrel.

'Help yourself, chaps,' Gerald instructed.

Moments later the first Heinkel tumbled from the sky.

Elspeth gazed at Andrew sitting across the table from her. It was just after three in the morning. 'How's the tea?'

'Lovely, thank you.'

She lit a cigarette while he stared morosely into his cup. 'A penny for them?'

He made a face. 'There's nothing in particular.'

'Worried about something?'

'No more than usual.'

A silence fell between them which Elspeth eventually broke by saying, 'You've never told me your story.'

He blinked. 'I beg your pardon?'

'Do you remember I told you my sorry tale some time back. I've never yet heard yours.'

'No,' Andrew said softly.

Elspeth waited patiently, but he didn't go on.

'I understand if you don't want to tell me. Some things are just too personal.'

How he enjoyed being alone with Elspeth Campbell. She was so relaxing to be with. He could have happily remained where he was, with her, for the rest of the night.

'It'll be strictly between you and me, Elspeth?'

'Of course.'

'No, I mean that. You mustn't breathe a word to anyone else. Members of staff in particular.'

'I won't. I swear.'

His expression became one of anguish as he spoke about himself and Rose.

It was more or less as she'd expected, Elspeth reflected as she got back into bed. She'd known there was something wrong between Andrew and his wife. Known it instinctively without having to hear the gossip that circulated from time to time amongst the staff.

There was the matter of separate bedrooms for a start. Understandable after the miscarriage, she supposed. And people of their class often slept apart, she knew that for a fact.

But not Andrew, not willingly, he simply wasn't the type. And so it had proved when he'd confessed his situation.

Her heart had gone out to him. How sad he'd sounded. Almost beaten somehow. It had taken a great deal of effort on her part not to weep on his behalf.

She'd already said her prayers earlier. But now she said them again, this time including Andrew.

'Get out, Dingo. Get out!' Tommy screamed into the R/T.

He'd seen Dingo's plane being raked with cannon fire, then, with smoke streaming from it, begin to spiral downwards.

The sky was filled with aircraft, a graceful ballet of death.

'Get out, Dingo!' he screamed again.

A figure detached itself from the doomed Hurricane, and seconds later a parachute billowed.

'Thank God,' Tommy breathed in relief. He could only hope no one shot Dingo before he hit the Channel.

He banked sharply to port as he glimpsed an Me110 zooming in on his tail.

Dingo was temporarily forgotten as the grisly dance went on.

Everyone looked round as Dingo strolled through the pub door. 'You bastards haven't got rid of me yet,' he grinned.

Tommy whooped and pounded the bar. 'Set 'em up for me old cobber!' he instructed a delighted Mavis.

There was a lot of back-slapping and hand-shaking before Dingo reached Tommy's side. 'It's sure as hell wet out there in that Channel,' he joked.

Tommy laughed, a trace of hysteria in his voice.

'And you know something?' Dingo queried.

'What?'

'I still can't bloody swim.'

'They've got the CO. Christ, they've got him!' Billy Moore's voice crackled over the R/T.

Tommy spotted Gerald's plane, identifiable by its distinctive markings, go belly up enveloped in smoke and flames.

He could see Gerald desperately trying to get out, but the canopy remained firmly in place.

'Dear God,' Tommy whispered. Gerald was being burnt alive.

It seemed an eternity before Gerald's plane eventually crashed into the sea.

*   *   *

'Time, gentlemen, please!' Mavis called out.

Tommy was sitting alone at the bar, Dingo having stayed in camp that night. The mood was funereal.

'You remain behind,' Mavis whispered to Tommy.

He only dimly heard her as he was lost in thought. What agonies Gerald must have suffered before he died, what excruciating torture. He kept thinking of his father's face, that being the result of burns. It was probably better Gerald hadn't survived.

The others present drank up and left, Mavis locking the door behind them. She poured herself a brandy and port before joining Tommy.

'I knew him from before,' Tommy said.

'The CO?'

'He came from the same village as me. I only met him once, mind, he was some years older. At his parents' house. I was seeing his sister Barbara at the time.'

Mavis had a sip of her drink, her eyes never leaving Tommy. Three of the squadron were now dead, two missing in action.

'Poor bastard,' Tommy choked, tears welling in his eyes.

Mavis put an arm round his shoulders and pulled him close. 'I can't say I knew him. He only came in here several times.'

'He was a decent bloke. I liked him a lot.' Tommy wiped away the tears. 'I suppose it was because of him I joined the RAF. Because of him and a Spitfire I once saw.'

'I'm sorry,' Mavis sympathised.

'My dad was in the Great War and never talks about it. Not unless you really push him that is. I'm beginning to understand why.'

She saw that his glass was empty. 'Another pint?'

'You wouldn't have any Drummond malt on the premises?'

'Drummond?' Mavis thought about that, then shook her head. 'I'm afraid not.'

Pity, Tommy thought. It would have been fitting to toast Gerald's departure with that.

'We've plenty others though.'

'No, it had to be Drummond. It's made in Dalneil where we both come from.'

He closed his eyes, again seeing Gerald fighting with the canopy and failing to release it. The long slow descent to the Channel and the final impact. A few minutes only, but they must have seemed like hours to Gerald. He shivered.

'Why don't you stay the night with me?' Mavis suggested softly.

Tommy stared blankly at her.

'Dan and his wife won't mind. I know they won't.' Dan Gilfeather was the owner of the Lamb and Flag.

'In your room?'

Mavis nodded. 'I have a double bed so we won't be cramped.'

Right then Tommy could think of nothing he'd like more. A warm body to hold and to hold him. 'All right,' he replied.

'Can you sneak back into camp in the morning?'

'That's isn't a problem. Some of the lads do it all the time.'

'Right then. Shall we go on up?'

Mavis stripped naked to stand in front of him. 'Well?' she smiled.

She was the first woman Tommy had ever seen fully unclothed. His mouth was dry, his pulse racing. 'You're gorgeous,' he said huskily.

Mavis gave a small laugh. 'Hardly that. I know I'm no great beauty. But I'm not too bad.'

'I think you're gorgeous.'

She came into his arms and he kissed her deeply. The smell of her was strong in his nostrils, the feel of her skin exciting in the extreme. He broke away, face red with embarrassment.

'What's wrong?' She frowned.

'There's something I have to tell you.'

She stared at him, waiting for him to go on.

He glanced down at the floor. 'I've . . . I've . . .' He coughed, this was awful.

Mavis smiled slowly as understanding dawned. 'Are you trying to tell me you've never been with a woman before?'

Still gazing at the floor, he nodded.

She should have guessed as much. 'That's all right.'

'I don't want to disappoint you. I know what to do but . . .' He trailed off.

'It doesn't matter, Tommy. Even if we don't do anything, I promise you. Now get those things off and come to bed before I freeze.'

He fumbled with his tie.

'Mavis?'

'What, Tommy?' she replied lazily.

'That really was wonderful.'

'For me too, darling.'

'Really?'

'Really.'

He snuggled up closer to her, marvelling at what had just taken place. How could you be prepared for such a thing? You couldn't.

'Are you sure that clock will go off?' he asked.

'Don't worry, it always does. It's never failed me yet.'

She caressed the inside of his thigh, and sighed. She'd had better lovers in her time, but that was where experience counted. Anyway, it was Tommy she'd wanted to sleep with, not Don Juan.

Minutes later she smiled, realising Tommy was fast asleep, she cradled in his arms.

Her last conscious thought was to hope he didn't dream of the CO.

'It's a letter from Tommy,' Hettie announced excitedly.

Jack sat upright in his chair. 'What does he say?'

'Hold on, Jack, I haven't even opened it yet.'

'Then hurry up, woman.'

Jack waited expectantly as Hettie swiftly read the single sheet of paper the envelope contained.

'Oh dear,' she whispered.

'What is it?'

'Gerald McTaggart, Barbara's brother, has been killed.'

Jack's lips thinned and whitened. 'But Tommy's all right?'

'Fine, according to this. Tired, but fine.'

Jack let out a sigh of relief. 'What else does he say?'

'Not a lot, there are only a few lines. All he's apparently got time for.'

Jack sank back into his chair, thinking about the McTaggarts. This would be a real body-blow for them. But at least Tommy was safe. It might be selfish on his part, but that was all he really cared about.

Hettie carefully refolded the sheet of paper and returned it to the envelope. 'I suppose a few lines are better than nothing,' she declared, trying to put on a brave face.

'Can I have the letter?'

She handed it to him.

'It seems like only yesterday he was a baby,' Jack said softly.

'Yes.'

Jack ran the tips of his fingers over the letter, trying to imagine the conditions under which it had been written. He knew only too well the sort of tiredness Tommy was referring to, appreciating the fact Tommy had actually forced himself, made himself find the time, to write.

'Would you like a cup of tea?' Hettie asked brightly.

'I'd love one.'

'And how about a piece of cake?'

'Even better.'

'I'll put the kettle on.'

Come home safe, son, Jack silently prayed. Please come home safe and sound.

'London's taking a right old pounding by all accounts,' Mavis declared to Tommy, placing a pint in front of him.

'Yes,' was the grim reply.

'It must be dreadful there.'

He'd seen the glow from the capital in the far distance during a night sortie. Bright red and orange, it might have been the gateway to Hell itself.

'You look exhausted,' Mavis stated.

'I am. I might even nod off right here at the bar.'

He reached for his glass, stopping his hand halfway on noting it was shaking. When he picked up his pint he spilled some.

'Is Dingo coming in tonight?' Mavis queried.

'Should be, a little later. He has something to do first.'

Mavis moved off to serve another customer.

They'd lost another member of the squadron that day, Tommy reflected. A replacement pilot who'd only joined them two days before. He hadn't seen the chap buy it, but several others had.

He'd been made up to Section Leader the previous week with Dingo flying as his wingman. They made a good team. And, so far, a lucky one.

Mavis returned. 'Did you ever write to the CO's parents as you thought you might?'

Tommy shook his head. 'I couldn't in the end. I did try but . . . just couldn't. I'll go and see them when I'm next in Dalneil.'

If he ever was, he thought to himself.

'How would you feel about Nancy taking meals with us?'

Andrew stared at Rose in astonishment. Really, this was going too far. 'Why should she do that?'

Rose shrugged, and glanced away. 'She's become almost part of the family.'

Anger flared in Andrew which he quickly brought under control. 'She's an employee, Rose, nothing more.'

'She is to me,' Rose stated defiantly.

Andrew recalled the small figure in the first painting Rose had done. There had been several paintings since, the same small figure in all of them. The face an amalgamation of his, Rose and Nancy's.

'Nancy brings me a great deal of comfort,' Rose said quietly.

'That's obvious.'

'We've become so close we're almost like sisters.'

Not sisters, Andrew thought, but mother and daughter. For that's what this was truly all about. Who would have foreseen when he brought Nancy into the house that this would be the outcome?

'The rest of the staff won't like it. They'll be jealous,' he said.

'That's their lookout.'

'And what does Nancy think about this?'

'I haven't mentioned it to her yet.'

'Then maybe you should.'

'I wanted to speak to you first, Andrew.' She shot him a pleading look that quite melted his resistance.

'It's very unusual to say the least,' he said gruffly.

'I know that.'

A few seconds ticked silently by. 'Do as you wish,' he growled eventually.

'And you'll be nice to her. Accept her at the table?'

'Of course I will.'

'Thank you, Andrew, I appreciate this.'

Rose got up and left the room, the last he saw of her that night.

The following morning a somewhat embarrassed Nancy joined them for breakfast.

Chapter 22

'David!'

Not caring what any of the others coming off shift might think, Bell flew across to where he was standing waiting and into his arms. 'Oh David,' she cried.

He squeezed her tight. 'Hello, darling. Surprise?'

A few passing female workmates giggled and tittered, but all were delighted for Bell.

'How long have you got?' she demanded throatily, not knowing whether to laugh or cry.

'Ten days. But I've already used up two of them.'

Bell frowned at him.

'I had to go to Auchgloan and see my folks. Now I've done that I can be with you.'

She took a step backwards to gaze him up and down. How handsome he looked in his uniform, quite the proper soldier. He'd lost a bit of weight, but it suited him. And his face had aged a little. The body that had embraced her had not only been leaner but tougher too.

'I presume you're not due back here till Monday morning?' he smiled, it now being Friday evening.

She nodded.

He encircled her waist and drew her off to one side. 'How do you fancy going away?'

Her eyes opened wide. 'Just the two of us?'

'That's right. I've managed to borrow a motor and enough petrol to see us through. There's a wee hotel I've heard of which I've booked us into. What do you say?'

Her mind was whirling. 'Are you suggesting a dirty weekend?'

He smiled lecherously. 'That's it.'

Bell caught her breath.

'I let slip to the owner that we're on our honeymoon. Which isn't true of course but they're not to know that. I thought it would make the whole thing easier.'

'You have got it all planned out,' she commented drily.

'I don't want to waste any time. Besides, I'm fed up going round the back of your house.'

Now she did laugh.

'It would mean we could actually go to bed together.'

The thought of that almost turned her legs to jelly. Anyway, why not? They'd made love together often enough, this was merely taking things one step further.

'Well?' he prompted.

'I'll have to pick up some things from home first.'

'Of course. I'll drive you.'

She hesitated. 'Will you mind waiting outside?'

He knew from his cousin Ronnie about Bell's parents and that she was deeply ashamed of them. The fact they were like they were didn't bother him in the least. He loved Bell which was all that mattered.

'Suits me.'

'Let's go then.'

'The car's over here.'

As they walked hand in hand towards the car she wondered what she'd tell her mother and father. By the time they reached her house she'd concocted a suitable story to explain her absence for the weekend. She'd say she was spending it with an old pal, as she occasionally did, who lived in a nearby village. Her parents wouldn't think to question that.

She asked David to park a little way further down the street before going inside.

Dingo yawned and then glanced at his wristwatch. It was ten past three in the afternoon and they hadn't been scrambled all day. 'Where the hell are the Jerry bastards?' he frowned.

'Don't complain. Enjoy the rest,' Tommy replied from the dilapidated armchair he was lounging in.

'I'm not complaining. Just curious, that's all.'

'Something's afoot,' Billy Moore commented from where he was sitting.

'Must be,' Dingo muttered.

When they were finally stood down they still hadn't been scrambled.

Andrew stared in concern into the contents of the toilet bowl. He'd passed blood, quite a lot of it too, which was worrying. He wondered if it was in any way connected with the intermittent pains he'd had in his stomach recently.

He was probably just run down, he decided. He hadn't had a proper break in God knows how long.

Maybe Dr Lesley had been right and it was an ulcer after all. But if so why hadn't it shown up in the hospital tests?

*   *   *

'It's a beautiful view,' Bell declared, looking out of the window of their double bedroom.

David came to stand beside her. 'It is that,' he agreed. 'But nowhere near as beautiful as you.'

'What a smoothie,' she teased.

He nuzzled the nape of her neck. 'Now we know what it's like to have a bed. Far more comfortable than the other, don't you think?'

'Oh yes,' Bell purred.

His hands covered her breasts causing her to moan. 'Stop that or we'll miss breakfast.'

'They'll understand if we don't show up in the dining room. We are supposed to be on our honeymoon, don't forget.'

'I'm not all that hungry anyway.'

'You should be after last night,' he chuckled.

'And you,' she retorted.

'We'll find somewhere to get a bite later on,' he said, one hand moving down to caress the swell of her buttocks.

They returned to the rumpled bed they'd just left.

'What's wrong with you?' Nancy demanded of Drew, back from school for the holidays.

He started, having been lost in thought. 'Nothing.'

'You had a face like fizz.'

'Had I?' he replied, pretending innocence.

'Are you bored, is that it?'

'No.'

'Then what?'

Drew shrugged. 'Why aren't you with Mum?' he queried, changing the subject.

'She's having an afternoon nap.'

He'd been thinking about his mother, guilt lying heavily on him. There were still times when he couldn't stare her straight in the eye.

'Are you bothered about something?' Nancy further probed.

He relented, and nodded.

'What?'

'I can't tell you.'

'I see.'

He turned away, desperately wanting her to remain with him, at the same time wanting to be alone. 'Things have changed quite a bit since I went away,' he commented.

She knew he was referring to her. 'Does it upset you?'

'Goodness no. I enjoy having my meals with you. Even if you don't say all that much. Only speak when spoken to.'

She blushed. 'I haven't got used to the situation yet if you want the truth. I don't want to . . . intrude I suppose.'

'Do you find Father daunting. Is that it?'

'Not really. He's kindness itself. And I owe him such a lot. Who knows what would have become of me if he hadn't come across me that day in Leithan.'

Drew reached out and touched her arm. 'I thought about you ever so much when I was at school. I had dreams about you.'

'Dreams!' she laughed, adding drily, 'I can imagine what sort.'

Now it was his turn to blush. 'I can't help dreaming, Nancy. Or what I dream about.'

'As long as they were nice dreams.'

'Oh yes,' he enthused. 'They were certainly that.'

She studied him for a moment, not for the first time trying to visualise the man he'd become. It was a pleasing picture.

'Can I come to your room tonight, Nancy?'

'No, you cannot,' she replied hastily.

'I'd like to talk.'

'And what else?'

'Nothing, I promise you.'

She smiled, knowing what his promises were like. Where she was concerned anyway.

'No, Drew, and that's an end of it.'

His disappointment clearly showed. 'I've changed my mind about what I said, Nancy. I would like to tell you what's bothering me. Why I had a face like fizz.'

She relented a little. 'Are you sure about that?'

He nodded.

It was asking for trouble. If Mr or Mrs Drummond were to find out . . . 'It's too risky,' she said.

'Please?'

The look in his eyes persuaded her. 'All right, but for no longer than half an hour. And, Drew, no funny business or you're straight out the door again.'

'You're a sweetie, Nancy.'

A fool more like, she thought.

Bell stood watching David walk down the street. That was it, his leave was over. Heaven knew when she'd see him again.

Thankfully there was a full moon which meant she could watch him for some distance.

Just before disappearing round a corner he turned and waved. She waved back, her mind crammed with the happy memories of the last week. Especially those spent in the hotel when they'd pretended to be on honeymoon. Memories that would stay with her for ever, no matter what.

And then he was gone from sight.

*   *   *

'Come in.'

Drew slipped silently into the bedroom and shut the door behind him. Once inside he stared around.

'It's certainly a lot nicer, and more comfortable, than the room you had before.'

It was Rose who'd proposed that Nancy move down into this bedroom which was on the level used by the family and guests. It was considerably larger than her previous one and, as Drew had rightly commented, far better appointed. For Nancy it was the very lap of luxury.

Drew crossed to the fireplace and gazed at the painting hanging above the mantelpiece. 'One of Mum's, eh?'

'She gave it to me.'

It was a landscape he recognised. What he failed to notice was the small figure almost obscured by foliage.

'Remember what I said, no more than half an hour.'

'Relax, Nancy, Mum and Dad are out as you know and won't be home for ages yet. We've nothing to worry about.'

'There's always Miss Campbell. She's often on the prowl at this time.'

'She's in the kitchen with Cook and the others. I checked.'

Nancy pulled her cardigan, a blue one she'd knitted herself, more tightly about her. It wasn't the best of fits. 'You wanted to talk, Drew?'

His face darkened. 'Yes,' he replied quietly.

'Then sit down.' She indicated a chair.

'And you?'

'I'll make do with the bed.'

'Can I bring the chair a bit closer? I don't want to have to shout across the room.'

She could see the sense in that. 'All right.'

Nancy perched herself on the edge of the bed and waited while he brought the chair over and placed it several feet from her.

He sat and lapsed into silence.

After a while he glanced up at her, his face filled with anguish. 'This isn't easy, Nancy.'

'Is it about me?'

He shook his head. 'No, Mum.'

'Your mother?' she queried softly, puzzled.

Drew took a deep breath . . .

'That's utter nonsense,' Nancy declared when he'd finally finished. 'You can't possibly have been responsible for your mother losing the baby.'

'But I *was*, Nancy. Didn't you hear me, I wished it to happen. And it did.'

'Pure coincidence, nothing more.'

'I can't believe that.'

'But it's true, Drew. Her miscarriage had nothing whatsoever to do with you. How could it possibly?'

'But I *wished* the baby away, Nancy.'

His newfound maturity of recent times had gone, vanished. He was again a little boy. And a terribly upset one at that. 'And you've been worrying about this ever since?'

'Yes,' he croaked.

She'd never heard anything so ridiculous. Poor Drew, what a burden he'd been carrying. 'I assure you, Drew, wishing the baby away didn't make it happen. As I said, it was just coincidence.'

'I blame myself, Nancy. I wished so terribly hard, you see. So terribly, terribly hard, and it came about.'

She slid from the bed to kneel in front of him, clasping one of his hands in hers. 'You're being silly, Drew.'

'No I'm not,' he replied defiantly.

'Oh yes, you are. You've got a guilty conscience about something that had nothing to do with you.'

His expression was one of utter wretchedness. 'Sometimes it hurts, Nancy, just thinking about it.'

'I agree you should never have made that wish in the first place, but in a way it was understandable. A new child was going to be born who'd put your nose out of joint, and so you were jealous. Right?'

He nodded.

'That sort of thing is common between brothers and sisters. Making that wish wasn't so awful, it was merely human. Millions of other boys and girls must have made the same wish.'

'But for *me* it came true.'

'Yes it did, but not because of your wish. What occurred was God's will and nothing else.'

Drew suddenly burst into tears. 'Oh, Nancy,' he sobbed.

'God's will,' she repeated.

Somehow, Nancy wasn't sure how, they were both on their feet, she holding him tight while he continued to cry.

His body shook in her arms.

'Nancy and I are going out after this,' Rose announced over dinner, speaking to Andrew but smiling at Nancy. 'There's a meeting in the village hall. We're discussing further ways of helping the war effort.'

'Very admirable,' Andrew commented with just a trace of sarcasm in his voice.

'We'll be gone for several hours at least. Won't we, Nancy?'

'I'd imagine so.'

'What sort of "further ways" do you have in mind?' Andrew queried, making conversation.

'Oh, I don't know. We'll just have to wait and see what's proposed.'

Andrew felt excluded at his own table which made him angry. It was Rose and Nancy, Nancy and Rose. He might as well have been a stranger. The barrier between him and the other two was almost tangible.

The rest of the evening stretched interminably ahead. He on his own. Not that it was all that different when it was just himself and Rose. Often it was as though she wasn't even there.

What were they talking about now? He forced himself to listen. Women's chat, nothing he felt he could contribute to.

Andrew excused himself before dessert was served. Rose wasn't put out in the least that he'd decided to leave them to it.

In fact, she seemed almost relieved.

'I had a letter from Irene this morning,' Bell said to Hannah McIlroy, working alongside her.

'How is she?'

'In the pink. Thoroughly enjoying life in the ATS which she says is enormous fun. The lucky blighter's been posted to London.'

'London!' Isa exclaimed.

'Trust her to get that posting.'

'But it'll be awfully dangerous there, what with the Blitz and all.'

'She's looking forward to it according to her. No matter what danger she might be in.'

'I hope she's going to be all right,' Isa frowned.

'Me too. There have been an awful lot of people killed there since the bombing started.'

'Ach, knowing Irene she'll probably have a whale of a time, bombs or not. You know what she's like, if she fell in a midden full of shite she'd come up smelling of roses.'

Bell laughed, that was true enough. And London would be full of men which would suit Irene down to the ground.

'You must miss her though,' Isa sympathised. 'The pair of you being best pals and that.'

'Aye, I do.' In fact she missed Irene even more than she'd thought she would.

They stopped talking abruptly when Balfour appeared, coming in their direction.

Tommy and Mavis were alone at the bar together, she having just locked up for the night. As was the custom that had grown up between them they'd have a few drinks to let Mavis catch up before going upstairs.

'I've been meaning to ask you.' Mavis smiled. 'What will you do when the war's over?'

If he came through it alive that is, Tommy reflected wryly. They'd lost another member of the squadron that morning to an Me110. His Section continued to be lucky without any fatalities.

'I suppose I'll go back to what I was doing before,' he replied thoughtfully.

'And what was that? You've never said.'

How strange war was, he mused. Mavis was right, she knew little about his life in Dalneil prior to joining up. Just as he knew little about her past, only that she came from Woking and was an only child. Neither of them had felt the need to exchange confidences, all that seemed to matter was the here and now. That's what war seemed to boil down to, getting through the day intact, not thinking about tomorrow, just staying alive.

He told her about his training as a traveller for Drummond's.

'That sounds a great job.'

'Well, it would have been when I got out on the road. If I'd stayed on that is. I'd have been well paid, had my own car and everything.'

He suddenly smiled.

'What is it?'

'Want a laugh?'

'I can always use one of those.'

'My burning ambition before the war was to be an African explorer and big-game hunter.'

She did laugh. 'You're joking!'

'No, that's what I desperately wanted to be. It was my dream.'

'Not a very practical one,' she commented drily.

'I suppose not. But I fantasised about it for years. I could just see myself with the gun and large hat.'

'Jungle Jim,' she teased.

'Something like that.'

'But why an explorer and big-game hunter?'

Tommy shrugged. 'I suppose it was the most exciting thing I could think of. Certainly a world away from Dalneil where I live.'

'A real hero, eh?'

'Oh yes. Carving my way through the undergrowth, rescuing fair damsels from killer lions, wrestling with man-eating gorillas, you get the idea.'

'As far as I'm aware gorillas are vegetarians,' she laughed.

'That may be so, but they're still dangerous beasties. Massive buggers.'

Mavis thought this a right hoot, but nice all the same. There was nothing wrong in having aspirations, after all. Even if they were daft ones.

'And what about you?' he asked.

She shook her head. 'I was just pleased to get a job when I left school. Being a barmaid was the first I was offered and that's what I've done ever since.'

'So why come to Laxworth?'

'No real reason. My mother started seeing another man and I felt in the way. I decided to move out of the area and eventually ended up here. No dreams in my case, I'm afraid.'

He finished his drink.

'Tired?'

'Aren't I always?'

She nodded her understanding. 'If you don't mind I'd like another before we go on up.'

'Have as many as you wish. I'm perfectly happy being here with you. There's no rush.'

She mustn't get too attached, she told herself. Not in the circumstances. That would be foolish.

But in the meantime . . . Well it was lovely having Tommy around – and in her bed.

Andrew gasped and bent over as pain exploded in his stomach. 'Christ,' he muttered through clenched teeth.

His senses swam, and for a few moments he thought he was going to lose consciousness.

'Mr Drummond. Mr Drummond!' Kelly exclaimed anxiously, hurrying over from where he'd been busy with some files.

Kelly grasped Andrew by the shoulders and manoeuvred him into his chair. 'What's wrong, sir?'

His stomach was on fire, a raging cauldron churning and bubbling. He'd had stomach pains in the past but nothing like this. It was excruciating.

'Would you like some water, Mr Drummond?'

Andrew nodded.

Kelly rushed from the office, swiftly returning with a glassful.

Andrew glanced up at the book-keeper, seeing the concern on the other's face. 'Thank you.'

He had a sip, then another. They didn't do any good. He took a deep breath and closed his eyes.

'What is it, Mr Drummond?'

'Indigestion,' he lied. If this was indigestion then he was a Chinese washerwoman.

Kelly nodded his sympathy, knowing Andrew had suffered from that in the past. 'Is there anything else I can get you?'

'No, thank you, Kelly.'

He'd gone weak as a baby, all his strength seemingly having drained from him. He'd also broken out in a cold sweat.

'I think you should go home, Mr Drummond, and have a lie-down.'

'There's a lot to do,' Andrew protested.

'Nothing that can't wait. Besides, look at the state you're in. You can't work like that.'

Kelly was right, Andrew thought. A lie-down was best. That and sleep if he could get it. Oh my God, but his stomach hurt. It was as if he'd swallowed a pint of acid.

'Help me up, Kelly.'

'Yes, sir.'

Kelly got Andrew to his feet where he swayed. He wasn't at all certain he could make it back to the house.

'You're going to have to come with me, Kelly.'

'Of course, sir.'

'Out the back way. I want as few people as possible seeing me like this.'

'I understand, sir.'

Andrew groaned when he took a step, sweat now running freely down his face. Lesley must have been right all along, he thought. This had to be an ulcer. Though it was still a mystery why it hadn't shown up on the tests.

It was a nightmare, Tommy's section and Red Section had been on a routine flight when they'd suddenly run into swarms of enemy fighters. The Jerry bastards were everywhere.

'I'm hit, I'm fucking hit!' Billy Moore screamed over the R/T.

Tommy was about to reply when an Me109 appeared behind him. He swore and took evasive action.

He glimpsed Dingo going into an attack, his cannons spurting flame.

'Coming to assist Section Leader,' Paul Wyborn announced calmly over the R/T.

Tommy threw his plane to port, and into a steep climb, hoping to shake off his pursuer. To no avail.

There was Paul Wyborn in his mirror now, lining up the Me109. Moments later the Me109 blew apart.

Relief surged in Tommy. 'Thank you, Paul,' he choked into the R/T.

'Waltzing Matilda . . . Waltzing Matilda . . .' Dingo started to sing.

Tommy almost laughed to hear that.

He pulled out of his climb and headed for cloud. But before he could get there an Me110 came into his sights. He instinctively fired, having the grim satisfaction of seeing the 110's fuselage become wreathed in black smoke and glycol.

He vanished into the cloud, only to almost instantly reappear again. The cloud had been a small one.

'Billy, where are you?' he queried.

There was no reply.

'Billy . . .'

'Billy's dead,' Dingo cut in. 'He got out but his chute didn't open.'

'Disperse, do the best you can,' Tommy instructed. If they remained where they were it would be curtains for all of them. The odds were simply too great.

And then it happened. His Hurry juddered and yawed as cannon shells ripped their way completely along its length. Tommy's right shoulder went suddenly numb and there was a spattering of blood on the sleeve of his flying jacket. Surprisingly, there wasn't any pain.

This was it, he thought, the plane hardly responding to the controls. He was a sitting duck.

And then he saw his attacker swooping in for the kill.

'Waltzing Matilda,' Dingo was singing again over the R/T. 'Waltzing Matilda . . .'

Chapter 23

'Let's get you into bed,' Elspeth Campbell said to Andrew, having taken over from Kelly.

'I think I can manage that by myself.'

Rose and Nancy were out, which was why Elspeth had assumed charge. It had given her a fright to see Andrew and the obvious pain he was in.

'Sit down,' Elspeth instructed in a strictly no-nonsense voice. When he had, on the side of the bed, she set about removing his shoes and socks.

'I'm going to send for the doctor,' she announced.

'No, I'll be all right. I promise you.'

She glanced up at him, her expression one of disapproval. 'That's plain silly, Andrew.'

It was too, he thought. Lesley should be fetched as soon as possible. That was the sensible thing to do. And yet he was reluctant, knowing that if an ulcer was confirmed then it probably meant an operation resulting in his being laid up for weeks.

'Now your collar and tie.'

Despite the pain he was enjoying being fussed over. It had been so long since a woman had done that to him. It gave him enormous pleasure, at the same time reminding him what he so missed from Rose. Not just lovemaking, but the day-to-day care and affection. The cherishing. How different it had all been before the last pregnancy and subsequent miscarriage.

Her hands were cool on his neck. He leant forward a little to give her better access to his back stud.

'That's better,' he declared, attempting a smile, when tie and collar had been removed.

'Now your jacket.'

'I told Kelly it was indigestion but I fear it might be an ulcer after all,' he said.

She paused to stare at him. 'I thought the hospital tests had disproved that theory?'

He shrugged. 'So did I. But what else can it be?'

She threw his jacket on to the floor, she'd tidy that away in a moment or two, then started on his shirt buttons.

'That's enough, Elspeth. Leave me my modesty,' he said when the buttons were undone to his waist.

'Get your trousers off.'

'Not while you're here!' he protested.

'You're acting like a big baby now. Get them off. I'll turn my back if you wish.'

It amused him to find he was embarrassed. Taking his clothes off in front of women, or having them taken off by them, had never bothered him before. Maybe it was because she was staff. There again, maybe not.

'Turn your back,' he said.

The pain had begun to ease he realised as he undid his flies. The trousers slithered to the floor and he scrambled under the bedclothes.

'You can look now,' he told her.

Elspeth quickly scooped up the trousers and jacket and put them away. 'Would you like a cup of tea?'

'No thank you.'

'Anything else?'

'A whisky I think.'

'Hardly the best medicine,' she commented drily.

He placed a hand on his belly and gingerly rubbed it. 'A whisky all the same.'

'No,' she stated emphatically. 'And I'll have no argument about that.'

'I'm your employer,' he reminded her. 'You'll do as I say.'

'Bully tactics, eh?'

He coloured slightly.

'You may be my employer but for now I'm your nurse, and nurse says no whisky.'

'What if I sack you?' he teased.

'Go ahead. You still won't get whisky.'

'Oh, all right,' he sighed. 'Now you're being the bully. The pot calling the kettle black.'

She grinned. 'Feeling any better?'

'A little.'

'Well, you stay there and rest quietly. I'm sending for the doctor.'

'I said not to bother.'

'And *I* said I'm sending for him.' She stared defiantly at Andrew. 'If it is an ulcer it isn't going away. At least not by itself. Ignore this and it might just happen all over again.'

She had another alarming thought. 'You don't think it's your appendix, do you?'

He frowned. That had never crossed his mind. 'Could be,' he admitted reluctantly.

'Then the sooner the doctor's here the better.'

And with that she swept from the room.

'Well, it definitely isn't appendicitis,' Lesley declared, having just given Andrew a thorough examination.

'What then? The ulcer you originally thought it was?'

Lesley shook his head. 'To be honest with you, Mr Drummond, I'm not sure. But it's hospital for you again, and this time you stay in until we find out what's what.'

'I can't do that. I . . .'

Andrew trailed off when Lesley held up a hand.

'I know you're a busy man, Mr Drummond, but certain things take precedence. We have to get to the bottom of this, no matter how inconvenient the process might be to you.'

Andrew stared hard at the doctor for a few moments, then slowly nodded, admitting defeat. 'When?' he asked.

'I'll get on the phone first thing tomorrow morning and then let you know. In the meantime stay in bed until this has completely passed. Understand?'

'Yes.'

'Good.'

Lesley packed away his bits and pieces, then stood. He had his suspicions but wasn't about to mention them to Andrew. This needed a specialist, not a local practitioner.

'Thanks for coming so promptly.' Andrew smiled.

'I'm glad I was able to. Another ten minutes and I'd have been off on another call.'

Elspeth Campbell met Lesley outside the bedroom and personally escorted him to the front door.

When she returned to Andrew's bedroom it was to find he'd fallen asleep.

'I'll be gone for a few days,' Andrew stated to Rose over breakfast later that week.

'Oh?'

It irritated him to see she'd hardly registered the fact. 'Business trip, that's all.'

'I hope you enjoy yourself, Mr Drummond,' Nancy said quietly.

Enjoy himself! He'd hardly be doing that. 'Thank you, Nancy,' he replied gruffly.

Rose began talking to Nancy about a paper drive she was organising for the war effort.

Andrew, as usual, felt totally excluded.

'Here, drink this.'

Jack gratefully accepted the hot toddy Hettie handed him. Albeit the fire was lit, he was sitting wrapped in an old travelling rug. He had a bad cold.

'This is the stuff for the troops,' he smiled.

'There's a good dollop of whisky in that so you can't complain.'

'As if I would,' he teased.

'Huh!' She then frowned when there was a knock on the outside door. 'Now who can that be?'

'Well, you won't find out unless you answer it,' Jack answered sarcastically.

She shot him a withering look. 'Very funny.'

Jack chuckled, sipping at his toddy as Hettie left the room.

My, that was rare, he thought appreciatively. It fair warmed the cockles of his heart. Something his mother had used to say about good soup.

'My God!' he heard Hettie exclaim.

There was the sound of excited voices and then Hettie bustled back into the room with Tommy in tow. 'Look who's here, Jack!'

'How can I look when I'm bloody blind, you daft eejit,' he retorted.

Hettie laughed, having momentarily forgotten Jack's disability. It had been a long time since she'd done that.

'Hello, Dad.'

Jack went absolutely still. 'Tommy?'

'Aye, it's me.'

The breath hissed from Jack's mouth. 'Welcome home, son,' he choked.

'He's wounded,' Hettie informed Jack.

'Wounded?'

'It's my arm, Dad. Nothing too serious. But it's put me out of commission for a bit.'

Tommy home, he couldn't believe it. 'Come here,' he rasped.

Tommy crossed over while a beaming and slightly tearful Hettie gazed on.

'Give me your hand, the good one.'

Jack clasped it. 'We wondered why we hadn't heard from you for a while.'

'Well, now you know. It's my writing arm that was hit.'

Wounded in the arm! Jack thanked God it hadn't been worse. 'Sit down while your mother fetches you a dram. I want to hear everything. And I mean *everything*.'

There was no chance of that, Tommy thought. Certainly not with his mother present.

'A dram sounds grand,' he replied.

Hettie hurried away to get it for him. She was excited fit to burst. All she wanted was a good cry.

McFarlane accepted Gypsy's reins from Rose. The horse had been ridden hard, but not cruelly so. And that's how it had been, more or less, since the beast's arrival. Much to his relief.

'A lovely crisp day to be out in,' he commented politely.

'It is indeed, McFarlane. I thought it might rain earlier but it's stayed away, thank goodness. I spotted some snowdrops which was nice. The first I've seen this year.'

'Aye, Spring isn't all that far off right enough.'

Rose patted Gypsy's flank. 'I want you to do something for me.'

'And what's that, Mrs Drummond?'

'Can we borrow a pony from somewhere?'

'A pony?' he queried, puzzled.

'I want to include one in my next painting. And I need a model.'

'You won't be riding it then?' McFarlane inquired craftily.

'Of course not. Why would I ride a children's pony? No, as I said, I only want it as a model.'

'I think I know where I can find a suitable Shetland for you. When would you want her?'

Rose thought about that. 'Is next week possible?'

'Oh aye, Mrs Drummond. The pony belongs to a lassie who's away at school, so I don't see any problem in having it whenever you wish.'

'Arrange it then, McFarlane. And agree payment if that's required.'

He touched his forelock. 'I'll do that.'

Rose left the groom and strode back towards the house. A pony with a child on it, she thought, smiling.

Mary.

'Yes, can I help you?'

The gaze was as fierce as Tommy remembered it. He hadn't been looking forward to this visit, but it was one he'd promised himself he'd make.

'I'm Tommy Riach, Mr McTaggart. I used to be a Sunday school teacher with Babs.'

Recognition dawned. 'Of course. The uniform quite changes you. Is it Babs you've come to see?'

'No, sir, you and your wife.'

Barney McTaggart frowned. 'And why's that?'

'May I come in?'

McTaggart stood aside and beckoned Tommy into the hallway. 'Anne, we've got a visitor!' he called out.

Tommy was ushered into the room where he'd previously met the family. He stood, cap in hand, feeling uncomfortable, while McTaggart vanished.

'Anne! Where are you, woman?'

Tommy noticed a silver-framed photograph of Gerald on top of the mantelpiece. Gerald whom he'd last seen being shot down in flames, struggling with a canopy that wouldn't open. He shuddered.

'Hello, Tommy.'

He turned to find Babs staring at him. 'Hello, I didn't hear you come in.'

'Fairy light feet, that's me.'

They both laughed.

'You're looking well,' she commented. 'Apart from the arm that is.'

'It's only a scratch.'

'I didn't know they put scratches in slings,' she retorted, slightly caustically.

'They got carried away.'

'Is that a fact.'

He hastily changed the subject. 'You're looking well yourself.'

'Thank you.'

How awfully young she seemed. A wee girl beside the woman that was Mavis Giddings. But it wasn't only that, it was him. His own youth had long since disappeared in the skies over southern England – and his innocence in Mavis Giddings' bed.

'You're here to see my parents?'

'That's right.'

'About what?'

He was about to reply when the elder McTaggarts appeared. Anne McTaggart's breath caught in her throat at the sight of Tommy's uniform. Then the moment was gone, and she'd regained her composure.

'I hope you don't mind me barging in uninvited,' Tommy apologised.

'Not at all,' Anne McTaggart replied. 'Will you stay for tea?'

Tommy shook his head. 'Thank you all the same.'

'Then please sit down.'

'I'd prefer to stand if that's all right.'

Barney glanced at his wife, then back at Tommy. 'So what's this all about?'

'I was in Gerald's squadron.'

Anne McTaggart sagged a little on hearing that.

'Did he ever mention me in any of his letters?'

'No,' Barney McTaggart replied quietly. 'Gerald wasn't a great one for letter-writing at the best of times. They became almost non-existent after the war started.'

This was the tricky part, where he had to tread carefully. 'I was there when he died.'

Anne McTaggart's eyes opened wide and a hand went to her mouth. Barney McTaggart's expression wasn't fierce any more, but grim in the extreme. He'd gone quite pale.

'How . . . how . . .' Anne McTaggart broke off, and sobbed.

'What exactly were you told?'

'Only that he was killed in action,' Barney answered.

Tommy nodded, it was as he'd thought. 'No more than that?'

'No.'

Anne McTaggart was staring intently at Tommy, her eyes full of pleading. He was about to tell her what she wanted to hear. That was why he'd come.

'It was instantaneous,' Tommy lied. 'He wouldn't have known anything about it, far less felt anything.'

Anne McTaggart started to shake, Barney putting an arm round his wife in support. 'Thank God,' he whispered.

'And you saw it happen?' That was Babs.

'Yes, I did.'

'Instantaneous,' Barney repeated. 'You hear such terrible stories. Pilots being . . .' he trailed off.

'I wanted you to know,' Tommy said. 'Now I'll leave you to it.'

'I'll see you out,' Babs volunteered.

Tommy was at the door when Barney called out after him. 'Thank you, son. We appreciate you coming here today.'

Tommy glanced back at them. 'Gerald was a brave man. I admired him tremendously. Brave, well liked and respected by his squadron. They don't come any better.'

Anne McTaggart managed to wait until Tommy had gone before collapsing, her husband catching her before she hit the floor.

Rose paused in her painting to glance over at Nancy who was staring into space. Nancy's brow was furrowed, her expression troubled.

Rose frowned. 'Nancy?'

She didn't answer, completely lost within herself.

'Nancy?'

Nancy started and turned to face Rose. 'Sorry. Did you say something?'

Rose placed her brush on the narrow indented ledge in front of the easel, and stretched slightly. She'd had enough for the moment.

'Are you all right?'

'Yes. Yes of course.'

'What on earth were you thinking about?'

Nancy coloured and dropped her gaze. 'Nothing really. Just the past.'

'You mean when you were a bondager?' Rose prompted softly.

Nancy nodded.

'A specific incident?'

Nancy sucked in a deep breath. 'A number actually. All bad.'

'Oh?'

'I was recalling one morning when I woke up feeling awful, really dreadful. My body ached and all my limbs were sore. I told Bill how I was and his reply was he didn't give a . . . well, that he didn't care. And I was to get out of bed right quick or it would be a leathering.'

'Oh, poor love,' Rose sympathised.

'Bill was like that, but then so were most of the men. Cruel as cruel. You had a day's graft to do and there were no excuses. He put his foot against my backside and kicked me on to the floor, telling me to get on with it and stop moaning.'

Nancy shook her head at the memory. 'I passed out three times that day, saved twice by my friend Annie McGillvary. She wasn't there on the third and I came round to find Bill about to hit me with his belt. I crawled away, pleading with him not to. But he still did.'

She paused, then said, 'You just don't forget things like that. They stay with you, haunting you, always.'

'It's he who should have been whipped,' Rose declared hotly.

'No, Mrs Drummond, that's just the way these men are. Bill was no worse than many. Though there are some with a kinder streak to them.'

'What sort of work were you doing at the time?' Rose asked, curious.

'Moving big boulders into place for a new dry stane dyke.'

'Dear God,' Rose muttered, thoroughly appalled. 'You shouldn't have been expected to do work like that.'

Nancy laughed bitterly. 'We women grafted as hard as any of the men, sometimes harder. There was nothing a man was asked to do that we weren't. That's how it is.'

Nancy dropped her gaze a second time.

'I'm so thankful to be here and out of all that. I can't tell you.'

Rose got up and went to Nancy, putting a comforting

arm round her. 'Well here you are now, and safe. There'll never be any more boulders and the like for you.'

Nancy shuddered. 'Thank you,' she croaked.

Rose decided to write a letter to the Secretary of State for Scotland. Ian Dalhousie was a personal friend of her father's. Something had to be done about this bondaging outrage, no matter how traditional it was in the Border counties. She would demand the situation be brought to the attention of the House.

Andrew emerged from hospital carrying the small case he'd taken in with him. It had been a far longer stay than he'd expected. Luckily he'd been able to telephone Rose with excuses about his continued absence. Not that he need have bothered, he thought bitterly, she hadn't seemed to care.

He went straight to the car and locked the case in its boot. It was a long drive home, he reflected. He only hoped he was up to it.

He stood for a moment and sucked in a deep breath. He felt so weak and wobbly on his feet and his head was spinning. That's what days in bed did for you.

There was a pub close by where he intended heading. He badly needed a drink.

Perhaps more than he'd ever needed one before.

'Are you alone?'

Tommy glanced up to find Bell Mathieson smiling down on him. He immediately rose. 'Sorry, I was lost in thought.'

'What happened to the arm?'

'Oh, it's nothing much. It'll soon heal.'

'It's nice to see you again, Tommy.'

'And you, Bell.'

'I'm with some friends over there.' She pointed to the other side of the pub. 'I noticed you and thought I'd come over to say hello.'

He gestured to the empty seat facing his. 'Will you join me for a bit?'

'I left my drink with the pals.'

'That's all right. I'll get you another. What's it to be?'

'Gin and orange would be lovely.'

'Coming up,' he declared, and strode off to the bar.

Bell watched his retreating back, thinking he was still as good-looking as ever. More so even. The uniform certainly suited him. It gave him a dashing air, reminding her of Errol Flynn in the pictures.

She recalled how she'd once been quite struck with Tommy Riach, even though he'd been younger than her. Still was, of course.

What a catch she'd considered him to be. Training as a traveller for Drummond's with excellent prospects in front of him. But that had never really been on. He was far too posh for the likes of her.

Anyway, she had David now. David who loved her and whom she was going to marry. It would be a fine life with David. Just dandy. She'd make sure of that.

Tommy returned with her drink, then went back again to the bar for his refill.

'So why are you in the pub? Is it an occasion?' he asked when he returned.

'Nope. We're just all fed up and decided to come out and get pished.'

He laughed at her bluntness. 'I know the feeling. I get it myself sometimes.' Only in his case it wasn't fed up but a combination of other things, not least fear and despair.

'How's Drummond's?' he queried.

'Ach, just the same. Well, not really. Some of the men have gone. A few called up, others joining. A couple of old fogeys have been brought out of retirement to help.'

'And Kelly, is he still there?'

'Oh aye, in all his glory.'

Bastard, he thought. That was how he always thought of Mister book-keeper Kelly.

'So why are you on your own?'

'Dad's got a cold and Mum won't let him out of the house. Otherwise he'd have been with me.'

'And so here you are.'

He smiled. 'So here I am.'

It was good being with Bell again, he'd always enjoyed her company. 'How's Irene?'

'She's in London.'

'London!' he exclaimed.

'With the ATS. She drives an ambulance for them. Having a whale of a time.' Bell giggled. 'Lots of men there, you see, which is right up Irene's street.'

'I can imagine.'

'That's why she went into the ATS in the first place. Said she wasn't doing that well round here where men were concerned.'

How at ease he felt with Bell, just as he did with Mavis. The two had a lot in common.

'How long are you back for?' Bell asked.

He shrugged. 'Depends on the arm. I'll rejoin the squadron when Lesley gives me the green light. Until then it's Mum's home cooking and the heady delights of Dalneil.'

'Will you go to the distillery? For old times sake, that is.'

He shook his head. 'I don't think so.'

'Pity, you're quite a smasher in that uniform. You'd have the lassies in bottling wolf whistling.'

Tommy grinned. 'Do you remember the Christmas party, when you and Irene had to walk me home?'

'Walk! We nearly had to carry you you were so far gone.'

'And we kissed. You and I.'

Bell blushed and looked away. 'I remember it fine. But that's a long time ago. There's a lot of water flowed under the bridge since then.'

'Aye, it has that,' he agreed.

There was a short silence between them. Then Tommy said, 'Tell me about your chap? I'd like to hear.'

Bell burbled on about David, their engagement, his conscription, and what their plans were when they eventually got married.

Tommy couldn't have been more pleased for her. A little wistful too perhaps. When they finally parted they'd spent nearly an hour together, an hour both had thoroughly enjoyed.

'Any idea where we are yet, Willi?'

The navigator of the Heinkel, poring over his maps, replied tersely into the R/T, 'None, Captain.'

Joachim Grüber swore and glanced out the side cockpit window. Nothing but blackness below, as far as the eye could see. Not even a single land light to give a clue as to their whereabouts.

They'd become separated from the others nearly an hour previously, going astray in thick cloud that had enveloped them. When he'd finally dropped below cloud level it was to find they were completely alone.

'So what do we do, Captain?' Wolf Kaplan, the co-pilot, casually inquired.

Joachim looked up at the heavy cloud layer high above the plane which totally obscured the night sky. It was that which was continuing to make it downright impossible for Willi to get a bearing.

'Another ten minutes, and then if we don't sight Clydebank we turn back.'

Wolf nodded his agreement.

The solitary Heinkel droned on.

Elspeth Campbell had been waiting for Andrew, certain he'd come and tell her what had happened at the hospital. She smiled when he appeared in the kitchen doorway.

'A cup of tea or cocoa, Andrew?'

He shook his head and produced a bottle of whisky from his dressing-gown pocket. 'I've been on this all evening. Far more appropriate.'

He collected a glass and then slumped on to a chair facing her. She watched as he poured himself a large dram.

'Are we celebrating?'

He barked out a short laugh. 'Hardly. The news was the worst possible.'

She frowned. 'How so?'

The smile he gave her was both tortured and strained. 'Not indigestion, not even an ulcer. I've got cancer of the stomach.'

She stared at him, appalled. 'Are they sure?'

'Oh aye. There's no doubt about it. I'm riddled with the damned thing. Well past redemption.'

'I'm so sorry,' she whispered.

He opened his mouth to speak, then shut it again without speaking. His eyes took on a misty look.

She knew instinctively that what she did next was the

right thing to do. Rising, she went to him and cradled his head between her breasts, her arms encircling his throat. 'How long?'

'Six months, a year. A little more if I'm lucky.'

She didn't know what to say. What could she say? Nothing.

'Not long, eh?'

Elspeth didn't reply.

The warmth and affection radiating from her were almost overpowering. Damn Rose, he thought angrily. Damn her to hell.

He knew women, oh only too well. Elspeth was his for the taking and had been for some time. What did infidelity matter now? Not a jot.

'Could you kiss a dead man?' he joked.

'Try me.'

He got up and took her into his arms. No further words were necessary.

'The ten minutes are up,' Wolf said.

Joachim grunted and glanced again out the side window. Still nothing but blackness.

'Kurt, let them go,' he instructed the bomb aimer through the R/T.

The Heinkel jerked as its deadly load fell free. Once it was gone Grüber banked the plane, heading for home.

Andrew, hands inside Elspeth's nightdress fondling her breasts, stopped on hearing a strange whistling sound. A whistling that grew rapidly louder.

Several seconds later he and Elspeth were knocked sideways as the first bomb landed on Dalneil.

Chapter 24

Andrew grabbed Elspeth before she fell over, while outside further explosions detonated.

'Jesus Christ, we're being bombed,' he exclaimed.

Elspeth's eyes went wide with fright. 'Bombed?'

He couldn't think of any other explanation. Besides, he'd heard bombs in Ireland though never the aerial variety.

His next thought was for Rose. Had the house been hit? He didn't think so. 'Wait here,' he commanded urgently, and dashed upstairs.

'Rose! Rose!'

She stumbled from her bedroom, hair dishevelled, nightdress gaping. 'What's going on?'

'Thank God you're all right,' he cried in relief.

'What's going on, Andrew?'

'We're being bombed.'

She stared blankly at him. 'Bombed?'

'That's right. Now get dressed while I see what's what.'

He ran along the length of that landing and then went up

another flight to the servants' quarters where several of them were anxiously milling around. If the situation hadn't been so serious he'd have laughed at the sight of Mrs Moffat in her night clothes. The large white cotton cap she was wearing, tied under her chin, was truly something to behold.

'Has anyone been hurt?' he demanded.

'I stubbed my toe,' Pattie Williams complained. 'It's sore.'

Andrew ignored that. Further inspection and inquiry revealed that everyone was fine and, as far as he could ascertain, there hadn't been any damage to the house.

He ran downstairs again.

Jack and Hettie had been fast asleep when the bomb landed in their back garden, blowing away the nearest wall. Their bedroom floor collapsed and the bed dropped through.

Hettie ended up half in and half out of bed. She was totally confused, coughing and spluttering from the swirling dust and plaster choking her throat.

'Hettie?'

She crawled over to Jack. 'What the fuck's going on?' he demanded.

'I don't know.'

There was a loud groan followed by a crash as their chimney stack toppled to the ground.

When Jack heard the following explosions he knew precisely what was occurring.

It was a sound he'd experienced only too often on the Western Front.

Bell too was fast asleep when the bomb crashed through their roof. She was still asleep when it exploded.

*   *   *

A distraught Rose was being cuddled by Nancy when Andrew rejoined her. 'Nancy?' he queried.

'Not a scratch, Mr Drummond. What's happened?'

Rose grabbed hold of Andrew. 'Stay here with me, Andrew. I need you.'

He shook himself free. 'We've been bombed I think, Nancy.' To Rose he said, 'The house doesn't seem to have been damaged. I'm going outside to see what I can.' He prayed the distillery hadn't been hit.

'No please, Andrew, stay with me.'

What a pathetic creature, he thought in contempt, then immediately regretted it. Rose was in shock which was completely understandable. 'You've got Nancy. She'll take care of you. I want to have a look at the distillery.'

'No, please stay, Andrew,' she pleaded.

'People will have been hurt in all this. I'll have to give what assistance I can. Now get everyone down to the kitchen and organise something. Do you hear me?'

Rose took a deep breath, then shook herself. 'Yes, Andrew,' she replied quietly.

There was a swift word with Elspeth, then he was out the back door. He stopped dead, appalled at the sight which greeted him.

The village was an inferno, at least half of it apparently on fire. Somewhere a woman was screaming. There was also an alarm bell of some sort clanging madly.

He turned in the direction of the distillery. 'Oh my God,' he croaked.

It was ablaze.

'We've got to get out of here before the whole damn building comes down,' Tommy said urgently to his parents.

'Is it that bad, son?'

'Worse than you can imagine, Dad.'

Jack cursed himself for his blindness. He felt so useless, so bloody useless.

Tommy picked up a coat that had been thrown on to the floor. 'Put this on, Mum.' He glanced around. 'I can't see your slippers.'

Jack, off the bed now, grimaced in pain as he stood on something sharp. He was still trying to take all this in.

He was one among many in what remained of Dalneil.

Andrew got as close to the distillery as he could, holding his hands in front of him to try and ward off the intense heat. The air was filled with the stench of burning materials.

The distillery was lost. There was no doubt about that. Drummond whisky had just been wiped off the map.

'Watch where you're going,' Tommy exclaimed as someone bumped into him.

'Sorry, pal. Didn't notice you.' And with that the figure was gone.

'My house, my bonny house,' Hettie whispered, staring in disbelief at the wreck which had been their home.

'Don't you worry, lass. We're alive and unhurt which is all that counts. I'll soon buy you another house,' Jack declared defiantly.

But it wasn't just the house, Hettie was thinking. It was many of the things in it. Personal items, mementoes of a long marriage. Keepsakes. They could never be replaced.

'Mr Drummond!'

Andrew turned to find Kelly there.

'You'd better get back in case the bond goes.'

Kelly was right, Andrew thought bitterly. If that went it would blow with the force of another bomb.

'Your house, Kelly?'

'A couple of broken windows, nothing more. And yours, Mr Drummond?'

'We escaped as well.' He stared again at the distillery. 'Which is more than can be said for here.'

'Aye,' Kelly agreed.

They both retreated to what they considered was a safe distance.

Andrew and Kelly stood helplessly by as the distillery continued to burn. At any moment they expected the bond to go up, but so far it hadn't.

'Listen,' said Kelly. Off in the distance was the clamour of a bell.

'Fire engine,' Andrew stated.

It was the first of many as every fire engine in that part of Perthshire converged on Dalneil.

Meanwhile Rose, Elspeth and Mrs Moffat had been busy. Masses of tea had been brewed, sandwiches made and the drawing room turned into a makeshift ward.

Christine had been dispatched to put the word round, and soon people began turning up at Drummond House, some injured, others, whose houses had either gone or were badly damaged, looking for a place to spend the rest of the night.

Rose and her staff did the best they could.

Andrew's mind was filled with memories. His own time running the distillery, the old days when it had been his father Murdo. He was in total despair.

He and Kelly glanced round when a fire engine came noisily towards them. It stopped and men jumped out.

Andrew didn't recognise the fire officer who came to stand alongside. 'This is Drummond's I understand?' the officer said.

Andrew nodded.

'And who are you?'

'Andrew Drummond, the owner. This is Mr Kelly, my book-keeper.'

'I see. Is the bond part of this building?'

'Yes it is.'

'Has it blown yet?'

'No.'

The officer's already grim expression became even grimmer. 'Where exactly is it situated, sir?'

Andrew told him, pointing it out.

The officer thought for a few moments. 'There's nothing we can do now. All I can suggest is we cordon off the immediate vicinity and wait for the inevitable.'

Andrew could only agree.

'Pity,' the officer said quietly, and with feeling, staring at the conflagration. 'I always liked a drop of Drummond's myself.'

Andrew had to smile.

'Hettie, Jack!'

Rose rushed across to them. 'Are you all right?'

'The house is a goner,' Jack replied with a tremor in his voice. 'But we're fine. Lucky I suppose.'

'Then you'll stay here for as long as it takes to get yourselves sorted out.' She held up a hand when Hettie started to object. 'You're as close as family, Hettie. I won't brook any argument.'

Tommy sat on a chair and held his head in his good hand. He was far more shaken than he'd realised. That was twice now he'd come within a whisker of death.

Rose called Jamesina Laing, the maid, over. 'Take the Riachs upstairs and put them in one of the bedrooms. See they get whatever they need.'

'Yes, Mrs Drummond.'

'I can help here,' Hettie protested.

'Later. Take care of Jack first.' She rounded on Tommy. 'What about you?'

He thought how magnificent she looked, remembering wryly that he'd fancied Rose Drummond rotten when younger. Still did, if he was honest. 'I'm OK.'

'Are you sure?'

'I might have only one arm functioning but I can put it to good use.'

Rose nodded her approval. 'Excuse me,' she said to Hettie and Jack, moving away as some ambulance men appeared at the door.

'I'll come up and see the pair of you shortly,' Tommy said to his parents as Jamesina began ushering them off.

'Mathieson . . .'

He rounded on the speaker who was Mrs Wilson, the local shopkeeper. 'What was that about Mathieson?'

'The Mathiesons, Tommy. They've all been killed.'

He went white.

'It was a direct hit apparently. The house and everyone in it went sky high.'

It was only a few short hours ago that he and Bell had been together, reminiscing, having a good laugh. And now she was . . .

'There's no mistake about that, Mrs Wilson?'

She shook her head. 'I'm afraid not, Tommy. I had it off

394

Mrs Farquharson who lives three doors down. There's just a hole where the house used to be.'

Tommy felt sick inside. This was a lot worse than losing his friends from the squadron. Far worse. This was personal in a way that that had not been.

He closed his eyes, picturing Bell as he'd last seen her. Recalling her hopes and aspirations for marriage with her David. Now she was gone; the marriage would never take place.

At least it would have been quick, he told himself. With a bit of luck she'd known nothing about it.

He was still thinking about Bell when the bond finally blew. It was the loudest explosion of all to occur in Dalneil that night.

Dawn had come and was long gone before Andrew returned home. He and Kelly had spent the last number of hours with firemen doing what they could. He was utterly exhausted, fit to drop.

Elspeth came hurrying over when she spotted him. 'You'd better have a seat and I'll get you some tea.'

'Whisky, Elspeth. Bugger tea, I want whisky.'

She didn't argue, but left him to find a bottle.

Andrew gazed around him. Rose and the staff had been busy right enough. The kitchen was filled with folk, others coming and going to various parts of the house.

He desperately wanted sleep, except that was impossible for the time being. There must still be a great deal to be done.

At least the house had survived, he thought. It would have been too much to bear to have lost that as well. And Rose was safe, another blessing to be thankful for.

'Mr Drummond.'

Andrew blinked, trying to focus. His eyes were stinging and watering from smoke. 'Tommy?'

'Aye, it's me. I wanted you to know Mum and Dad are upstairs. Mrs Drummond has given them a room.'

'They're all right then?' How often had he asked a variation of that question since this had started.

'It was a close shave but we weren't hurt in any way. The house is a wreck though.'

Andrew nodded his understanding, relieved to hear that Jack and Hettie hadn't come to any harm.

'I saw the distillery on the way here. I'm sorry,' Tommy said.

Andrew was suddenly too choked with emotion to reply. The distillery had been like an extension of himself.

Then Elspeth was by his side, holding out a huge whisky. He took it and swallowed half in one gulp. The stinging in his eyes increased but that didn't matter.

'I hear Clydebank outside Glasgow has been flattened by a Jerry raid,' Elspeth said.

'Clydebank?'

'They must have been after the shipyards there.'

What had happened to Dalneil must be connected in some way, Andrew thought, though how he couldn't fathom for the moment.

'Can I have a word, Mrs Drummond?'

Rose paused in what she was doing. 'Yes, Miss Campbell?'

Elspeth drew her aside and explained what she was proposing.

Andrew tapped on the door softly, then opened it a bit and stuck his head round. 'Can I come in?'

Rose glanced at him. This had been Elspeth's request,

that Andrew move back into her bedroom for the time being. His room was needed for Jack and Hettie.

'Of course.'

He slipped inside and closed the door again.

'You look terrible,' she commented.

'You don't look so clever yourself.'

They both laughed, and that broke the ice.

'I'm sorry about this,' Andrew apologised. 'But Miss Campbell says it's necessary. In the short term anyway.'

'She's quite right.'

'I'll use the spare quilt and sleep on the floor so as not to disturb you, Rose.'

She hesitated for a moment. 'You'll do no such thing,' she replied quietly. 'You'll sleep in the bed with me.'

He regarded her steadily. 'Are you certain about that?'

'Yes,' she snapped in reply.

Later, when they were lying side by side, she said, 'What are we going to do, Andrew?'

He considered that. It was a question he'd been asking himself. 'I honestly don't know, Rose.'

'Is the distillery completely destroyed?'

'Yes. Completely.'

Reaching out she took his hand and held it. 'I know how much it meant to you, Andrew. It was everything.'

He smiled. 'Not quite everything, Rose. You and Drew always came first.'

On hearing that Rose started to cry silently.

'Don't, Rose.'

'I can't help it,' she sobbed.

Pulling herself over she laid her cheek on his chest. And like that, they both fell asleep.

Outside their bedroom door Elspeth halted to stare at it. From inside came the faint sound of steady breathing.

Shoulders slumped she continued on her way to her own bed.

Mrs Wilson had said there was only a hole left where the Mathiesons' house had been, and that was exactly right. A hole filled with debris while other debris lay scattered around.

The bodies of the family, if found, had already been removed. The bodies or ... Tommy swallowed hard ... bits and pieces of them. Whatever had been left.

'Oh, Bell,' Tommy whispered, a huge lump in his throat.

He stood there for a good half-hour before retracing his steps to Drummond House.

Some of the rubble was still smoking as Andrew picked his way through the wreckage. He stopped in front of what remained of the pot-stills, unrecognisable now, just heaps of melted copper. Like all pot-stills they could never be replaced as such, each one being unique in shape and what it produced.

He remembered the first time Murdo had taken him into the distillery to show him round. He'd been a shaver then, quite uninterested in the goings on.

And that was how it had been through his youth and twenties. The distillery was to be his brother's one day after all. His future lay elsewhere.

And so it had been until Peter's death on the Western Front, and Murdo's on hearing the news. Then it had become his inheritance and his views towards the distillery had totally changed.

Andrew shook his head in disbelief. Yesterday at the same time the distillery had been intact, now it was a smouldering ruin. His, and his family's, livelihood had literally vanished in a puff of smoke.

What could he pass on to Drew now? Nothing. Oh, there was the house and capital in the bank. That remained. But the inheritance was no more.

He felt it was his fault somehow. And yet commonsense told him that was nonsense. He had no control over a German plane bombing the village, though why it should have done so was still unknown. The theory doing the rounds was that a plane *en route* to Clydebank must have got lost and jettisoned its load. Dalneil, wrapped in blackout, had just been the unfortunate victim.

Perhaps the lost theory was true, maybe it wasn't. He doubted they'd ever find out. All that was of concern was that the bombing had taken place with, for the village, catastrophic results.

He turned and stared out over Dalneil. How could it ever recover from this? That was something it was far too soon even to think about.

'Drew!' Rose exclaimed in astonishment.

He flew into his mother's arms. 'The headmaster called me into his office and told me what had happened. He said Dad had got a message through to him that you and he were safe and well, and not to worry.'

'So why are you here?'

'I wasn't going to remain in school after this. I wanted to come home and the headmaster finally agreed after I said if he didn't I'd run away anyway. I caught the train to Pitlochry and took a taxi from there. The driver wouldn't accept any money when he found out where I was going and why.' Drew paused, then stated, 'I'm home to help, Mum. To be with you and Dad.'

She held him close and stroked his hair. How thankful she was she hadn't become pregnant by Andy Somerville. That would not only have been cheating Andrew but Drew as well.

How selfish she'd been. She could see that now. Selfish and cruel out of morbid self-pity.

She felt truly ashamed.

'Hello.' He'd at last managed to corner her alone. How tired she looked, he thought. There were dark bags under her eyes while her hair had gone listless and dry.

Nancy smiled. 'Hello, Drew.'

He touched her, as though making sure she was actually there and not merely a figment of his imagination. 'I was worried sick about you. I knew Pops and Mum were fine, Dad sent a telephone message, but of course no mention was made of you.'

'It was terrible, Drew, really terrible,' she stated, tight lipped.

'I know. I've seen.'

'But you weren't there. It was as if the whole village was alight. I'll never forget it till my dying day.'

'I can imagine.'

Nancy ran a hand over her face. She'd hardly stopped during the past few days, and what sleep she'd had hadn't been good. Restless sleep disturbed by vivid dreams and nightmares was all she'd snatched.

'Come and sit down over here,' he suggested. They were in a small sitting room containing a sofa and chairs.

'I shouldn't really. There's so much to do.'

'Take a break, Nancy. If only for a few minutes at least. I insist.'

She smiled at the dominance in his voice. 'All right.'

He sat alongside her. 'I'm back to help out. Do what I can.'

'How long for?'

'As long as it takes.'

'But school . . .'

'Damn school,' he interjected vehemently. 'This is far more important. The family and you that is.'

She was touched by that. And surprised at just how pleased she was to see him. 'Have you had something to eat?'

He shook his head. 'I'm not hungry. I'll get something later.'

Nancy closed her eyes for a moment, feeling incredibly weary. There were still people in the house with nowhere else to go. People who had to be taken care of.

'I noticed the army's here,' he said.

'They've been terrific, organising all sorts. As have the other services. They've all been magnificent.'

'That's good.'

She named a few people. 'They were killed. Did you know them?'

He nodded.

'And others were maimed. One wee lassie lost both her legs. She's only six years old.'

Drew couldn't think what to say to that. It was appalling. How easily that could have been Nancy, or himself if he hadn't been off at school.

'You hear of the war,' Nancy went on. 'But it's all distant. Happening elsewhere. This brings home what it's really like. Not whist drives and coffee mornings, or knitting balaclavas and sweaters, but people you know, and are acquainted with, being killed and having their limbs blown off.'

'Aye,' he agreed softly.

Nancy took a deep breath. 'Now I must get on. I can't stay here chatting for ever.'

He smiled. 'I'll come with you. I'm here to help, remember.'

She matched his smile. 'If you wish.'

'I do, Nancy.'

He gazed deeply into her eyes and she into his. In that moment she knew their lives were inevitably intertwined. She'd considered it a bit of a joke before, a young lad with a crush on an older girl. But it was more than that, far more. Drew had been right all along.

'Let's get to it then,' she declared, rising.

They'd come in their many hundreds, folk from round about, and further afield, to pay their last respects to the dead of Dalneil. The church was crammed to bursting, those who couldn't get in standing outside, rank upon rank.

Tommy was there with Jack and Hettie, the three of them squashed together towards the front of the congregation. The service was the most heart-wrenching Tommy had ever heard.

When the names of the dead were read out he bowed his head when Bell's was mentioned. Bell from bottling who'd kissed him when he was drunk. Bell with the earthy sense of humour and ready laugh. Bell whom he'd never forget.

As the concluding words were being spoken there wasn't a dry eye in the church. With the exception of Jack Riach that is, for whom tears were impossible. But inside he was crying.

'Amen,' John McLean, the minister, solemnly intoned.

Outside a single army piper began to play 'The Flowers Of The Forest'.

The traditional Scottish lament, composed after the national disaster that was the Battle of Flodden.

Chapter 25

'Well, look who the cat dragged in!' Dingo Roberts exclaimed in delight when Tommy appeared in the Lamb and Flag.

Mavis beamed at Tommy from behind the bar.

'What are you having, sport?' Dingo queried as Tommy joined him.

'A pint would be nice.'

'It's on the house,' Mavis purred.

'Thank you.'

They stared at one another for a few seconds, then Mavis moved away to the pumps.

'How's the arm?' Dingo inquired.

Tommy flexed it. 'Good as new. Well . . . almost.'

They both laughed.

Tommy was pleased to be back, the last few weeks in Dalneil had been awful. A great sense of despondency had settled over the village as its inhabitants tried to gather up the pieces and get on with life.

'We heard about what happened,' Dingo said, his face creasing with concern.

'Not very pleasant,' Tommy mumbled.

'I can believe that. I take it you and your folks were OK?'

'We lost our house. A bomb landed in the back garden almost demolishing it.'

Dingo whistled softly. 'That was a bit rude of whoever dropped it.'

Rude, Tommy thought wryly. The understatement of the year. 'There was a lot of damage done. People killed. I doubt the village will ever really recover.'

Mavis placed his pint in front of him. 'You're a sight for sore eyes,' she declared.

'You too, Mavis.'

Dingo glanced away, allowing them to have a few private words together.

'Can you stay the night?'

He shook his head. 'Maybe tomorrow. I'll have to get settled in again first.'

'I understand.'

There was a yearning inside him for Mavis which had been with him all the way down from Scotland. Not just her body, though that would be more than welcome, but she herself. He'd missed her more than he'd realised.

She reached out and touched him lightly on the hand, her expression more eloquent than any welcome back speech.

'Are you serving, Mavis?' a customer called out.

'Excuse me.'

'Of course.'

Tommy looked round as he sipped his pint. There were many RAF uniforms, most of their wearers unknown to him.

'There have been quite a number of losses I take it,' he said quietly.

Dingo nodded. He reeled off a list of names that made Tommy blanch. 'Herbie too,' he muttered.

'Gone West with the others.'

Herbie Ostrove had been considered the best pilot in the squadron, a potential ace if ever there was. Now he too was gone.

Death was everywhere, Tommy reflected bitterly. So many pals, friends, acquaintances, flying off into the wild blue yonder never to return. When would that happen to him? It was surely only a matter of time.

Tommy shook himself. He mustn't think like that. Nothing was a foregone conclusion. His number might never come up. To believe it was inevitable was almost inviting it to happen.

'You'll be in charge of Green Section as I'm leading your old one,' Dingo said.

'Uh-huh.'

'No one in that section you're familiar with. They're all new boys.'

'Great,' Tommy muttered unenthusiastically.

He stayed for about half an hour before returning to camp where he found out he'd be flying in the morning just as he'd expected.

'What do you think?' Hettie asked Jack, having just read him a letter that had arrived in the morning post.

'Writing propaganda films?'

'That's what they say.'

'Based in Hertfordshire.'

'They'll provide accommodation close to the studios.'

Jack barked out a laugh. 'I wonder if they know I'm

blind? It's funny if you think about it, a blind man writing films.'

'No more than a blind man writing books and plays.'

She had something there, especially with the plays.

'Well?' Hettie demanded.

'It would certainly sort out our short-term problem of living with Andrew and Rose. It's kind of them to put us up but we can't go on accepting their hospitality for ever.'

'That's true enough,' Hettie agreed.

'How would you feel about living in England?'

She considered that. 'I don't really know. Their way of life is so very different to ours. There again . . .' She broke off.

'What, Hettie?'

'It would take us away from Dalneil for a while. I think that would be a good thing.'

'It would also mean we were closer to Tommy. Hopefully we'd be able to see him more often.'

'Aye, there is that advantage,' Hettie nodded.

They both lapsed into thoughtful silence.

'You can't keep moping around like this,' Rose chastised Andrew. 'You must find something to do.'

'Like what?'

'Something. Whatever.'

Every day he went to what remained of the distillery, stayed for a bit, and then came home again. He was still getting used to the idea that it was no more. He reached for the decanter.

'And you can cut back on that! It's only eleven in the morning, for God's sake.'

Andrew smiled inwardly. What did it matter how much he drank? It didn't in the slightest. The grim reaper was waiting no matter what.

He eyed Rose dyspeptically. He hadn't yet told her about the cancer, unable to bring himself to. And perhaps he never would. Keep it a secret.

He poured himself a dram.

'Andrew!'

He drank it off and immediately poured another.

Rose swept from the room in disgust.

'Propaganda films!' Andrew exclaimed.

'That's right.'

'Living in England. Hertfordshire,' Hettie added.

Andrew shook his head in bewilderment. 'When did this happen?'

'The letter came the other day and I've been thinking about it since then,' Jack explained. 'I've decided to accept their offer.'

'I hope it's not because you're staying here and feel in the way,' Andrew retorted. 'Because I'll be bloody angry if it is. You're welcome here for as long as you like. And that's both Rose and I speaking, not just me.'

Jack was deeply touched by that speech, knowing Andrew meant every word. 'Hettie says it would be good for us to get away from Dalneil for a while and I agree with her. That's the main reason for us going.'

'And because we'll be closer to Tommy,' Hettie added.

Andrew grunted. That seemed reasonable enough. 'As long as it is.'

'So when will you leave?' Rose asked.

'They want Jack there as soon as possible. So we thought next Monday.'

'So soon!' Rose exclaimed.

'It's high time I got back to work anyway. I don't like doing nothing.'

Rose glanced at Andrew who suddenly looked slightly uncomfortable.

'We can't thank you enough for what you've done,' Hettie said.

'As if you wouldn't have done the same for us if the boot had been on the other foot,' Andrew replied. 'You know you would.'

'And what about you, Andrew, when are you going to start rebuilding?' That was Hettie.

'Rebuilding?' he queried softly.

'Well, aren't you?'

He glanced down at the carpet so that none of them could see his expression. 'I suppose so,' he mumbled.

Jack frowned. 'Just suppose so. What kind of talk is that?'

Jack didn't know of his condition either, Andrew thought. No one in the room, apart from himself, did. There was a great black hole inside him which he felt he might tumble into at any moment.

'Well, Andrew?' Rose prompted.

'It's early days yet. There's lots of time to think about that.'

Jack's frown deepened. 'That's not like you, Andrew. Is it a case of money?'

Andrew shook his head. 'No, Jack, it's not.'

'Then what?'

Andrew was desperately trying to think of a plausible answer when he was saved by the appearance of Christine.

'Telephone for you, Mr Drummond.'

'Pardon me,' he muttered, and hastily left the room.

He used the telephone call as an excuse to absent himself from the house for a while.

'Why hello, Mr Drummond, you haven't been here for

ages.' McFarlane smiled when Andrew showed up in the stables. He noted Andrew was dressed for riding.

'How's Moonbeam?' Andrew queried, crossing to the gelding and scratching its ear. Moonbeam whinnied in recognition and appreciation.

'Just fine, sir. It took a bit for him to settle down after the bombing like, but that was only to be expected. He's his old self again now.'

'Good,' Andrew murmured. He fished some sugar lumps out of his pocket and gave them to an appreciative Moonbeam.

'You're taking him out I presume, sir?'

'Yes indeed, McFarlane. So if you'll saddle him up for me.'

'Of course, sir.'

Andrew gazed about him. He'd always enjoyed the smell of stables. There was something comforting about them. Something womblike in a way.

'Mrs Drummond hasn't been riding much recently,' McFarlane commented, heaving Andrew's saddle from its rack.

'No, I don't suppose she has.'

McFarlane was secretly pleased about that. He'd never forgotten what Rose had done to Strumpet. Neither forgotten nor forgiven her.

A sudden pain stabbed Andrew's stomach making him wince. He'd passed blood again that morning and he was losing weight. There were times when the thought of the cancer worried him almost out of his mind, other times when he felt quite ethereal about it. He'd considered confiding in Jack before he went off to England, then decided not to. Jack would leave unsuspecting they might never see one another again.

'The beast could do with a good long gallop, sir. I hope you'll give it to him.'

'I shall, McFarlane. I'm right in the mood for one.'

McFarlane nodded his approval. Such a gentleman Mr Drummond, a joy to work for.

'Right then,' Andrew said when Moonbeam was ready, and swung himself into the saddle.

'I'll be waiting for your return, sir.'

Andrew put all thoughts of cancer, and everything else, out of his mind as he urged Moonbeam forward.

It was over an hour later when Andrew came to a halt by the side of the main road leading to and from Dalneil. The weather was closing in, he observed, glancing up at a leaden grey sky. There would be rain before long. And heavy rain too by the looks of things.

He'd best get back, he decided. He didn't want to get caught in a downpour. Why add the possibility of a cold to the problems he already had? Besides, the ride had tired him out. A cup of tea and a lie-down was what he needed.

Off in the far distance lightning flickered. He waited for the sound of thunder which eventually came. A low rumbling, interrupted by another, larger, lance of lightning.

Not just rain but a storm, he concluded, as more thunder rumbled. A storm that could quite quickly be upon him if he was reading the signs correctly.

He was about to turn for home when a car came into view, one he recognised as belonging to Dr Lesley.

Lesley drew up alongside and rolled down his window. 'Hello, Mr Drummond.'

'Hello, doctor.'

'Thunder and lightning, we must be in for it.'

Andrew smiled. 'So it would seem.'

Lesley was staring keenly at Andrew. 'I've been expecting you to call on me.'

'You've had the results from the hospital then.'

'Oh aye. Several weeks ago.' He hesitated, then said, 'I really am very sorry.'

'A far cry from indigestion, eh?'

'A far cry,' Lesley agreed sympathetically. 'How do you feel?'

'So so.'

Lesley nodded. 'Much pain?'

'Some.'

'If it gets worse I can give you pills to ease it. And after that . . . I have a mixture that'll help.'

'Laudanum?'

'Old fashioned I admit. But it does the trick.'

'I'll bear the pills and mixture in mind, doctor.'

'How has Mrs Drummond taken it?'

'She doesn't know yet.'

Lesley frowned. 'When *are* you going to tell her?'

'When I decide to,' Andrew prevaricated.

Lesley wasn't really surprised. People dealt with these things in their own way. That was his experience. 'If you need me I'm always on hand. Day or night.'

'I appreciate that. Thank you.'

This time thunder cracked like a cannon discharging. 'I'd best be getting on then,' Lesley said.

Moonbeam was moving restlessly beneath Andrew, the noise both alarming and frightening him.

Andrew nodded and Lesley nodded in return.

Pills and mixture, Andrew reflected as Lesley drove away. There was clearly going to be a great deal of pain in the months ahead.

Of course there was always another way to avoid that altogether. It was certainly something to think about.

'Having a fly one then?'

Elspeth Campbell started and turned to find Andrew staring at her. She was at the rear of the house, not far from the kitchen door.

'It's my coffee break so I thought I'd come outside and watch the storm.'

A huge bolt of lightning zigzagged across the heavens followed almost instantly by a massive peal of thunder.

'That's close,' she commented, having another puff on her cigarette.

It was the first time they'd been alone since the night of the bombing and Elspeth suspected that Andrew had been purposely avoiding her. She searched his face for unease at her presence but couldn't detect any.

'How are you, Elspeth?' he asked softly.

She shrugged.

That told him a great deal. Although it didn't show, she was right, he had been avoiding her. What had nearly happened that night still troubled him.

'The Riachs are leaving tomorrow morning,' he said.

'So I understand.'

'I shall be driving them to the station and while I'm away you might arrange for my things to be moved back into the room they were using.'

She went very still inside, having wondered about that. She hadn't wanted to put Andrew and Rose together again but at the time it had made sense in the circumstances.

'I see,' she replied quietly.

The first drops of rain began to fall. Soft rain that was a prelude to what was to come.

'Have you . . . told her yet?'

Andrew smiled. That was the second time today he'd been asked that question. 'No, I haven't.'

'Don't you think you should?'

'When I'm ready, Elspeth. Whenever that might be.' If ever, he added silently.

She finished her cigarette, grinding it out on an empty matchbox and sticking the remains inside. 'Hiding the evidence,' she joked.

He noticed again those graceful hands of hers which so fascinated him. 'We'd better get in or we'll be soaked through,' he said.

'Can't you sleep?'

'No,' Tommy mumbled in reply.

Mavis reached out under the bedclothes and laid a hand on his shoulder. She was exhausted after their lovemaking and had actually dozed off only to waken again. 'What's wrong?'

Tommy twisted on to his back. 'I've been thinking about Dalneil and a girl I knew there.'

'Oh?'

'Her name was Bell Mathieson.'

'Was?'

'She was killed when one of the bombs scored a direct hit on her house.'

'I'm sorry.'

'I liked Bell. She was fun.'

Jealousy blossomed in Mavis. 'Did you know her well?' she asked casually.

Tommy laughed, having detected the jealousy. 'She wasn't a girlfriend, Mavis, though she did kiss me once when I was pissed.' He then related the story of the

Christmas 'do' and how Bell and her friend Irene had walked him home.

'And she worked at the distillery?'

'In bottling, the pair of them.'

There was a pause, then Mavis said, 'It sounds as if she was special to you?'

'Special?' Tommy mused. 'I suppose she was, in a way. She was part of my growing up. The period between school and the RAF. My youth, you could call it.'

'You're hardly an old man now,' Mavis teased.

'No? I certainly feel like one some days. War does that to you.'

'I can understand that,' she sympathised softly.

'You wake every morning whilst on active duty wondering if it's going to be your last. That takes its toll, Mavis, believe me.'

She ran a hand over his chest, thinking how much she'd come to care for Tommy Riach. She couldn't bear the thought of something happening to him.

'Bell was to be married,' Tommy went on. 'I never met the chap but they were daft on one another apparently. We spoke the night before she died and she talked about him and their plans together. It must have broken the poor sod's heart when he got the news.'

Tommy drew in a deep breath and closed his eyes. It was wonderfully safe here in bed with Mavis. Safe, and peaceful.

'Well, that's it then,' Andrew said as the train rattled into Pitlochry station. 'You've a long journey ahead of you.'

'We've got plenty of sandwiches and tea thanks to your Mrs Moffat,' Hettie said with a smile.

Andrew kissed her on the cheek. 'Don't forget there

are telephones in Hertfordshire. You can ring once in a while.'

'I won't forget. I promise.'

The train belched a great hiss of steam as Andrew turned to Jack. 'Don't let being a big film writer go to your head now.'

Jack laughed. 'I doubt it'll be quite Hollywood.'

'But knowing you, that's probably where you'll end up.'

'That'll be the day.'

Andrew had been prepared for this to be hard, but it was proving even more so than he'd expected. He and Jack had been friends a long time, bosom pals. Now it wasn't merely au revoir, but adieu.

Andrew startled Jack by wrapping his arms round him and squeezing him tight.

'Have you turned into a poof or something!' Jack exclaimed in alarm.

Andrew laughed and released him. 'Not on your life. Now get on board before you're left behind.'

Once that had been completed and their cases safely stowed on the overhead rack Andrew stepped back on to the platform and closed the carriage door. There was a lump in his throat the size of an egg.

Hettie let down the strap and leaned out of the window. 'Thanks again for all you've done, Andrew. You know how much we appreciate it.'

'Give my regards to England and all the Sassenachs,' he joked. 'And watch Jack round those actresses. We don't want him being led astray now.'

Hettie laughed, knowing there was about as much likelihood of that as there was of him regaining his sight.

The green flag was shown and the engine driver tooted his whistle. A sad, lonely sound, Andrew thought.

'Goodbye, Andrew!' Jack called out.

'Goodbye, old bean. Bye, Hettie.'

He waved till Hettie pulled herself back into the carriage, then dropped his arm.

'Goodbye, old bean,' he repeated in a choked whisper.

'What are you doing?' Rose demanded.

'Miss Campbell's orders, ma'am. Mr Drummond's things are to be returned to the room where the Riachs were.'

'Indeed,' Rose commented caustically, thinking she'd have a word with Miss Campbell about this.

And the sooner the better.

'Why, Andrew?'

Rose had purposely waited till after dinner to speak to Andrew, deeming that the most appropriate time.

He glanced across at her, having been thinking of Jack. 'Why what, Rose?' He knew precisely what she was referring to.

'I thought . . . Well, I thought . . .'

She was embarrassed, he noted, rather pleased in a way. He waited for her to continue.

'You've gone back to the other room, Andrew.'

'That's correct. Jack and Hettie have now left so it seemed the natural thing to do. Restore the status quo so to speak.'

Rose swallowed hard. 'I see.'

Andrew got up and crossed to the decanter from which he poured himself a dram. 'It's odd to think we'll soon run out of this,' he said. 'It's hard to imagine myself ordering cases of someone else's whisky, there being no more of our own available.'

Rose hung her head, shame and guilt strong within her.

They hadn't made love since sleeping together again. Once or twice she'd thought Andrew might attempt to do so, but he hadn't. As for herself, she hadn't been able to suggest it or make an advance of any kind in that direction, though, in truth, she'd wanted to.

She should apologise, she thought. Try and explain. But how could she explain what she herself didn't really understand. The loss of their baby, Mary, had played such havoc in both their lives.

'I hope Jack and Hettie are having a comfortable and speedy journey. It's such a long way,' Andrew commented casually.

'Yes.'

'With as little hold-up as possible. The train services have been dreadful since the war started. Understandable I suppose.'

'The war has upset and changed a lot of things.'

'Not least Dalneil,' he said softly.

'At least they'll be closer to Tommy where they're going.'

Andrew had a sip of whisky. His stomach had been playing up all day, and at one point he'd thought he was going to vomit. But thankfully the moment had passed.

He wondered what Rose's reaction would be if he told her about his cancer. Shock, horror no doubt. Maybe even hysterics. They had been married many years after all. And it had once been good between them.

He thought of Elspeth Campbell. Oh, what a temptation that was. A temptation to which he'd so very nearly succumbed.

What if he had, what then? He didn't know the answer to that.

'Drew will be home soon for Easter,' he said.

'Not long now,' Rose agreed.

What would become of Drew after he was gone? he wondered. What future now lay in store for the lad? What career? He had no idea.

He visualised the bombed-out rubble that had been the distillery, his heart sinking at the picture conjured up. Rebuild, Hettie had suggested. How could he do that when under the sentence of death? There simply wasn't time. Rebuilding was a long-term project, providing he could get hold of the materials which was doubtful in wartime. As for new pot-stills, securing the copper for those would be nigh on an impossibility.

And even if he succeeded in having new pot-stills made, adhering as close to the original shapes as he could, the whisky produced would be different. That was how it was with pot-stills. Each was unique and an individual which couldn't be re-created.

She deserved this, Rose thought. It was all her own fault. She had no one to blame but herself. The laugh was, she'd never stopped loving Andrew. Not for an instant. Even if she hadn't wanted him in her bed or being intimate with her.

'I think I'll go out for a walk,' Andrew declared.

'But it's late!'

Later than you realise, he thought wryly.

When he'd gone Rose remained staring into the fire. After a while she got up and went to her bedroom which now seemed an incredibly lonely place after Andrew's presence of the past few weeks.

Her own fault, she repeated to herself as she started to undress.

Mavis stopped and sucked in a deep lungful of air. 'Hmmmh,' she sighed dreamily on exhalation. 'That's good.'

Tommy, standing beside her, smiled. Her expression was almost beatific as the wind whipped her hair. 'A penny for them?'

'I enjoy working in the pub, but it's wonderful to get a day off and get out for a change. To be amongst the elements.'

'Even if it's raining?' he teased.

'It can rain and snow and chuck down hailstones for all I care. As long as I'm outdoors away from all that smoke and fug.'

He laughed. The pub did get that way at times, particularly later in the evening. There were occasions, with so many cigarettes and pipes being puffed on, you could hardly see from one end of the bar to the other.

He glanced up at the low, lowering sky. The rain had started a few minutes previously and from the looks of it was going to get a lot worse.

He took her hand in his and gently squeezed it, relishing just being in her company. How happy she made him, and, somehow, at ease with himself. If a coin has two sides then he was one, Mavis the other. Each different, yet part of the same whole.

'It's fortunate for me the weather's so bad today so I can spend it with you rather than flying.' All flying had been suspended until further notice.

She smiled her agreement.

The wind had brought colour to her cheeks, he noted. It suited her. She looked exhilarated.

'Do you mind getting wet?' she asked.

'Not in the least.'

She laughed. 'Me neither.'

The rain was getting heavier now, rattling against their coats like machine-gun fire. 'What are you thinking about?' he queried.

'Nothing. Nothing at all.'

Using his free hand he traced a line down her cheek. 'We're very lucky, you know.'

'How so?'

'To have found one another. Don't you think?'

'Yes,' she murmured huskily.

The wind suddenly gusted, making her stagger. Tommy immediately reached out and grabbed her in support. He drew her to him and held her close.

For almost a minute they remained like that, staring into each other's eyes. Neither stated what was in his and her mind. It was all too obvious.

It was hours later, the pair of them thoroughly drenched, before they returned to the Lamb and Flag. As days off went, it couldn't have been more of a success.

The sort of day that lingers in the memory for years afterwards.

Chapter 26

T he clock in Andrew's study chimed midnight. The witching hour, he smiled thinly to himself.

He was drunk, the almost empty whisky bottle by his side bearing witness to that. And he didn't care. In fact, he didn't think he cared about anything any more.

Not true, he chided himself. Of course he did. He cared about Rose, and he certainly cared about Drew, both now fast asleep upstairs.

Andrew sighed, and ran a hand through his hair. The pain had been bad that day which was why he'd started early on the whisky, preferring that, for the time being anyway, to Lesley's pills. Besides, whisky was far more enjoyable than any pill he could imagine.

'Oh, Dad,' he whispered, thinking of Murdo. 'I wish you were here to talk to. Advise me what to do. How to cope with this thing.'

Murdo's death had been swift, instantaneous almost. One moment alive, the next dead of a heart attack.

Well, it wouldn't be like that with him. He wouldn't have such luck. His would be a long lingering death filled with agonising pain. The very thought of it made him break out in a cold sweat.

Pills, mixture, was that what it had all boiled down to? A life as rich and exciting as his ending with pills and laudanum. There was a certain irony about it really. Perhaps this was his punishment for all the bad things he'd done – murder included.

Murder that had happened so very long ago, reprisal for another murder, that of his beloved Alice whom he'd intended marrying.

Hers had also been a horrible death. Burning alive in a house engulfed by flames. He shuddered just thinking about it.

What a different life it would have been if Alice had lived. She instead of Rose would even now be the mistress of Drummond House. That would have meant no Drew of course, but undoubtedly there would have been other children.

Andrew shook his head. He couldn't wish away Drew. The wee laddie had been born and was his. Loved and cherished by him. His heir.

Andrew laughed mirthlessly. Heir to what? Oh aye, there was plenty of money in the bank, and the house of course. But the distillery was gone. The distillery that should have been passed on to Drew. As it had been passed on to him by Murdo before that. And his father . . .

How he bitterly regretted getting Rose pregnant the second time. Everything between them had been fine up until then. And might still be if the baby had been born. There again, the foetus had been that of another male child, while Rose's heart had been set on a girl. Mary, as she'd called her.

Who knew what knock-on effects a baby boy would have had? The answer to that was unknown, a mystery. But he didn't think it would have been as bad as losing the baby altogether. That had been a tragedy of immense proportions, for Rose and him. Immense.

He reached down for the bottle, holding it in front of him and studying the label. Drummond's Finest Malt, Best Speyside. Perhaps the best malt in all Scotland. Now defunct.

He swore volubly, emptied the remains of the bottle into his glass and tossed the bottle aside.

He recalled his ride out the day of the storm when he'd talked to Lesley. He'd told himself then there was an alternative to the pills and mixture, and there was. Release from all this in the length of time it took to pull a trigger.

Oh, it was an option all right. He had the means to hand. All it would take was to click the bullets into the chamber and point the barrel at his head.

Boom! For a fleeting second he might hear the noise, then nothing. Oblivion. Eternity.

He laid his glass aside and came to his feet. Crossing to the bureau he opened a drawer and there it was. The Webley revolver he'd brought back from Ireland as a souvenir. And beside it the box containing four rounds of ammo, just one of which would be sufficient.

He caressed the revolver with his fingertips, then grasped the butt.

Andrew smiled in memory. This was an old friend carried daily by him throughout his entire posting in Ireland. A friend who could now come to his aid if he so wished.

Don't, son.

Andrew started. He knew that voice. Knew it only too

423

well. The hairs rose on the back of his neck and he sucked in a deep breath.

Slowly he turned but there was no one there. He was alone in the study.

'Murdo? Dad?'

Silence.

'Is that you, Pa?'

Silence again.

And then he felt it, a pressure of some sort. Not alarming in the least, rather reassuring. A warm glow that seemed to encompass him. A presence and glow not of this world.

Don't, son, the voice said again. And still there was no one else present.

'Why not, Pa? It would be easier.'

That would be cowardly, son. Don't.

The glow had become a heat that was making him tingle from head to toe. He'd never felt more alive than he did at that moment.

'I won't, Dad. You have my promise.'

The heat abruptly left Andrew's body and the sense of a presence withdrew.

He shivered. Was he going mad? Had he imagined the whole thing? Too much whisky perhaps?

No, he thought with absolute certainty. Murdo had been with him. Returned from beyond the grave and whatever lay there.

He placed the Webley back in the drawer and shut it. Nor would he ever be tempted to open that drawer again.

He'd promised. A promise he'd keep.

Tommy was drained as he and Dingo entered the Lamb and Flag. Paul Wyborn had been shot down that afternoon during a sortie over France. Both he and Dingo had seen

Paul's parachute open so by now Paul would be a prisoner of war. In the bag for the duration.

At least Paul was out of it, Tommy thought. At least he'd survive. The conditions in the POW camps may be appalling, so rumour had it, but incarceration in one was preferable to the fate that so many of their comrades had met.

Ruffles, Dan Gilfeather's wife, was behind the bar polishing glasses. Ruffles was a nickname given to her years before on account of her fiery, and quick, temper. A local had said to her one night, Don't get your feathers ruffled, Gilfeather, and that's how the nickname had come about. She'd been Ruffles to all and sundry ever since.

'Hello, boys.' She smiled. 'What's it to be?'

'A couple of pints please,' Dingo retorted, heaving himself on to a stool.

Tommy looked along the length of the bar but there was no sign of Mavis, and it wasn't her night off.

'Upstairs in bed. She's feeling poorly,' Ruffles informed him when he inquired.

Tommy was immediately concerned. 'How poorly?'

'Flu I think. Or something similar. Came down with it earlier so I packed her off to her room.'

Ruffles smiled at Tommy. 'I was just about to take her up some soup. Would you like to instead?'

'Yes please.'

'Then come on through and I'll give it to you,' Ruffles said, serving Dingo.

'What about your pint?' Dingo queried of Tommy.

'I'll get it shortly. I won't be long.'

And with that Tommy followed Ruffles to the kitchen.

*   *   *

'Can I come in?' Tommy asked, poking his head round Mavis's door.

Damn! Mavis swore inwardly. What a sight she must look. She didn't want Tommy to see her like this. But the damage was already done.

Tommy entered the room without waiting for a reply. 'I've brought you a bowl of soup,' he explained.

She shook her head. 'I couldn't eat a thing.'

'But you must to keep up your strength.'

'I couldn't, Tommy. Honestly. I've no appetite at all. The very thought of food . . .' She trailed off and pulled a face.

Frowning, he set the tray he was carrying atop a chest of drawers, then crossed and sat on the edge of her bed.

'You shouldn't be up here this time of day. What will people say!' she admonished.

He shrugged. 'It's an errand of mercy. Quite understandable in the circumstances.'

'And I'm a mess!'

'Well, I hardly expected you to be all dolled up ready for a night on the tiles,' he joked.

She smiled at that.

Mavis was pale as anything, he noted, with dark smudges under her eyes. Her brow was dotted with perspiration.

'So how are you?'

'Weak.'

He grunted.

'And very hot.'

He felt her forehead which was burning. 'Ruffles says it's flu.'

'It could be.'

'Have you sent for the doctor?'

'Not yet.'

'Then why don't I go back downstairs and ring him.'

'I happen to know he isn't there just now. He's out delivering a baby and will be tied up for hours yet. I'll ring in the morning if I'm still bad.'

He stared at her, his anxiety clearly showing. 'Is there anything I can get you?'

'I could use some water. My glass is empty.'

He immediately rose, picked up the glass and went over to her washing jug and basin, filling the glass from the jug.

'Here,' he said, placing the rim of the glass against bloodless lips.

Mavis drank her fill then lay back on the pillow. 'This is quite unlike me. I just don't get ill very often.'

'Well, you are now. So you stay in that bed until you're better. Hear?'

'I hear.' What a truly lovely man he was, she thought. If only things had been different and there hadn't been a war on. There again, she'd never have met him if it hadn't been for the war.

'Could you take a hot toddy?' he asked. 'It would do you the world of good.'

She pulled her hand out from under the bedclothes and grasped his. 'That would be sweet of you.'

'Then a hot toddy it is, I'll go and fetch it. In the meantime don't run away.'

She laughed at that, the idea of her running anywhere in her present condition being so ridiculous.

'What are you doing!' Tommy exclaimed in alarm on returning with the toddy. Mavis was squatting by the side of the bed.

She coloured. 'I had to use the gazunder.'

'You should have waited till I got back.'

'I didn't want you to see. It's embarrassing.'

427

'Daft woman,' he chided, hurrying over. 'If you have to go you have to go and that's all there is to it. What if you'd fallen over, for God's sake!'

'Then I'd have got up again.'

'That's not the point.'

Her head was swimming and she felt even weaker than when she'd been tucked up. She swayed slightly.

Tommy instantly had her by the arm. 'Have you finished?'

She nodded.

'Then let's get you back under those clothes.'

He smoothed the quilt having first readjusted her pillows. 'How's that?'

'Better, thank you.'

Her hairline was damp he noticed, which, surprisingly, he found rather erotic.

'We're like an old married couple,' she joked.

Using his foot he pushed the gazunder out of sight. He'd empty it later. 'Nothing wrong in that.'

She didn't think so either. It was a most enjoyable experience. She wasn't used to being looked after. Certainly not by a man. And a lover at that.

'Let's get some of this toddy down you,' he declared.

She drank about half and then said she couldn't swallow any more. He laid the glass aside.

'What about your pals in the bar?' she asked. 'They'll be missing you.'

For some reason that angered him. 'I can be with them any night I want. I'm here now with you because you need me. And here I stay.'

That touched her deeply. 'What if I fall asleep?'

'I still stay. You may want the pot again. Or something else. Are you hungry?'

'Not in the least.'

'Have you had anything at all today?'

'Ruffles brought me a lightly boiled egg earlier that I managed to get down. But it was a struggle. I just don't have any appetite at all.'

He went back to the jug and basin, picking up the towel that was there. He used that to mop her forehead and neck.

'There,' he declared when he was finished.

'At this rate I'll lose pounds,' she smiled. 'Which is no bad thing.'

'Rubbish,' he admonished. 'You've got a lovely figure. Just right in my opinion. You don't want to get skinny with your bones showing through. Horrible.'

'You've quite cheered me up, Tommy. Thank you.' She smiled again.

'Have I?'

'Oh yes,' she breathed, wishing he was in bed beside her. Cuddled up close as they often were when they slept together. 'Do I really have a lovely figure?'

'Absolutely gorgeous.'

'My bottom's rather large.'

'Not so.'

'And my thighs . . .'

'Are a knockout,' he interrupted. 'Smooth as silk and shapely as can be.'

'You've got a nice body yourself,' she told him. 'With a beautiful bottom. Women like beautiful bottoms. It's a huge attraction in a man.'

'Well well,' Tommy murmured. He'd had no idea.

'And you always smell nice. Some chaps pong no matter what, but you never do.'

'I think this is a mutual admiration society,' he laughed.

'Well, if it is it's because we're so . . .' She trailed off.

'So what, Mavis?' he prompted.

She desperately tried to think of the correct word, not wanting to admit too much of what was in her mind. She didn't want to frighten him off. 'So compatible.'

He stared at her. Compatible? 'I suppose we are,' he replied softly. He hadn't thought of it like that before. But yes, they were.

'Tell me a story about Africa?' she requested.

'Africa! But I haven't been there yet.'

'That doesn't matter. You must know a lot about the place. Make one up.'

His mind raced, recalling Edgar Rice Burroughs whom he'd read years ago. Perhaps it was then the whole great dream had started. He wasn't sure. Edgar Rice Burroughs and, later, H. Rider Haggard.

'King Solomon, of old, had a fabled diamond mine whose whereabouts somehow became lost through the centuries . . .'

Mavis snuggled down deeper under the covers, closing her eyes to listen.

'Then, in Victorian times, a map was discovered . . .'

Tommy woke, sore and stiff. With a sudden jerk, realising where he was, he sat upright and glanced anxiously at the bedside clock, breathing a sigh of relief to see he hadn't overslept.

Pale morning light had invaded the room, it being not long after dawn. He rose and quietly stretched.

Mavis was breathing regularly, her eyes firmly closed. Just as she'd been before he too dropped off. He placed the chair he'd been sitting in back in its original position, then, ever so gently and lightly, touched her forehead.

It was warm, but no more than it should have been. He noted that the dark smudges under her eyes had disappeared.

Tommy smiled to himself. It seemed Mavis was on the road to recovery.

'Come in, Green Leader, this is Control.'

Tommy flicked on his R/T. 'Receiving you loud and clear, Control.'

'You are diverted to West Malling, Green Leader. We're fogbound here.'

Tommy frowned. Damn! he inwardly swore. This was a nuisance. He wanted to get back to Laxworth and Mavis.

'Is that certain, Control?' he queried.

'Quite certain, Green Leader. Please confirm.'

'Confirmed, Control. Am now making for West Malling.'

The R/T order had been heard by the rest of the section so Tommy didn't have to repeat it.

'Breaking right, chaps. Here we go.'

The section came on to its new course.

'I'm sorry, sir, I can't get through to that number.'

Tommy grimaced in disappointment. This was the third time he'd tried to phone the Lamb and Flag and the third time he'd failed.

'Thank you very much, operator.'

'You're welcome, sir. I'm sorry.'

Tommy hung up. He was desperate to know how Mavis was. Of all days to be diverted and then not be able to get through on the telephone. He just hoped Mavis was all right.

He returned to the Officers' Mess where a party was in progress, it being one of the West Malling-based pilots' birthday. A boozy, riotous affair which was bound to result

431

in a few sore heads in the morning. He was determined he wasn't going to be among them.

Later, he attempted one more call, that too proving unsuccessful.

Tommy stared in disgust out of the window of the temporary billet he'd been allocated. It was a pea-souper which meant that West Malling was now also fogbound. He seethed with impatience, anxious about Mavis.

The 'drome remained fogbound for the rest of that day during which he attempted a number of times to ring the Lamb and Flag.

On the sole occasion the operator did manage to get a connection no one answered.

'Can I come in, Dad?'

Andrew smiled at his son, home for the holidays, standing framed in the study doorway. 'Of course.'

Drew closed the door behind him.

'So what can I do for you?'

'I thought we might talk.'

Andrew raised an eyebrow. 'About what?'

'The distillery.'

Andrew's face clouded over. That was the last thing he wished to discuss.

'Can I sit, Dad?'

'Aye, help yourself.'

There was a fine fire going which Andrew had positioned himself to one side of. Drew now pulled a chair across and positioned himself at the other side.

'It's a terrible loss,' Andrew stated quietly. 'I still haven't come to terms with it. As long as I can remember it's been there, and now it's gone. For ever.'

Drew's brow furrowed. 'For ever? Surely not?'

Andrew shrugged.

'Aren't you going to rebuild?'

Andrew became uneasy. He could hardly explain the reason why he hadn't considered doing that. Why it was impossible.

'Well, Dad?' Drew prompted.

'Some things are just meant to be, son, and there's nothing we can do about them.'

Drew couldn't believe he was hearing this. It was so unlike his father. 'But of course there is! You can rebuild.'

'With a war on? I'd never get the materials.'

'Surely from somewhere?'

Andrew sighed. The very guts had been knocked out of him, he thought. He was a shell compared to the man he'd once been. And, in a way, he felt ashamed.

He studied Drew. The lad was a credit to him and Rose. He'd been a bit of a tyke when younger. Spoilt if he was honest. But Drew had outgrown that. A young man was emerging, one of promise. He and Rose could be proud of themselves.

Andrew shook his head. 'Not a chance.'

'But you could try.'

'I'm telling you . . .'

'You must *try*, Dad,' Drew interjected hotly.

'Anyway, it's early days yet.'

'Not too early to start thinking about it, making plans. For the future if they have to be, but at least making plans. Doing something.'

There was a silence between them during which Andrew stared morosely into the fire.

'This is important to me, Dad,' Drew went on after a while. 'More than anything I want to carry on after you, just as you did after Grandpa Murdo. I've set my heart on it.'

'Have you indeed,' Andrew murmured.

'Yes I have. I've even got ideas of my own.'

That surprised Andrew. 'What sort of ideas?'

'We only distribute in this country, Britain that is. And even then not a huge amount into Southern England. When the war's over we can expand our market. First into Southern England, then abroad.'

'Abroad?'

'America to be precise. I'm certain the Americans would take as much as we could give them. We need the capacity of course, but we can acquire that by rebuilding on a far larger scale than the old distillery.'

Andrew stared at his son in amazement. Well well, he mused. It would seem he'd spawned a tiger.

Excitement gripped him. America! Now why hadn't he thought of that? The reason was obvious. Capacity, as Drew had pointed out. That had been his limitation. It had simply never crossed his mind to expand, being content to let things go on as they'd always been.

'What do you say, Dad?'

'Interesting premise, I'll give you that.'

'It's a golden opportunity we have here. One we should grasp with both hands.'

We? Andrew chuckled inwardly. Whatever else, the lad was certainly serious about all this. Particularly his own involvement.

'I was thinking earlier about a lecture you once gave me,' Drew stated, slightly changing tack.

'Oh?'

'About the people who work for us and our responsibility towards them. If you don't rebuild they'll be permanently out of a job. And think of the effect that'll have on Dalneil.'

Andrew blanched. That was below the belt. True, mind you, but still below the belt.

And yet, the fact remained, he was a walking, talking dead man. He just didn't have the time left to rebuild.

But Drew did. Drew had a whole lifetime ahead of him.

'I'm worried about Dad.'

'In what way?'

Drew leant on the mantelpiece in Nancy's bedroom, having come to pay her a visit on leaving Andrew. Nancy had been reluctant to let him in, but had eventually been persuaded to do so.

'He doesn't look well. Have you noticed?'

Nancy thought about that. 'Can't say I have.'

'Well, I've noticed. I swear he's lost weight. And there's a tinge about his skin that isn't at all healthy.'

'Now you mention it,' Nancy frowned, 'his appetite isn't as good as it was. Your mother commented on that only recently.'

Tommy nodded. 'It's losing the distillery if you ask me. It's eating him up inside. That's what's bothering him and making him unwell.'

'Poor man,' Nancy sympathised.

'Well, I may have done something about that.'

'You?'

Drew smiled. 'The chat I had with him tonight has certainly given him a great deal to think about. He was quite bubbling with enthusiasm when I left his study.'

'So what did you say?'

Drew repeated the conversation he'd had with Andrew. When he finally finished Nancy was staring at him in admiration. Where was the boy of only a few years ago? This was a man talking. And an ambitious, far-sighted one at that.

'What do you think?' he demanded eagerly.

'It's a terrific notion.'

'And it'll work. Believe me. I just know it will. Oh, it'll take a long while to come to fruition, even if we started rebuilding tomorrow. Whisky takes time to mature before you can sell it to the public. It could be ten years from now, more, before the first bottle of Drummond's malt reappears in the shops and pubs. But reappear it must, and will.' His jaw jutted forward. 'I'm determined about that.'

'Why don't you kiss me,' she whispered.

He was smiling again as he moved towards her.

How many nights now had she waited for Andrew? Elspeth had lost count.

Sighing, she lit another cigarette. She'd hang on another half hour before returning to bed.

He hadn't come to the kitchen in the early hours since the night of the bombing, the night they'd come so very close to making love.

She would have to speak to him soon, she decided. She had to know where she was. She couldn't go on fretting like this.

Her heart leapt when there was a sound from outside in the corridor. Andrew?

But it wasn't. The kitchen door remained resolutely shut. Whatever had caused the sound, it hadn't been him.

The minutes continued to tick slowly by.

Chapter 27

Tommy and the section had been fogbound at West Malling for two days, then, on the third, had flown a sortie from there, returning at long last to Laxworth. At no point during this time had he managed to get through to the Lamb and Flag.

He now strode into the pub, coming up in surprise, and relief, to see Mavis busy behind the bar.

'Home is the hunter!' Dingo called out, giving Tommy the thumbs-up sign.

'How are you, mate?' Dingo asked as Tommy joined him. Dingo's section had landed considerably earlier than Tommy's which was why he was in the bar before him.

'Fine. And you?'

'Never better.'

Mavis served her customer and hurried across, eyes shining at the sight of Tommy.

'I thought you were at death's door?' he joked.

'Whatever it was I had passed quickly. I was up and about the afternoon after you left me.'

'I've been trying to ring but couldn't get through.'

Mavis nodded. 'There has been trouble with the phone lines, but I think it's sorted now.'

He wanted to take hold of her, clasp her in his arms. Tell her how much he'd missed her.

'I'm off to the dunny,' Dingo announced, deeming it polite to leave the lovers alone for a few minutes.

'Thank you for what you did,' Mavis said.

'It wasn't much.'

'Oh yes it was. It was appreciated I can tell you.'

He didn't know what to answer to that.

'Can you stay tonight?'

'I thought you'd never ask.'

She laughed and, reaching out, briefly touched his hand. A touch that was also a caress.

'I was worried about you,' he admitted.

'The doctor came but couldn't diagnose exactly what was wrong. It wasn't a cold, he said, or flu. Though the symptoms were similar to flu. He gave me some medicine and a few hours later I was back on my feet again.'

'Good medicine.' Tommy smiled.

'Maybe. But the best medicine was having you with me. That was an enormous comfort.'

There was a slight hiatus while they stared at one another. 'Now what are you going to have?' Mavis asked eventually.

'We should get married.'

Mavis went very still. Then, slowly, she turned to face Tommy. It was later that night and they were in bed together.

'Married?'

'I love you, Mavis.'

A thrill ran through her to hear those words. 'And I love you, Tommy,' she replied softly.

'If it wasn't for the war I'd propose here and now. There's no doubt whatsoever in my mind that I want you to be my wife. But how can we get married with a war on? We could be married one day, you a widow the next. I couldn't ask that of you. It just wouldn't be fair.'

She stroked his cheek, still damp from their recent lovemaking. 'How little you know of women, Tommy.'

'Is that so?'

'That's so,' she smiled. 'I'll happily marry you, no matter what.'

He sat up on an elbow. 'Are you serious?'

'Never more so. We love each other and that's all that counts.'

'But if I was killed . . .'

'Then it happens,' she cut in. 'There's no way of telling whether it will or not. But if it doesn't, think of all the time we'd have wasted.'

'We could go on just as we are for now.'

'We could. Except, what happens if you're re-posted?'

Tommy bit his lip. That was always a possibility. The war could drag on for years yet. The chances of his remaining at Laxworth indefinitely were very small if it did.

'If we were married I could follow you to wherever. There's always a need for barmaids.'

He studied her, thinking the last thing he wanted was for them to be parted. Even the few days he'd spent at West Malling had been torture.

'Are you absolutely certain about this?' he demanded.

'Absolutely.'

'No doubts . . . ?'

She interrupted him by laughing. 'None whatever.'

'Then will you marry me?'

'I'd be honoured to.'

A great whoof of breath escaped him. Then he was holding her tight, squeezing her against him. Now all that remained was the matter of where and when. The sooner the better they both agreed when he put that to her.

'Let's go and tell Ruffles and Dan,' she suggested. 'I have to tell someone.'

'But they're in bed.'

'So we'll wake them. They won't mind.'

Tommy released her and slipped from underneath the covers, Mavis getting out the other side. She put on her dressing gown, he trousers and shirt. They left the room hand in hand.

Ruffles and Dan Gilfeather were so excited by the news they insisted on opening a bottle of champagne, and a second bottle after that. As Dan commented, owning a pub did have its advantages. Like being able to lay your hands on champagne after closing time.

Andrew, hands deep in pockets, stood hunched, staring for the umpteenth time at the remains of the distillery. His mind was whirling, thinking about that conversation with Drew, wondering . . . wondering . . .

'Hello, Mr Drummond.'

Andrew started, and turned to find Kelly there. 'Why, hello, Kelly.'

'I was out for a constitutional and found myself wandering up here. It's something I often do.'

Andrew gave the book-keeper a wry smile. 'Me too.'

'It's a bit like visiting a cemetery I suppose,' Kelly said. 'Paying your respects, that sort of thing.'

Andrew nodded that he understood.

'Lovely day,' Kelly declared, glancing up at the sky. 'It promises to be a fine summer.'

'Let's hope it is.'

'And how are you, Mr Drummond?'

'Not too bad. And yourself?'

'Bored, if the truth were known. But I imagine that's how it's going to be from here on. No one else is going to employ me now. Too long in the tooth I'm afraid.' He sighed. 'When the distillery went so did my working life. I'm on the scrapheap now and there I'll stay.'

Andrew felt for the man.

'Still, it could always be worse,' Kelly murmured.

Aye, Andrew reflected, thinking of himself. It could be. 'Do you know the legend of the Phoenix, Kelly?' he asked.

Kelly frowned. 'Isn't that the bird who dies and then gets reborn again?'

'The very one. It literally rises again out of the ashes of its own funeral pyre. At least that's how I remember the story.'

Kelly regarded Andrew quizzically. 'Is there a relevance here?'

'Possibly,' Andrew mused. 'Let's go for a walk. I've something to discuss with you about which I wish your opinion.'

It was an enormous undertaking, Andrew reflected. He'd been doodling on a pad of paper, roughly sketching out how the new distillery might look. Of course he'd need an architect to do the job properly, this was just to give him some sort of idea.

A new distillery would have to be fully up to date which meant mechanisation wherever possible. The bottling department, for example, would be entirely updated, machines doing the bulk of work previously done by hand.

Naturally some processes couldn't change, they would be performed in the traditional manner. Had to be.

His thoughts were interrupted by a tap on the study door. 'Come in!'

It was Elspeth. He knew instantly from her expression what this was all about.

'I took the opportunity while Mrs Drummond and Nancy were out,' she stated.

He nodded. 'Take a seat.'

'I'd rather not, if that's all right.'

He laid his pencil aside and studied her. 'What's on your mind, Elspeth?' As if he didn't know.

'I want to know where I stand. About you and me that is.'

'And you have every right to,' he murmured. 'But please take a seat. I'm hardly the boss on this occasion.'

Elspeth hesitated, then crossed to a chair.

'Drink?'

She shook her head.

He decided he wouldn't have one either. His stomach was tender and he'd passed blood again that morning. Best leave well alone for the time being.

'I should have spoken before now,' he said.

'Yes, you should, Andrew.' Her tone was accusatory.

He dropped his gaze for a few moments, thinking about how he should phrase this. 'It's obvious I'm extremely attracted to you. Have been for quite some time. I certainly wasn't trying to simply take advantage of you.'

Tears came into Elspeth's eyes. 'You've made me feel so cheap.'

'I'm truly sorry about that, Elspeth. Honestly I am.'

'Then what happened? Why have you never approached me again since the night of the bombing? Is it? Is it me? Something I did? Something I said?'

Andrew shook his head. 'Attracted as I am, I realised it would be a mistake.'

'Why?'

'Because . . .' And here it was, the nub of the matter. 'Because I still, despite everything, love my wife.'

Elspeth jerked as though she'd been struck.

'That may sound ridiculous, considering how she's treated me, but nonetheless it's fact.'

Elspeth glanced away, tears now streaming down her face. 'How little you must think of me.'

'That's not so!' he exclaimed. 'I happen to think very highly of you. Very highly indeed. But I don't love you, I love Rose.'

Damn, he was going to have to have that drink after all. He got up and went to where he kept a bottle and glass. One of the last bottles of Drummond in the house. Galling as it might be, he was going to have to order a case or two of another brand.

'Do you want me to leave? My job that is?' she asked.

He thought about that. 'Not really. But I would understand if you did.'

He suddenly laughed. 'It's ironic really. I was quite the rake when younger, there were women galore. When it came to them I don't think I had a scruple in my entire body. It just shows you how we all change.'

'If that's how you feel why did you do what you did the night of the bombing? Was it because of what you'd been told at the hospital?'

He leant back against the bureau, feeling incredibly weary. Not just a physical tiredness, but a fatigue of the soul. 'I suppose so. I was full of self-pity that night. About my cancer, about my marriage. You were sympathetic. But more than that, I'd found something with you that I'd once had with Rose and which has been missing for years. Something I desperately needed, particularly that night of all nights.'

Elspeth didn't feel so bad any more. What he was saying made sense. She could understand it.

'It wasn't some kneejerk reaction,' Andrew went on slowly. 'At the time it seemed almost inevitable. But it would have been wrong, believe me.'

'I do,' she whispered.

He had a gulp of whisky, shuddering as it coursed its way down his throat. 'I should have spoken sooner, I know. You shouldn't have had to come and beard me literally in my den. Call it cowardice if you will. Call it whatever. I apologise.'

'You still haven't told Rose, have you?'

He smiled cynically. 'No.'

'Why not?'

He shrugged. 'I'm not certain I shall tell her.'

'But you must! You can't leave her in the dark. That's not fair.'

'I can do whatever I wish,' Andrew replied softly. 'Certainly where that's concerned.'

'But you said you still love her.'

'And I do. But Rose's affections for me have long since withered on the vine. Look at it this way, perhaps it's a case of what she doesn't know won't upset her. Anyway . . . I haven't decided yet. I may or I may not. I'll see.'

There were the beginnings of new lines on his face she realised. 'Are you in much pain lately?'

The cynical smile returned. 'It varies from day to day.

Whisky helps, though sometimes it gets too much for even that.'

Now Elspeth dropped her gaze. 'If there's anything I can do . . .'

'There is.'

'What?'

'Stay on until it's all over. I said I'd fully understand if you went, but I would like you to remain.'

'Why, Andrew?'

'Because . . .' He trailed off and frowned. 'I'm being selfish again, aren't I? Selfish and unfair. You must do what's right for you.'

Elspeth wiped away her tears, then snuffled into a hanky she produced from a pocket. 'Your Rose is a fool,' she said quietly. 'A bloody fool in my opinion. She doesn't realise what she's chucked away.'

'Compassion, Elspeth, remember the miscarriage. If anything's to blame it's that.'

She'd have to go to her room and wash her face, Elspeth thought. That and compose herself. 'You're a good man, Andrew Drummond,' she stated simply.

He laughed. 'Hardly that! Quite the contrary I should think.'

'But you are. And I wish you had fucked me that night. I'll always regret you didn't.'

Her using that word shocked Andrew. And yet, wasn't that, attraction or no, exactly what it would have been?

'I still go down to the kitchen in the early hours if you ever need companionship,' she said.

'No strings?'

'None. I still enjoy being with you, talking . . .' She bit her lip, and shrugged awkwardly.

'And I you.'

She hesitated for a few seconds, then said, 'I'll let you get on. I can see you're busy.'

'Thank you.'

She left him with a far lighter heart than she'd had on entering the study.

'My God!' Hettie exclaimed, reading the letter that had just arrived in the morning post.

'What is it?'

'Tommy's getting married a week on Saturday and wants to know if we can come!'

Jack was stunned. '*Married?*'

'So he says. A girl called Mavis Giddings. It's to be a civil ceremony.'

Jack was totally lost for words. He hadn't even known Tommy was courting, neither of them had.

'Well, I'll be buggered,' he managed eventually.

'Can we go?'

'Of course we'll bloody well go. Wild horses wouldn't keep me away.'

'I've got to sit down,' Hettie declared.

Jack rubbed his chin. Tommy getting married? This was a turn-up for the book. He just hoped it wasn't one of those fleeting wartime romances that would end in tears.

Please God it wasn't that.

'What are you and Kelly up to, locked away in your study hour after hour?' Rose demanded.

Andrew tapped the side of his nose. 'That's for me to know and you to wonder about.'

He was teasing her she realised. 'Oh come on, Andrew, spill the beans?'

'No,' he replied, shaking his head.

'*Pretty* please?'

He laughed. She was in as playful a mood as he. 'It's a secret.'

'Oh, one of those, eh?'

'Exactly.'

'But a man shouldn't have secrets from his wife.'

'And why not?'

'He just shouldn't, that's all.'

He wagged a finger at her. 'Are you saying you don't have secrets from me? Because if you do I won't believe you.'

Her eyes flew open in pretend innocence. 'Cross my heart and hope to die. Not a one.'

This was the Rose of old, he thought, smiling. How relaxed it made him feel.

'Come on,' she urged. 'Give.'

'It's a plan,' he declared.

'What sort of plan?'

'A plan I was asked to draw up by the War Office.'

That was obviously a lie. 'And when did they do this?'

'Some while ago. I had a telephone call from Winnie himself.'

Now it was becoming outrageous, but fun. 'I see.'

'Is that you, Andrew old chap, Winnie said. And then went on to tell me what he wanted.'

'Which is?'

Andrew leant forward in his chair and winked conspiratorially. 'A plan to bring about the downfall of Hitler.'

'Really!'

'Really,' he nodded.

'And how are you going to do that?'

'That's the secret.'

'And how did they get your name?'

'From Kelly. He's really a member of . . .' Andrew broke

off in apparent confusion. 'I can't say. I'm sworn not to.'

'Another secret?'

'That's right.'

Rose's lips were twitching with amusement. 'That makes you very important.'

'Indeed.'

'And Kelly?'

'Indeed again.'

'And you won't tell me?'

'Can't, Rose. Promised Winnie.'

Andrew thought he'd better get out of this while the going was good, while he was ahead. As an actor had once told him, important rule of the theatre, always know when to get off the stage.

A glance at the clock told him it was getting late. He rose, and stretched. 'It's bed for me.'

'I'll go on up shortly.'

Andrew turned to leave, then stopped. 'Oh by the way, I shall be spending a few days in Glasgow next week.'

She frowned. 'Glasgow?'

'On business.'

'But we don't have a business any more. It was blown up, remember?'

'Secret business, Rose. Winnie and the plan.'

What was he really up to? she wondered. It certainly had nothing to do with whisky. She was intrigued. And then she had a terrible thought, one that made her go quite cold inside. Was it another woman?

'Andrew?'

'What, Rose?'

'Can I come with you?'

That rocked him. 'To Glasgow?'

She couldn't hold his gaze, dropping hers to stare at the carpet. Had she left it too long? She didn't know. Perhaps she had.

'Rose?' he prompted.

'We had such a wonderful time when we last went there . . .' She swallowed, then added in a croak, 'Together.'

He couldn't believe he was hearing this. 'Is that what you want?'

'Yes,' she replied in a whisper he almost didn't catch.

Andrew took a deep breath, his mind whirling. 'What about the room accommodation?'

She looked up at him, her eyes bright. 'A double will do. If you wish it that is.'

A double, sharing a bed again with Rose. This time not merely out of convenience but at her request. Could it possibly be . . .' I haven't fixed a date yet. I'll let you know when I do.'

She nodded. 'Fine.'

'Do you have preferences?'

'No.'

'Because it doesn't matter to me.'

'Nor me, Andrew.'

'Probably the Thursday and Friday.'

'Whatever.'

'And the hotel, which do you fancy?'

'The one we went to before.'

He stared hard at her, still not believing he was hearing what he was hearing. 'All right then.'

She glanced away, aware that her face was slightly flushed. 'I'm looking forward to it.'

'Goodnight, Rose.'

'Goodnight, Andrew.'

He shook his head all the way upstairs to his room.

*   *   *

'So what do you think?' Mavis demanded of Ruffles. She'd been given the day off to go and buy her wedding outfit.

'Turn round.'

Mavis slowly did so.

'It's beautiful,' Ruffles breathed.

Mavis laughed. 'Hardly that, but the best I could do. With clothes rationing rumoured about to come in the shops are stripped bare. I was lucky to find anything at all.'

She was wearing a navy suit whose jacket had a nipped waist, rounded collar, short, slightly ruffled sleeves and a narrow cuff. There were neat covered buttons at the front.

The skirt was fitted at the waist, dropping to a slight flare at mid calf. The shoes were navy suede courts.

The entire ensemble was set off by a small navy hat, rayon-draped at the front, trimmed with feathers and perched at a jaunty angle.

'I still say it's beautiful,' Ruffles enthused. 'Tommy will be proud of you.'

'Do you really think so?'

'I'm certain of it.'

There was a warm glow inside Mavis as they began eagerly discussing accessories. And other necessities. Something borrowed . . .

'The Clyde by night and moonlight,' Andrew declared. He and Rose had been to Rogano's restaurant where they'd had a wonderful fish meal. After which he'd suggested they go for a stroll that had eventually brought them to the banks of Glasgow's main river.

The meal itself had been a somewhat constrained affair, as had their journey down by car. In a peculiar way they might have been strangers, or old friends thrown together after a terribly long time apart. Which, as Andrew had reflected earlier, was more or less what they were.

'Is it too late, Andrew?'

He didn't look at her, but continued staring out over the water. And he didn't reply.

Rose was finding this difficult, but had known she would. 'It's as if . . . I've been in another place. Of this world, but not of it. I've been hurt, confused and angry.'

He still didn't respond.

'I've treated you so badly, Andrew. What happened wasn't your fault, and yet I acted as though it was. I've been extremely cruel.'

'Yes,' he agreed.

Rose winced.

'And now?'

'It seems to have passed. At least I think it has. I'm seeing things more clearly. The anger and confusion have somehow lifted, gone away. I'll never get over Mary, that went too deep. But now I've come to terms with it.'

She hesitated, then said softly, 'I love you, Andrew. Even when I was hating you I loved you.'

'And I've never stopped loving you, Rose.'

The relief that washed through her then was almost tangible. 'Truly?'

'Truly.'

Her hand sought out his. 'So can we start again? A new beginning?'

'If that's what you want.'

'It's what I want more than anything, Andrew. I swear it.'

He turned to her and took her into his arms. How he'd so longed to hear these words, desperately craved to hear them.

'Just one thing, Andrew. I have to know.'

'What?'

'Is there someone else? I mean, I could hardly blame you if there was.'

'No, Rose,' he replied truthfully. 'There isn't.'

'Oh, Andrew.'

He held her close, her cheek pressed against his chest. For a while they remained like that, then he kissed her.

Later, they made love. Not the frenetic wild abandoned kind that had been their intermittent couplings since the miscarriage, but a tender, caring union that was far more fulfilling.

When they finally fell into a blissful sleep their bodies were intertwined.

'I now pronounce you man and wife.'

Tommy turned and gazed deep into Mavis's eyes, she into his. Beside him Dingo was beaming broadly. Ruffles, matron of honour and second witness, did the same.

Hettie, watching the ceremony, thought this one of the happiest moments of her life. She buried her nose in the already sodden handkerchief she was carrying.

Jack, who thoroughly approved of the match, having told Hettie he could tell from Mavis's voice that she was a good woman, was praying that the war would soon be over and Tommy would come out of it unscathed.

Chapter 28

T hat was it, Andrew thought, laying his pen aside. He'd written down everything he could think of about running a distillery, every piece of advice. All done for Drew's benefit when the time came.

He stared morosely at the almost filled ledger, the facts, figures, tricks of the trade. You name it and it was there. A dead man's guide, he reflected bitterly.

Drew would never be able to rebuild the distillery as the lad envisaged it. That might have been possible if the old distillery had been covered against acts of war, but it hadn't. Not one penny piece had come their way, or would come, in insurance money.

In due course an amount would be settled by the government by way of compensation, but nothing like the distillery's true worth. A gesture, nothing more.

He did have capital of his own of course, a considerable amount tucked away in the bank and various investments, but not nearly enough for an expanded rebuilding programme.

Another small distillery could be built, but not one incorporating modern methods.

Andrew sighed and closed the ledger. He would ensure that it was given to Drew when he was gone. A legacy of sorts.

Kelly had been brilliant, helping him with all manner of details a book-keeper specialised in. Together they'd been working incessantly for months now.

There was a tap on the study door. 'Andrew?'

'Come in, Rose.'

She entered carrying a cup of coffee with a biscuit on the saucer. 'That's the last biscuit for a while,' she announced cheerfully. 'They've become rarer than gold dust.'

He smiled at her, thinking how good it was between them again. Rose had asked if they could have a new beginning, and that's exactly what it had been.

'I'm finished for the day,' he declared as she placed the cup and saucer on his desk.

She regarded him with surprise. 'So early?'

He spread his hands. 'It's done. Completed.'

'Whatever that is,' she retorted, still in the dark as to what Andrew and Kelly had been up to week after week.

'You're looking particularly lovely this morning,' he said.

'Am I?'

'Most decidedly. You always look lovely. But today, for some reason, you look even more so. Has Nancy done your hair differently?'

'Not really. It's just a variation.'

'Whatever, it suits you.'

He went suddenly chalk white as the pain erupted in his stomach, pain far more intense than any he'd so far experienced.

With a groan he clutched himself and bent over till his forehead was resting on the desktop. It was sheer agony.

Rose was instantly by his side. 'Andrew, what's wrong? What's the matter?'

For the moment he couldn't answer. All his willpower was intent on coping with the raging hell boiling him alive.

She grasped him by the shoulders. 'Andrew?'

His vision was blurred and he was seeing double. Black spots were dancing before his eyes while her voice seemed to be coming from a long way off.

'Pills,' he managed to gasp at last. 'In the drawer.'

Pills, what pills? She frowned, tearing at the nearest drawer. The bottle revealed was brown, the writing on the label recognisable as Dr Lesley's.

'Two,' Andrew instructed through gritted teeth. 'With whisky. Quick, woman.'

She shook two pills on to the palm of her hand and then flew to the whisky bottle. Not their brand, the last of the Drummond having long since gone. She slopped out a huge one.

'Here,' she said, holding the pills to Andrew's mouth.

He swallowed them with a large gulp of whisky. Then he swiftly drank off what remained in the glass.

'More,' he croaked.

Rose didn't know what was going on, totally mystified by all this. Up until then Andrew had succeeded in keeping his attacks from her.

'I'll call the doctor.'

'No,' he jerked out.

'But you're ill.'

'No doctor,' he repeated, writhing on his chair.

His face was now covered in sweat, skin the colour of mud. His hands were pressed tight against his middle.

Rose was at a loss what to do. Ring for Miss Campbell? Ring for someone! And why wouldn't he let her telephone the doctor?

In that moment Rose knew something was terribly wrong. Terribly, terribly wrong.

'Leave me,' Andrew muttered.

'But, Andrew . . .'

'I said leave me!' he almost shouted. 'I'll be with you shortly.'

He was groaning horribly as she shut the study door behind her.

It was over an hour later before Andrew joined a distraught Rose. He was still in pain but the pills and whisky had taken effect, the spasms now nothing like they had been.

'I think you owe me an explanation,' she stated simply.

Yes, it was time for that, he thought. Time, because there wasn't all that much of it left to him.

'You'd better sit down,' he said.

An appalled Rose listened to what he had to say.

Rose was sitting at her vanity table removing her make-up. In the mirror she watched Andrew undressing.

Her mind was still numb from his news. Andrew with cancer, dying. She hadn't yet fully taken it on board.

'I'm tired,' he declared, undoing his tie. 'I feel I could sleep for a month.'

Rose blanched. According to him it would soon be for a lot longer than that.

He stared at her, and smiled. 'You took it well.'

'Did I?'

'I half expected hysterics or something of the like. But no, you were cool, calm and collected. I was proud of you.'

She glanced away, breaking eye contact in the mirror. Perhaps he might not be so proud of her when the shock wore off. She might well have hysterics then.

He hesitated, then said softly, 'Every moment left to us is precious, Rose. We must use them wisely.'

'Yes,' she agreed.

'Spend as much time as we can together.'

'Yes.'

He came across to stand behind her. Gently, he stroked her neck. 'At least we made up, Rose. We've that to be thankful for. I never thought we would.'

Her heart lurched inside her. Reaching up she took his hand and, bringing it to her mouth, kissed it.

Later, when Andrew was asleep, Rose began silently to cry.

'Well how about that!' Tommy muttered as he and Mavis left the village hall where they had been to the weekly pictures on Saturday night, the main attraction being *The Emperor's Candlesticks* starring William Powell and Maureen O'Sullivan. The B feature, a short, had been written by his dad.

'Talk about propaganda,' Tommy went on, referring to Jack's offering. 'That was laying it on with a trowel.'

'Probably what he was asked to do.'

'Probably,' Tommy agreed. The film had been about fighter pilots in the Blitz, the leading male a quite unbelievable hero who'd knocked Jerries out of the sky like ninepins.

'Do you think he had you in mind?' Mavis teased.

Tommy laughed. 'I hope not. For if that's the case he got it entirely wrong.'

'I enjoyed it nonetheless. I think it caught the spirit of the RAF.'

They talked about Jack's film until arriving back at the small cottage they were renting. A modest affair built of red brick, Peppercorn Cottage had a sitting room, kitchen, toilet/bathroom and two bedrooms. It had come fully furnished, the owner, a widowed lady, having decided to go and live with her sister in Oxfordshire for the duration.

Once inside Tommy closed the blackout curtains before switching on the lights. He gazed about him with satisfaction. It may not be much but for the present it was his and Mavis's. Their first home.

'It's lovely having a night off,' Mavis declared, turning on the gas fire. 'I wish I had more.'

'You don't have to keep on at the Lamb and Flag you know. I earn enough to keep us both.'

'Just about,' she laughed. 'Anyway, my money comes in handy. You can't deny that.'

'You still don't have to work there. I'd prefer you home every evening.'

'I'd get bored, Tommy. I'm used to working. Hanging around the house twenty-four hours a day would drive me crackers.' What she didn't say was that working helped keep her mind off the danger he was in daily while flying. To have dwelt on that wouldn't have done her any good at all.

'Would you like a cup of tea?' she queried.

'Love one.'

'Coming up.'

Mavis disappeared off to the kitchen and Tommy slumped into an easy chair. He'd ring his dad during the coming week, he decided. Let Jack know he'd seen the pic. Jack would be pleased about that.

Talk about Biggles, he thought, and chuckled. Biggles was tame compared to his dad's hero.

That idiot wouldn't have lasted five minutes in the real

Blitz. Heroes there had been a-plenty. But none, in his experience, as stupid and gung ho as that.

It was propaganda after all, he reminded himself. What was that expression? Theatrical licence. Yes, that was it. Theatrical licence.

He'd enjoy pulling Jack's leg.

'Mum, what's wrong with Dad?'

Rose went very still. 'Why do you ask?'

'I went to the toilet after him and there was blood in the bowl. It obviously hadn't flushed properly.'

Rose's mind was racing. She and Andrew had agreed not to tell Drew the truth for now. There was time enough for that when Andrew's condition became obvious.

'He's got piles,' she lied smoothly.

'Since when?'

'Drew!' she admonished. 'That's not the sort of question to ask. And don't mention them to your dad. It's a touchy subject.'

Drew grinned, thinking this highly amusing. 'I won't.'

Rose casually changed the subject.

'You're coming on really well.'

Nancy beamed at Drew who, during the long summer months, had been teaching her her letters. 'Am I?'

'You know you are, Nancy. Why, you read that entire page without hesitating or stumbling once. You've improved no end and are continuing to do so all the time.'

She laid the book to one side. 'At least I'll be able to read your letters when you go back to school.'

'*And* write a reply.'

She hugged herself with pleasure. She, Nancy Thompson, being able to read and write. Who'd have believed it!

She thought back to her early days and especially those with Bill McCabe. What a contrast to the life she now led. Chalk and cheese. Poverty and luxury. It still amazed her how she'd fallen on her feet. She owed the Drummonds, particularly Mr Drummond who'd hired her in the first place, everything.

And one day she'd be one of them, a member of the family. Drew swore that would be so. That they'd marry when he was old enough.

'I'll miss you so much when I go back to school,' Drew said.

'And I'll miss you.'

He stared at her, drinking her in. There would never be another woman as far as he was concerned. No one else but Nancy would ever interest him. They'd been born for one another. Soulmates.

'Now, let's have another page,' he declared.

She pulled a face. 'Do I have to?'

'Yes,' he replied, pretending to be stern. 'You haven't finished the day's quota yet.'

'Bully,' she teased.

'That's me. Now get on with it or else.'

'Or else what?'

'The strap. Across your bare bum.'

She squealed. 'You wouldn't do that to me?'

'Just try me, Nancy Thompson.'

She was giggling as she picked up the book again.

'Andrew!' Elspeth exclaimed in surprise. 'It's been ages.'

He rubbed a hand across a bristly cheek. 'I was lying awake and didn't want to disturb Rose. So here I am.'

'Just like old times,' she smiled. Though not quite.

'Any chance of a cup of tea?'

'Of course.'

Elspeth stubbed out her cigarette and then got up and crossed to the stove. 'I've missed our chats,' she said, her back to him.

He didn't respond to that, but instead sat.

'How are you?' she asked, aware of his silence.

'So so.'

'Is that good or bad?'

'It varies from day to day, Elspeth. Some are worse than others.'

She glanced at him in sympathy. 'I'm pleased you and Rose have settled your differences. You've told her I presume?'

He nodded.

'How did she take it?'

'Remarkably well, considering. She's been quite stoical. At least on the surface that is.'

'And underneath?'

'She cries at nights and thinks I don't know. But I do. I hear her.'

'I'm sorry,' Elspeth commiserated.

Andrew shrugged.

'So why couldn't you sleep?'

He gave her a wry smile. 'Memories running through my mind. Things that happened in the past. Conversations. Relationships. Places. Recalling things I've experienced.'

He paused, then added softly, 'They say that when you're drowning your whole life flashes before you. Well it was a bit like that with me tonight.'

'I see.'

The wry smile became somewhat disjointed. 'It wasn't that unpleasant. In fact I rather enjoyed lots of it.'

Elspeth poured the fresh tea into a cup, then brought it to him. Sugar and milk were already on the table.

Sitting down again she lit another cigarette. 'I'm smoking more and more of these damn things,' she commented.

'Even to the point of sneaking out for a fly one?' he jibed.

She knew he was referring to that day in the storm. 'Yes.'

'Oh well, if you like them why not. A little bit of what you fancy never does any harm. At least, that's always been my belief.'

She glanced away. That had struck home. She knew what she fancied all right, except that was now never to be. More than once recently she'd told herself she was mad to stay on here, why torture herself! The simple answer was Andrew wanted her to stay and so she would.

'And how are you?' he asked.

She knew precisely to what he was referring. 'Fine.'

Their eyes met and understanding flowed between the pair of them. How different things might have been if it hadn't been for Rose and Andrew's feelings towards his wife. But Rose, and his feelings, existed, and that was that. For the second time in her life she was a loser where love was concerned.

'I want you to order another couple of cases of whisky,' he stated.

Elspeth raised an eyebrow. She'd taken receipt of two cases only the previous week.

Andrew noted the raised eyebrow and smiled. 'It helps,' he explained.

She so wanted to comfort him. For it to be her in his bed instead of Rose. To care for him during what time remained. She nodded that she understood.

Andrew yawned. Strangely, he was dog tired but not at all sleepy. He sipped his tea.

'Is everything running smoothly in the house? No trouble with any of the staff?' he inquired.

'Everything's hunky dory, and no, there isn't.'

'Good.'

She stared at him through a haze of cigarette smoke. 'I know it's none of my business, but are things really all right between you and Rose again?'

He guessed she meant in bed. 'Yes,' he replied firmly.

Elspeth flushed.

'In every respect,' he qualified.

'Then you did the right thing in not . . .' She trailed off.

'Whether or not Rose and I had made up it was still the right thing, Elspeth.'

'Then I'm glad it's worked out as it has for you.'

He appreciated how much it cost her to say that. 'Thank you.'

He suddenly didn't want any more tea. What he did want was to be back with Rose.

Andrew got up. 'It's been good talking again.'

'For me too.'

'Don't stay up too late. You've got an early rise.'

'I'm used to that. Staying up late and the early rise.'

He smiled. 'I suppose you are. Goodnight then, Elspeth.'

'Goodnight, Andrew.'

When he'd gone she went to the cupboard where the cooking sherry was kept and poured herself a glassful.

And when that was drunk she poured herself another.

Drew was curious, it was so unlike his father to ask him to go for a walk. Just the pair of them. He couldn't recall Andrew ever having done that before.

Andrew halted and sucked in a lungful of air. God, but the air was beautiful round here, he reflected. He was so used to it he normally never noticed how clean and pure it was. 'Shall we turn back now?'

'If you want, Pa.'

Andrew glanced sharply at his son. Drew normally called him Dad, Pa was what he'd always called Murdo. A different generation, a different mode of address. 'It's school again soon, are you looking forward to it?'

'You must be joking!'

Andrew laughed, he'd been none too fond of school either. 'Oh well, it's something that has to be done. A necessary evil we all have to endure.'

They began retracing their steps. 'Is there a reason for this walk today?' Drew asked.

Andrew considered his reply. 'I've always thought of myself as a reasonably good father. But up until the bombing I was a busy one. The distillery took up an awful lot of my time. Now I have plenty to spare it would seem to me a good idea if we get to know one another a little better. Do a few things together. What do you think?'

Drew was delighted. 'I'd like that.'

'As the saying goes, sometimes you don't see the wood for the trees. You forget what the really important things in life are. They get pushed to the background in the frantic day-to-day living and business.'

What an odd mood his father was in, Drew thought. He didn't think he'd ever seen him like this before. He'd always considered Andrew a slightly austere, even remote, figure. That appeared to have changed. He suddenly felt closer to Andrew than he'd ever done. It was an enjoyable experience.

'I thought we might take a ride out tomorrow,' Andrew suggested.

'In the car?'

'If you wish. Though it was the horses I had in mind.'

'You know I hardly ride.'

'You did when younger. Anyway, it's not something you forget. So, what do you prefer, car or horses?'

'Whatever. Either would be nice.'

'Then horses it is. And the day after that we'll go for a spin in the car.'

'Can I drive?'

Andrew smiled. 'I'll begin teaching you. How's that?'

Drew's face was radiant. He couldn't wait to tell Nancy. 'Great, Dad. Absolutely great.'

Andrew had the impulse to take the lad's hand, but of course Drew was far too old for that.

He felt an enormous sense of satisfaction and well-being as they continued on their way.

'Tommy?'

'Go back to sleep, love.'

It was still dark, but then it always was when Tommy got up to go to the 'drome.

'I was trying not to disturb you,' he said, shrugging into his flying jacket.

Mavis smiled lazily. They'd gone to bed early the previous night, but it had been hours before they'd actually got to sleep. Glorious hours that even now made her squirm with pleasure. 'Shall I make you breakfast?'

'You stay where you are. I'll get something there. If I'm smartish that is.'

'Come here, Tommy.'

He crossed to her, taking the hand she offered up to him.

'Be careful.'

'I always am.'

'Hurry back.'

'I always do.'

He bent and kissed her on the mouth, swiftly avoiding the arms that tried to encircle him. 'I must go. There isn' time for that.'

Once outside the cottage he started to hum a jaunty tune as he headed for the camp and 'drome.

'I need some of that mixture,' Andrew stated to Dr Lesley.

'The pain's worse?'

Andrew nodded grimly. 'It's with me all the time now. And past the whisky and pills stage. I require something stronger.'

Lesley rose and went to his medicine cupboard. 'You could always be admitted to hospital, Mr Drummond You'd be more comfortable there.'

'No,' Andrew declared defiantly. 'I remain at the house That's how I want it.'

Lesley shrugged. 'Suit yourself.'

Andrew had every intention of doing just that.

Lesley handed Andrew a large clear bottle filled with green liquid. 'One tablespoonful when necessary. It'll make you drowsy, and it is habit-forming, I have to warn you about that.'

Andrew barked out a laugh. 'I don't think I have to worry too much about long-term effects. Do you?'

Lesley smiled cynically. 'I don't suppose so. But I have to warn you nonetheless.'

Andrew slipped the bottle into a pocket. 'Thank you doctor.'

'And if there's anything else don't hesitate to either ring o call in. I'll of course replace that bottle when it's empty.'

'Thank you again.'

En route home Andrew stopped the car and had a quick, surreptitious swig. It tasted foul. But what the hell, that didn't matter. All that did was it worked.

'I'm sorry, Rose, I really am,' Andrew said, pulling himself away from her.

'That's all right.'

'The mind is willing, very much so, but my body seems to have other ideas.'

She reached out and grasped his shoulder. 'Don't worry, Andrew. I understand.'

'I do love you, Rose.'

'I know that. And I love you.'

He'd lost so much weight these past few weeks, Rose was thinking. It was frightening. It wasn't so obvious when he was dressed, but stripped it was all too evident.

'Just cuddle me,' she whispered.

'It seems that's all I'm good for now,' he replied bitterly.

'No it's not.'

This sort of thing simply didn't happen to him. He never let a woman down, even drunk he was usually capable of performing. A great black cloud descended on him.

When Andrew made no move Rose shuffled over the bed and took hold of him. 'I said not to worry.'

It had never occurred to him this might happen. Stupid really, he should have realised it was a possibility. Laudanum did deaden the senses after all. Numb things. On the other hand, it might just be he was too ill, his body beginning to pack in.

'Maybe tomorrow night,' she said.

'Maybe.'

'Whatever, as I said, it doesn't matter. We have one another and that's all that does.'

He laid his cheek on her breasts and closed his eyes.

She began gently to rock him as though he was a baby.

Mavis had been ringing up at the till when Dingo entered the pub. Turning round again she found him at the bar staring at her.

'Hello, Dingo,' she smiled.

He didn't smile back while his grim expression became even grimmer.

'Mavis, can we be alone for a moment?'

Her own expression froze. 'Oh!' was all she could think of to reply.

She knew what was coming next.

Chapter 29

'He's dead, isn't he?' a wide-eyed Mavis asked.
She and Dingo were in the Gilfeathers' parlour which Dan had said they could use. The look on their faces had told Dan this was bad news and he'd handed Dingo a bottle of brandy before they'd gone in.

Dingo nodded.

It was her worst nightmare come true. She felt as though she'd been hit full on the forehead by a hammer. 'How?' she croaked.

'It was over the Channel. We were escorting bombers back from a raid when we ran smack into several flights of Me109s and 110s.'

Dingo paused and sucked in a deep breath. He'd have given anything not to be saying what he was. 'The weather was foul, really bad. Visibility appalling and the rain hammering. It was some of the worst weather I've ever encountered out there.'

Mavis swallowed hard. Tommy! she was screaming inside her head. Tommy! She had to force herself to listen.

'There were fighters everywhere, absolute pande-
monium. Pinky Smith saw it. Tommy's Hurricane disinte-
grated, then blew up. There were flaming bits flying in all
directions according to Pinky. But no parachute.'

Mavis sobbed.

'I'm so sorry, Mavis. Jesus Christ and all his Angels, I
am.'

Dingo fumbled with the bottle and poured two large
shots. 'Have this,' he urged, going to her.

Mavis's head was bowed. When she raised her face it was
tear-streaked. 'Oh, Dingo,' she whispered.

'It would have been over in an instant, Mavis. You must
remember that. And take comfort from it if you can.'

She could see Tommy as he'd been that morning before
leaving her. Recall his words precisely. It just wasn't possible
he was gone.

'Drink up,' Dingo croaked, thrusting the glass into her
hand. Brandy spilled over the side of the glass as she raised
it to her lips.

Mavis was a woman absolutely stricken. 'I loved him
so much.'

'I know. And he loved you.'

'We had . . .' She sobbed. 'Such a short time together.
No time at all really.'

'But you had it, Mavis. That's the main thing. It's
something to treasure for the rest of your life.'

He threw brandy down his throat. The next moment
Mavis had wrapped herself round him and was crying
uncontrollably.

After a while he called Ruffles and they took her up to
her old room where they put her to bed.

Mavis smiled as she came out of a deep sleep. She could

hear Tommy moving about, getting ready to go to the 'drome.

'Tommy?'

When she opened her eyes she found herself not in Peppercorn Cottage but in the Lamb and Flag. And Tommy wasn't there.

The room, apart from herself, was empty.

'You're doing really well,' Andrew enthused to Drew who was driving the Austin.

'Am I?'

'Top-class.' Andrew laughed. 'Give it a month or so and you'll be good enough for Monte Carlo.'

Drew knew he was being teased, but nicely so. Surprisingly he'd discovered Andrew to be a patient teacher having expected otherwise.

'Change down now,' Andrew advised.

Drew did so.

'Your clutch movement has improved tremendously. That was smooth as silk.'

Drew visibly swelled. 'Can we go out again this afternoon?'

Andrew laughed again. 'If you wish.'

'Driving's great fun, Dad. Even more so than I thought it would be.'

'Careful on the corner here. Concentrate . . . That's it, roll her round the bend.'

'Easy as pie,' Drew beamed.

'Just don't get overconfident, lad, or you'll start to make mistakes.'

'I won't, Dad. I promise.'

'Fine.'

Dalneil came into view, for which Andrew was thankful.

They'd be home shortly and he could have some more mixture. The last dose was beginning to wear off.

When they got in he'd have a sleep, he promised himself. Sleeping was something he was doing more and more of recently. He seemed to spend half his time in bed.

Sleeping . . . and dreaming.

Jack had his own office in the studios where he and Hettie worked together as they'd always done. It was nowhere as peaceful as Dalneil, continually being surrounded by hustle and bustle, but somehow they managed.

Jack was in the middle of dictating when the telephone rang. He sighed, another bloody interruption. Hettie laid her notebook and pencil aside and rose to answer it.

'Why hello, Dingo!' Hettie exclaimed in surprise.

Jack frowned. They only knew one chap with such an outlandish name, Tommy's best man. Now why should he be . . . A terrible sense of foreboding hit Jack with all the strength of a hammer blow.

'I see,' Hettie muttered, voice strained almost beyond belief. 'I see.'

Jack clasped and unclasped his hands. It took all his self-control not to demand there and then what was being said.

The exchange was brief, and then Hettie hung up, her eyes filled with tears. Slowly she turned to stare at Jack.

'Well?'

'It's Tommy . . . he's . . . he's been killed.'

Jack's expression remained impassive, but inside he was a tempest of emotions. 'Are they sure?'

'Yes.'

He swallowed hard, then swallowed again. 'Oh, lassie,' he choked.

Hettie flew to him, sank on to her knees and buried her face in his lap. Her entire body began to shake.

'Tommy,' Jack whispered. His son. Their son. Their wee boy.

He didn't want any details, not right now anyway. If indeed there were any. That was for later.

'Tommy,' he repeated, still in a whisper.

'Mavis couldn't ring herself, she's in too much shock,' Hettie wept.

At that moment they were two babes lost in the wood, clinging to each other for support.

Hettie continued to cry and shake. Jack didn't realise it, but he was shaking also.

He started to sob.

There was a full moon that night with millions of stars twinkling down. Mavis was sitting in darkness by the window gazing up at this panorama.

Someone had called earlier but she hadn't replied to their knocking. She presumed it to have been Dingo but hadn't wanted to talk to him. Not him or anyone else.

'I think I'll stay in bed for a while,' Andrew said to Rose, she having risen about ten minutes previously.

She was instantly by his side, trying, and failing, to keep the concern from her face. 'Shall I have some breakfast brought up to you?'

'No thanks. I'm not hungry.'

'But you hardly ate any dinner last night. It isn't good enough, Andrew.'

'Nag nag nag,' he joked. 'You're turning into a shrew, woman.'

'Sorry,' she mumbled. 'I'm only trying to do what's best.'

'I know.' He smiled weakly. 'And don't think I don't appreciate it. I'm just not hungry, that's all. No appetite whatsoever.'

'A slice of toast perhaps? Could you cope with that?'

He shook his head. 'I doubt it.'

There was a look in his eyes which caused her enormous pain. It was one of total resignation. Where was the dashing Andrew of yesteryear? The man in bed was a pale shadow of that.

'Why don't you come back and talk to me after you've eaten?' he suggested.

'I'll do that.'

'You could bring a cup of tea. That would be nice.'

'I shall, Andrew.'

He watched her do her toilet and dress, savouring every delicious moment of it.

When she did return with the tea he was sound asleep and remained so till early that afternoon.

Nancy's job was a great deal easier since Rose and Andrew had become reconciled, Rose no longer incessant in her demands of her. Life was far less arduous and considerably more pleasant.

She was *en route* to the kitchen for coffee and a natter with Cook when she passed an open doorway, glimpsing a pensive Rose inside staring into space.

'Mrs Drummond?'

Rose started. 'Yes, Nancy?'

'Is there anything you want done?'

Rose thought about that, and shook her head.

'Shall I join you for a bit?'

Rose's reply was to gesture to an empty chair which Nancy crossed to and sat on.

'Are you worried about Mr Drummond?'

Rose studied Nancy, and didn't reply.

Nancy flushed slightly. 'It's none of my business I know, but he obviously isn't well.'

'He's dying,' Rose stated matter of factly.

That shocked Nancy who'd had no idea. '*Dying?*' she whispered.

'Of cancer.'

'Oh, Mrs Drummond, I am so sorry.'

Rose glanced away. 'Yes, so am I.'

'Is there nothing can be done?'

'Nothing I'm afraid. It's only a matter of time.'

The rest of the staff had been talking for a while now, saying Mr Drummond wasn't his usual self, that he was peaky, listless, that he'd lost weight. They'd all put it down to the destruction of the distillery.

'Does Miss Campbell know?' Nancy queried, thinking that if the housekeeper did she hadn't let on to anyone.

'No. You're the only one. And I'd be obliged if you'd keep it that way, for now anyway.'

'Of course, Mrs Drummond. My lips are sealed.'

Rose gave Nancy an ethereal smile. 'You're a good lass, Nancy Thompson. I've often thought if my baby, Mary, had lived she might have grown up like you. A lass to be proud of.'

That embarrassed Nancy. 'Thank you,' she mumbled.

'Don't thank me, it's true. You'll make someone an excellent wife in time.'

Nancy hoped Rose still thought that when, one day, she became her daughter-in-law.

'I've been sitting here wondering about Drew,' Rose mused.

'Oh?'

'You see, he doesn't know either.'

Nancy was already aware of that. 'Shouldn't he be told?'

'That's what I've been mulling over. He'll have to be eventually of course, but now or later? That's the question.'

There were a few moments' silence while they both considered that. 'May I say something, Mrs Drummond?'

Rose nodded.

'Have you any idea how much longer Mr Drummond has?'

'That's the problem, Nancy, the doctor can't be specific. But it might be only a matter of weeks.'

'Then how would you feel, how would Drew feel, if Mr Drummond suddenly went without Drew having any inkling it might happen? That would be awful, surely? It seems to me it would be better to bring him back now, at least for a bit, to say his goodbyes. To be put fully into the picture. He is grown up after all. Not a little boy any more.'

Nancy was quite right, Rose thought. On both counts. She made up her mind there and then. 'I'll write to Drew later today,' she said. 'And his headmaster. I shall say there's a family crisis and he's needed at home. I'll then explain the situation when he gets here.'

Rose breathed a huge sigh of relief, glad that was settled. Better by far to be safe than sorry.

Poor Drew, Nancy was thinking. This was going to be terrible for him. She'd have to give him every support.

'What are you doing here?' Ruffles queried in surprise.

Mavis shrugged. 'I can't sit around the cottage moping any longer. I need to occupy myself. So I've come back to work.'

'But it's far too early for that.'

476

They were behind the bar and Mavis couldn't help but stare at the spot where Tommy had so often stood. A lump rose into her throat which she tried to swallow back.

'Mavis?'

'Sorry, Ruffles?'

'I said, it's far too early for that.'

'I have to come back sometime, so why not sooner than later? I need to keep active otherwise . . .' She took a deep breath. 'I think I'll go off my chump.'

Ruffles nodded her understanding. 'All right, if it's what you want.'

'It is.'

'Then you can start tonight. In the meantime, how about a cuppa?'

'Smashing.'

'And a piece of . . . wait for it, chocolate cake. Don't ask me how I came by the chocolate either. It's a secret.'

The evening shift was hard, so many of the customers sympathetic when that was the last thing she needed. But after a while, as the beer flowed, things became easier. By the end of the shift it was almost like old times. With one exception.

Tommy hadn't come in. Nor would he ever again.

'Are you cold?'

'Bloody freezing.'

Elspeth smiled. 'Let me put more logs on the fire for you.'

Andrew grunted his appreciation.

'Where's Mrs Drummond?'

'Gone out to one of her war effort meetings. She won't be long.'

It wasn't really chilly in the room but Andrew was

obviously feeling that it was. Elspeth squatted by the fire and began piling on logs. The wood was sweet-smelling apple.

'I've always admired your hands,' Andrew mused.

That took her aback. 'Really?'

'They're very elegant. Real woman's hands. It was one of the first things I noticed about you when you came for your interview.'

Elspeth gazed down at her hands which she'd never considered out of the ordinary. Elegant? It was a lovely compliment, though she didn't see them to be.

'How are you today?' she asked.

'Tired, but then I always am recently. All my energy seems to have disappeared.'

'What does the doctor say?'

Andrew barked out a laugh. 'What can he say! Nothing. It's merely a progression of what's wrong with me. Tiredness and inertia.'

She felt sorry for him, and tried not to show it. 'Would you like a rug round you?'

He shook his head. 'That's for cripples and the extreme elderly. I'm neither.'

'But you said you were cold?'

'I said no thank you, Elspeth.'

'Sorry, I was only trying to help.'

He sniffed. 'Now that I think about it, I could use a whisky. Nothing beats the cold better than that.'

She made a mock gesture of obedience. 'Your wish is my command O master.'

He laughed. 'Are you taking the michael?'

'Of course.'

He wondered yet again what it would have been like to . . . He thrust that thought from his mind. Those days were over, Rose could testify to that.

'Will you join me?'

'I'm working, Andrew.'

'And I'm still the boss who makes the rules and can break them when I so choose. Have a drink and keep me company.'

She smiled. There had been that ring of authority in his voice which had always brought her out in goose-bumps. 'What shall we talk about?'

'Whatever. It's up to you.'

She couldn't help herself. As she walked past him she laid a hand lightly on his shoulder.

For a few minutes anyway she could pretend she and not Rose was his wife.

'Hello, Dad.'

Andrew opened his eyes and smiled at Drew. 'Hello, son. Good journey?'

Drew shrugged. 'All right I suppose.'

They stared at one another. 'Mum's told me,' Drew said eventually.

'Aye, well there it is.'

'Oh Dad,' Drew whispered.

'None of that now. I expect you to act the man who'll soon be taking my place as head of the family. Fortitude, as they used to say when I was young, you must show fortitude.'

Drew had been tense, wound up about this meeting, but now he suddenly relaxed and was completely at ease. 'I'll try.'

'Good,' Andrew growled, nodding approval. 'Now sit down. I want to tell you about a ledger I've been writing up as a notebook of sorts.'

Drew frowned. What was this? He listened intently as Andrew explained.

479

*   *   *

'Was it bad?'

Drew shook his head. 'Not really. I fully expected it to be but somehow it wasn't. If anything it was rather jolly actually.'

'Jolly!' Nancy exclaimed. Drew had come to her in her room directly after his conversation with Andrew.

'Sounds bizarre I know. But that's how it was. The old man just wouldn't let it get soppy or maudlin.' Drew's face crumpled. 'Oh Nancy. I still can't believe it.'

He went to her and she took him into her arms, holding him tight and then stroking the back of his head.

'Mum says he could go at any time,' Drew choked.

'I know.'

'It's so . . . horrible.'

'Death is something we all have to face up to eventually, Drew. I think we country folk are more aware of the fact, and accept it more readily, than others. It's part of the natural way of things.'

'I suppose it is.' He paused, then said, 'I'm so pleased you're here, Nancy. It makes it a lot easier for me.'

That pleased her.

'I shan't go back to school until it's over.'

'But he might last for some time, Drew. There's no knowing according to Dr Lesley.'

Drew's body stiffened. 'I don't care. I'm staying here and that's all there is to it. I shall tell Mum that.'

She eased his head back and stared into his eyes. She saw great sorrow there. And love. Love for her, love for his father now going through such a terrible ordeal. She'd promised herself she'd comfort him all she could. And that was a promise she'd keep.

'Come back here late tonight,' she said softly.

He stared at her in surprise. 'Here. What for?'

'You can sleep with me.'

Delight lit up his face. 'Can I?'

'But we have to be careful. Do you understand? We have to be very careful.'

'You have my word on that.'

'It would be a disaster if I fell pregnant. Especially now.'

'You won't,' he assured her. 'I have the means to make sure you don't.'

He trembled in anticipation.

As for Nancy, she was smiling knowingly.

The bar was empty, it being lunchtime. Mavis was polishing glasses and generally tidying up. Lunchtimes were usually slack, often passing without a single customer coming in. When she'd finished this she'd polish the brasses, she decided. Anything to keep her from thinking.

She stopped what she was doing when she heard a plane roar overhead, the engine unmistakably that of a Hurricane. The lead plane quickly followed by others.

Mavis thought of the lads up there, all of whom she probably knew. How many would be coming home again? All of them, she fervently prayed. Please God, all of them.

There was the hint of tears in her eyes as she bent again to the task in hand.

Ireland. For the past few days Andrew hadn't been able to get Ireland out of his mind. But mostly he was remembering that bastard McGinty, the Fenian he'd killed for murdering Alice and her family. An eye for an eye he'd decided, and so it had been. McGinty and his family for Alice and hers.

It was a deed he'd have to pay for, he'd always known that. But he didn't regret what he'd done. And never would.

No one had more deserved what had happened to him than McGinty.

Ireland with its green lushness and soft rain. Happy times, except at the end.

Faces from those long-ago days floated before him. Where were they now? How had they fared? He'd never know. All he could do was speculate.

Dublin was a fair city, as the song said. And the maids oh so pretty. He smiled in recollection.

One maid in particular, Alice Fortescue. His Alice. Alice who'd been burnt alive because she was a Protestant.

He shook his head, the dreams and memories continuing to flood through his mind.

'Can I come again tonight?' he whispered, having first glanced around to ensure no one was in hearing distance.

Nancy smiled at him. Truth was, there was nothing she wanted more. She'd forgotten just how good it could be. And with Drew, far better than anything she'd previously known.

She swelled inside with tenderness and love, wishing he was older and they could get married. But that would come in time. Meanwhile they just had to be patient.

'I'll be expecting you.'

Drew beamed at her.

'And don't forget to come prepared.'

'Cross my heart and hope to die.'

'Nancy!'

They both started. That was Rose calling.

'Tonight then,' Nancy crooned.

'You can count on it.'

'And make it late. I don't want anyone seeing you.'

'Late it'll be.'

'If you don't fall asleep that is,' she teased.

'No fears.'

'Nancy!'

He watched her hungrily as she hurried off.

'Why don't you go away from here?'

Mavis slowly laid her cup back on its saucer and stared at Ruffles. 'You mean Laxworth?'

'That's right. Far away. Make a new start.'

Ruffles glanced across at the clock. There were still five or six minutes left to opening time.

Mavis shook her head.

'Why not? It would surely be for the best.'

Mavis gave Ruffles a wry smile. 'I might, but not yet. It's far too soon for that.'

Ruffles sighed. 'Well, at least move back into your old room. It can't be good for you being alone in that cottage. You've said yourself, all you do is mope when you're there.'

Mavis thought of earlier when she'd been packing up some of Tommy's things, a job she'd been putting off knowing how hurtful it would be. Well, she'd been right about that. Every item of clothing and personal effect she'd touched had been like a knife stuck in her.

And she'd re-read yet again the letter sent her by Hettie and Jack, the pair of them promising to come and visit when they could. They'd been as devastated as she, though, of course, in a slightly different way. They'd lost a son, she a husband.

'I prefer the cottage, Ruffles. But thank you all the same.'

Ruffles sighed again, sure that was a mistake.

Neither said another word until it was time to open up.

* * *

Mavis went over to where Dingo was sitting by himself in a corner. 'Can I join you? It's my break.'

'Surely, Mavis. Surely.'

Once seated she gazed quizzically at him. 'What's wrong with you tonight? You're unusually quiet.'

'Thinking of home, Mavis. That's all.'

'You mean Australia?'

'That's right. She's a beaut place, you know. Real beaut. I miss her like buggery.'

'Tell me about it.'

'I don't want to bore you, Mavis.'

She smiled. 'You won't. Tell me about it.'

His eyes took on an excited gleam. 'I was born on a cattle station in the Northern Territory. Born and raised there where the skies are blue and the earth red as rust.'

'Were you a cowboy?'

Dingo laughed. 'We call them stockmen. Or jackeroos. And yes, I have been one in my time. Now there's an exciting life. Lonely on occasion, but exciting too.'

When her break ended Mavis knew an awful lot about Australia, pleased as she returned behind the bar that she'd managed to snap Dingo out of his melancholy mood.

He was a good man Dingo, as Tommy might have said. One of the best. He couldn't have been kinder since . . .

Taking a deep breath she headed for a customer waving an empty pint pot at her.

'I'll take over here for a bit,' Dan Gilfeather announced gruffly to Mavis. 'There's someone in the parlour to see you.'

That surprised her. 'Me?'

'Yes, you. Now on you go.'

Mavis couldn't imagine who it might be. She was about to ask Dan if he knew who it was when he moved away from her to attend to a customer. Wondering, she left the bar.

The parlour door was ajar so she went straight in, coming up short in total shock when she saw the person standing there. Her jaw dropped open and her eyes bulged. It seemed to her that for several moments her heart stopped beating.

'Just call me Lazarus.' Tommy smiled.

Chapter 30

'What happened?'

'You fainted,' Tommy sympathised, stroking her brow. She was on the easy chair he'd half carried, half dragged her to.

She gazed at him in wonderment. 'Is it *really* you?'

'It's me all right, Mavis. In the flesh.'

'But you're dead. Dingo said you were.'

'And so I should be. It's little short of a miracle that I'm not. Now before I explain would you like a glass of water? Or a brandy perhaps?'

She grasped hold of him. 'No, don't leave me. I couldn't bear that.'

Already bent over he now squatted beside her, and resumed stroking her brow.

'How?' she asked simply.

'What did Dingo tell you?'

'That your plane exploded.'

Tommy nodded. 'That's right. It did. Or so I've

presumed anyway as I've no recollection of the actual event. I remember the plane being hit, then a God Almighty noise. The next thing I knew I was floating face upwards in the water with a bloody great submarine alongside.'

'Submarine?'

'Somehow I must have been blown free in the explosion.'

'But Pinky Smith said there was no sign of a parachute opening.'

'It didn't. It was still on my back when the sailors hauled me on board. Somehow, and it *is* incredible, I not only survived the explosion but also falling from that height. The impact when I hit the water alone should have finished me off, but didn't.'

Mavis was desperately trying to digest all this. As Tommy had said, it was little short of a miracle.

'The weather was appalling,' Tommy went on. 'Visibility dreadful, the rain coming down in sheets. That's no doubt why I wasn't spotted by our lads still in the air. I mean, who survives an explosion like that must have been? I certainly haven't heard of anyone doing so. And not only survive that but also the impact of hitting the Channel. And yet I did, on both counts.'

'So where have you been all this time?'

'To the Aegean. I'm not allowed to be specific.'

'The Aegean!'

'There and back. It was an amazing coincidence that the submarine was just where it was and that I came down so close to where it surfaced. If I'd been any further away chances are they wouldn't have seen me in that weather. The whole thing is miracle upon fluke upon coincidence.'

He broke off and laughed. 'Talk about luck! I must have used up ten lifetimes' worth that day.'

'But why the Aegean?'

'Ah, well the sub had surfaced for a reason. It was on a secret mission and the purpose of its surfacing was to send off its last radio message. From that point until returning to Portsmouth it was under strict radio silence. Hence the reason no one knew they'd picked me up.'

He took his hand away from her brow, lifted one of her hands and kissed it. 'We docked in Portsmouth yesterday and I came straight here. I didn't telephone or telegram because I thought it better this way. I haven't even been to the camp yet, though, by now, they know I'm on my way.'

She couldn't think what to say to all this, it was far too bewildering. All that really mattered was that Tommy was alive and well, and here with her.

'You could have given me a heart attack,' she chided gently.

'I'm sorry.'

'No, don't be. It's just . . . well . . . walking in and seeing you there.' She shook her head.

'I wasn't even hurt, neither in the explosion or fall into the Channel. Not a scratch.'

'And the submarine just surfaced beside you?'

'It was already coming up when I hit the water apparently. The officer on the periscope actually saw me go in.'

Mavis sucked in a deep breath. She could now desperately use that brandy Tommy had offered her but didn't want to let him out of her sight while he fetched it.

'Do you still love me?'

She smiled.

'You haven't taken up with anyone else thinking I was dead?'

'That deserves a smack, Tommy Riach.'

He was staring at her, hard. 'There was a Divine intervention that day, Mavis. What other explanation is there? You and I weren't meant to be parted just yet.'

'Kiss me, Tommy,' she whispered.

He encircled her with his arms and their lips met. For Mavis the world was suddenly a good place to be in again.

Andrew opened one eye and gazed at Rose sitting by his bedside reading a book. 'Let's have a party,' he suggested brightly.

Rose was astonished. 'A what?'

'You heard, a party.'

'But . . . why? You're ill.'

'Of course I'm ill, but that doesn't mean to say I wouldn't enjoy a party. In fact, I know I'll thoroughly enjoy one.'

Rose was flabbergasted. Andrew hadn't been out of his bed all week, and now this. It was ridiculous! 'And who do you intend inviting to this soirée?'

'The staff.'

'The staff!'

'That's right. Mrs Moffat can lay on a buffet and there'll be oodles to drink. I can't think of anything nicer.'

Rose laid her book aside. 'Are you sure you're up to it?' she queried quietly.

'You don't have to worry about me. I'll be there with bells on. Ring-a-ding-ding!'

She had to laugh, and did. 'Will we have music?'

'We'll use the gramophone, and you and I shall trip the light fantastic.'

She studied him, thinking how awful he looked. His face had become almost cadaverous. 'I can't exactly see you dancing, Andrew.'

'I'll dance,' he insisted stubbornly. 'You can bet your boots on it.'

She couldn't imagine why he wanted to give a party for the staff. It just didn't make sense.

'I shall wear black tie, you your prettiest gown and jewellery. It'll be a wonderful night.'

'I'm not so sure about this, Andrew,' she prevaricated.

'Well, I am. And that's an end of it.'

It was obvious how determined he was. 'And when shall we hold it?'

He frowned, considering that. 'Speak to Mrs Moffat and ask if this Saturday is all right? Tell her no expense is to be spared. And by that I mean if she has to pay out backhanders to get anything then she's to do it.'

'You mean the black market?'

'Precisely!' he beamed. 'Sod rules and ration books. Money talks, and we can afford it.'

'You're something else, Andrew Drummond,' she laughed.

'I should hope so. But then so are you, my darling. Something very, very special.'

Even after all she'd put him through, she thought bitterly. Well that was all over and done with. Forgotten. She hesitated . . . maybe not forgotten, but certainly in the past. An episode she'd always feel guilty about. And ashamed of.

'I'll have a word with her now,' Rose declared. 'If you're sure it's what you want?'

'I am. Completely sure.

'And decorations, Rose,' he added as she was about to leave. 'Have Miss Campbell organise those.'

He wondered if there was any champagne in the house.

Saturday evening arrived, and Andrew and Rose came down together, arm in arm. He was wearing black tie as he'd said, Rose a stunningly simple black sheath without frills or fripperies that came to just above the knee. This was offset by a diamond choker and matching bracelet. Her hair, having been cut some while back, was equally simply styled, parted in the middle to fall curling into the nape of her neck.

Andrew's weight-loss was all too obvious, his clothes hanging on him. Nonetheless he was in a happy, buoyant mood as he and Rose entered the kitchen where they were immediately applauded by the staff.

The kitchen was hung with paper bells and streamers with lines of fairy lights sparkling overhead. Truly, a magical kingdom, Andrew thought on seeing it all.

The staff were in their Sunday best, for once not a uniform in sight. Mrs Moffat, resplendent in a brown concoction, reminded Andrew of a tea cosy.

'Speech!' Jamesina Laing called out, and blushed at her own forwardness.

'Quite right, a speech,' Elspeth Campbell seconded. She was smiling broadly, but secretly worried this was all going to be too much for Andrew, as indeed was Rose.

By now the staff knew the truth about Andrew's illness, all of them heartfelt in their sympathy. At Rose's request, not one of them had mentioned it to Andrew.

Andrew shook his head. 'This isn't a night for boring old speeches, I refuse to inflict one on you.' For a brief moment his expression changed. 'Except to say thank you for the hard work and loyal service you've given Mrs Drummond and me over the years. Now eat and drink up, and get that gramophone playing! I want to hear music.'

Andrew gazed about him, thinking how splendid this all was. For some reason he was reminded of his youth, though there had never been any such parties for staff that he could recall. Neither in the kitchen nor any-where else.

Elspeth came forward and handed Andrew a glass of whisky. 'For you, Mr Drummond. I think you'll find it rather special.'

He raised a quizzical eyebrow, but Elspeth didn't elaborate.

'Drummond!' he exclaimed in delight on tasting it. 'Where on earth did you get this?'

'In the cellar. I found a bottle that had been mistakenly placed in a wine rack. It's goodness knows how old but still good. I tasted it just to make certain.'

Andrew laughed. Nothing could have pleased him more. This time he had a proper swallow, smiling as its mellowness warmed its way down his throat.

'Thank you, Miss Campbell.'

She gave him a small nod of acknowledgment.

Mrs Moffat had excelled herself with the buffet, having taken Rose's instructions to heart. Nothing but the best had been provided, and there was stacks of it.

'Now drink up!' Andrew called out. 'I want everyone to have a good time.'

Rose put an arm round Andrew and pulled herself even closer to him. Looking into his eyes she smiled, he smiling back. They were the very epitome of a happily married couple.

Pattie Williams cranked the gramophone and put on a record, filling the kitchen with lively dance music. To much amusement Jamesina Laing and Lena Johnstone, the latter already a bit tipsy, lacking male partners, got up together. Andrew clapped his approval.

'I haven't enjoyed myself so much in years,' he whispered a little later to Rose.

'Me neither.'

'Truly?'

'Truly.'

Not giving a damn about the others present he kissed her full on the lips.

Nancy appeared beside them when the kiss was over. 'I hope you don't mind, but I took the liberty of filling a plate each for you.'

'Why thank you,' Rose murmured. Nancy was about to move away again when Rose said, 'Stay with us for a bit. We'd like your company.'

Almost as though she was one of the family, Nancy thought. Which some day she would be. She obediently took her place at Rose's side.

The whisky was working wonders, Andrew reflected, as dram followed dram. He could feel all his old strength returning. Why, it was almost as if he was young again. His feeling of well-being continued to grow and grow.

It was shortly after that Andrew, having long since demolished the food given him, turned to Rose. 'Our dance I believe, my dear.' The record that had just started playing was 'The Anniversary Waltz'.

Nothing could have been more perfect, she thought, allowing him to take her hand and lead her forward into the centre of the kitchen.

Then they were in each other's arms and gliding round the floor. A couple completely in love.

For the space of a few minutes it was as though time stood still.

Andrew lay staring at the ceiling while beside him Rose was fast asleep. It had been a tremendous party, he reflected. All that he'd hoped for.

After Rose he'd danced with Mrs Moffat and then Elspeth, at the conclusion of which he'd given in and had to sit down.

And so the night had passed and midnight chimed, that, Rose insisting, being their cue to go on up and leave the others to it. Andrew hadn't objected, tired by then and wanting his bed.

Reaching out under the covers he touched Rose, gently running his hand up and down the swell of her buttocks, his mind filled with memories of their marriage.

How contented he was. How very complete. It struck him he couldn't have asked for a more perfect day. Or happier one.

He wasn't sure if he'd dozed off or not, but gradually he became aware that there was someone else in the room. A shadowy figure standing at the end of the bed.

Andrew frowned. Wondering who it was. Strangely he was quite unperturbed or afraid. Merely curious.

The figure shimmered and became clear. It was his father, Murdo, smiling at him.

'Hello, Pa,' Andrew whispered.

It's time to go, son. I've come to take you with me.

'Go?'

Aye, lad, go.

Andrew half turned to stare at Rose's outline. He touched her again, his hand lingering for a few moments before he withdrew it.

'Goodbye for now, my darling.' He smiled. 'But just for now.'

Darkness was giving way to light, light that quickly became brighter and brighter.

'Ready, Pa,' he said.

Postscript 1

1946

'That's it, we're away,' Tommy declared as the last line was cast ashore. He tightened the arm he had round Mavis, drawing her even closer.

'The start of your awfully big adventure,' Mavis replied teasingly.

'That's right. Destination Cape Town.'

Slowly the S.S. *Samson* began to get under steam, its decks crowded with passengers waving their goodbyes to those who'd come to see them off.

There was no one there to do that for Tommy and Mavis. Jack and Hettie had left for America the previous month, bound for Hollywood where Jack had been contracted to one of the big studios. To Jack's amazement Andrew's long-ago prediction had come true. The propaganda films he'd written during the war had made a big impression in the film capital and no sooner had hostilities ceased than a telegram had been winging towards Jack with an offer.

He and Hettie had discussed the matter long and hard. It meant totally uprooting themselves after all. In the end they'd agreed to take the chance, the sort, as Jack had put it, that only came along once in a lifetime. While they were gone their house in Dalneil would be rebuilt, ready for their return, should that either be for good or merely a holiday.

As for Tommy, shortly after his Aegean episode he'd been promoted and posted to Yorkshire as a flight instructor, and there, much to Mavis's relief, he'd remained till the end of the war.

Dingo was home in Australia, having also survived, the last letter they'd had from him promising he'd visit them in Africa when, and wherever, they eventually settled.

'I can hardly believe this is happening,' Tommy exclaimed. 'It's always been my dream and now it's about to come true.'

'Well, part of it anyway,' Mavis cautioned. 'Going to Africa is one thing, being an explorer and big-game hunter quite another. I'm not traipsing through the bush while you play at being Jungle Jim. That is simply not on.'

'I know,' Tommy sighed. 'You've made that clear enough.'

'I won't have you surviving the Jerries only to be eaten by a hungry lion or swallowed whole by a monstrous snake.'

'Stop nagging, woman,' he teased.

The ship's horn hooted its farewell, a sad sound, yet, conversely, a joyful one too. A door was closing, a new one opening.

They stayed on deck until, at long last, there was nothing remaining to be seen of England.

'Let's go below and get unpacked,' Mavis suggested.

'But first we stop off at the bar.'

She smiled. 'If you insist.'

'I insist. This calls for a celebration.'

The toast was to absent friends, and the exciting future that lay ahead.

In Africa. Land of Tommy's dreams.

Postscript 2

1953

There had been many despairing times when Drew had thought this day would never arrive, but arrive it finally had. The re-opening of Drummond's Distillery. The new, far larger building rising, Phoenix-like, from the ashes of the old.

His grandfather Willie had been their saviour. On learning of Drew's plans from Rose, and the lack of money to carry these plans properly through, Willie had made a gift of a large amount of capital to Rose, telling her it would have come to her anyway on his death. Rose had promptly made it available for the rebuilding.

The next great stumbling block had been materials, extremely difficult, and sometimes nigh on impossible, to get in post-war Britain. But somehow, by fair means and occasionally foul, the materials had been acquired and workmen set to their task.

Kelly, the book-keeper, had been an invaluable help to Drew, assisting him every step of the way. Kelly and the detailed ledger Andrew had left.

And so the new Drummond's Distillery had been born, everything that Drew had envisaged. A modern building filled with modern machinery and a potential output far exceeding the previous one.

There was still a long way to go of course, years before the first bottle of Drummond appeared back in the shops and other outlets. But for now that was irrelevant. All that mattered was that the distillery was up and running again.

'Pleased?' Nancy queried with an amused glint in her eyes, knowing only too well that he was.

'What do you think?'

'That today's the second happiest of my life.'

'And the first?' he teased.

'Our wedding day.'

He paused, then said softly, 'That's exactly how I feel.'

All about them people were milling, village folk and assorted worthies. Those who'd been employed previously had been rehired, breathing life back into a Dalneil shattered by the bombing. The village was alive again, the distillery's not the only rebuilding to have taken place.

Rose broke away from Willie and Georgina to come over. Holding her hand was Mary, Nancy and Drew's daughter. Nancy was pregnant again, and this time they were hoping for a boy whom they'd agreed to call Andrew after his father and paternal grandpa. A male to carry on the long Drummond tradition of malt whisky-making *par excellence*.

Drew bent and scooped up the youngster. 'Are you enjoying yourself, angel?' he asked.

Mary nodded.

'Have you had something to eat?'

'Yes, Daddy.'

'Good.'

Rose glanced about her, then back at Drew and Nancy, the latter whom she'd welcomed into the family with open arms. Her eyes were bright, the hint of a tear glistening in them. 'I want to say something,' she said huskily.

'What's that?' Drew queried.

'Your father would have been proud of you this day. Proud fit to burst.'

'Thank you,' Drew choked in reply. That meant an awful lot to him.

'And so am I.' She looked at Nancy. 'Of both of you.'

'What about me?' Mary demanded.

Rose chucked her under the chin. 'We're all proud of you, my poppet. Wee Mary.'

For a moment Rose's face clouded, then cleared again. If only Andrew had been here to see this, she thought.

And then a strange feeling took hold of her. And she knew, without doubt, with absolute certainty, that he was.

FLOWER OF SCOTLAND

Emma Blair

'Emma Blair is a dab hand at pulling heart strings'
Today

In the idyllic summer of 1912, all seems rosy for Murdo
Drummond and his four children. Charlotte is ecstatically
in love with her fiance Geoffrey; Peter, the eldest, prepares
for the day when he will inherit the family whisky distillery;
while Andrew, gregarious and fun-loving, is already
turning heads and hearts. Nell, the youngest, contents
herself with daydreams of a handsome highlander. Even
Murdo, their proud father, though still mourning the
death of his beloved wife, is considering future happiness
with Jean Richie, an old family friend.

The Great War, however, has no respect for family life.
As those carefree pre-war days of the distillery fade,
with death, devastation, revenge, scandal and suicide
brought in their wake, the Drummonds are plunged
to the horrors of the trenches in France. Yet those
who survive discover that love can transcend class,
creed and country . . .

THE PRINCESS OF POOR STREET

Emma Blair

An enthralling saga of love, courage and defiance ...

They called it Black Friday in Parr Street when the factory closed. Glasgow's slums were caught in the depths of the Depression and whole families felt the cruel sting of despair. Vicky Devine's father, George, was devastated, but young Ken Blacklaws had steel in his veins: 'I'm going to make something of my life,' he would tell her with passion and a dangerous fire in his eyes. Maybe that's why Vicky loved him so much.

Beautiful Vicky, her love gained strength and defiance in the midst of bleakness and hardship. But as Ken ruthlessly fought his way out of poverty, his ambition knew no bounds. In his lifetime, he would break the law and Vicky's heart, but he could never break her spirit ...

Other bestselling Warner titles available by mail: